UNTIL IT
FADES

ALSO BY K.A. TUCKER

Ten Tiny Breaths
One Tiny Lie
Four Seconds to Lose
Five Ways to Fall
In Her Wake
Burying Water
Becoming Rain
Chasing River
Surviving Ice
He Will Be My Ruin

UNTIL IT FADES

a novel

K.A. TUCKER

ATRIA PAPERBACK
NEW YORK LONDON TORONTO SYDNEY NEW DELHI

ATRIA
PAPERBACK

An Imprint of Simon & Schuster, Inc.
1230 Avenue of the Americas
New York, NY 10020

First Atria Paperback edition July 2017

ATRIA PAPERBACK and colophon are trademarks of
Simon & Schuster, Inc.

For information about special discounts for bulk purchases, please contact Simon & Schuster Special Sales at 1-866-506-1949 or business@simonandschuster.com.

The Simon & Schuster Speakers Bureau can bring authors to your live event. For more information or to book an event, contact the Simon & Schuster Speakers Bureau at 1-866-248-3049 or visit our website at www.simonspeakers.com.

Manufactured in the United States of America

10 9 8 7 6 5 4 3 2 1

Library of Congress Cataloging-in-Publication Data

Names: Tucker, K. A. (Kathleen A.)
Title: Until it fades : a novel / K.A. Tucker.
Description: First Atria Paperback edition. | New York : Atria Paperback, 2017.
Identifiers: LCCN 2016052121 (print) | LCCN 2016058519 (ebook) |
    ISBN 9781501133381 (softcover) | ISBN 9781501133398 (eBook)
Subjects: | BISAC: FICTION / Romance / Contemporary. | FICTION / Romance / General. | FICTION / Contemporary Women. | GSAFD: Love stories.
Classification: LCC PR9199.4.T834 U58 2017 (print) | LCC PR9199.4.T834 (ebook) | DDC 813/.6—dc23
LC record available at https://lccn.loc.gov/2016052121

ISBN 978-1-5011-3338-1
ISBN 978-1-5011-3339-8 (ebook)

for the fairy-tale lover in all of us

UNTIL IT
FADES

Chapter 1

■ ■ ■

March 2010

The Subaru station wagon comes to a sliding halt in a parking spot out front of the Balsam County police station, the fresh blanket of snow coating the asphalt making the streets slippery.

And my stomach sinks with the realization that I've been tricked by my own mother.

"What happened to going to the *mall, Mom*?" She's been quiet since we pulled out of the driveway; I just assumed she was pissed at me. These days, she usually is.

"Did you honestly think we'd just pretend that nothing happened and go shopping?" Her eyes remain focused ahead as she says, "I had to get you in the car somehow."

I've seen her pull this same trick on our golden Lab, Bingo. He thinks he's going to the park, so he eagerly jumps into the backseat, his tail wagging and his tongue lolling, only to end up at the vet. Falls for it every damn year.

This is so much worse than a trip to the vet.

Shutting off the engine, she unfastens her seat belt. "Okay. You know why we're here."

When I don't unfasten my seat belt, she reaches over and pushes the release button for me. Her expression is stony, her tone is worn-out. "I reported Mr. Philips to the police yesterday. They need your statement, so we are going in there and you are telling them everything *right now*."

"But . . ." My stomach drops at the same time that heat crawls up my neck. "You promised that you wouldn't do this!"

"I made no such promise, Catherine."

Oh, my God . . . I need to warn Scott before she forces me in there.

It's like she can read my mind. She snatches my phone from my grasp.

"That's mine! Give it back!" I dive for it, but she holds on to it tight, slapping my hands away.

"The police will want this for evidence."

"That's an invasion of my privacy." I'm doing my best to put up a calm but defiant front. Inside, I'm screaming. Because there *is* evidence on my phone that I should have deleted. That Scott told me to delete and I assured him that I did, but I haven't yet, not all of it. Not the message where he told me I was beautiful. I love lying in my bed and rereading that one.

"Just drop this already. *Please, Mom.* Or how about let's just go to the principal. Let him fire Scott if he thinks he needs to. Okay?" I plead.

My mom's face contorts. "The principal is his *father*. The superintendent is his *uncle*. And his mother *is* a Balsam! You think they'll want this to get out? They'd just find a way to sweep this under the rug."

Which is exactly what Scott and I were hoping for when, two nights ago, my mom heard me tiptoeing down the stairs and followed me—quietly, in her nightgown and housecoat—outside and around the corner, to where Scott was waiting for me in his car.

I'm not sure what made her more angry—that she caught me sneaking out to meet up with my English teacher, or that I tried to sell the "he's helping me with my assignment over spring break" excuse to her, standing on a sidewalk at one in the morning.

"Besides, it's too late. The police are investigating." She takes a deep, calming breath. "I have an obligation, Cath. This is what good parents are supposed to do when they find out that a thirty-year-old man has taken advantage of their teenage daughter."

I squash the urge to roll my eyes. That'll only infuriate her. "*Nothing happened.* And, besides, age of consent is sixteen. Stop making it sound like he's some dirty old man." Scott is fun and handsome and could pass for early twenties. He wears ripped jeans and Vans, rides a motorcycle, and listens to The Hives and Kings of Leon. I'm far from the only girl in school to fall for him. I've been infatuated with him from the very first day I sat down in his class.

"He's your teacher! And what kind of idiot do you take me for? I know exactly what's going on, so stop lying to me." She reaches for her door handle.

And I know I'm not going to get anywhere with her by continuing to deny this.

"But Mom . . ." I seize her forearm, feeling the muscles tense beneath my grip. I'm fighting to keep my bottom lip from quivering. "*Please.* I love him. And he loves me." He's told me so. Quiet whispers in between stolen kisses after school lets out and he's helping me with my portfolio for college applications. Loud shouts in between our tangled breaths the two nights I've managed to sneak away and ride my bike to see him.

There's the faintest flicker of pity in her eyes before they harden. "You're barely seventeen, Cath. It's a crush, that's all. It won't last. It's *not real.*"

"No, this is different."

"Whatever he's told you, whatever promises he has made, they're all lies. You're a pretty, young girl and he will tell you whatever you want to hear if it means he gets sex."

"You're wrong."

"Even if I am, it doesn't matter because you *cannot* be with him, Catherine!"

"You are just . . . impossible!" I smack the dashboard with my hands, tears of frustration burning my cheeks. She's not listening. She doesn't care how I feel. She doesn't care how happy he makes me.

Her eyes are now focused on the windshield, on the thin blanket of snowflakes settling against the glass. The car didn't even have enough time to warm up in the five-minute drive over. "One day you'll see that I'm right. Until then, you need to stop being so selfish."

Selfish! "But we aren't hurting anyone!"

"Really? What do you think this mess is going to do to our family? We all have to live here! And your brother and sister have to go to the same high school. The rumors and the gossip and . . ." She heaves a sigh. "I'm sure people are already wondering about our parenting abilities. We will be the topic of conversation at every dinner table from Belmont to Sterling after this."

"Yeah, because *you* reported us!" For someone who's so worried about her image, I'm surprised she's not just as eager to keep this quiet as Scott and I are.

"God dammit, Catherine!" My mother explodes. "You are so desperate to be treated like an adult. Show me you deserve it and start acting like one. Take responsibility for your own actions."

"Fine! I'll end it with him!" Even as I shout the words, I know it's an empty promise. I'm not ending anything with Scott.

"Oh, it's ending, all right. And one day, when you're a parent, hopefully a *long* time from now, you'll understand why I'm doing this."

One day, when you're a parent . . . Next to "because I said so," that's her party line. But wasn't she ever seventeen and in love? "You can't do this. You're going to ruin his life. What if they put him in jail?"

"That's where he belongs, if he's preying on his students."

"He's not *preying* on anyone."

"Please. It's you today, and it'll be some innocent fifteen-year-old tomorrow."

I hear what she doesn't say—that I'm not all that *innocent.*

I huff out a sigh. "It was just the once."

She shakes her head angrily. "Has this been going on since you broke up with that boy?"

I avert my gaze.

"Why couldn't you have just stayed with him?"

What? "You *hated* Ethan!" I've never seen Mom as happy as she was the day I told her that I'd dumped my cigarette-smoking, Mohawk-sporting boyfriend of three months, by far my longest relationship before Scott. She didn't even ask why, or if I was okay. She didn't care.

"I'd welcome him back with open arms at this point," she mutters.

"I don't want Ethan." I haven't given him a moment's thought since the day I ended things. In hindsight, I don't know what I ever saw in him. He's failing half his classes and will likely still be playing video games and bagging groceries at Weiss in ten years' time.

I don't want him, or any of the other boyfriends I've been with either. That's what they all are. Boys.

Scott is a *man*, and he makes me feel smart and beautiful and talented. He treats me like we're equals. We talk about everything from art to music to places around the world that he wants me to see with him. He makes me think about my future.

Our future.

"We're moving to Philadelphia after I graduate next year. Scott will get a teaching job there, and I'm going to go to college for art. He's been helping me with my portfolio. Mom, you should see it, it's kick-ass." This is the right angle. College is all she talks about at home.

Cath, where are you applying?

Cath, you won't get in anywhere decent with these grades.

Cath, you can't make it without a college education.

She sighs, drops her gaze to her lap.

"I told you, we're in love." I hold my breath. Maybe this is all just a scare tactic. Maybe she'll sigh again and then tell me to put my seat belt back on and—

"Get out of the car. They're expecting us."

Hot tears stream down my cheeks. "What's Dad going to do when he finds out that you brought me here?" I'm grasping at straws now, and we both know it. Mom and Dad were fighting about me behind closed doors last night, so she must have told him her plan. He may have disagreed with her, but even he knew that she'd do what she wanted to anyway. That's just how she is.

That he wasn't at home this morning is telling. Not that he's around much to begin with.

She collects her purse and keys and steps out of the car without a word.

I consider holding the door locks down and taking a stance, but I know that it's futile. One way or another, Hildy Wright always gets her way.

So I wipe the tears with the back of my hand and throw open the car door. "I hate you!" I scream, using all my strength and anger to slam the door shut.

Maybe I can still run.

Can they actually make me talk?

Do I need a lawyer?

Heavy footfalls crunch in the snow behind me and my back tenses. "Everything all right here?" Sheriff Kerby asks in his smooth, authoritative voice.

"Yes, Marvin. We're just here for Catherine to give her statement." Mom and the sheriff have been in the same bowling league for twenty years. Of course she'd go directly to him.

I take a deep breath and turn to face the older man, his cheeks rosy from the blistering-cold winter wind. He has a kind smile, but I don't let it fool me. He's about to help my mother ruin my entire life.

But the Philipses do have a lot of sway around here, I remind myself. And people love Scott. They loved him back when he was taking the Balsam High baseball team to the state championship, and they love him more now that he gave up a teaching job in Philly to move back home and teach here. Maybe that will be enough to get whatever bullshit charges are coming dropped. Scott said it's technically just a misdemeanor and those get tossed all the time, so maybe nothing big will come of it. Then, we'll have the last laugh. And when I move to Philly with him?

My mother will be dead to me.

With grim determination and what feels like a lead ball in my stomach, I march up the steps to the station.

She's wrong. Scott and I are meant to be together.

It *is* real.

And I will never forgive her for this.

■ ■ ■

December 2010

I sit with my hands folded in front of me, fighting the urge to shrink into my seat as I quietly watch Lou Green drag her pen down the length of my résumé. Misty warned me that the owner of Diamonds would seem a bit intimidating, with her stern face and harsh tone.

I so desperately need this job that I've been unsettled by nerves all last night and this morning. By the time I stepped through the diner's doors fifteen minutes ago, overwhelmed by the buzzing voices and clanging pots in the kitchen and the potent smell of hot pancakes and sizzling bacon, my stomach was churning fast enough to make butter.

It doesn't help that Lou's interviewing me in a booth, smack-dab in the middle of all the bustle, where countless sets of eyes can survey me with abandon—some merely stealing glances, others downright staring.

Are they always so interested in potential new staff? Or is it just an interest in me, the high school slut who tried to put Scott Philips in jail?

"So you have no waitressing experience." Lou says it so bluntly, I can't tell if she's merely stating a fact or pointing out a reason why this interview should end now.

"No, ma'am. But I'm a fast learner."

"Aren't they all," she murmurs dryly, more to herself. "You livin' with Misty?"

I nod. "For about three months now." In the apartment she shares with her long-haul-truck-driving father who's home one night a month. I moved out of my parents' house on my eighteenth birthday, when my mother could no longer force me to stay. It's her legal duty, after all, to house her children until they reach the age of majority. And Hildy Wright is all about the law.

"And how's that goin'?" Lou asks.

"Fine." For the most part. Misty isn't the sharpest tool in the shed and she rarely shuts up—a nightmare early in the morning when I prefer to drink my coffee in quiet solitude and she's all bubbly. But I can't complain because she's given me a place to live and she'll be the reason I get this job, if I do. Plus, she's pretty much the only friend I have left.

From the expression on Lou's face, I can only imagine what she thinks of Misty. Her opinion can't be all bad, though, given she hasn't fired her, and she humored her request to interview me.

"I see you were a cashier at the Weiss in Balsam, from November of last year until March?"

"Yes. That's right. Five months."

"What happened?"

"It wasn't a good fit." I swallow the knot that's forming, thinking about the day the manager, Susan Graph, pulled me into her office to hand me my vacation pay and tell me that it would be best if I didn't come in anymore, due to what was going on in my personal life. This, after only a month earlier giving me a glowing employee review. The worst part about it is that I have to shop there because it's the only grocery store in Balsam.

"I can work any shifts you want. Early mornings, midnights . . . anything." I'm trying not to sound too desperate, but I don't think I'm succeeding. Then again, maybe employers like desperate employees— we'll put up with just about anything. And I *will* put up with just about anything. Misty makes good money in tips. The kind of money I need so I can save up and get as far away from Balsam County as soon as possible. I've been waiting for a job opening here for months.

"How will you get here? Do you have a car?"

"With Misty, for now. And I figured I could buy something cheap after a few months." Diamonds is a fifteen-minute drive from Balsam, on Route 33, way too far to bike.

Lou's pen shifts back to my education. She frowns. "You haven't finished high school?"

"No, ma'am."

She peers up at me from behind thick-rimmed glasses, her curly mouse-brown hair framing her face in a short crop. If I had to guess, I'd put her in her midfifties, though it's hard to say. "Don't you know how important having your high school diploma is?"

I swallow against the rising shame. "I do, but . . . I decided to take a year off." I'd thought of lying about it on my résumé, but Misty warned me that Lou'd fire me for lying if she ever found out.

Plus, there's no way Lou hasn't heard about "the Philips mess," as my mother likes to call it. Everyone around here knows about it. It's been the talk of the local news since Scott was arrested nine months ago.

"People makin' it hard on you, are they?" She poses it as a question, but I get the feeling she already knows the answer.

I nod.

"That whole business with that teacher is . . ." Lou purses her lips, and I grit my teeth, waiting for her to say something like "What kind of girl are you?" or give me a stern "You should be ashamed of yourself" frown. She would be far from the first. I've heard it plenty and from every direction, it seems, especially after I recanted my statement ten days later—after I learned that no DA would force a seventeen-year-old "victim" to testify—and the charges against him were dropped. At the store, where Scott's family and friends have more than once passed by me, making comments about how I deserve to be punished for trying to ruin his reputation, how I should stick to boys my own age, how someone needs to teach me to close my legs. At school, where the many students who adore Scott trailed after me in the halls, hissing "slut" and "skank" and "attention whore." Walking down Main Street, where strangers point me out to their friends.

I've become a local celebrity, as ridiculous as that sounds.

"You and him . . . it's over and done with, right?" Lou says instead.

I open my mouth to deny that it ever started, but her eyes narrow, as if calling me on the lie. And so I answer with a small nod instead, even as my throat tightens and the first prickles of tears touch my eyes. Great, I'm going to cry in my interview. I'm sure Lou will be chomping at the bit to hire me now.

But the whole ordeal still stings today, even more than it did the day Scott was let go on bail and wouldn't answer my phone calls and texts. I convinced myself that he had no choice but to avoid me, that it must be a condition of his release.

And it was . . . partly.

The rumors began quickly and spread like a stomach virus at a day care, just as nasty. Whispers in art class—but not so quiet I couldn't hear them—about how I had thrown myself at him and then accused him of rape; how he turned me down and I was so mad I decided to destroy his life; how I was a stalker who'd lingered around his house late at night, hoping to catch a glimpse of him. If anyone considered the alternative—that Scott and I *had* been together, that I'd been forced to give a statement—they kept it to themselves.

The charges were dropped and Scott's job was reinstated, only he was no longer teaching my art class. He was no longer glancing my way as we passed in the halls.

It was as if what we'd had, had never happened.

As if I didn't exist.

Lou clears her throat. "Well, that's for the best. Nothing was ever going to come of that, anyway."

"No, I guess not," I agree softly. Too bad it took me so long to see.

A waitress strolls past with a plate of fried onions and my stomach does a full flip from the smell.

"You okay? You're awful pale all of a sudden."

"I'm fine." I glance over at Misty, punching an order into the computer. She grins and gives me the thumbs-up. I wish I could be as confident as her.

A woman at the table two over from us is staring at me. That's Dr. Ramona Perkins, my dentist. Or ex-dentist. In April, we got a phone call to tell us that her office was reducing its patient load and that she would no longer be able to accept my family for appointments. In a town of three thousand, Perkins Dentistry is the only office. Now my family has to drive almost thirty minutes away, to the far side of Belmont, to get their teeth looked after.

My mother was in shock at first, given she started with Ramona's father, John Perkins, when she moved to Balsam twenty years ago. But after a few questions, she found out that Dr. Perkins is best friends with Scott's mother, Melissa Philips.

The other two women have the decency to look away, but Dr. Perkins spears me with a haughty glare and then offers loudly, "Wives will have to hold on to their husbands when they come in here, with that one serving them."

"You know what? I think we're better off talkin' in my office." Lou heaves her squat, plump body from the booth, collecting my résumé on her way past, not so much as glancing Ramona's way. She leads me through the kitchen, where a heavy-set, ebony-skinned man is flipping pancakes through the air with one hand and stirring a pot of grits with the other with deft precision. "That's Leroy. He's the head cook around here."

"But she takes me home at night and does my laundry. Occasionally refers to me as 'husband' too." Leroy winks, and then his face splits into a wide grin.

I force a returning smile, but I'm afraid it's unpleasant at best because the overpowering stench of grease from the deep fryers is making saliva pool in my mouth.

"Three tables of four just came in," Lou warns him. "Don't know why it's so damn busy all of a sudden. I should be out there coverin' tables. We'll wrap this up quick. Here's my office, right . . ."

I lose her words as I shove through the door marked STAFF RESTROOM, making it just in time to dive for the toilet before my oatmeal makes its reappearance.

Lou's waiting for me when I step out a few minutes later, her arms folded over her ample chest, the look on her face unreadable but alarming all the same.

"The smell of sausage must have gotten to me."

"You can't handle the smell of breakfast sausage and you want to work in a diner?" I can almost hear the "you idiot" that she mentally tacked on to the end of that.

"I don't know what happened. I guess I'm just really nervous." I *really* need this job. "I promise it won't happen again."

She twists her lips in thought and then heaves an exasperated sigh. "Stay here." She disappears into her office and returns a moment later. "I keep a box of these in my office. Between all my waitresses, we have at least five scares like this a year. I'd rather make my girls know one way or another than have them droppin' dishes and forgettin' orders all day long because they're eaten up by worry for the wonder. So do me a favor. Go on back in there and pee on this."

I stare at the thin foil-wrapped package she just shoved in my hand, feeling my cheeks burn. "No . . . I'm not . . . This isn't . . ." I'm on the pill.

"You a hundred percent sure of that?"

I quietly do the math in my head. It's been how long since . . .

Oh, my God.

"Yeah, thought so. Go on, now." Lou ushers me through the door with a forceful hand, pulling it shut behind me.

With a flushed face, I quietly fumble with the wrapping, though I don't know why. It's not like she doesn't know what I'm doing. "This must be the worst interview you've ever had?" I call out with a weak giggle as I position myself on the seat, stick in hand, hoping I'm doing this right.

"Nope. A girl from out near Sterling has you beat. Cops came in and arrested her right after she finished tellin' me how trustworthy she is. Turns out she robbed her previous employer the weekend before."

"I guess she didn't get the job." And, I suspect, neither will I.

Over the flush of the toilet, I hear Lou call out, "Two minutes for the results!"

I take my time washing my hands as I wait, avoiding the little strip that sits on the back of the toilet, forming its answer. The sense of failure overwhelming me. I spent a lot of time getting ready for today's interview, ironing a simple white blouse I borrowed from Misty, curling the ends of my ash-blonde hair so it falls nicely over my shoulders. Misty said Lou likes subtle makeup so I skipped the black eyeliner and stuck with lip gloss rather than the bright pink that I usually wear.

Pots are clanging and loud voices are calling out orders in the kitchen. "I know you're busy. It's okay if you have to take care of your customers. I'll show myself out."

There's no response, and I start to think that Lou is gone until she calls out, "Time's up!"

Taking a deep breath, I reach for the stick with a trembling hand.

"No, no, no . . ." My back hits the wall and I slide to the floor, my eyes glued to the second dark pink line. There's no mistaking it.

Oh, my God.

But how? I'm on the pill! Granted, I missed a few here and there, especially over the past couple of months.

Hot tears roll down my cheeks as I grip the test, thinking back to the only night this could have happened. I was so hurt . . .

So drunk.

So stupid.

As if I haven't fucked up my life enough. How am I going to do this? I can't live at Misty's with a baby, and there's no way I'm crawling back home. I don't have a job and now who the hell is going to hire me?

The door opens without warning and Lou steps in, peering down at me with my arms wrapped around my knees, sobbing uncontrollably. It doesn't take a genius to figure out the results, I guess.

She hesitates, but only for a second. I get the impression Lou isn't the type of person to beat around the bush. "Do you know who the father is?"

Fair question to ask the town slut, I guess.

I bob my head.

"How far along are you?"

I quietly do the math. "Seven weeks, maybe? Or eight?"

"You gonna tell him? Get him to help?"

"I don't know."

"It's only right."

I avert my gaze to the faded rose linoleum floor. I think I've suffi-ciently screwed up my chances at getting this job.

Misty comes barreling into the tight space. "Leroy said you were—" Her voice cuts off when she sees the test in my hands. "Oh, no . . . Cath!" Her hands go to her stomach, pressing against it. "Oh no, oh no, oh no!" After a moment, "This is all my fault!" She looks about ready to burst into tears.

"You're not exactly equipped to be blamed for this, Misty," Lou points out.

"No, but I'm the one who convinced DJ to bring his friend from New York to that party, so he and Cath could meet."

"*DJ*, your ex?" Lou spits out his name. I'm guessing she dislikes him. Most people do. DJ Harvey is a snake disguised as a hot guy. If cash goes missing from your house at a party, you can bet it's in his pocket. If there's a fistfight and he's around, you can bet he provoked it. Smashed window or spray-painted wall? Check for his fingerprints. I never understood how Misty could ignore the shadiness. It has only hurt her reputation.

Misty's blonde curls bob with her nod.

Lou sighs. "And I suppose the guy who got arrested with him is this friend from New York?" Everyone around here has heard about DJ and another guy getting busted for dealing marijuana and coke in Belmont the very next day after that party. It was a reprieve for me, because it gave people something else to talk about. Misty was smart enough to dump DJ right away, though she cried for a week after.

Another head bob.

Another heavy sigh. "On second thought, I wouldn't be too quick to say anything. No one needs to know your baby's daddy is a drug dealer. Not like he's gonna be able to support you from jail anyway, and it sounds like he's gonna be there awhile."

"People saw me get into his van, though." Actually, they saw Matt *drag* me into his van after I lunged for a girl who spat in my hair. In all the months of gossip and sneers since Scott was arrested, it was the first time I had physically lashed out. I was drunk and so angry; I couldn't help myself.

Matt lit a joint and we hung out in the back of his VW van for hours, complaining about how fucked up life is as the party raged around us. It felt good talking to someone who didn't know a soul around here besides DJ and didn't seem to give a shit whether I slept with my teacher or not.

He wasn't bad-looking and had me laughing by the time he leaned over to kiss me . . .

And now I'm pregnant.

As if I haven't provided these people with enough to gossip about.

Not that I should be worrying what people say or what they think about me anymore. I have a bigger issue now. Another human being to take care of, when I can't even take care of myself.

"Don't matter what they saw, as long as you don't admit to anything. It's none of anyone's business," Lou tells her. "Misty, you've got tables to take care of. And you keep your trap shut about this if you're a real friend, got it?"

Misty offers me a sympathetic smile and then ducks out of the bathroom.

"Okay, let's get some saltines and water in you to settle that stomach, and then you can sit down with the menu. It's big, but the sooner you learn it, the faster you can move from hosting and bussing to waiting on your own tables."

Wait . . . I stare up at the woman who hovers over me in the tiny but clean staff restroom. "You want me to work?"

She shrugs. "Better to stay busy than to leave free time for regrets, I always say."

"But, I mean, you're *actually* giving me the job? *Why?*" I can't help sounding incredulous.

She twists her lips. "Well, I'd say you need this job more than you did when you walked through my door twenty minutes ago, wouldn't you?"

"Yeah, but . . ." Dr. Perkins's words come to mind. "Aren't you worried what your customers will say?"

She snorts. "I don't have any use for *those* kind of customers. They're the same kind who think I shouldn't be married to my husband for the color of his skin. Besides, anyone who can't see how that teacher used you for his own needs is a damn fool." She rests her hands on her hips. "So, do you want the job or not?"

"Yes." I furiously wipe the tears from my cheeks with my palms.

"Well, all right, then. And no more cryin'. Leroy doesn't allow cryin' in the kitchen. Gets him all flustered and then he starts droppin' pancakes. Ask Misty, she'll tell ya."

I force a smile and pull myself to my feet, trying in vain to ignore that voice in the back of my head, screaming at me.

Telling me how badly I've fucked up my life.

Chapter 2

...

May 2017

Tonight is a night of firsts.

And lasts.

As in, I will *never* agree to a blind date *ever* again.

"So I says to the guy . . ." Gord's fleshy hands wave over his dinner plate—he's a hand-talker—"I says, 'Walkin' out that door without buying this car would be a travesty I can't allow you to suffer.'" He pauses and leans in, to build suspense, I guess, before slapping the table. "He drove off the lot with a mighty-fine Dodge that same afternoon."

Gord Mayberry, future owner of Mayberry's New and Used Vehicle Dealership when his father croaks—information he shared three minutes into our date—is a self-proclaimed master car salesman. The doughy thirty-five-year-old has regaled me with countless dealership stories while sucking the meat off his rib bone dinner, and I have smiled politely and nibbled on my french fries, struggling to keep my gaze from the prominent mole perched above his left brow, the two dark hairs sprouting from it begging to be plucked.

I wish I didn't have to drive so I could drown my disappointment in a bottle of cheap house chardonnay.

Why Lou thought her nephew and I would mesh, I can't figure out. I'm trying my best not to be vain, to get beyond the utter lack of physical attraction, and focus on the positives—the man owns a house, he has a great job, he's educated. He has all his teeth.

He'd provide well for Brenna and me. A helluva lot better than I can do on my own.

And seeing as I'm a twenty-four-year-old truck stop diner waitress with a tattered suitcase's worth of baggage in tow, who hasn't so much as kissed a man in over three years, maybe I don't have a right to be judgmental.

The server comes around to set a dessert menu on the table and clear our plates, earning my soft sigh of relief that I'll be going home soon. "Can I get you something else?"

Gord yanks the napkin out from where he tucked it in his collar and rubs his sticky BBQ sauce–covered fingers against it. "I'll have some of that divine blueberry pie of yours. How about you, Cathy?"

"No, thank you. I'm full." I stifle my groan. He's one of those people who assume Catherine and Cathy are automatically interchangeable. Maybe I'll tack on a "Gordy" to see how he likes it.

"Watching that gorgeous figure of yours, aren't you." He grins and reaches across the table. I panic and quickly occupy my hands with my dishes.

"Thanks, doll. But I've got it," the middle-aged woman chides with a wink, collecting the cutlery from me, freeing my hands for Gord's waiting grasp.

I tuck them under my thighs instead.

He finally relents, leaning back into his side of the booth, checking his sparse blond hair in the window's reflection. He's not fooling anyone with that comb-over. "So . . . *Catherine Wright.*" His emerald-green eyes—really, the only appealing attribute this man has—study me with a mixture of curiosity and amusement. We've sat at this table for almost an hour and he has yet to ask me a single thing about myself.

And I know exactly what he's thinking right now.

The Catherine Wright.

Gord may be a decade older than me and from the much larger Belmont, but I'd be stupid to think he doesn't remember the stories from way back when. That he hasn't heard *all* about me. Or at least the troublesome teenage version of me. The one who couldn't possibly have changed enough after all these years for people to just forgive and forget.

Hell, for all I know, that's why he agreed to this blind date. Maybe he's banking on the hope that I haven't changed at all and that he has a chance of getting laid tonight. I'm betting it's been a while for him, too.

"Yup. That's me." I meet his gaze with a hard one of my own. One that says, "I dare you." Actually, I *do* want him to dredge up things better left in the past. It'll give me a good excuse to walk out and end this train wreck of a date.

I see the decision in his eyes a moment before he averts his gaze to the bottle of ketchup on the table, his fingers wrapping around it absently. "My aunt Lou says you've been working at Diamonds for seven years now."

I guess we're not taking a trip down memory lane just yet.

"Six and a half years." Since the day after I found out I was going to have Brenna, through my entire pregnancy.

I was carrying a plate of grits in one hand and an open-face turkey sandwich in the other the day that my water broke. As far as truck stop owners who have to deal with amniotic fluid all over their tile floor during the dinner rush go, Lou was pretty sympathetic.

He lets out a low whistle. "I don't envy you, on your feet all day, servin' tables for tips. I mean, Aunt Lou's doin' all right, but that's because she owns the diner. But I see those older ladies who've been workin' at it awhile and"—he ducks his head and glances over his shoulder for, I assume, our waitress—"they don't weather well in that kind of job, all haggard by the time they hit forty."

Working at Diamonds when I'm forty is not something I want to be thinking about right now, so I push that fear away and offer a tight smile. "It's a job for now." It's more steady than seasonal work at the resort, more stable than the Hungry Caterpillar café or the Sweet Stop or the dozen other little tourist stops in Balsam, and it pays a lot more than a place like Dollar Dayz. I shudder at the thought of standing behind the counter at the local dollar store all day, ringing up discounted nylons and aluminum foil for the local elderly, for $7.25 an hour.

Sure, between the housing subsidy, the food stamps, and other government help I qualify for each month, I'd still get by, but just barely.

Gord drags the last of his Dr Pepper through his straw, making a slurping sound. "Not exactly a *dream* job, though."

"Some of us don't have the luxury of chasing after our dream job." *Our parents don't hand us businesses and futures.* Truth is, there aren't a lot of career options in Balsam, Pennsylvania, to begin with. Sure, we're the county seat, but we're a tourist town of three thousand—a lot more during the summer and winter seasons—with one grocery store, one gas station, two schools, two churches, a few inns, a main street of tiny shops, cafés, and restaurants that operate on limited hours throughout the week. Oh, and a pool hall to give the locals something to do. Plus, I didn't exactly win over Balsam-area employers enough early on in life with my "false accusations" to warrant much consideration from anyone who's hiring. I still count myself lucky that Lou ever gave me a chance when she did.

He frowns, obviously picking up on the edge in my voice. "I just meant that you need something better for the future. You have that little girl to take care of."

Despite his condescending tone, his words—just the mention of Brenna—make me smile. The one bright spot in my life, in the form of a rambunctious five-, soon-to-be six-year-old. "We're doing fine."

"I hear her daddy ain't around."

I force my smile to stay put. "Nope."

He leans in, as if he's got a secret. "So, he's a drug dealer?"

This is the problem with where I live. Small towns, small lives.

Big mouths.

I clear the irritation from my throat, hoping he'll take the hint that I don't talk about Brenna's father.

Sliding a toothpick between his front teeth, he works away at a piece of dinner. "You know, some people still think you and that teacher had somethin' goin' on after all, and it's *his* kid."

Gord has not taken the hint.

I glare at him until he averts his gaze to the ketchup label.

"Course, they also say it wouldn't make much sense what with timing and all, now would it?"

"Not unless I had the reproductive system of an elephant."

He scratches his chin in thought. "He moved out of state, didn't he?"

"No idea." Just after Christmas of that horrible year. To Memphis, Tennessee, with Linda—his ex-girlfriend, who he had reconciled with about two months after charges were dropped. The woman who is now his wife. They've since had two children together. A few of the more spiteful Philips family members still love to talk out loud about Scott every now and then, when I'm passing by them carrying plates to customers, or in line at the bank or grocery store. I think it's their polite way of saying, "Look how happy he is despite you trying to ruin his life."

I do my best to ignore them, because I'm not pining over a man who hurt me so deeply, who cared more about saving his own skin than protecting mine. It took a few years for me to understand how badly Scott used and manipulated me, to accept that I was a vulnerable and infatuated teenage girl that he took full advantage of.

Now I just count my blessings that he's far enough away from me that I don't have to see him. I heard he's come around a few times at Christmas, but otherwise his visits seem rare. Shockingly—and thankfully—I've never once run into him.

"So your daughter's daddy . . . he don't even want to see his little girl?"

"Nope." If he's somehow heard that she exists, he's made no efforts to reach out, which is exactly how I want it to be.

"I'll tell ya, you need to be gettin' money out of him, is what you need to be doin'," Gord says, poking at the air with a stubby index finger in a scolding manner.

"I don't want his money and I don't want him in our lives." And I don't need this guy—or anyone, for that matter—telling me I should want otherwise. We can do this on our own, Brenna and I.

Gord pauses to stare at me, and I feel him weighing my words. "Well . . . I guess you're your own woman."

"I've learned to be."

"I do like that." Gord winks at the waitress as she delivers his slice of pie. Scooping up a forkful, he shoves a large chunk in his mouth before continuing, bits of crust tumbling out. "You gettin' on with your family now? Aunt Lou said you had a rocky go of things with them. Didn't they boot you out or something?"

I don't bother to hide the flat stare at him, though in truth I'm more annoyed at Lou. Sure, she's the reason I'm standing on my own two feet right now, but that doesn't give her the right to discuss my personal past at length with her nephew before sending him off on a date with me.

Gord's hands go up to pat the air in a sign of surrender. "Okay . . . okay. No need to get your panties in a bunch. I didn't mean no harm." Gord waves his fork in the air between us, a smile filling his face. "You know . . . there just might be a job for someone like you at Mayberry's. I'm thinking of hiring my own personal assistant. Play your cards right and you could find yourself with a bright future ahead of you. You know, benefits and stuff. You wouldn't need no welfare." He pauses, watching me, waiting for my reaction.

I think this is the part where I'm supposed to start gushing and thanking him profusely for saving me from my lackluster future.

I force a smile and remind myself that this is Lou's beloved nephew that she speaks so highly of, and I have to bite my tongue.

He eats his pie and rambles on about *his* town of Belmont, twenty-five minutes south of Balsam. How it's got a Target, a movie theater, shopping mall, and four grocery stores instead of just the one Weiss; and it's closer to Route 33 South, which gets him to Philadelphia in an hour and twenty minutes; how there's more opportunity and I should seriously consider leaving my stagnant little tourist town and move closer to him.

I smile and pretend to listen, happy not to be answering any more questions about my personal life. When the waitress drops off the check and he quickly collects it, I breathe a sigh of relief that he's going to pick up the tab. This night has already cost me a dinner shift and a babysitter.

"Halfsies is twenty each," he announces, leaning his bulky body to the left to pull his wallet from his pocket.

Right.

Except he had pie and a bottle of Bud to go along with his Dr Pepper and full rack of ribs, so it's not really even. Not even close. I could argue, but instead I count out the bills because I want to be done with this guy as quickly and politely as possible, and get home to Brenna.

He grins as he collects the money and sets it next to him on the table. I know what he's doing—making it look like he's paying for the full check. "That was one heck of a meal."

I should tell him about the purple chunk of blueberry skin sitting on his front tooth.

I *really* should.

Instead, I climb out of the booth and slide my arms into my black faux-leather jacket. It's early May and the days are growing longer and warmer, but there's still a chill to the air.

Though I try for a quick wave and getaway at the restaurant door, Gord insists that I need an escort to my car at the back of the parking lot. So I spend the entire way hugging my purse, clutching my keys, and praying to God that he doesn't try to kiss me. There is no way in hell my lips are going anywhere near this guy.

"This is me," I announce, stopping in front of my black Grand Prix.

He shakes his head with mock dismay, his eyes roaming the body, settling on the rust that eats away at the rear wheel well. "You've got to be kidding me."

"It still works." Thanks to the help of my friend Keith, who knows enough about cars to fix whatever ails it and takes payment in the form of beer IOUs. I owe the guy about twenty cases by now.

Gord slides a business card out of his pocket and hands it to me. "You need to come by my store. I'll get you into a good, safe car for a steal. As little as five."

"Five *hundred*?" That's more than what I paid for this car, a 2000 model with a hundred and thirty thousand miles on it.

He chuckles, but it carries a superior twinge. "Well, I guess we could see what arrangements can be made for the woman Gord May-berry is dating."

Oh, God. He just referred to himself in the third person.

His hot, sweaty hand closes over mine, and I immediately tense. "I had a great time tonight, Catherine."

"Really?" *Were we on the same date?*

"Oh, believe me, I had my reservations. Plenty of people warned me about you when I told them we were going out. You know, especially because of that whole Philips thing."

That whole Philips "thing."

Gord's gaze lingers over the simple black dress that peeks out from beneath my open jacket. I chose it because it flatters my slim, toned frame and, back when I was getting ready for my blind date and had real hope for Lou's "tall, successful blond" nephew, I wanted to look good.

"I'd like to do this again," he says, taking a step closer.

I plaster on my friendliest smile as I take a big step back. "How about I call you?" I am never calling him. Ever.

If he realizes that's a standard blow-off line, I can't tell. "I'll be waiting. Anxiously." His green eyes drift down to my mouth and he hesitates for a second before swooping in, so fast that I barely have time to turn my head. His wet lips land on my cheek.

With an awkward giggle, I pry my hand from his grip and duck into my car, slamming my palm against the door lock before he gets the foolish idea to try again.

Ugh. Thank God this night is over.

Chapter 3

■ ■ ■

March 2010

"Go to hell!" I kick my shoes off at the door, purposely leaving them astray.

"Don't you dare speak to me like that! I am your mother. You will respect me!" My mom is hot on my heels as I storm into the kitchen.

"Why should I? You don't respect me. You don't give a shit about me."

"I did what I had to do." She grabs my arm, pulls me back to face her. "He was going to ruin your life!"

"No, you have ruined my life. If people at school hear about this . . ." I shudder at the thought. Balsam High has a total of six hundred students, and they have nothing to do except gossip. Plus, I swear, half of them are in love with Scott.

"You didn't seem to care what anyone at school thought when you were sneaking out and whoring around."

My mouth drops open. Did my mother just call me a whore? Anger wells deep in my throat, and I blink back the tears. "Well, we can't all be a frigid bitch like you, I guess."

The slap she delivers is biting, and I'm sure the sound carries past the kitchen in this 1950s backsplit. It's the first time she's ever hit me. I'm stunned with surprise, frozen as the sting blossoms on my cheek.

And then my hand is swinging, the sound equally cringeworthy.

She reaches up to cup her reddening cheek, her face filled with shock.

"No wonder Dad's never home. He can't stand you either." I spin on my heels and march up the stairs to my room, ignoring the fear on Emma and Jack's faces, as they sit perched at the top, listening to every word.

■ ■ ■

"What was that you said? I can barely hear you over that noise." There's just the faintest twinge of a German accent in my mother's voice, a remnant of her life in Berlin before she moved to America with my grandparents at ten years old, but you have to listen hard to catch it.

I let my car coast toward the stop sign. "Sorry. It's a crack in my catalytic converter. Or something like that." Keith says he doesn't have the equipment to fix it and it's going to cost me a small bundle at the shop. Maybe I should take up Gord Mayberry on that deal for a new car, after all. "I said I'll be by at six thirty with Brenna." My parents take Brenna every Saturday, giving me a chance to pull an all-day shift on the busiest day of the week without losing a large chunk to a babysitter.

She sighs. "Why don't you just drop her off on Friday nights from now on, so she's not sitting at the diner while you work?"

"I don't want to impose on you and Dad any more than I already have."

"She's our granddaughter, Catherine. It's never an imposition."

Right. Then why does she make it feel like it is, every Saturday that I pick Brenna up and she goes through all the things she couldn't do that day because of Brenna's short attention span. That's always been my mother's MO: offer the help and then not so subtly complain about it. "I'll see you tomorrow morning, then."

"We'll be here."

My shoulders sag with relief as I toss my phone to the passenger seat. I have that same reaction after every conversation with her. I can't see us ever growing to be friends, but at least we're on speaking terms again. There was a long stretch of time—almost five years—where I would have nothing to do with her, or Dad by default.

Gord used the term "rocky relationship" earlier. I'd call it more "volcanic." I'm still trying to work around the rock-hard layers of mistrust, wariness, and resentment that formed after it finally exploded.

Our issues started long before the day my mother brought me to the police station. I remember questioning her rules as early as nine, when my best friend at the time, Mary Jane, invited me to a sleepover and my parents wouldn't let me go "because they said so," even though *all* of my friends were going and there was nothing about Mary Jane or her family that would warrant concern. My father left the parenting—and most decisions—up to my mother. He worked steady afternoons on the line at the paint factory, leaving before I came home from school and asleep for breakfast.

My mother didn't see value in things like playdates and sleepovers, cuddling and bedtime stories. That was American culture fluff that she didn't have when she was young, and she "turned out well." She valued good grades in school, which I could never quite achieve, and a strict regimen of household chores, which I never could do to her satisfaction. She believed that it was her job to deliver constructive criticism with a heavy hand, and that coddling her children with praise would spoil them for adulthood.

In many ways, my mother was thirty-five going on seventy for as long as I can remember: strong-willed and unable or unwilling to adapt to change. Couple that with her old-world European values, taught to her by parents who had her in their late thirties, and we were destined for failure.

It wasn't until I was fourteen that I truly rebelled. I could never measure up to her expectations, and I guess I decided to make a point of intentionally not trying. By the time I hit sixteen, they were at their wit's end with me. I was skipping school and failing classes, missing curfew because I was out somewhere getting high and meeting boys. More, they were terrified of how I might influence Emma and Jack, my younger siblings. Emma, three years younger than me, was about to enter high school and had been groomed for the role of honor roll student and future class valedictorian.

And then I met Scott in my junior year and I started settling down—on account of his good influence, ironically.

None of that mattered, though, when Mom found out about us.

Now . . . we've come to an understanding. She was right in one sense—Scott never really loved me.

I'm sitting at the corner of Rupert and Old Cannery Road—the quiet route that will get me back to Balsam—and pondering my tumultuous relationship with my parents when a red sports car zips past in a noisy blur.

"Idiot," I mutter. That driver is easily doing double the speed limit, and on a foggy night like tonight, where the thick white plumes hang over the cracked pavement, and on a road like this, with its sudden, sharp curves and uneven dips, it's especially dangerous. Probably another city guy heading to his chalet for the weekend, reveling in the mild spring weather. We have plenty of them around, with the Poconos so close.

I glance at the clock on the dashboard again as I try not to speed along the dark, winding road, hoping I can make it home by ten so I don't have to stop at the bank for more cash to pay Victoria. Tonight has already cost me too much, given that Lou forced me to take the night off work, promising me that I'd be thanking her when I stroll in tomorrow morning for my shift.

I'm not sure how I'm going to maneuver around that awkward conversation. Lou has been trying to set me up with Gord for years. And for years I have declined the offer, afraid of this exact situation. Lou's the type of person who might consider my rejection of her nephew a personal affront upon her.

I guess my loneliness had finally weakened my resolve when I agreed.

I've practically been revirginized, having not slept with a man since the night Brenna was conceived. The last man I kissed was Lance, the truck driver who broke the final straw of my faith in men. Lance was a handsome regular who came through Diamonds twice a week—on Mondays, on his way to the West Coast, and on Thursday mornings, on his way home. He flirted with me for almost a year before I finally agreed to sit with him over my break. It quickly escalated to a break in his truck's cab, where we snuck off for a hot and heavy make-out session.

That's where I discovered the picture of his wife and son tucked into the driver's seat sun visor. It took months to shake my guilt, afraid that I'd now be labeled a "home wrecker" on top of everything else. After that, I put a hundred percent of my focus back on Brenna and ignored my own needs.

Which is what I'll be doing from now on, instead of accepting blind dates with car salesmen.

With a groan, I slow around a bend in the road, thankful that after so many years taking this quiet route to Diamonds for work, I've memorized each bumpy dip and dangerous turn like the back of my hand.

That's why, when I spot the dim, flickering red lights ahead, my brow furrows with worry.

Because I know that the road curves to the left at an almost ninety-degree angle right there.

I hit my brakes and throw my high beams on as I ease my car closer. The fog eats up most of the light cast, forcing me to pull up close, until the other car's license plate disappears from sight beneath my hood.

Turning on my hazards, I check my rearview mirror for headlights—so few people take this road that it's unlikely someone will come upon me—and then I grab my safety flashlight and step out onto the road.

And my stomach tightens.

I don't need to see the front of the red sports car to know what happened. The thick old oak that meets its hood already tells a bleak story.

And that car was going too fast for the story to end well.

"Hello?" The word breaks in my throat as I rush toward the front of the car—a Corvette, I think—on shaky legs, dialing 911 on my phone. The engine's hiss is the only response I get.

"I'm on Old Cannery Road," I tell the dispatcher who answers the call, my voice quivering. My toe hits a piece of metal debris from the car, sending it skittering away along the narrow gravel shoulder.

The dispatcher asks how many people are involved. My gasp answers him as I round the driver's side and the beam of light lands on a body, partially ejected through the windshield. By the haircut and size, it's a man. And he's not moving.

Is there a passenger? the dispatcher asks. I don't know, I tell him, because I can't see the other side. Because *this* side doesn't really exist anymore. It's just a heap of rumpled, smoking metal wrapped around a body now.

I'm operating on pure adrenaline, circling the back of my car to get to the other side, my two-inch heels sinking into the mud, remnants of last year's bulrushes brushing against my sleeve.

Yes. I think I see a shadow behind the spiderweb of cracked glass.

"Emergency services will be there in approximately four minutes. Get back in your car, ma'am, where it's safe," the dispatcher directs me.

"Four minutes," I repeat to myself, disconnecting the call. My gut tells me that it won't mean anything to the driver. But what about the passenger? It looks like the driver's side took the brunt of the impact with the tree after it left the road. Still, this side isn't without damage—the door no longer fits its frame.

Slipping the flashlight's rope over my wrist to free my hands, I take a deep breath and yank on the handle. Miraculously, the door creaks opens without too much protest.

A man sits inside, his head hanging forward, unmoving. I turn my flashlight inside to assess the situation. His forehead is coated in blood, so much blood, and it's running down the side of his face into his short, scruffy beard. He must have collided with the dashboard. That's the issue with these fancy old cars: no air bags. His seat belt still stretches across his chest. At least he was smart enough to wear it.

I reach forward now to press my hand against his chest, my fingers trembling. It rises and falls with shallow breaths.

He's still alive.

"Hello?" I whisper, as if afraid to startle him. "Can you hear me?"

No answer.

I inhale deeply through my nose. Something smells like it's burning. Hopefully it's just an oil drip. But what if it's not? God only knows what kind of fluid is leaking over that hot engine. If it ignites, this car will go up in flames within minutes. If there's anything I've learned while listening to chatter in a truck stop, it's how fast a car can burn once a spark catches.

"Hey! Can you hear me?" I call out, louder this time, my panic creeping in where there was only shock a moment ago.

The slightest groan escapes his lips but otherwise he doesn't stir. He's still unconscious.

I waffle with indecision for five heartbeats. "I'm just going to unfasten your belt." I carefully reach over his body to press the seat belt release button, afraid to bump him and cause more injury.

Has it been four minutes yet? I pause to listen, my ears perking for a hint of a siren. None.

But my ears do catch something else.

That distinctive whoosh of flammable liquid when it ignites.

This car is on fire.

And if this man doesn't wake up and get out of here, he's going to burn alive.

Full panic sets in. "Wake up! You need to wake up, now!" I yell, giving his broad shoulder a squeeze. He's a big guy, all the more so in this crumpled car.

The flames are now visible, curling around and licking the hood, beginning to radiate an intense heat. A putrid odor curls my nostrils, and my stomach spasms with the realization that it's likely the driver's flesh against those flames that I smell.

A voice inside my head screams at me to run, to get back home safe and sound to Brenna. That I've done all that I can do and now it's time to save myself.

I reach in to grasp the far side of his waist. "Wake up! I need you to wake up!" I cry, tugging on his massive body, earning his grunt but nothing more. I'm probably hurting him, I could be causing serious damage, but I don't have a choice. It's nothing compared to what the flames will do.

But it's futile. He's easily double my weight; there's no way I can lift him.

Giving up on that angle, I yank on his right leg, pulling it free to hit the gravel. "The car is on fire! Wake up!" I'm a broken record of screams as I reach in to tug on his left leg, the heat from the flames flushing my skin, growing warmer by the second as thick, choking smoke begins to form. But his left foot seems to be pinned beneath something I can't see, and I can't free it no matter how hard I yank.

Tears of frustration slip out as the heat becomes almost unbearable. He still hasn't woken up and I've run out of time. "I'm sorry. I can't do this!"

He's not waking up, and I have to leave him, one leg hanging out of the car.

One step toward safety. It's not enough.

"I'm sorry," I sob, cringing against the fire's heat as I take a step back. I have a child I have to get home to. There's nothing I can do here. And I can't die for this man.

I take another step back, feeling the bulrushes brush against my back.

He coughs and lifts his head to rest against the back of the seat.

"Hey! Hey!" I scream with renewed hope, diving forward once again, my fists grabbing hold of the lapel on his jacket. "The car is on fire! You need to wake up!"

His eyes are still closed but he's wincing. From the intense heat or pain, I can't say.

"I need you to pull your foot free, right now! Please! *Please!* If you don't, you are going to die!"

Something must finally trigger inside his head. He begins shifting his trapped leg this way and that, a grimace twisting his lips as he tries to free it. I reach down and grab the top of his boot to help, distinctly aware of the smell of burning rubber.

Finally, it pops free.

Grabbing his muscular thigh with both hands, I yank on it until it slides out to settle next to his other. "Stand up!" I reach in again, disregarding the blood and broken glass and any worries for injuring him more as I rope my arms around his waist.

"Get out of the car!" With all my strength, I pull.

Suddenly I'm falling backward.

Into the bulrushes, rolling through the ditch, this man's bulky weight on me both crushing and exhilarating as we tumble in a messy heap to land in an inch of swamp water, the cold temperature a pleasant contrast to the intense heat from the fire.

I look over my shoulder in time to see the flames rolling into the car through the dash and gaping windshield, the roar not quite loud enough to drown out the sound of sirens approaching.

■ ■ ■

Keith hands me a white cloth. I accept it with a nod, my eyes on the smoldering heap of metal ahead. It looks like the fire department finally has the fire under control. They used everything they had—water, foam, and an entire truck's worth of men. They moved fast, but not fast enough to save the looming oak tree ahead.

Or my car, parked too close behind.

"Where did they take him?" The paramedics came running when they saw me waving my arms from the ditch. We were still too close to the fire, and they were afraid that the flames would spread to the brush, so they worked fast to get the injured man on a stretcher and out of harm's way.

"Belmont for now but they'll probably airlift him to Philly."

Airlift. How bad are his injuries? And how much worse did our tumble into the ditch make them?

Beside me, Keith's police radio chirps with a series of codes. He answers the dispatcher with a few quick words of his own before turning his attention back to me. I'm so glad he was on shift tonight. "Your parents have Brenna?"

"She's with a babysitter. I was supposed to be home . . ." How long ago now? It feels like it's been hours. My gaze drifts to my burned-out car. The only thing salvageable from it was my purse, sitting in the backseat. Even if it were drivable, I can't fathom how I'd get behind the wheel right now. "I need to get home." I look at Keith. I'll never get used to seeing the gangly neighborhood kid who I made out with behind the school gym when I was twelve and then proceeded to ignore for the better part of my teenage years because he wasn't "cool," who's now my best friend, carrying a gun and a badge.

He's still on the lean side, and at twenty-five he barely passes for twenty-one out of uniform. Facial hair isn't even an option for the poor guy; it grows in in blond patches.

He reaches down to settle a comforting hand on my shoulder. "Text the sitter and let her know you'll be home in a half hour, tops. I'll give you a ride as soon as backup comes. They're on their way. Just a few more minutes."

I manage a soft "thank you," as I focus on the cloth in my hands, now splotched with blood, most of it not mine. I can't imagine what the rest of me looks like.

Keith leans his back against the cruiser, his gaze drifting over the wreckage. We don't see this sort of thing very often in our small community. "Damn, Cath. That was crazy, what you did tonight. Brave . . . but fucking crazy."

"I couldn't just let him die."

"Yeah . . ." He sighs. "It could easily have gone another way, though."

"He would have burned alive," I whisper hoarsely. It's the only answer I can give, because I can't let myself think of what *could* have happened. My throat tightens every time the thought of Brenna waking up without a mother tomorrow edges into my thoughts. And I know it's only the beginning. No matter what happens to that guy—whether he lives or not—I will be playing a horrific game of what-if for months to come.

Keith shakes his head to himself, his eyes on my Grand Prix. "I definitely can't fix that."

I groan.

Three more cruisers roll up behind us then, their lights flashing but no sirens. No doubt the town's CB radio junkies will have heard about the accident by now. They'll be jumping in their cars and trying to get close to the scene soon enough. I'm surprised someone from the *Tribune* isn't here yet.

"All right, give me a quick minute and then I'll take you home. Unless you've changed your mind about the hospital?"

I test my right wrist. Agonizing pain shoots through my forearm, but at least I can move it. "It's just a sprain. I'll be fine," I promise through gritted teeth. It must have happened when we tumbled into the ditch, though I didn't feel a thing. It's swollen to almost twice its normal size, and the paramedic who cleaned the scrapes on my legs wanted to take me in, but I refused. I've never wanted to go home more than I do right now, to shower the blood and ditch water off my body and curl up with Brenna's small, warm body, and *not* worry about how the hell I'm going to get to work without a car or serve platters of food without the use of my right hand.

Keith opens his mouth, no doubt to argue with me.

"Please, Keith."

He sighs. "Yeah, give me a minute." He marches toward the approaching officers, while I climb into his cruiser, yanking the door shut to trap the heat in, my single shoe resting on my lap, the heel snapped off. The other one is lying somewhere out there, lost in the tumble.

I wrap the soft gray blanket Keith gave me around my body, and watch and listen quietly from the passenger seat as the firefighters mill about, their bright yellow suits an oddly comforting sight. A middle-aged man with gray wing-like stripes at his temples, in black pants and a jacket that reads CORONER on the back, arrives. I can't imagine the gruesome sight left on the hood of the car. I close my eyes at the very thought and instead listen to the car radio, alive with chatter, most of it code that I can't understand. I doubt it's seen this much action in decades.

A few minutes later, Keith slides into the driver's side. The car's still running, the heat pumping out to warm my wet body. "So, we haven't released your name to the media yet—"

"Don't! Please. I don't want to give this town any reason to talk about me." It's guaranteed to dredge up the past, and that's something I'm hoping Brenna never hears about, until *I* decide to tell her. *Many* years from now.

"I know. That's what I told everyone."

I reach up to pull my seat belt across and hiss with pain as I bump my injured wrist.

He watches me quietly for a moment. "What are you going to do about work?"

"I'll figure something out. I always do." As much as it makes me cringe, I do have some savings that I can use to keep us afloat. That took me forever to accumulate.

"Maybe your parents can help?"

I spear him with a look. There's no way I'm asking my parents for money. I'm sure they're up to their eyeballs in debt anyway, putting Emma through four years at Columbia. At least my little brother, Jack, earned a scholarship to Minnesota.

He heaves a sigh. "But you're going to tell them about this at least, right?"

When I don't answer, he groans. I make Keith sigh and groan. A lot.

"Are you really that surprised?" Keith, who still lives with his parents and has what I consider an abnormally close relationship with them, just doesn't understand why things are the way they are between us. He's constantly offering his advice on ways to "fix our problems," no matter how many times I tell him that some things will always be broken beyond repair.

"Come on, Cath! What do you really think she's gonna say?"

"That I can't help but make poor life choices?" My mother's reedy voice is already filling my head. *How could you put a stranger before your daughter!*

I push away the guilt edging in with that thought, because I'm asking myself the same question.

"I don't think she'll do that this time."

"*I* do."

"Well, that doesn't mean you're right."

"Don't you dare, Keith." Keith lives three blocks away from my parents and he has no problem sticking his nose in other people's business.

With a heavy sigh, he agrees. "Whatever you want, Cath. But them finding out about this through someone else isn't gonna help things between you guys."

"They're not going to find out because I'm not telling anyone. And you're not releasing my name."

"Right." He pulls a three-point turn and edges past the other cruisers on the shoulder.

"Besides, Emma and Jack are in the middle of final exams. I don't want this to distract them. God knows she'd blame me if they didn't both get straight A's."

"She wouldn't blame you."

"She needs to assign blame in every situation. It's her MO." For most of my childhood, that blame fell on me. Jack tripped and fell? I wasn't watching him carefully enough. Emma lost her glasses? They were obviously buried somewhere in the sty that was my half of our shared room.

We round the bend in the road and all I can see are lights. Red and blue flashing lights from the police blockade and, beyond them, the hazy glow of headlights in the fog. At least a dozen, with the hint of more approaching in the distance. More than I would expect for a Balsam County car accident, as tragic as it may be.

Keith slows the car, allowing the officers to move the barricade enough to let us through. Beyond us, cameramen and reporters fill the open lane, filming.

I frown, taking in the line of media vans with names of TV stations painted on their sides. Local stations . . . Philly stations . . . one from New York City . . . CNN? "Why are there so many news stations? Why would they be here for this?" This isn't exactly worthy of national coverage.

"Do me a favor and pull that blanket up over your head for a minute?"

I don't argue because hiding under a blanket sounds like a fantastic idea right now.

Keith hits a button and that odd-sounding "get out of the way" police horn blasts into the night, forcing people to the side so we can pass. After a moment he says, "You can come out now."

I emerge to a dark, quiet road. "Keith? What's going on?"

He hesitates, stealing a few glances my way while driving. "The guy you pulled out of the car tonight? He's not just any guy, Cath. That's Brett Madden." There's a note of reverie in his tone.

"Brett Madden," I repeat, frowning as I pick through my thoughts. The name sounds so familiar.

Keith shoots a "come on" glare my way. "*The* Brett Madden. Captain of the Philadelphia Flyers?"

"The football team?"

He chuckles, his deep dimples filling his slender face. "The hockey team. The one that just swept two teams in the play-offs and is practically guaranteed to win the Cup this year. Or *was*, at least." He shakes his head to himself.

"I think I heard the guys at work talking about him."

"Likely. He got a hat trick in last night's game. The guy's a legend on the ice. Ask Jack about him."

My brother, who's at Minnesota on a hockey scholarship, would definitely have heard about him. "Okay. So he's a hockey player."

"No. He's not just 'a hockey player.' He may be the best player the NHL has ever seen," he corrects.

But I can tell just from Keith's tone that there's more. "And . . ."

"And he's also Meryl Price's son."

"Meryl Price?" That's . . . I gasp. "*Oh, my God.*" My body flushes as a new wave of shock washes over me. I just watched a Meryl Price movie last weekend. The one that earned her her latest Oscar.

Keith slows the car as we pass through another especially thick patch of fog. "Exactly. He's a pretty big deal to the media." I feel his eyes flickering to me. "And you just saved his life. So we can withhold your name, but that mess back there? You're not going to be able to avoid it forever. They're vultures, and your fifteen minutes of fame are coming whether you like it or not."

I shrink into my seat, my stomach turning. "I've already had my fifteen minutes. I'm good."

Keith gives me a sympathetic look. "Not like this, you haven't."

Chapter 4

■ ■ ■

"Mommy?"

Between my lingering shock and the throb in my wrist, I was sure I wouldn't fall asleep, but I guess I did because when I hear Brenna's childish voice, it hurts to open my eyes. So I don't, simply reveling in her warm body snuggled next to mine.

Two hot little hands grip my cheeks. "Why are you in my bed?"

"Just because," I murmur, smiling.

"Because you didn't want me getting up and going to your bed?" It's a nightly ritual, a half-awake girl stumbling from her room to mine, to crawl in with me for the rest of the night. I've gotten so used to it, I anticipate the sound of her bare feet padding across the linoleum.

Now I crack open my eyes to take in her rich brown irises up close. I have brown eyes, too, but Brenna's are a darker shade than mine and they have a ring of hazel around the pupils. She also has an olive complexion to my pale pinkish hue, and thick waves of golden blonde locks to my poker-straight, thin ash-blonde hair. "Because I didn't want to wait."

I was almost two hours late getting home last night. Keith took care of paying Victoria for the extra hours—her eyes looked like they were going to pop out of her head when I walked through the door all covered in blood and mud—and then because it was too late to walk he drove her home, leaving me to struggle out of my ruined dress. I caught a glimpse of myself in the bathroom mirror before climbing into the shower and immediately regretted it. I looked like I belonged in a horror movie, the fortunate lone survivor of a massacre in the Everglades.

It wasn't until the water running over me turned cold that the reality of what I had done hit me. Yes, I saved a man's life. But more important, I risked leaving Brenna an orphan. I risked my life to pull a giant unconscious man—a complete stranger—out of a burning car.

What if the car had exploded? I would have been incinerated trying to accomplish the impossible.

Even though, thanks to some God-granted miracle, I *did* accomplish it.

But first, I gave up. I had walked away, leaving him there to burn.

That's when my forehead fell against the shower wall and the tears began, first quietly, in a steady hot stream, then mixed in with ragged sobs. I couldn't describe my emotions at that moment, the relief and guilt so tightly entwined, both flaring for attention.

I bagged my ruined clothes and made sure all traces of the night were gone from the bathroom, a difficult feat with only one operational hand. Once I struggled into my pajamas, I decided I couldn't wait to be close to my little girl. I couldn't carry her into my double bed, so I slipped in behind her in her twin, pulling her slumbering hot body close to me, and struggled to keep my body from trembling as the sobs tore from my chest.

She studies me intently now, an adorable scowl line forming between her brows. "Your eyes are puffy."

"Are they?" I smile, make my voice sound light. "I guess I'm just tired."

The phone rings from the living room.

"I'll get it!" she exclaims, scrambling off the end of the bed and tearing down the hall. Ever since she turned five and I told her she was old enough to answer the phone, she runs for it like a dog at the dinner bell.

I close my eyes and smile, listening to her squeaky, childish voice as she tries to sound mature.

And I thank God that I'm still here to hear it.

"It's Grandma!" Brenna hollers.

I groan as I peel myself off the mattress, checking the clock to see that it's just past eight. I left a message at Diamonds for Lou last night, explaining in vague terms that I fell and sprained my wrist and apologizing profusely about not being able to make it in this morning. I didn't bother calling my mother; it was too late, anyway. I simply texted her with the same ambiguous excuse, letting her know that I wouldn't be dropping Brenna off.

"She's coming, Grandma . . . yeah." Brenna's small, naturally athletic body is curled up in the forest-green La-Z-Boy I snagged from the local Goodwill store, twirling the old-school coiled phone cord within her fingers, also from Goodwill. I may be the only person in the entire state of Pennsylvania still using a rotary phone.

How long before Brenna demands something from this century to talk to her friends on? A few years, maybe?

My throat thickens with the mental flash of a teenage version of Brenna sitting in that same chair, and for the second time in mere minutes, I thank God that I'm here to imagine that.

"Hey, Brenna, can you get me an ice pack from the freezer?"

"For what?"

I hold up my aching, mangled wrist. The night has given it time to swell even more and turn an angry mottled black and blue.

Her eyes widen in that expressive, childlike way. "What happened?"

"I fell." I nod toward our fridge with a whisper of "go" before the onslaught of questions start.

Taking the receiver in my left hand, I settle into the chair. "Hey, Mom."

"Are you insane? You climbed into a burning car?" My mom's shrill voice fills my ear, catching me off guard.

Panic sets in. Did the police release my name against my wishes? "How did you—"

"Keith was jogging by and ran into your father. He told him."

"Oh." I sink into the La-Z-Boy with a wave of overwhelming relief, even as I remind myself to call and yell at Keith the moment I hang up with her. What was he thinking? I'll bet passing by my parents' house isn't even his usual route, especially right after a midnight shift.

But at least the reporters haven't figured it out. Yet.

I smile my thanks at Brenna as she settles the ice pack on my lap, already wrapped in a tea towel to lessen the bite of the cold. She clambers into the small space beside me in the chair, her tongue curling out as she grins. A telltale sign that she's proud to be helping me.

"Keith said you weren't going to tell us?"

"It's not a big deal."

"Not a big deal! Have you turned on your TV? The story is *all over* the news." Before I can answer, she hollers, "Ted, turn up the volume!"

Reporters' voices fill the background and I picture my parents, sitting at the kitchen table with their coffees in hand, already dressed for the day when most people would happily sit in their robes and enjoy a lazy Saturday morning.

All over the news. Great. I glance over at the old tube TV sitting in the corner, resisting the urge to search out CNN. While I probably don't censor myself as much as I should in front of Brenna, she doesn't need to be exposed to that first thing.

"I mean, seriously, your car is right there, on TV!"

"Yeah, it's toast." Burned toast, to be more specific. "What else have they said?"

"Just that there was a witness. But they haven't released your name."

"And I don't want them to. *You* haven't told anyone, have you?"

"No, of course not. Keith asked us not to," she answers with a hint of indignation in her tone. I swear, the guy walks on water as far as they're concerned.

"Okay, good. Please, don't. Tell anyone, I mean. Especially not Emma and Jack."

"I wouldn't. They're still taking their exams. I don't want this affecting their grades."

It's not an outright accusation, but I hear the hidden tone behind it. Less than an A would be due to Catherine's recklessness. *I told you so, Keith!*

"I don't want this circus in Brenna's life." I use my five-year-old as a scapegoat, but in reality, *I* can't handle it.

"Circus?" Brenna's eyes widen, hopeful. "We're going to a circus?"

I shush her with a kiss on the forehead.

"Be realistic. You won't be able to stop this, Cath."

"I'm going to try." Keith is right, the police don't have to officially release my name. But word of mouth will out me, and in a town this small and connected, it'll out me pretty damn fast. Considering who Brett Madden is, I'm afraid "circus" might be an understatement.

"I just . . . We . . . What were you thinking, climbing into a burning car? You could have died." Her normally even voice breaks with a rare show of emotion.

"It wasn't *fully* on fire . . . yet," I mumble, closing my eyes. I can't really fault her for her reaction. The only time I ever lose my temper with Brenna is when she's doing something dangerous. Just imagining her with a broken leg is enough to make me want to lock her up in our house for good.

"What was on fire?" Brenna chirps next to me.

I lean away from her prying ears, hoping she can't hear my mother through the receiver. "I wasn't really thinking at the time."

"Obviously."

"Mommy! What was on fire?" Brenna tugs impatiently at my arm. I let out a hiss of pain. "Brenna, careful!"

"Keith said you hurt your wrist but refused to let him take you to the hospital?"

I sigh, wondering how long it will take my hand to heal before I can use it to throttle my dear friend. Isn't it against some police code to run—literally—to my parents like that? "I had to get home to Brenna. It's just a sprain."

"You don't know that, you're not a doctor. If there's a hairline fracture, it won't heal well. You'll only make it worse. You won't be able to work. Then what will—"

"Okay! Okay." I hold up my wrist to examine it. It does look bad. "I'll figure out something."

"Ted! Get the keys. We're going to Cath's." To me, she says, "I hope you're dressed."

"You don't have to . . ." I begin but realize that she's already ended the call.

I frown at the receiver, long after the dial tone fills our quiet living room.

■ ■ ■

The Philadelphia Flyers head coach wears a somber expression as he addresses the media, seemingly unaffected by the steady stream of flashbulbs and clicks. "The franchise's thoughts and prayers are with the players and their families. We've been told that Brett is in stable condition. We pray for a speedy and full recovery for him. And Seth . . ." He pauses, his voice growing shaky, the first sign of raw emotion I've seen from the gruff, stony-faced man. "He was an exceptional hockey player and human being. He will be missed by everyone."

A reporter asks a question about game one of the Eastern Conference finals, scheduled for next Friday, and if the coach thinks the team still has a real shot, even though they've lost arguably their two best players. My dad jabs at the Mute button on the remote before I hear the answer. "There goes our chance at the Cup." A deep scowl settles across his weathered forehead. "Idiots and their sports cars."

I glare at him, the mental image of the driver lying across the hood of the car still too fresh in my mind.

"Don't tell me he wasn't speeding," he adds, but he has the decency to look sheepish over his callous remark.

I most certainly can't say that he wasn't speeding, as I told Keith last night, but that doesn't really help matters. I tip my head back and drain the last of my coffee. At least I managed to get caffeine in my system in the five minutes it took my parents to show up at my door-step. Besides that and telling Brenna to get dressed, I didn't manage much else.

"I wonder if Jack is awake yet. He'll be devastated when he sees the news." Mom makes a beeline for the mug I just emptied and returns to the sink with it. She wasn't inside for thirty seconds before she was running the tap for last night's pile of dirty dishes. I'd like to think it's solely because she realizes I'm incapable of washing them given my injury, but I know it has more to do with her psyche being unable to handle a mess. Mom is what most would call obsessive when it comes to tidiness. I think she actually has a mental condition, though it has never been diagnosed. I've caught her gaze drifting to a dozen different places in the past ten minutes, no doubt tallying the ways my standards are much too low for her. And my standards aren't even that low, com-pared to Misty's or even Lou's. But I do have a five-year-old. That's akin to housing a tornado most days.

Plus, in a house as small as mine, there's no hiding a mess, short of stuffing it under a bed. It's more a cottage than a house—a tiny four-room structure of seven hundred square feet, with a combined living room–dining room–kitchen as soon as you walk in and two bedrooms off the back, the bathroom sitting in between them. A front porch gives a little extra living space during warmer months, but being be-hind Rawley's Pool Hall means that the view—a brick wall covered in graffiti and a Dumpster almost always overflowing—leaves much to be desired. Then again, that's the reason we can afford the rent.

I spent months searching for a place while waiting for Brenna to be born. I looked in Belmont, and Davenport, and every other town within easy driving distance to the diner. Everywhere except Balsam. While I wasn't going to Philly, I was adamant that I'd at least stay away from here.

Belmont turned out to be too expensive for me, and not everyone is keen on renting to a single eighteen-year-old pregnant girl. But I found two decent apartments within my price range in neighboring towns. Both times, the landlords seemed willing to rent to me. I filled out the paperwork and provided checks for first and last months' rent. Then suddenly the apartments were unavailable. It didn't take a genius to figure out they'd realized who I was and didn't want the hassle that they assumed would come by renting to me.

I was beginning to think I'd be homeless, and then Lou walked me over to a booth one day to introduce me to a customer named Mr. Darby, who had a tiny white-clad cottage covered in creeper vines during the summer months for rent, not far from Main Street.

In Balsam.

It's on the outskirts, away from the well-groomed downtown core, the area designed to appeal to both tourists and the wealthier residents, which Balsam has plenty of. This part of town is for the small minority like me—locals who don't quite fit in with the rest of the aesthetics. I took the house because I had no choice. I took it figuring I'd find something else eventually.

I guess it's fate in a way that I'm still here, because there are definite benefits to living a four-minute drive from my parents now that we're on speaking terms again.

"We really should get going, unless you want to be sitting in the ER all day." My mother's gaze drifts over my T-shirt and plaid pajama pants with a look that says, "You weren't going to go out in that, were you?"

"I'll be ten minutes at most."

"Brenna, would you please bring this to Grandpa." My mom hands Brenna a glass of water, warning in a grave tone, "Two hands and go slow."

Brenna takes the task seriously, her steps tiny, her eyes glued to the glass, all the way across the room to my dad, who watches her with a wide, genuine grin on his face.

I can't help but smile on my way past them.

When I found out I was pregnant, I didn't tell my parents. I wasn't talking to them anyway, and it was just one more way their elder daughter had disappointed them. It's not like I was going to move home. It made more sense to find my own apartment and apply for government assistance and Medicaid. As a single eighteen-year-old pregnant girl, I was pretty much a shoe-in for it.

I was about six months along and unable to hide my swollen belly behind an apron when they finally learned the news from a neighbor who had seen me at work. I'm not sure what infuriated my mother more: the fact that she heard they were going to be grandparents through third-party whispers or that she actually had to ask who the father was.

My mother showed up at Diamonds, berating me for yet again dragging the Wright family name through the mud.

There wasn't much I could say to ease her anger, and I had no interest in doing so. With more than a touch of spite, I admitted that her first grandchild was conceived in the back of a Volkswagen van, thanks to countless Solo cups' worth of beer and heartbreak. That I had no plans of including the father in our lives. That I could do this alone.

That she could leave because I considered myself an orphan.

That I hated her.

All I wanted to do was hurt her, after all. Just a fraction of how badly she had hurt me.

I didn't hear from her again until after Brenna was born, when she showed up at Diamonds, demanding to see her granddaughter. I refused. I'd survived the hardest months of my life alone—with the help of Misty, Lou, and Keith—and I wasn't going to give her what she wanted simply because she wanted it. I might have given my dad some leeway—he was just going along with whatever his wife insisted on—but they were a package deal, and if I'd inherited anything from my mother, it was her stubbornness.

She even showed up on my doorstep once. I called the cops. It was enough to make her never try that again, the experience too embarrassing in a town where souls thrive on gossip.

That was definitely a low point in our relationship.

I basically hid Brenna for years. From this town, from my parents.

We'd play in our backyard on weekends and go to the park and library only during weekdays. I'd go to the grocery store on Monday mornings. I kept to myself and avoided anywhere I thought my mother might be. She's a regimented person—weekly shopping, gas, library every Saturday morning—and she sticks close to home when she's not working. Aside from the few times I passed one of their cars on the main street, I was successful.

My little brother, Jack, is the force that finally pulled us back together. He and Brenna, really. Almost six years younger than me, he was twelve when I left, and fourteen when he rode his bike to my house after school to see me for the first time, unbeknownst to my mother.

He held Brenna before anyone else in my family even saw her.

He and I are much more alike than me and Emma, who in many ways is a mini version of my mother. But he also has a healthier relationship with my parents than I ever did—maybe because he's the baby, or maybe because he's the boy, or maybe because things changed once I left. After nearly two years of secret visits to my house, he confessed to them that he was in contact with me and with his niece. He even showed them pictures.

Brenna was getting older. She was becoming a little person. A smart little person. She was starting to ask questions: "Where does Uncle Jack live?" "Do I have grandparents?" And "Why don't we see our family on Christmas, like the families on TV?"

She met my parents for the first time just days before her fourth birthday, on the same front-porch steps I'd stormed away from years before, her little hands grasping for the American Girl doll my dad held out for her. Anyone could see the elation on her face, that her world was expanding beyond just me and Jack.

That's when I finally realized how selfish I'd been, withholding her from them. I wasn't just hurting them. I was hurting her.

A silent understanding passed between my mother and me that day—a truce of kinds. We've never actually talked about what happened, but communication has always been a problem for us anyway. I'd call what we have now "civilized."

That they dropped everything and rushed over here to take me to the hospital today? This is far from normal for us.

It takes me twenty minutes to get ready, the struggle with the most mundane tasks of pulling a shirt over my head and brushing my long hair beyond frustrating given my handicap.

When I emerge, my dad is still glued to the news. "It's over. We're finished for the season. Probably for the next five years," he grumbles.

"That's what happens when you give young men who already think they're invincible all that money." Mom's head is in my fridge, rearranging the condiments. Brenna's laundry has been sorted and folded, the worn floors look like someone's run a mop over them, and the books on my shelf and the shoes by the door are straightened. She moved fast, to get all that done while I wasn't watching.

I'm equal parts thankful and affronted.

"Stable condition . . . what does that even mean? Why won't they tell us more? I think fans have the right to know! We're the ones buying the goddamn tickets and the merchandise that pay these insane salaries! Hell, he could have a dozen broken bones in his body." My dad isn't one to say much, except when he's agitated.

He must be *really* agitated right now.

He turns to me, a freshly brewed cup of coffee in hand. "What do you think, Cath?" He lifts the mug to his lips before I can warn him against drinking it.

As his mouth twists with disgust with the first sip I cringe, offering a soft "Sorry." I picked up the single-serve Keurig at a garage sale for ten dollars, thinking I'd scored an amazing deal. Turns out the seller was looking to make a quick buck off trash, and I now have the worst coffee brewer known to man.

Shaking his head to himself, he sets the cup on a side table, dismissing it entirely. "How bad off did he seem?"

"He was pretty banged up." God only knows what internal damages he sustained.

"Did he tell you who he was?"

"No. He wasn't conscious."

My dad frowns. "What about when you helped him get out of the car . . . He must have said *something*."

"No. He never woke up."

"Well, he must have. I mean . . . the guy's two hundred and twenty pounds of solid muscle and you're . . ." His gaze slides over my slender five-foot-four, hundred-and-ten-pound frame.

I shrug. "I don't know. I was pulling on him and screaming, and then all of a sudden we were tumbling into the ditch. I guess he could have woken up just for that second? It was so hot in there, that probably brought him around. You know, self-preservation and all. I mean, he was seconds from dying, otherwise." The more I think about it, he *must* have come to and lifted himself out.

"Who was seconds from dying?" Brenna chirps, pirouetting through the space.

I rope my good arm around my daughter and plant a kiss on her forehead, reminding myself that those little ears are always perked. "Can you go and make your bed for me, please?"

My eyes trail her slight body as she trots off, excited to have another task. That should occupy her for at least three minutes.

When I turn back, I find both my parents simply staring at me. They've been doing that a lot since I opened the door for them this morning. "What?"

They share a look. It's my mother who answers, naturally. "We just can't believe you did what you did. We're—"

"I know, okay? I don't need a lecture. It already makes me sick to my stomach, just thinking about it. It was stupid and risky and I should have thought more about Brenna and—"

"Cath!" my dad hollers. He shakes his head at me in disbelief. "She's not trying to give you grief!"

"I was going to say that what you did was selfless. And brave." Then my mom does something so foreign, so unlike her—unlike us, and our relationship. She reaches for my shoulder and pulls me into an awkward hug. "You should be proud of what you did."

I simply stand there, stiff and confused, by both her actions and her words. Do I feel *proud*? No, 'proud' doesn't seem like the right word. Relieved that I don't have Brett Madden's death weighing on my conscience is more like it. And that feels selfish.

"Yes, what you did was crazy and reckless, and we"—she cuts her words off with a sharp inhale, as if she's catching herself—"you should be proud. We are proud."

I can't say when the last time was I heard those words come out of my mother's mouth. If I had to wager, I'd say that I've never heard anything that resembled them.

I feel my cheeks flush. "I guess I am, maybe, a little? I don't know. I just don't want the attention this is going to bring. For me and Brenna, and you guys. I'm afraid of what it'll turn into." I remember waking up to the sound of glass smashing, as someone threw a brick through the living room window. And how my dad lost his job at the paint factory after his supervisor, a good friend of Scott's father, cited him on a bunch of bogus infractions. And how Emma wasn't awarded the academic award when she graduated from eighth grade that spring, even though her marks were far higher than the next-best student. My mother was right—the Philips family practically owns this town, and they didn't seem to be the type to simply let things go and move on.

"This is very different from what happened before." My dad's knowing look tells me he hasn't forgotten it either. He got another job fast enough—on an automotive line, this time.

"I know, but I don't want to give people a reason to drag that all out."

My mom sighs. "Well, there's no point stressing over it now. We got through it once, and we'll get through it again. At least there's no shame this time around."

I purse my lips. The way she uses the word "we," she makes it sound like we did it together. We didn't. There was the Wright family, and then there was me.

Now's not the time to remind her of that, though.

"But you do have to get in touch with this hockey player. Or his family." My mom smooths her thin sweater over her curvy hips, where she's beginning to grow thick as she approaches her midfifties. "He owes you a new car. They have plenty of money. I'm sure he'll be more than willing to replace it. If not, I'll get Hansen involved." My mother has worked as a paralegal at Belmont's prominent civil law firm of Jeremy Hansen & Robert Shaw for the past twenty-eight years, and it has become second nature for her to look for the monetary gain behind every situation.

My shoulders tense. "I am *not* asking Brett Madden or his family to buy me a new car. And Hansen is absolutely *not* getting involved." At one point that bottom-feeder had my mother convinced that they had civil cases against Scott, the school board, and the paint factory where my dad had worked. She would have gone through with suing them all, too, had my dad not promised divorce. He was as tired of the circus as the rest of us.

Given the chance, Hansen will have Brett Madden served with papers as soon as he's up to receiving visitors from his hospital bed.

"Well, you need a car, Catherine. How else are you supposed to get to work?" The rare moment of affection has passed, and the Hildy Wright I know is back, her arms folded over her chest, that patronizing tone edging her words. That one that tells me she's about to take control, to harp on the issue until she gets her way.

"Hildy . . ." my dad warns. He's a calm, quiet man. He rarely raises his voice, and when he does, it's because he's had enough of my mom being, well, herself. He and I are much more alike, both introverts. He's always preferred working his shift and then enjoying a night with a beer and the sports highlights.

"Don't get offended." She heaves a sigh. "I'm not trying to manage your life. I'm just thinking about your welfare. And Brenna's."

"And I'm not?" I take deep, calming breaths, reminding myself that my mother isn't evil. That she does care about me. She just shows it in a way I don't appreciate. "I will tell people about the accident if and when I'm ready, and there is no way *anyone* is bringing up the idea of replacing my car with Brett Madden or his family. That is *my* decision to make, and I've made it." I say it slowly and calmly but firmly.

"And we respect that. Don't we, Hildy?" my father says, again in that warning tone.

"Why do we need a new car?" Brenna chirps, wandering back into the living room, breaking up the tension in the room.

"Mine doesn't work anymore, sweetie," I explain. It's not even worth the deductible I have to pay on insurance. There is no replacement value. I wouldn't be surprised if I get a disposal bill from the town for it.

"We'll revisit this conversation later," my mother promises under her breath. My dad rolls his eyes. After years of bending to her will, he's finally growing a spine.

"First things, first." Mom reaches down to grab her purse. "You need to get that wrist X-rayed. It could be broken. You *really* should think about seeking compensation for that, too."

I open my mouth, about to tell her that I'll find my own way to the hospital, that I don't want her involved because I don't trust her to respect my wishes, when my dad clears his throat, catching my gaze. In his eyes, I see only concern. "One thing at a time. Let's just worry about getting your wrist looked at."

"You can drop me off if you want. I'm probably going to be stuck there for hours."

"No, we're staying. Through *all* of it." His expression says this isn't negotiable.

And for once, I'm relieved.

Chapter 5

. . .

I spot three news station vans in the parking lot as soon as we pull in. It's not surprising that they'd choose Diamonds as the ideal place to squat, given that we've been voted the best truck stop diner in the state of Pennsylvania for the last ten years straight.

Still . . . I'm not sure what those reporters know. Keith's words from last night have kept cycling through my mind all morning, making me skate around every answer I gave the doctors and nurses at the hospital, making me eye everyone through a suspicious lens.

It'll be fine, I tell myself.

"I just need to grab my paycheck. Two minutes." I reach for the door handle, hoping to make the stop quick and painless, wanting desperately to get back to the safety of my tiny home.

"I'm hungry. Aren't you hungry?" Mom's eyes narrow as she takes in the sign that sits atop the diner. At least a dozen of the flashing red bulbs that outline the diamond-shaped appendage have burned out.

"Chicken fingers and french fries!" Brenna hollers from next to me in the backseat. "I want chicken fingers and french fries!"

Mom turns to me, her gaze rolling over the beige binding that the hospital wrapped around my wrist to help support it while it heals. It only took four hours at the hospital to tell me it's a bad sprain. "It's been a long morning. Why don't we have lunch here? Our treat."

True to my dad's word, they stuck by me the entire time, entertaining Brenna in the waiting room while I had X-rays taken and saw a doctor. And, surprisingly, my mother made no more comments about Brett Madden buying me a new car or compensating me for lost work. It could have been the whispered words exchanged between my parents as they lagged behind us in the hospital parking lot. Whatever it was, I'm grateful.

But I don't know that sitting in Diamonds, where people know me and are bound to ask questions about what happened, is the best idea.

"Please, Mommy! I'm *starving*! And we haven't eaten here in *forever*!"

Brenna's dramatic flair—and her pouty bottom lip—ends any possible protest from me. "Okay." I sigh. "But I need you to do me a favor and not repeat anything you may have heard me and Grandma and Grandpa talking about today."

She peers up at me with wide, serious eyes. "Like what?"

"Like . . . Just, anything." The last thing I'm going to do is give my five-year-old a rundown of everything she *isn't* supposed to talk about. Hopefully she's already forgotten. She's pretty good at keeping secrets, I'll give her that.

The buzz of voices envelops me the second we step inside the busy roadside restaurant, and I can't help but begin calculating how much tip money I'm losing by not working my shift today. My electricity bill for the month, at least. And because I left them one waitress short at the last minute, Lou's working the floor, apron on and cheeks flushed.

"We'll grab Number Fifteen," I tell Jessica, the sixteen-year-old Lou just hired as a hostess, and she leads my family to a corner booth where the sun beats through the window. After such a long, cold winter, all of us could stand some warmth.

Brenna runs toward Lou instead, wrapping her arms around my boss's thighs in a hug. For better or worse, Diamonds is her second home. She has spent plenty of time watching me wait tables when a babysitter fell through or when Lou was short staffed and begging me to cover a busy dinner hour at the last minute. In many ways, Lou filled the role of grandmother in the early years, plying my daughter with enough hugs and ice cream sundaes to win her eternal love.

By the tight brow and small sniff of discontent coming from my mother, I can tell that the special bond between the two of them hasn't gone unnoticed.

"What are you doing in here today, Miss Busybody?" Lou sets her tray of ketchup bottles on the counter so she can reach down to ruffle Brenna's hair.

"Mommy was in a car accident so we had to go to the hospital but now we're here with Grandma and Grandpa and I want chicken fingers and french fries because I'm *starving*."

"Car accident?" Lou's eyes flash with a mixture of worry and suspicion as she looks first to me, then to my bandaged wrist, and I can almost see the wheels working inside her head, replaying the voice message where I said that I fell.

Clearly, I was wrong and should have specified *exactly* what Brenna wasn't supposed to repeat. I fight the urge to groan. "I'm so sorry about leaving you in the lurch like this. It's just a bad sprain, at least. I should be back to normal soon."

"Doctor said at least two weeks, likely three," my mother throws in, her eyes on the dessert tent card menu tucked into the condiments stand.

Lou sighs. "Well, at least you're all right. I guess this happened on your way home from your date with Gord?"

Ugh. I'd completely forgotten about him until now.

My father perks up. "Date?"

"Yes, with my nephew." Wiping her hands on her apron, Lou only now takes in my parents, her polite mask usually reserved for customers who she doesn't know sliding on smoothly. "Hello. I hope you're both well." They haven't seen each other in years, since the last night my parents came in here, demanding to meet Brenna. Lou told my mother what she thought of her for how she handled the entire Scott Philips incident—it wasn't complimentary—and my mother told Lou that since her only son is in prison for armed robbery—of Diamonds—she had no business pretending she knew how to raise a child.

That dagger was well placed on my mother's part.

Lou threw a dagger of her own, telling my mother she was no longer welcome at the diner.

"We're fine. Thank you for asking." Hildy Wright has a mask of her own, and it's firmly in place now.

There's a sudden clatter in the kitchen, and Lou uses that as her excuse to escape the awkward situation. "I'll give you a few minutes to look over the menu." Reaching down to ruffle Brenna's hair again, she adds, "And Leroy will start on those fingers right away. Extra crispy, just how you like them."

"So? Who's this nephew you went on a date with?" Mom casually asks while she rearranges the sugar packets so they're grouped by variety and tidy in their holder.

"We can talk about that *later*." My parents catch my pointed glance at Brenna, who will no doubt repeat every unflattering comment word for word to Lou if asked.

"Are the wings still good here? I remember them being good." Dad slips on his reading glasses and draws his finger down the length of the menu.

"Same recipe." Leroy learned his lesson once, tinkering with the ingredients in the Diamonds burger patties. He'll never try that again.

"Well, then, that was easy." He pushes the menu away, folding his glasses and tucking them in his shirt pocket, before letting his gaze wander over the place.

Mine follows. There are plenty of regulars, but a lot of new faces, too. And I can spot the news crews right away. Three tables of them, the cameramen in casual attire—jeans or cargo pants, brown suede jackets—sitting across from their counterparts, the more polished reporters, dressed in button-down shirts and pressed trousers, ready to hop in front of a camera with sixty seconds' notice should the need arise. Each one grasps a white porcelain coffee mug as if its contents are the only thing keeping them alive.

I doubt they've slept since hearing about the accident.

Their very presence makes me anxious.

"Relax, kid. Everything will be fine." Dad reaches over and pats my forearm. "And no matter what happens, you just hold your head up high. You have every reason to." He ends that on a husky note.

"Thanks, Dad." I could have used that same sentiment seven years ago, but I'll gladly accept it now, with a smile.

"What are you doing here!"

I'm so on edge, I jump at Misty's sudden outburst beside me. Her giant round eyes—too large for the rest of her features, really—take my family in with curious interest as she slides a plate of fries in front of Brenna. "To tide you over," she whispers with a wink before turning back to me. "I thought you weren't coming in today."

"I'm just here to grab my check. And eat."

"Right. Lou asked me to take your orders." She scrunches her button nose as she sees my wrist. "Ow! How'd you do that, again?"

"Oh, I fell. Clumsy . . ." I try to cast it off as no big deal.

"But I thought you were in a—"

Dad shoves a french fry into Brenna's mouth, cutting her off before she outs me again. Thank God, too, because every last regular in here will hear about it before I leave if Misty catches wind. She has a hard time keeping secrets. That she's never said a word about Brenna's father to anyone—as far as I know—is no small miracle.

"So, how has it been today?" I ask, steering the bubbly blonde off the topic of my wrist.

"*Busy.* Especially with all these newspeople coming in and out of here. Did you hear about that accident last night with those two hockey players? Oh, my God!" She presses her notepad to her ample chest, the top button popped to earn herself a few extra bucks in tips from the single truckers who come through here. While I'd never describe Misty as beautiful, with her apple cheeks and her expressive blue eyes, she has a certain cuteness factor that seems to attract a lot of guys. She's never searching too long for the next date, that's for sure. "It's absolutely horrible! Someone said that the driver burned to death! Ugh! Imagine seeing that. How awful!"

"I'll have a pound of wings," my dad announces, his eyes flickering to me before turning to my mom. "Hildy?"

"A chicken Greek salad, please."

Misty gives her head a little shake, as if just remembering that she's here to take an order. "Of course. The usual, Cath?"

"Sure," I mumble, though I can't possibly stomach a club sandwich, my appetite still missing.

"'Kay! I'll ring these up straightaway!" she chirps, ever oblivious.

"She's . . . cheery," my mom says, though I don't doubt she's using another word in her head to describe Misty, and it's not an entirely flattering one.

Lou has reappeared from the kitchen, her arms loaded with a tray of glasses for the drink fountain. I feel the urge to get up and help her, but I wouldn't be much use right now, and she'd only yell at me to sit. She's a fifty-nine-year-old lady, but she has more energy than most of the waitstaff at Diamonds.

"Turn it up!" Jimmy, a Saturday regular, hollers, pointing at the flat-screen hanging over the serving counter, where someone's flipped the channel over from the baseball game to CNN.

The diner can hold ninety-six customers, and I swear, every last head turns to take in the charred wreckage of the Corvette that flashes across the screen, surrounded by police tape. The fog and the darkness helped dull the raw tragedy of the scene last night, but now in broad daylight, nothing can hide. Not the singed bulrushes, not the blackened trunk of the oak tree where the bark caught fire. I wonder if it will survive that wound.

A woman with high cheekbones and flawless olive skin stands to the right of the screen, giving the camera the opportunity to capture the bleak scene in the background.

"After sweeping Boston and Florida in four games apiece, Philadelphia Flyers right wing Seth Grabner and Captain Brett Madden were on a break before the Eastern Conference finals begin next Friday, and driving to a team gathering at franchise owner Sid Durrand's mountain house when the accident occurred. As you can see behind me, there is a near ninety-degree bend in this side road. Police believe that foggy conditions and speed may have been factors in the crash that left Grabner dead and Madden in the hospital. Police are reluctant to release details, but they have confirmed that a witness was at the scene of the accident." The screen pans to poorly lit video footage from last night, of Keith weaving around the barrier in his cruiser, a person with a dark gray blanket over her head sitting in the passenger seat.

I feel the blood drain from my face.

That's me.

"This witness is being credited for saving Madden's life, pulling him from the wreckage before the fire could claim him."

"Oh, my God!" Misty gasps, gaping at the TV along with everyone else. "Do you think it's someone we know?" she asks, to no one in particular.

"The Balsam County Sheriff's Department has not yet released the name; however, we suspect that the person is the driver of this car." The camera pans and zooms in on my Grand Prix.

I'm torn between the urge to run out the door and crawl under the table. In the end, I accept that neither is an option and simply sink into my chair.

It's a Grand Prix, though, I remind myself. There are plenty of them. There's no reason to automatically tie that car to me. And it's not even really recognizable as a Grand Prix, what with the damage. Misty, who's been in the car plenty, hasn't so much as glanced here. If she hasn't made the connection yet, I'm probably safe.

I feel eyes boring into my face.

Lou, staring intently at me from across the way.

I duck my head as she approaches, focusing on the menu that Misty forgot to collect. I memorized it front to back years ago and nothing has changed except the prices.

"Cath, why don't you come back to the office with me for a minute, to get that paycheck of yours." There's that tone, the one where I know I can't get out of this so I shouldn't bother to argue. And I never argue with Lou, even though sometimes she gives me more grief than my mother ever did.

Not until she pulls her office door shut behind me, enclosing us in the cramped room, does she speak again. "Catherine . . ."

She uses my full name only when she's annoyed with me, which is rare.

I sigh. "Yes?"

"That was your car on the news."

I mock-frown. "Why would you think that?"

"Because of that zebra-striped tissue box thingy sittin' in the rear-view window. You've had it for a good year now."

Now my frown is real. Lou has an uncanny sense of awareness. How does she remember these things? Will anyone else remember that?

Will I be outed by a decorative metal box?

"What? I've been admiring it. Anyways, that doesn't matter." She nods toward my wrist. "That happened last night, helpin' that man out of the car?"

I hesitate, then finally give her a single nod.

Her desk creaks loudly as she leans her weight against it, folding her arms over her ample chest. "Spill it. Tell me everything. Start from the beginning."

When I'm done, Lou is staring at me with that same stunned look that my parents wore earlier.

"What?"

She gives a headshake. "It's just . . . That must have been terrifying."

"Every time I think about it, I want to puke. And then I feel guilty about feeling guilty about it, and I want to be sick all over again."

"That's understandable. You're still out of sorts. A few good nights of sleep will help."

"Yeah. Maybe." I don't know how many good nights of sleep I'll be getting, given that I'll be worrying about money. I sigh, my eyes wandering around the small office, taking in the cotton candy–pink beanbag chair in the corner. It faces an old TV and DVD player, a stack of Disney DVDs next to it. Lou brought that in for Brenna, so she can hang out somewhere quiet when she gets bored with her coloring books out front.

Lou must be able to read my mind. "You gonna be able to manage with the bills?"

"I have some savings, if I need it." A meager few thousand that has taken me two years of scrimping, never touching, to squirrel away under a loose board in my bedroom, because I'm afraid I'll get cut off of government assistance if they see it sitting in a bank. It's money that is meant to go toward a future life. A better life for Brenna and me, whatever that looks like.

I *will* need it now, though.

Lou leans back and slides her hand into the top drawer of her desk. She taps my paycheck against the desk's surface several times, her gaze lost in thought, then hands it to me, and reaches back inside. "Here." She pulls out a wad of cash. "You're going to need another car."

I'm already shaking my head, but she thrusts the cash into my hands, folding my fingers over it. "Consider this an advance on your paycheck. It's all I've got on me right now."

After almost seven years, I know Lou well enough to know that when time comes to write me a paycheck, she won't be accounting for this. "No, I can't. It's not right. I'll manage. I'll—"

"Take it. I insist." She pushes it forward again. "It'll make *me* feel better. I'm doing it for purely selfish reasons."

If there's one thing Lou is not, it's selfish. The woman would give me the shoes off her feet if I were barefoot.

With resignation, I thank her and slide the cash into the envelope with my paycheck, fully intending to hand it right back to her once I'm healed.

I trail her through the kitchen and back out into the dining area. She leaves me at the service area to check on her tables, and I wander over toward my parents, throwing a hello to several regulars on my way. When they ask why I'm not working—because I haven't missed a Saturday shift in over two years, since Brenna was in the hospital with the flu—I simply hold up my bandaged hand and say, "I fell."

Technically, I'm not lying.

Thankfully, the TV channel has been changed back to sports highlights, and the quiet buzz in the restaurant carries with it plenty of mundane conversations that have nothing to do with Brett Madden. Or me.

And the reporters sitting mere feet away, sipping their coffees and biding their time for a clue, aren't the wiser.

Yet.

■ ■ ■

"I'll open it!" Brenna snatches my keys from my hand and runs for the door with them, my mom trailing behind her.

"Make sure the key is *all* the way in before you turn it or you'll snap it again!" I holler after her. The last time she tried to unlock the door, I had to fork over a hundred bucks for new locks.

"I know, Mom!" she exclaims with exasperation.

"Independent. Just like you were." A soft smile takes over my dad's face, as it always does when he's watching Brenna.

"Thanks again for lunch, and for taking me to the hospital. I guess . . . I'll talk to you later. I don't know if I'll be back at work next Saturday or not, so I'll let you know about babysitting Brenna." I turn to head for my front door.

"Hey, listen." My dad clears his throat. "So have you decided what you're going to do about a car?"

I groan. As much as I hate the idea of draining my savings, I know I have no choice but to face the inevitable. "I figured I'd call Keith to check out a few with me, so I don't get hosed with a lemon."

"Why don't I come by tomorrow and take you into Belmont. We can get an idea of what's out there. Just you and me," he adds quickly. "Your mom can stay here and look after Brenna."

"Really?" This is the most time I've spent with my parents—without the buffer of my siblings at Christmas—in years. "Are you sure you have time?"

He frowns. "Of course I'm sure. I'll come by around noon. We'll . . . we'll figure this out."

I don't really know what that means, but it feels good to have his offer of help. "Yeah, okay. That'd be great. Thanks."

He opens his mouth to say something, but hesitates. "It's all going to work out. Things will be back to normal in no time."

I force a smile.

If only I believed him.

Chapter 6

■■■

"When are you going to finish the attic?"

"When my wrist is better."

"Oh, yeah." Brenna's big chocolate eyes slowly drift over the half-completed sketch before moving on to the next page, her small hands struggling with the size of the book. "Can we give Stella a doggy pool? I was thinking she might like that in the summer."

I smile at my daughter, curled up in her sheets with her favorite stuffed dog beside her. "Yeah, I think she would, too. Right here?" I point to an empty spot on the left of the doghouse I drew for the husky Brenna wants so badly.

"Yeah. And maybe a tree over here, so she can have some shade."

"That's a great idea."

With a wide yawn, Brenna pushes the scrapbook toward me. "When can we go and see the Gingerbread House again?"

"I don't know. Right now you need to get some sleep."

"Okay, Mommy." She wraps her arms around my neck and squeezes tight. "I hope your wrist feels better soon."

"Me, too." I shut off the lights and head for the kitchen to pour myself a tall, cold glass of SunnyD, my one and only true vice next to coffee. It's juvenile and *so* unhealthy, but it reminds me of hot summer Saturday afternoons when Jack was just a baby and my dad was in charge of keeping my sister and me fed and watered. I suppose I'll have to graduate to something more mature at some point.

For now, though, I wash my painkillers down with it.

Brenna's bed creaks noisily as she flips back and forth, trying to settle. Another ten minutes or so and she'll be asleep. As desperate as I am to turn on the news station, I don't want her overhearing the reporters. She's a smart kid with a short attention span, which is the only reason why she hasn't already tied this terrible accident everyone's talking about to me yet. But she still may put two and two together and make "Mommy's the one who pulled the guy from the burning car" out of it. So far, everyone assumes it was a man who rescued Brett Madden, and that has kept them from making the connection to my "accident." But as far as Brenna's concerned, I'm superwoman and fully capable of such a feat.

So I wait for the creaking to stop, flipping through my sketchbook, studying the countless hours of work to kill time.

The only class I ever enjoyed—and excelled at—was art. Not just with Scott as my teacher, either. I was sketching from a young age. I'd draw the people around me, houses in the neighborhood, clothes. I loved to create. I never thought it could amount to a future for me. Not until Scott Philips started praising me and filling my ears with all kinds of ideas. Whispers of school where I could do this all day long, and how a few years of that could turn it into a career in fashion, or home design, or digital art . . . the sky was the limit for me in his eyes. I lapped it up, excited.

I stopped sketching after Scott Philips turned my world upside down. I didn't so much as touch a pencil. I figured he'd been lying to me about all that, too.

Then, a year and a half ago, a loose real estate flyer landed on our doorstep. It was for a sprawling Victorian house down on Jasper Lane that I knew well. I'd fallen in love with it as a child on a cold winter day when my parents packed us into the backseat of their car and we toured the town, admiring the Christmas lights.

It was Christmas at that time again, and though Brenna was only four years old, I bundled her up and we drove down so I could see the place. It had a FOR SALE sign on it and they were hosting an open house.

I couldn't help myself. We went inside.

It was everything I'd imagined, and more—with tall windows and detailed moldings, polished rosewood floors and delicate wallpaper. It was *huge*—three stories and enough space for ten people to live comfortably.

Brenna said it looked like a gingerbread house and asked if we could move there. I laughed and asked her what the two of us would do with such a giant house. She shrugged and said that we didn't need to use all of it. We could let others borrow it if they needed a place to stay.

"What, like a little inn?" I asked.

Her face scrunched up. "Can you have a dog at an inn?"

"It'd be ours, so I guess we could do whatever we want."

"Okay," she said, a twinkle of excitement in her eyes. "Then let's buy it and make it an inn." So simple.

If only I had the money to pay the astronomical price they were asking.

I chuckled, though inside me frustration swelled. This was just another thing on a long list of things that I would never be able to give Brenna.

Every night for the next week, Brenna asked me questions about our inn. What would her room look like? Would we eat with the guests? Where would she put her toys? Could she have a playroom? What would Stella's doghouse look like?

A week later, I was in Dollar Dayz, cutting through the art supply section, and I noticed this twelve-by-twelve-inch sketchbook.

I bought it.

And that night I began to draw the Gingerbread House for Brenna.

If I could give her nothing else, I could give her this—a way to imagine it.

A year and a half later, it's brimming with drawings. Of cottage gardens and lush bedrooms, of grand wraparound porches with people sitting around bistro-style tables, drinking their coffees. Of a kitchen sizzling with home-cooked meals. Of a peaceful lakefront, quiet in the morning and full of laughter in the afternoon.

Somewhere along the way, I found a part of me that I had lost. I found the ability to dream again. And the Gingerbread House became my dream, too.

Of a beautiful house that was so impeccably decorated that guests would be in awe as they stepped inside. Of a life where I could sit on that porch and watch Brenna roll through the grass with the dog she asks Santa for every single Christmas.

For years, I've hated Balsam. Not for its quaint main street, lined with charming shops and decorated by a canopy of mature trees and overflowing planters. Not for the picturesque landscape that surrounds it, nestled within a valley south of the mountains and surrounded by forest and lakes. Not for the odd sense of calm in the air, even as the streets come alive on weekends with countless tourists.

At first it was simply because I was a teenager, and most teenagers don't fare well in small towns like this. And then it was because of how the people in this quaint, picturesque little valley town treated me.

Now that I've come to terms with my life—I'm probably never leaving here—I've been able to step back, to look at Balsam through a different lens. To try to convince myself that maybe it's not so bad. The children's parks are clean and well maintained, the streets are quiet and safe. Keith complains that his shifts consist of driving drunk tourists back to their hotels and listening to the same people try to finagle their way out of speeding tickets, but that's not so bad. I may have wanted to escape, but then again, all these people are desperate to leave their big city lives to escape *here*. Maybe *I'm* the lucky one. Maybe there's a way I can still make a great life for Brenna and me here.

I realize that the inn is an impossible dream, but it has given me something to think about besides paying bills and work, and worrying about whether or not I'm a good mother. It's almost therapeutic, working on it at night, when I'm bone tired from a busy shift and sitting alone in my living room.

Only silence comes from Brenna's room now, so I tuck away the sketchbook in the side table drawer. Taking a deep breath, I do what I've been dying to do all day: I hit the Power button on the remote control, my stomach rolling as I scroll through the channels to find the news, afraid of what I might hear.

That Brett Madden took a turn for the worse.

That he didn't make it.

I finally stumble on a Philly news channel. It's a generic sports recap. The dull buzz of two commentators arguing over a referee call fills my tiny living room. It reminds me of weekends at home when I was younger. There was always a sports channel on in the background when my dad was around.

Someone says "Brett Madden" on the television and everything else fades into the background. They're showing a hockey game, the last game the Flyers played, and the camera follows a man wearing a construction orange-and-black jersey with the number 18 and the name MADDEN printed across the back in white, as he weaves around players like a dancer, his movement graceful but lightning fast. Once, twice, three times, he sinks a puck into the net, and the crowd goes wild.

Despite my father being an avid fan and my brother a talented player, I don't know hockey. I don't like it much, either, and yet even someone as ignorant as me can see that Brett Madden is truly gifted.

Because it's not enough to be born into extreme wealth and family fame.

They show several seconds of the team colliding into a tangle of sweaty bodies at the end, the joy they feel palpable. The camera pans to a shot of two men embracing on the edge of the rink. It's impossible to identify them if not for their jerseys, which read MADDEN and GRABNER.

My stomach clenches. This was their last game before the accident. Twenty-four hours later, one of them would be dead.

The camera flips to the newscasters again to discuss the accident, highlighting the main details as if everyone hasn't already heard them a hundred times. I keep waiting and hoping for more information on how Brett Madden's doing, but they have nothing more to give and seem more focused on his contract and what this devastating loss may mean to the Flyers' chances at a Stanley Cup.

The screen then flips to a taped interview of Brett. I stare at the broad-shouldered man filling the screen, dressed in a black tuxedo and wearing a dazzling smile, his wavy sandy brown hair combed back to curl at the ends. He's answering questions about his children's charity work with eloquence while flashes go off. He has a deep, smooth voice, the kind you feel in your chest.

I have no idea what a typical hockey player looks like, but he looks every bit the movie star right now, facing the camera with the comfortable ease of someone who has spent time in front of it. And I suppose he has, being Meryl Price's son.

This man . . . I stare at him and think he cannot possibly be the same man hunched in the passenger seat of that crumpled car, unconscious and bleeding profusely from his forehead.

He cannot be the same man I begged and pleaded and screamed at, to please get out of that car.

He cannot be the man I tumbled with into the swampy ditch.

He cannot be the man I saved.

He's utterly flawless.

Again, I assume it has to do with the infinite amount of money at his disposal growing up and a certain social grooming that comes with being in the spotlight, but there isn't a hair out of place, a tooth crooked or yellowed—or missing, as is apparently the case for many hockey players according to Jack. And his eyes are a dazzling aqua blue with green flecks circling his pupils. They're much like his mother's eyes, which have won over millions on screen.

It's hard to picture him as Meryl Price's offspring. Where she is slender, almost to the point of frailty, he towers over the male reporter holding the microphone to his mouth, his jacket tapering at a slender waist in comparison to his broad chest, the sleeves straining around his arms in that way that tailored suits tend to around built guys. Where Meryl Price's nose could be described as almost hawkish, his is strong and bends ever so slightly to the right, likely broken at some point. I guess that could be considered his one flaw, but it only makes him look more masculine.

He must take after his father. Who is his father, anyway? Another movie star? There was a time, long ago, that I was actually in the know on the latest celebrities. The young, hot ones, anyway. Never sports, though. From the buzz around Diamonds today, I heard that Brett was a first-round draft pick out of high school, not spending even a day playing for the farm team. I would have been sixteen. Already well on my way to troubled pastures.

The segment on Brett Madden ends with the sportscasters offering their condolences to the family of Seth Grabner, and then the news cuts to a special broadcast on the conflict in Syria.

And I begin to flip through the channels, in search of every last scrap of information I can find on Brett Madden.

Chapter 7

■ ■ ■

"You're still in your pajamas! Get dressed! Scoot!" I usher Brenna toward her bedroom on my way toward the front door, doing a visual sweep of all the things already out of place in our tiny house, silently cursing my parents for being fifteen minutes early.

"Keith?" I frown, peering over the massive bouquet of white flowers that fills the doorway—lilies and roses and a half dozen other flowers I can't even identify—to the blond boy-next-door haircut peeking out from behind. He needs two hands to hold the vase.

"I have to put these down. Seriously, they're giving me hives," he complains, forcing me back as he steps in and heads for the kitchen table.

I shake my head at the cruiser parked out front. That's twice since Friday that I've had a cop car parked at my house. "You can't keep showing up here in that thing. People will talk." People like Gibby, the gangly twenty-six-year-old busboy standing next to Rawley's Dumpster, his eyes glued to me as he takes long drags of his smoke.

"Yeah, well, when I took my oath to serve and protect, I don't remember agreeing to be a florist delivery boy." Keith sneezes.

"You're allergic to lilies, aren't you?"

"Is that what those things are?" he grumbles, dusting his hands against his uniform, only to sneeze again. "Great. My car is full of it."

I pluck the white envelope that sits perched on top and rub my thumb over the Philadelphia florist stamp with curiosity. "Who are these from?"

"Who do you think?" He grabs a tissue and blows his nose. "Madden's family has been harassing us since yesterday for your name, and since you refuse to let us give it to them, a truck showed up at the station this morning with orders to deliver these to 'the woman who saved his life.'"

"You told them I'm a woman!"

Keith shrugs. "You didn't say we couldn't do that."

I spear him with a glare before shifting my focus back to the card, nervous flutters stirring in my stomach.

"Well? Open it!" He pushes, turning to grab Brenna in a hug as she launches herself at him. "Hey, Squirt."

Just as quickly, she dismisses him in exchange for the flowers, reaching to touch the nearest petals. "Who are those from?"

"Some people your mom helped. Nice, huh?"

I tune out their chatter as I fumble with the envelope to peel it open. A standard card sits inside that simply reads,

Eternally grateful,
                    The Madden Family

Okay, so it's . . . short and sweet. But a nice gesture. Probably arranged by their publicist. But it's the thought that counts. And they did go to some trouble to get them to me. And there isn't really an appropriate way to express yourself through a third party–written two-by-three-inch card. And I'm sure they're all still at the hospital, overwhelmed and unable to focus on anything but Brett.

"Can I see? Can I see?" Brenna's little hand grabs for the card.

I lift it out of her reach. "Brenna, can you go straighten your room before Grandma gets here?"

"But, I already—"

"Shoved everything under the bed. Go on."

She grumbles under her breath as she stomps back the way she just came.

"Have you heard more? How is he?" I ask.

Another sneeze. Poor Keith. "Still in stable condition, last I heard. His mother was filming in Australia so she just got in late last night on a private jet. They brought in heavy security, too. Reporters are all over the hospital, but they're not giving them any information."

I nod toward the arrangement. "This was a nice gesture."

"You really should let me tell them who you are. I mean . . ." He glances around at my house, then at my hand. "You saved the guy's life. He could at least buy you a new car."

I treat him to a flat stare, earning his sheepish grin.

"Yeah. So your mother may have stopped by and asked me to talk to you." He shrugs. "She's not wrong, though. If someone pulled me out of a burning car, I'd want the chance to at least say thank you. My conscience would need that closure."

I shrug. "Maybe not everyone's like you." It's a weak argument, I realize, as I find myself agreeing with him. If roles were reversed, not being able to thank the person would likely drive me crazy.

"Word is he's a decent enough guy."

"I'm not worried about him not being a decent guy."

Keith looks at me through soft, knowing gray eyes. "What can they say that hasn't already been said?"

I drop my voice to a whisper. "Seven years ago, yeah. Do you really want Brenna hearing that her mother tried to seduce her teacher? Or that her dad is in prison for dealing drugs?" I was right to think that people would remember seeing me with Matt and put two and two together to make "Cath is having that scumbag's baby." I took Lou's advice and didn't confirm the rumor one way or another, the likelihood that Matt would ever hear about it almost nonexistent. After all, he was from New York City and in jail. DJ—also in jail—was his only tie to Balsam, and DJ's family moved out of the area not long after their son's arrest.

But now, with all this media attention . . .

Keith sighs. "Consider this your second chance. A way to redeem yourself, if you feel like you need it." With a glance over his shoulder toward Brenna's room, he lowers his voice and adds, "She's gonna hear it all one day. Let this become part of the story. Let it overshadow the rest."

Keith always has a way of making me look at things in a different light. How did I get so lucky to have him as a best friend? It was random, really. Two weeks after buying my Grand Prix, it broke down in the grocery store parking lot. I was eight months pregnant and fighting tears, not sure how I'd pay for whatever was wrong with it. Keith was there, picking up snacks for a party at a friend's. I barely recognized him, it'd been so long since our awkward make-out session, and we never ran in the same circles. He was into soccer and volunteering at his church. I was into boys and art and general mischief.

Turned out it was the battery. He boosted my car for me so I could get home and offered to bring by an extra one he had sitting in his garage. A new one was going to be a hundred bucks—might as well have been a million to me back then—so I agreed, assuming he'd be by the next day. He showed up in my driveway with the battery an hour later, along with soda, chips, and a double-chocolate cake for the pregnant girl.

He's been my best friend ever since, an even better friend to me than Misty if I'm being honest.

I sigh. "Look, I'll probably let you release my name to the family. Eventually. And not because I expect anything from him." I hesitate, reading the card once more before setting it on the table. "I'm just not ready yet. But if they call again, you can pass along my thanks for the flowers."

A knock sounds on the door then, and Brenna flies out of her room screaming, "I'll get it!" before I can take a step.

My dad steps in first, his arms filled with a large box. "What're you doing here?" He quickly sets the box onto the floor and holds out a hand. If there was ever a guy my dad wished I would marry, I'm sure it's Keith.

"Keeping the streets safe, one flower delivery at a time," Keith answers dryly. "I gotta get back to the station, now. See ya, Squirt." He rubs Brenna's head on his way past, nodding toward my mother. "Hi, Mrs. Wright."

"Now, Keith. I've told you about calling me Hildy." She smiles and winks before the floral monstrosity on my table steals her attention. "Who are these from?" She collects the card from the table, reads it, and sniffs with mild dissatisfaction. "Well, I guess that's a start."

I roll my eyes and nod toward the box in the middle of the floor, frowning. "What's that?"

"A coffeemaker that won't kill your guests." My dad waves toward the door. "Come on. Let's hit the road."

■ ■ ■

"So you decided to take me up on my offer." Gord's smile is smug as he approaches, sliding his hands around the inside of his pants to tuck in his button-down shirt, the buttons pulling across his belly. The twinkle of satisfaction in his eyes makes me wary, makes me think that he's sure I'm here for more than just a car.

Suddenly, I'm afraid that Gord might dive in for another kiss, so I step in close to my father until our shoulders bump together. He heard all about the horrible date on the drive over, and he promised to play interference. I didn't even want to come to Mayberry's, but I have five hundred dollars in my purse from Lou, and while I intended on giving it back to her, reality says I'll need it if I want to buy something that doesn't leave me stranded on a dark road late at night. In that case, there's really only one car dealership I can spend it at.

Dad steps forward to take Gord's hand, saving me from my discomfort. "I'm Ted, Catherine's father. Lou said you'd be able to give us a good deal?" That's my dad—right to the point.

"Yes, sir. I have just the vehicle in mind for your lovely daughter. And can I say how lovely she is?" His hands are up and waving again. Gord's switching into car salesman mode. Or maybe "impress the future father-in-law" mode. I can't be quite sure. Either way, it's making my skin crawl.

Gord frowns at my wrist. "Now what'd you go and do to yourself? Did that happen when your car went into the ditch?"

"Uh . . ." I didn't think to check with Lou on exactly what she told him, but she's obviously lied for me.

"Poor thing. Aunt Lou said you were having a rough go of things and I needed to be extra nice. Like I wasn't gonna be, anyway." He tacks on a big toothy grin, and I press myself closer into my father's side.

I keep my dad between us at all times as Gord leads us toward a 2010 navy blue Ford Escape with an $8,000 price tag scrawled across the windshield in orange. "Now, I know you said 'car,' but I can't help but feel that a special lady like Cathy, and that precious little girl of hers, should be in a safer vehicle."

"I completely agree." My dad is reaching for the door handle.

I've already tuned them both out. "This is *way* out of my price—"

"How many miles on the gallon do you get on this?" Dad asks, cutting me off, scanning the interior.

"Not as bad as you might think. It's only had one owner, low miles and mainly highway drivin', no accidents." Gord has turned all of his attention to my father, assuming he's making the decision for his "lovely daughter." "It's in mighty fine shape. I even considered drivin' it home myself when it rolled into the lot last week and I took a listen. Thing purrs like a kitten." A fake laugh bursts out of his mouth as he pats the hood. "A powerful V6 engine kinda kitten."

"And this price, I assume it's *before* this great deal you're offering us?" Dad's left brow arches. A trademark move of his that says Gord needs to do better than eight grand if he wants a hope in hell of making a sale today.

Gord waves his words away. "We'll talk numbers after. How 'bout I grab the keys and we can take it out for a spin."

Before I can say, "No, thanks," my dad is agreeing and Gord is ambling toward the office.

"Dad!" I hiss. "I only have twenty-seven hundred dollars and no bank is going to give me a loan. We're wasting our time, and his."

"Now, listen." He pats the air in a calming motion. "Your mother and I talked about it last night. I'm done with my car loan payments and . . ." A stern frown pulls at the deep grooves in his forehead. He had hardly so much as a hint of wrinkles before I left home. "Look, Catherine. I know we've had more than our fair share of differences, and sometimes I wonder if we handled everything wrong. In fact, most times I know we did. Your mother just—" He presses his lips together. "We want to help you. You and Brenna. Keep your savings and let us do this, at least."

"But this is too much." I look at the price, then the SUV, then him, a knot forming in my throat. Even with all three of us out of the house, I know my parents have always floated in the lower end of middle class. We had decent clothes but always purchased on sale. We went to the local T.G.I. Friday's for dinner, but only on special occasions and only on two-for-one entrée nights. Between my braces, Jack's hockey, and Emma's tuition, my parents are probably still weighed down by debt. There's no way they have this much kicking around.

"We'll manage."

"But I—"

He cuts me off with a gruff, "You can pay us back down the road." It's a brush-off, though I can tell he doesn't really mean it. "You can't support your family without a decent car. End of story."

I eye the SUV again. Not a spot of rust on it. Four doors, which makes getting Brenna in and out of it so much easier. But the clincher is a safer vehicle for Brenna. Especially now, after seeing how that sports car crumpled when meeting with a tree.

I nod, because I can't quite voice the "okay."

The door jangles as Gord steps out, keys dangling in his fingers.

"You sure you don't want to give him another chance? He seems to have taken a liking to you," my dad muses. "Maybe he was just nervous."

I watch Gord approach us with that odd, oafish lumber of his. "Yes, I'm sure I never want to go on a date with him again."

"Could mean a better deal today if he thinks he might get a date tomorrow."

I turn to shoot a glare at my dad, only to see his teasing smile. "Please don't barter me off like cattle when we negotiate this price down," I whisper.

"I'll try not to." Dad chuckles, roping an arm around my shoulders. It feels unfamiliar.

And so comforting.

Chapter 8

■ ■ ■

"How many times do I have to tell you, *go home!*"

"I'm fine, really!" I scrub at a spot of ketchup on Table 32 with my left hand. It's a simple act, but today it feels cumbersome. My right wrist is slowly healing, enough that I was able to grip the wheel to drive my "new to me" Escape today. "I don't need to write orders down, you know that. And Carl doesn't mind clearing my tables and helping me carry out food. I've already told him I'll split my tips with him." Our dishwasher-busboy Carl graduated high school last year—barely—and has absolutely no direction in his life, besides his one life goal to not work at his parents' gas station.

Lou glares at me, her hands resting on her hips, and I already know that idea's not being received well. "That boy will take his pay as expected and—"

"I don't mind, Lou! I just . . . I can't stay home." I pause to look up at her, to plead with my eyes. "I will literally go insane." It's odd that when you're constantly on the go, all you want is a day to do nothing. To lie on the couch in your sweatpants and watch TV and stuff potato chips into your mouth. But I've had six days of that and I can't handle one more hour of television and being alone with my thoughts. I'll start smashing dishes, just to give myself something to clean up.

"For the record, I think it's a terrible idea." She huffs a sigh, and I know that I've won. "Here. I have something for you." She reaches into her apron to pull out an envelope.

As soon as it lands within my grasp, I know what it is. I open my mouth to object, but she cuts me off. "When some of the regulars heard that you were in an 'accident'"—she emphasizes that excuse with a wide-eyed look—"and couldn't work, they started a little 'Catherine fund' tip jar. It's not charity!" she's quick to add, as I feel my cheeks flush. "They've all been there before, and they just wanted to make sure to keep you afloat until you were back on your feet."

I feel eyes on me and turn to find Steve and Doug, two truckers who meet here every Friday afternoon during their long-haul runs from somewhere in the Midwest, watching. I'd have known that they were two of the regulars who chipped in, even if Steve hadn't just thrown me a wink and a nod before turning back to his coffee.

"It's not charity," Lou repeats. "It's kindness, and you never turn your nose up at that."

I finally tuck it into my apron pocket with an embarrassed "Thanks." At least the diner's not too busy right now, so I don't have an audience.

She glances around, then lowers her voice. "Have you heard anything more from the family?"

I shake my head, scooping up a stack of menus and tucking them under my arm. "Nothing since the flowers." The Maddens still haven't spoken to the media, leaving reporters salivating and coming up with all kinds of speculation of their own. Reports that have kept me in a constant state of near-apoplectic shock—everything from claims that Brett is paralyzed and will never walk again, to lying in a medically induced coma, to having one foot in the afterlife.

I'm sure there are critical issues also being covered right now, like the Syrian rebels, and the devastating floods in Argentina, and a world hunger crisis, but I have been watching the Brett Madden Show. All Brett, all the time.

And I've learned a ton.

He's twenty-six. He'll be twenty-seven on September 2. His father is not a movie star or an NHL player or famous for anything other than being Meryl Price's husband. Richard Madden was a stagehand who won the actress's attention while she was filming in Toronto. After a whirlwind romance, they married, and she was pregnant not long after. It was important to both that their children stay grounded, so Richard Madden quit the movie industry and became a stay-at-home dad to Brett and his younger sister, Michelle, while Meryl's star kept climbing.

It's Brett's father, a huge fan of hockey himself, who put Brett in skates at three years old and discovered his uncanny talent. California wasn't the ideal location to nurture their son's burgeoning skills, so they bought a house in Richard's hometown near Toronto, where they could build an ice rink in their backyard during the cold winter months and live in relative peace.

Brett is half-Canadian. Hell, he basically *is* Canadian; he grew up there. Of course they have places all over the States, too, and the family has moved back full-time since.

The media loves Brett, almost as much as they love his mother. Every newscaster makes a point of mentioning how down-to-earth and charming he is, and the countless postgame interviews he grants rink reporters—moments after stepping off the ice, still out of breath and drenched in sweat—show nothing more than a humble guy who counters any praise he's given with kind words about his teammates' skills.

He's generous, too. The video of the charity event he spoke at? It's for a fund he has spearheaded, helping children from broken and dysfunctional homes learn how to play hockey. The charity even supplies their skates and their gear.

And he doesn't seem to be all about the money, whether that's because of his values or that he simply has so much of it that it's no longer motivating. Apparently he was offered a lucrative modeling contract at sixteen—I'm not surprised—but turned it down. He was also offered a role in a movie with his mother, without any acting experience. He turned that down, too.

He was drafted into the NHL and has been breaking records ever since. Three years ago, he signed an eight-year, seventy-one-million-dollar contract with the Flyers. And now people are wondering if Brett Madden will ever put on skates again.

Some hockey experts have already written him off, assuming that the ambiguous third party–reported injuries to his leg are serious and he'll never bounce back fully.

Maybe that's why his family hasn't spoken out yet.

Lou yanks the menus from my grasp. "I guess that makes sense. They must be preoccupied with worry over him. The last thing they want to be doing is talking to those hounds."

As if some kismet force is listening and feels the need to respond to our unanswered questions, the news channel cuts to a live broadcast from the hospital in Philly. I feel all the blood drain from my face as Brett Madden is pushed out in a wheelchair by a man whom I now recognize as his father.

"Oh, my God." *Is he paralyzed?*

What if falling down the hill paralyzed him? Or how I recklessly yanked at him as I tried to pull him out of the car? What if *I* caused that?

With a grimace and help from his father, Brett pushes himself out of the chair and my entire body sinks with relief. Crutches appear out of nowhere.

Countless flashes fill the screen as a horde of reporters waits to capture his statement. Meryl Price stands just behind him and to the side, well within the camera's angle. She's wearing a simple black blouse and jeans, her bombshell blonde hair pulled back in a sleek ponytail, and noticeably less makeup on than she has for the red carpet. She looks like she hasn't slept in days, the bags under her eyes poorly masked by makeup. Still, she somehow exudes glamour.

Brett's younger sister by sixteen months, Michelle, who's had several small roles in movies already and is said to have a promising acting career ahead of her, stands next to her mother, looking equally tired.

A week after the accident and Brett Madden's face is still banged up, both eyes mottled with shades of blue. His sandy brown hair hangs over his forehead, poorly disguising the bandages beneath. Yet he still looks more well put together than any man sitting in Diamonds right now, even with the scruffy facial hair. Somehow I first missed the cast on his left leg, peeking out from a slit in his track pants. That's the leg that was trapped.

The way he approaches the microphone, his face scrunched in pain, I can tell being out of that chair pains him.

And yet, even in his current shape, leaning against crutches for support, he stands tall, regal, and strong, his shoulders so broad that they dwarf the podium in front of him.

Yes, he definitely must have regained consciousness in those last seconds before tumbling out of the car with me. There's just no other way I could have gotten him out.

Somewhere in the background, the bell from the kitchen rings to announce a plate of food. I ignore it, gawking openly at the television, my stomach wild with butterflies as I wait anxiously to hear what Brett Madden has to say. Normally, Lou would be hollering by now, never one to let food sit idle under the heat lamps, but she's standing right beside me, her attention riveted.

"Good afternoon," Brett says, and the camera flashes explode in the room again. "I will give a brief statement and then answer a few questions for you today. After that, I ask that you give my family and me the space to recover and deal with a tremendous loss in my life." He sounds somber but calm and collected, his deep voice unwavering. Not at all like a guy who nearly died a week ago. Whose friend and teammate *did* die.

He swallows hard, the bob in his throat prominent. The only sign that he is affected.

"I should not be standing here today. I count myself extremely lucky to be doing so, after last week's tragic car accident that claimed the life of my good friend, Seth Grabner. My thoughts and prayers go out to his family and friends, and to the fans of the Philadelphia Flyers and the National Hockey League, who have lost an incredible player and man. I would like to thank the doctors and nurses at St. Mark's for providing me with such excellent care." He pauses, takes a deep breath, and I can't tell if it's due to physical discomfort or because of what he has to say. Not until he blinks away a slight sheen over his eyes several times, and then I realize this is all emotional pain. My heart tightens. "I will be with my teammates in spirit through the rest of the play-offs. They've worked hard and they deserve to hold that Cup." He accepts a bottle of water from his father, and I notice the slightest tremble in his hand. Nodding toward someone beyond the TV camera, he says, "I'll take a few questions now."

I strain my ears to hear the first one. *"Do you expect to be on the ice at the beginning of the next season?"*

Again, I see his throat bob with a hard swallow. I can't imagine standing in front of these people and fielding their questions. "We remain optimistic that I will make a full recovery. Next question."

Not exactly an answer as far as next season goes.

Another unseen person shouts a question out, *"Can you tell us about your injuries?"*

"They hurt," he answers bluntly, then offers a charming smile as a light chuckle rolls through the audience. "As you may have noticed, I have some broken bones and cuts, but I somehow escaped serious injury. And worse." He shakes his head to himself. "It's all rather miraculous, really. They made me sit in that chair over there for insurance purposes while I'm on hospital property, but I don't plan on spending any more time in one than I have to. Still, the doctors have insisted that I spend the next week or two off my feet. I'm not about to argue with them." He points at someone.

"Was alcohol a factor in the crash?"

"No." The word flies out of Brett Madden's mouth fast and firm and with more than a hint of anger.

"The Flyers are playing their first game of the Conference finals against the Toronto Maple Leafs tonight. Will you be at the Wells Fargo stadium to help bolster their confidence?"

"I'll be at the games as soon as my doctor permits it. But they don't need me there to win. There is a whole team of very talented players who will succeed."

"At any point did you think you were going to die while inside the car?"

"I wasn't conscious through any of it, so no." He abruptly stops, presses his lips together.

That same reporter asks, *"Reports say that the car was already burning by the time emergency vehicles arrived. How did you get out of the car, then? Did it have anything to do with the unidentified person at the scene of the accident? Did he pull you out?"*

The muscles in Brett's thick neck cord with tension and he nods to himself, as if he were expecting that question.

My stomach tightens. That's me they're talking about. They still think it's a "he." Good. Let them keep thinking that.

But what is Brett going to say?

What do I want him to say?

A part of me—a big part—would prefer he simply pleads ignorance or outright lie. Maybe use the very useful "no comment."

I hug the menus to my chest with my good arm, waiting with everyone else to hear about this "mysterious person."

Meryl Price catches her son's attention with a graceful hand on his arm. He covers the microphone and leans down to allow her to whisper something. She shoots him a stern look of warning.

Oh, to be a fly on that podium right now.

Removing his hand from the microphone, he seems to struggle with his decision. The camera zooms in suddenly, as if the operator has guessed that whatever Brett Madden has to say will be that much more impactful when viewers can feel the weight of those intense aqua blue eyes framed by a fringe of thick, dark lashes. "Yes, *she* did." That smooth voice, that practiced speech, cracks with emotion. "It was a woman who pulled me from the car before I burned to death, and I would really love to thank her in person, so if she's watching this . . . let the Balsam Sheriff's Department release your contact information to me. *Please.*"

That pleading tone is like a spell, gripping me. I find myself whispering, "Okay," before I realize it, then clamping my mouth shut and glancing around to make sure no one heard me.

Shouts fill the room as reporters struggle to get their question heard. Cameras flash and click. But Brett offers a quick, "That's all, thank you," and eases himself into the wheelchair. With his father pushing and his mother and sister at his side, he leaves through a side door.

And I can't help but feel the shift in the air around me.

The news channel moves to a live report from a blonde female reporter. "Brett Madden addresses the media for the first time since last week's tragic car accident that claimed the life of Philadelphia Flyers right wing Seth Grabner. Police have so far withheld details about the accident, but Madden himself has just admitted to being pulled from the wreckage by an unidentified female. The question remains, who is this good Samaritan, and will she finally reveal herself? Well, Raven News may be able to answer Brett Madden's plea, as our reporters on the ground have uncovered information about the black sedan seen at the scene of the accident." The screen flashes to my burned-out car. "Stay tuned for more from investigative reporter Camaria Wilkins shortly."

Lou leans in to whisper. "Your license plate. I'll bet someone from the towing company leaked it."

I don't want her to be right, but Lou's always right. She's notorious for it. Tension courses through my body as I accept that the sand in my hourglass of anonymity is close to expiring. I'm about to be outed as the "she," and if the reaction in that press room was any indication, there's no way the media's not going to latch on to this story in a big way.

Lou's hand settles on my shoulder. "I think it's time you head out."

I don't argue with her. I simply go to the back to grab my purse, hoping I can make it to school to get Brenna before the news breaks.

Chapter 9

. . .

"Carrots don't actually give me night vision. That's just something parents tell their kids to make them eat their vegetables." Brenna scrunches her nose up at her plate.

"You're right."

Her brows jump a moment before excitement dances in her eyes. "So . . . I don't have to eat them?"

"Oh, you still do. Or I'm going to make you watch me eat this." I hold up the Oreo cookie—Brenna's favorite and the last one in the house.

She scowls at me but pops a carrot into her mouth, because she's afraid I'm not kidding. She earned her sweet tooth from me, after all.

I sit down across from her.

"You forgot your plate."

"I'm not feeling well." My stomach has been in knots since leaving Diamonds.

"Because of your wrist?"

I sigh. "Yeah. Because of my wrist." How much longer before I find myself explaining things I hadn't planned on telling her for years? What's it going to be like for her at school? What are kids going to say to her about her mother?

Oddly enough, she seems to have accepted that it's just me and her. That a daddy doesn't fit anywhere in this equation. That doesn't mean she hasn't asked—who he is, where he is, is he dead, why doesn't he live with us. I've successfully danced around the answers, telling her that sometimes daddies aren't around and that's okay, because that just means I get to love her twice as much.

My phone begins ringing and Lou's name appears. It's five P.M. A mere three hours after Brett Madden's live statement. Part of me doesn't want to answer the phone, but my gut tells me I should.

Lou's agitated voice fills my ear. "That sniveling nephew of mine! I'm so sorry, Cath! I can't believe he would do this!"

I don't know that I've ever heard Lou so upset before. "What did he do?" A sinking feeling tells me it has to do with me.

She groans. "Turn on Channel Seven."

Oh, God. I already know this is going to be bad.

I had warned my parents not to answer any questions about anything related to me or the accident that might be coming soon. I should call Jack and Emma to tell them the same thing—they still have no idea that I was involved. At least Emma is smart enough not to say anything without first checking with me. I *hope* Jack is smart enough, but either way, he's in the middle of his last exam, so I'll have to wait.

I flip on the TV in time to see Gord's chubby-cheeked, hairy-mole face fill the screen, a prominent shot of Mayberry's store signage in the background. A female reporter stands next to him.

". . . Oh, it's her all right, the woman I'm dating. Last Friday night, we were having dinner in Belmont, not five minutes away from my store, Mayberry's New and Used Vehicles." He enunciates each word of the name slowly and loudly, turning to face the camera as he promotes his store.

Blood rushes to my ears. I can hear Lou saying something through the receiver, but I ignore her, tuned in to the TV.

". . . She got into her black 2000 Grand Prix at around nine thirty, on her way home to her sweet little daughter. I've been tryin' to get her into something better, but she loves that car! Anyway, she was takin' her usual route home on Old Cannery Road . . ." My teeth grit as the weasel both outs me and presents himself as someone who knows everything there is to know about me. Gord Mayberry has hit a new low in the ranks of slimy car salesmen. ". . . and she came upon Mr. Grabner's car. Poor thing, she sprained her wrist somethin' fierce, tryin' to get Brett Madden to safety. You should see it, all swollen and bruised and wrapped up in bandages. She's a single mom and waitress over at my aunt's diner, Diamonds, out on Route 33, so you can imagine how devastating somethin' as simple as a sprained wrist might be."

"Mommy! Who are they talking—"

I cut Brenna off with a sharp shush as I turn the volume up to listen to Gord hang me out to dry.

The reporter shifts her microphone to ask, "Stats put Madden at two hundred and twenty pounds. She must be a strong woman, to pull an unconscious man of that size out of a car."

Gord belts out one of his awful fake laughs. "No! That's just it! Cathy's a tiny wisp of a thing. It's a damn miracle. Oh!" His hand flies to his mouth. "Sorry for cussin' on the air. Anyway, divine intervention is what I call it. But it's just like my girl to help others. She's come a long way from her wild teenage years, I'll tell ya."

"'Wild teenage years'?" the reporter repeats, and I swear her face lights up like a kid discovering a treasure trove of sweets.

"Oh, yeah. That affair with her high school teacher, the Philips guy. Affluent family around these parts, so it was an especially big shock to everyone. Course, she recanted her statement, so who knows what actually happened, but some say that *somethin'* happened."

"Brenna, go to your room right now," I somehow manage to get out. I'm going to lose my lunch, and it's been hours since I ate.

I hear her whine of "why?" somewhere in the background, but I'm too focused on the TV to answer.

Here we go again.

Only this time it's going to be *so* much worse. This is going to make national news.

"Anyhow, she came in on Sunday with her father—good man—and I set her up with a nice Ford Escape from right here, at Mayberry's New and Used Vehicles. Hopefully she'll think twice before parkin' too close to a burning vehicle next time, am I right?" Again, that fake chuckle, this time embellished with a snort.

"Well, thank you so much for taking the time to speak with us, sir."

"Yeah, don't forget. I'm Gord Mayberry, from Mayberry's New and Used Vehicles. And no problem at all. I don't know why my Cathy wouldn't just tell people what happened. She deserves to be recognized. She's the only reason Madden is alive right now!"

The camera cuts to the reporter, though Gord rambles in the background. "Divine intervention in the form of a young, single mom and waitress from Balsam, Pennsylvania, is apparently what saved Brett Madden's life. We'll be back with more on this developing story, heard on Raven News first."

A pizza commercial airs as Lou's sigh fills my ear. "Do you know the idiot called me up all proud of himself, lookin' for praise for getting both of our family businesses free advertising. I swear, that boy has the same screw loose in his head as his daddy. I don't know what's wrong with him."

There are at least a dozen things I could name that are wrong with him, but I have bigger things to think about.

Gord just handed me to the media on a silver platter. "Why would they air that? What kind of reporting is that?"

"It's Raven News. Are you really surprised?"

"No, I guess not." They're notorious for being bullies and reporting on events without actual, confirmed proof. "But—"

Knuckles wrap on my front door.

"I'll get it!" Brenna hollers, skipping from her bedroom.

"No!" I don't mean to yell at her, but I'm too freaked out to keep my voice level. I didn't even hear the steps creak, a telltale warning that someone is here. "Come here and finish your dinner." To Lou, I say, "Give me a sec. It's probably Keith." I set the phone down on the table and head over to answer the door.

It's not Keith.

It's the same reporter who was just on TV with Gord, and she's now standing on my front stoop, a microphone in hand, a monstrous camera angled directly on me behind her, the bright beam of light capturing what I'm sure is a ghostly pale face. "Catherine Wright! We've received reports that you are the woman who pulled Brett Madden out of a burning vehicle. Is this true?"

She shoves the microphone into my face, waiting.

I'm frozen, caught in that lens like a deer in headlights for two . . . three . . . four seconds, before I snap out of it and step back to slam the door in her face, fumbling with the dead bolt, my hand trembling.

I'm such an idiot. I should have checked the porch through the blinds before I opened the door. But I've never had to before. No one but Keith ever just shows up.

"Mommy, what's going on?" Brenna stares at me with wide, fearful eyes. She's not used to seeing me like that. I always strive to keep a calm, cool head around her.

"Nothing. Stay put." I slink over to the living room window and push the blinds open a crack to peek through. The news van is parked next to the Dumpster in the pool hall parking lot, and a photographer is taking pictures of my tiny ramshackle house.

I sense Brenna coming up beside me and I pull her away just before her tiny fingers go for the blinds. "No. Stay back!"

"Why?"

"Because I said so." I cringe the moment the words come out of my mouth, because I always hated that answer coming from my own mother. I promised myself I'd never use it, and I've been good about that up until now.

Lou's loud voice carries from my phone, calling my name. I forgot about her.

"Reporter. On my doorstep. The same one that interviewed Gord." I was obviously watching a replay if the woman had time to get here from Belmont.

"Oh, Lordie." I can just picture Lou rubbing at the frown line between her eyes. "They're like hounds after blood."

"How did they find me so fast?"

"They had someone in the DMV run your plates." She says it so matter-of-factly.

"Isn't that illegal?"

"Like they'd care if it was. They want this story."

I sigh. "What do I do? They're still out there."

"They're trespassing and invading your privacy. Call Keith."

Another sigh. "Right." I don't like taking advantage of my friend-ship with him, but I don't have much choice. I peek out the blinds again. "Okay. I guess I'll see you tomorrow."

"Are you nuts? You're not coming in here."

"But it's Saturday." I make triple what I would on any other day.

"That envelope I gave you should more than cover it. And I have it in my mind to make my no-good nephew fork over some money to help cover what you'll be missing on account of his big mouth. You mark my words."

There's no point arguing with Lou, and besides, I don't have the en-ergy. A week of poor sleep, nightmares, and constant worry has finally taken its toll on me, drawing dark circles under my eyes and weighing down my weary body.

"Keep me updated about what's goin' on, ya hear?"

"Yeah." I hang up with Lou and see the slew of missed calls from my mother and Misty. No way in hell can I deal with Misty right now.

The news anchors fill the TV screen again. "Police are still not releasing the name of the woman who pulled Brett Madden from a burning car last week, but local sources have named twenty-four-year-old Catherine Wright as the driver of the 2000 Grand Prix."

"Mommy!"

"This isn't the first time Catherine Wright made headlines. Back in 2010, she claimed she had an affair with her—" I squeeze the Power button on the remote control so hard that the plastic body makes a cracking sound as the TV shuts off.

"Why are they talking about you? What were they going to say?" Brenna's big eyes peer up at me. "What's an . . . affair?" She tests out the word on her tongue for the first time.

I'm not ready for this. How much easier it would be if this had happened four years ago, when she was still blowing raspberries and throwing oatmeal at the wall, happy and oblivious. "Just . . . Go and finish your dinner. Please, Brenna." I toss the remote to the couch, fighting tears of dread.

■ ■ ■

"Damn, I can't watch this." Keith only flipped on the TV a minute ago but he shuts it off now, the five-to-one score for Toronto painful to see. Anyone who was hoping the Flyers would rally in memory of their two players will be sorely disappointed.

He peeks through the blinds. "We can keep a car on Rawley's for the night, as long as they don't get called away on an emergency."

"Are the reporters gone?"

"No, but they're out on the street now."

"How many?"

He hesitates. "More than one."

I groan.

"Not much we can do about it unless they're disturbing the peace. You know, all that journalistic rights bullshit." Keith isn't a fan of reporters, either, but that has more to do with them pestering him for story leads than any past interest they've had in me.

"What about *my* rights?" I mutter, wandering over to my kitchen cupboard.

Keith offers me an apologetic smile. "You know they're not going to stop until they get their story. As soon as you leave the house, they'll be on you, with cameras."

I sigh, reaching for the bottle of chardonnay from the cabinet above the fridge, a Christmas gift from Emma. It's seven bucks at the grocery store, not exactly high end. Still, wine is a luxury these days, so I've been holding on to it for a special occasion.

And SunnyD just isn't going to cut it tonight.

"Want some?" I wave it his way, earning his grimace. "It's not chilled, but I can put some ice in it."

He tosses his phone and keys on the kitchen table. "My night's clear now, so yeah, I can stick around for a bit. As long as you never tell the guys."

I scan his jeans and button-down shirt. I'm used to seeing Keith in uniform, so maybe it's that, but he looks different tonight. More put together than usual. "What were you doing when I called, anyway?"

He waves my question away with, "Ah, nothing. I was just going to meet up with someone, but I can do that anytime."

I'm dumping ice cubes into two glasses when it finally clicks. The cologne, the chain around his neck . . . "You had a date tonight, didn't you?"

"Like I said, no big deal." He heads into Brenna's room to tuck her in and say good night. Thankfully, as soon as Keith showed up, she quickly forgot about everything else.

Great. Now I feel bad. Keith had to cancel his date because of me. Keith rarely ever goes on dates. The guys around the station give him the gears about it constantly. I know because I overhear some of it when they come into Diamonds.

My phone chirps with a text from its resting spot on my table, and my shoulders instinctively tense. Raven News got hold of my home number and started calling me every five minutes until I unplugged the old rotary phone. I may have to power this one off next, if they've managed to find it.

It's not Raven News, though. It's Jack.

I turn my phone on after my last exam to find out that my sister saved my idol's life. Are you fucking serious????

I sigh. Looks like news has reached Minnesota, and likely the entire rest of the country. I guess that means Emma has heard by now, too. She's not done with exams until next week. Luckily, it would take a nuclear bomb to disrupt her study schedule.

I punch out, *Sorry. I didn't want to distract you. I'll call you tomorrow, promise.*

Of everyone in my family, Jack's the only one I've never gone out of my way to avoid. But this isn't the kind of thing you text about, and I'm not up to answering a million questions just yet. Misty has already lit up my phone with a slew of messages. I made her the same promise, though I'll be stretching that "tomorrow" out as long as possible.

Brenna's giggles carry from her room, so Keith is suitably distracted. I do what I promised him I wouldn't. Grabbing the remote, I turn the TV back on, lowering the volume so far that I have to stand right in front of it to hear the reporter. ". . . Our sources have confirmed that the Grand Prix removed from the scene of the accident is registered to Catherine Wright of Balsam County. We know that she was driving her car on Old Cannery Road at the approximate time of the accident, and that the woman who called nine-one-one identified herself as Catherine. We have yet to speak to the single twenty-four-year-old mother and waitress, who has refused several of our attempts to get her side of the story."

"And you *won't* be speaking to me," I grumble under my breath, scowling.

"Catherine Wright made local headlines seven years ago as a junior at Balsam Public High School when she claimed to be romantically involved with her art teacher, Scott Philips. Philips's father was the principal of the school at the time. She recanted her statement after Philips's arrest, and all charges against him were dropped, despite records detailing several inappropriate interactions between Wright and Philips."

How the hell did they get arrest records already?

"Philips, who was charged with the misdemeanor of corruption of a minor—"

Keith's fist slams against the Power button on the television. "What are you doing?"

I toss the remote to the couch, that deep burn of shame settling into the pit of my stomach. A sensation I haven't had to feel in some years. "That didn't take long."

Grabbing me by the shoulders, Keith spins me around and pushes me to my dimly lit kitchen table. The electricity bills in this drafty little house are higher than they should be, and so I bought those energy efficient lightbulbs in an attempt to counter the costs. The only noticeable change so far has been poorer lighting.

I nudge his wineglass toward him, shuddering from the chill of the ice. "How is that jerk Gord Mayberry allowed to just go on TV and say that?"

The chair's legs drag across the worn linoleum as Keith sits down. "There's not really a law against it. Maybe if he had made a false statement there'd be more we could do."

"Alluding to us dating is a false statement." I can't keep the grimace from my face.

It matches the one that flashes across Keith's. "Yeah . . . not gonna lie, hearing that made my stomach turn. You haven't given any guy the time of day for *years*, and then you go out with *him*?"

I shoot him a soured look as I ease into the chair across from him. "It was a blind date. I don't know why I ever agreed to Lou setting us up. I guess I thought I could actually meet someone."

An awkward silence hangs in my little house for a long moment as I take a sip of my wine, feeling Keith's weighty gaze on me. We talk about a lot, but our dating life has always been an unspoken subject. Neither of us has ever had to draw the line to make sure it doesn't come up. It's like we both intentionally avoid it.

For different reasons, though, I think.

While he has never come out and said it, I've seen the looks, I've noticed the way he's always available for me, how he answers my calls and texts immediately, without fail. Even when he's in the middle of something police-related and can't really talk.

I'm not the only one who's noticed either. Misty's convinced he has a diamond ring tucked away in an underwear drawer, sized for my finger. Every once in a while, when I'm especially lonely, I consider what it would be like if we were something more. But the thought always ends when I remind myself that I don't feel that way about him. I'd be settling, and that's not fair to Keith.

"What the hell's with these, anyway?" Keith holds up the crystal glass in his hand.

"What? I found them at a garage sale. They're nice!" And they were only fifty cents apiece.

"They're made for children."

"They don't make wineglasses for children."

"Then why are they so small? Come on, it's like a shot glass!" To prove his point, he brings the rim to his lips and finishes it in one gulp, contorting his face into a sneer that I can't help chuckling at. That's Keith, always able to make me laugh, even in shitty situations.

"Sorry . . . next time I'll make sure I have beer." My eyes wander to the window, and unease creeps back in. There are people waiting for me beyond those curtains.

That reality puts a damper on the momentary relief.

"Tell you what, I'll do a drive-by during my next shift and shake Mayberry's tree a bit. Give him a good scare for taking advantage of the situation."

"He'll probably try to sell you a car while you're at it," I warn.

"I'd love to see him try." He nods toward the street. "So? Shitty reporter practices or not, that's not going to go away. I'm guessing there will be ten more out there by the morning."

I sigh. "I know."

"You can't avoid it, Cath. What are you going to do?" Keith is notorious for being my voice of reason.

"What *should* I do?"

"Just give them what they want."

"And that is . . . ?"

"The story. Tell them what happened, say your piece, and be done with it."

"I'm not Gord Mayberry. I don't want to be on TV."

"Like I said that night, you're getting your fifteen minutes of fame whether you like it or not, so just get ahead of it now, while you still can. They're going to tell the world about Catherine Wright." He leans forward in his seat, a soft expression taking over his typical nonchalant face. "Make sure they tell the right version."

I shake my head, the dread of my past rearing its ugly head. I thought that part of my life was over.

"You were in high school. High school kids do *stupid* stuff all the time. Hell, I just arrested a fifteen-year-old last week for shoving potatoes in his neighbor's tailpipe."

"Not even close to the same thing."

"I know you think you're still some sort of social pariah, but honestly, you're the only one who hasn't moved on. Everyone else has."

"This is just going to remind them." I sigh. "I don't want to go back to that. You don't know what it was like, not being able to go anywhere without feeling people talking about you, glaring at you, judging you . . . *Knowing* that you're the topic of conversation around tables and at parties. And that was when I was seventeen and the paper couldn't publish my name. Now there are going to be millions of people talking about Catherine Wright."

"So you slept with your teacher when you were a teenager. You saved a guy's life, too. Which part do you think people are going to be more interested in hearing about?"

We were friends for two years before Keith got the nerve to ask me what really happened between Scott and me, if I had made it up. When I told him that I hadn't, he believed me instantly. "Get out ahead of this and show them who you are now. A responsible, loving, selfless mother, and incredible woman." His voice cracks over those last two words.

I drop my gaze to where my fingertips grasp the grooves in the crystal, the emotion in his words pricking me a little too close for my liking. "I don't know . . ."

Keith hesitates. "Brett Madden called the station."

"Right. Of course he did." In all this, I hadn't even thought of *him* seeing the broadcast, but it stands to reason that he'd be watching the news, too. "What did he say?"

"He wanted to know if it was really you, or if Gord was just some jackass looking for airtime."

"And? What did you tell him?" I can't hide the anxiety from my voice.

"He's desperate to talk to you. To thank you. So stop being such a chickenshit. After what you did for the guy, it's kind of pathetic."

"Okay," I hear myself blurt out, taking both of us by surprise.

Keith's brows shoot up. "Okay?"

A flutter stirs in my stomach. "Yeah. I mean, it's all out in the open now so . . . May as well talk to him, right? You could give him my number and . . . I don't know . . . tell him to call me?" What's it going to be like to talk to him? Even after what happened, I can't help but admit that I'm a bit starstruck.

Keith toys with the empty glass on the table. "Yeah, okay. I could do that."

My gaze drifts to my worn La-Z-Boy and the old rotary phone sitting on the table next to it, unplugged. "My cell number."

He chuckles. "I figured as much."

"Okay." I'm going to talk to Brett Madden. Maybe I'll even meet him? A second, stronger wave of flutters hits me, thinking of the man standing at that podium on television today.

Keith shoots a glare my way, and I realize I've started biting my thumbnail, a nervous habit.

"What do you think he's going to say?"

"Uh . . . 'Thanks for pulling me from a burning car'? 'Thanks for saving my life'? 'I owe you one'? Something along those lines, anyway. Just a wild guess, though." His phone chirps and he immediately reaches for it, only to frown at his screen. "Shit," he mutters under his breath.

"Something wrong?" Please don't tell me that Keith has to leave. I feel safer having him here.

"Nothing. Just . . . I told my date that I had to work late and I guess she found out that's not true."

I'm about to ask why he lied to her but decide against it. People around here assume we have something going on, and if she's heard those rumors, then it would stand to reason that he not tell her he's bailing on her because of me. "Who is she, anyway?"

His mouth twists in a grin, making him look even more boyish. "Her name's Cora. She's a paramedic. Just started a few months ago."

"Not from around here, then?" I'd remember if we'd gone to school with a person by that name.

"Nah. Grew up south of Pittsburgh."

"First date?"

Keith's expression is neutral, unreadable. He's a master of that. "Third. Or fourth? Can't remember."

That's his way of saying he's not at all serious about her, or wants me to think he isn't, anyway. A part of me—the selfish part—is relieved because it means I'm not going to lose his undivided attention just yet. But at the same time I want him to be happy. It's just not going to be with me. "I'm glad you've met someone."

His phone chirps again, and he begins punching out a text as he mutters absently, "Not sure that's going to go anywhere now."

"You should just call her and explain the situation. Not over text," I push, adding a soft smile.

"Huh?" A deep frown creases Keith's forehead, a look of confusion fills his eyes. "Oh, right. Yeah, I'll talk to Cora later."

I guess he's not texting Cora, then?

He climbs out of his seat and heads for the window to peek out the blinds. "So, okay. Cath, don't get mad."

Wariness slips down my spine as I watch him reach for the dead bolt. "Whenever you say that, I usually have a good reason to be pissed with you."

He opens the door. Muffled voices sound beyond. "Careful on that," Keith warns someone. "The last thing you need is to break your other leg."

A man's smooth chuckle sounds and I feel the blood drain from my face. I jump to my feet, so fast that the chair topples over, two rungs cracking as the back hits the linoleum.

But I couldn't care less about my broken chair right now because Brett Madden is suddenly standing in my doorway.

Chapter 10

...

I've only ever met one famous person before, and "famous" is a big stretch. I can't even remember her name. She played the precocious little girl in the Campbell's soup commercials when I was just a kid. There were at least three different ads, and I used to see them on television ten times a day. It felt like that, anyway. This girl and her family vacationed in a Balsam-area summerhouse one July and our paths crossed. She was a snot, plain and simple, her nose so high in the air I'm surprised she didn't trip over the curb. The moment her eyes touched you, it was obvious what she thought: that she was better than you.

That was my one and only foray into knowing a celebrity. And now Brett Madden is standing in the front door of my tiny ramshackle rental cottage, and I am in a pair of two-sizes-too-big gray track pants and a graphic cotton T-shirt with Grumpy Cat on the front, and my hair is pulled into a messy bun on top of my head, and I am going to kill Officer Keith Singer for surprising me like this.

Brett looks much the same as he did in the news conference earlier today, other than swapping out his black shirt for a light blue and gelling his hair slightly. His face is just as scruffy. That's a hockey play-off thing, from what I'm learning. It does a solid job of hiding the chiseled jaw I know is beneath, but it doesn't take away from his eyes, which are piercing, much more so than they seemed through the television screen.

Maybe it's because now they're trained on me.

As covertly as possible, I reach up to smooth and tuck the stray strands of hair that hang around my face behind my ear. When it was Keith, I didn't really care what I looked like. Now, I'm toying with the idea of excusing myself and darting into the bathroom.

Brett sighs. "He didn't tell you that I was coming."

Before I can respond, Keith pokes his head in. "I was just about to." He has his even-toned cop voice on now, the one he uses when he's working or talking about police-related matters. I spear him with a look that says he's a lying bastard, but it doesn't ruffle him. Keith can deadpan, even when he knows he's in the wrong. "I'll be out here on the porch, keeping an eye on the vultures. If you need me, holler." He pulls the door shut behind him.

And I'm alone with superstar and media heartthrob Brett Madden.

I want to ask so many questions. Mainly, what is he doing here? Why did he leave his bed—his doctors told him to rest for the next few weeks—only *hours* after being released from the hospital?

And yet I can't seem to form a single word.

All I can do is stare at this imposing man standing in my living room, until he begins to shift on his crutches.

"I saw the news break, so I left Philly and headed here. I knew that mess out there was going to happen, and fast, once they had your name. I'm sorry, I should have just said 'no comment' and left it at that." His naturally deep voice sounds different, slightly off, a touch unsteady.

Still, it somehow vibrates inside my chest. I can actually *feel* his voice.

"Why didn't you?" I manage to get out in a croak. I remember him hesitating during the press conference, his mother giving him that disapproving look that all mothers somehow master without training, myself included. Was she warning him not to?

He sighs, shakes his head. "Honestly, I don't know. I guess I just thought that, if that was the only way I could reach you . . . I'm sorry." Sincere eyes peer down at me. Even all banged up, he's entrancingly handsome.

I feel a blush creep in under the weighty gaze. "It wouldn't have mattered anyway. They had my license plate number so it was only a matter of time." Another long pause hangs between us, until I nod toward the front door. "How bad is it out there?"

"Depends. Are you ready to talk to a reporter?"

"No. Not particularly."

"Then I'd suggest you stay put." His eyes skim over my tiny house, stalling plenty, and making me wish that Keith could have at least given me five minutes' heads-up to straighten up the place.

What must he think of my cramped space and kitschy thrift store finds, with his multimillion-dollar houses and fast cars and, I'm sure, designer *everything*. I'm dirt-poor by comparison.

I take a deep breath and force myself to stand taller, to not compare myself to that, to not be ashamed. I've worked hard to get here, and all on my own, with a child in tow. That's something to be proud of.

He nods toward the last vase of flowers on the side table, where Keith moved them for fear of an allergic reaction, though the lilies are long gone. "My mother said that she sent flowers."

Last week while I was car shopping with my dad, Mom decided that the bouquet from the Madden family was "too ostentatious" for my table, so she and Brenna spent the afternoon arranging flowers in jars and glasses, and then strategically placing them along windowsills and side tables. There wasn't a flat surface in this place that didn't include flower petals. I've been changing the water daily, and plucking out the overripe blooms one by one, trying to preserve them as long as possible.

"Yes. Please tell her thank you. They were beautiful." An absurd voice in my head wonders if I'll ever get to thank her for them in person, but I quickly dismiss it. Not likely, given who she is.

After a moment, his gaze lands on me again and the most awkward tension settles in the air. Or maybe it was there from the moment he stepped through the door and I'm only just noticing it, now that the initial surprise of him in my doorway has faded.

He shifts his stance and winces in pain. "Do you mind if I grab a chair?"

I finally snap out of my daze. He's not even supposed to be on his feet, and here I am making him stand at my door. "Oh, my God. Yes. Please." I rush to pull a chair out for him, inhaling a light waft of cologne on my way past. A wave of déjà vu hits me. He was wearing that cologne the night of the accident. My senses didn't process it then, but they obviously cataloged it for future reference because I'm instantly drawn to it, breathing in the scent of him, horrific memories or not.

I step back to make room, silently assessing how tall and broad he is as he hobbles closer. They say television distorts your body, adds twenty pounds. I'm thinking they've got it backward, because he feels larger than life right now.

How the hell did I ever get him out of that car?

He's peering down at me, scanning my slender arms and bony shoulders, like he's thinking the exact same thing, but he doesn't voice it, easing himself into the chair with great difficulty, propping his crutches against the table next to him.

I move Keith's dirty glass to the sink, feeling Brett's warm, probing blue eyes on me the entire time. I can't help the heat from crawling up my face, so I duck over to the sink and busy myself with rinsing dishes, waiting for my cheeks to cool. "I don't have much to offer, but do you want a drink?"

He groans. "I'd kill for a cold beer."

"How about cheap white wine that makes you cringe?" I *really* need to start stocking beer in my fridge.

When Brett doesn't answer, I glance over my shoulder to see his amused expression. "I'm not selling it very well, am I?"

"Not really."

My eyes drift to his hand, resting casually against the worn wood-grain tabletop, its massive size all the more pronounced next to my dwarf wineglass. "You probably should avoid alcohol anyway right now, being on meds?"

"You're probably right," he murmurs, a secretive twinkle in his eye that brings another uncontrollable and embarrassing flush to my cheeks.

I turn away from him, this time to wash my hands. "We have milk . . . water . . . ," my eyes drift to the coffeemaker my dad got me, "coffee that won't poison you . . . tea . . . SunnyD."

"They still make that?"

"They do."

"I think I was about seven when I had that last." He chuckles.

"It's my daughter's," I lie, embarrassed. I can't imagine the women he associates with drinking anything but martinis, vintage wine, and organic smoothies.

After a pause, "Let's go with the kid juice."

I set to getting him a glass, the simple task taking longer on account of my wrist.

When he speaks again, his voice is much softer, more hesitant. "You were yelling at me that night, weren't you. When I was in the car?"

A long, shaky breath sails from my lips. *Yes . . . Until my throat was raw. So he did hear me.* "You wouldn't wake up."

"All I remember is driving along that road and the fog, and Seth talking about the new lines and how it was a bad idea for the coach to switch them up. Then suddenly a woman was screaming at me from somewhere far away. And it was hot."

I nod absently as I pour his drink. "I've never felt anything like that fire before. When the entire car went up, I was afraid the bulrushes in the ditch would ignite from the heat alone."

"How long did it take you to get me out?"

"I don't know. It was all a bit of a blur. Emergency response was there in about four minutes, and I managed to get you out just before they came." *I gave up on you. I turned and started to walk away. Did you hear my screams of "I'm sorry," too?*

Maybe that's why I'm struggling to meet his gaze now. Everyone's praising me for saving his life, but I was going to leave him there to die.

I've had my back to this man for far too long and now I have no excuse, unless I decide to wash my sink load of dishes.

With a deep breath, I walk over to the table to set his glass down in front of him. Then I turn my attention on righting my chair, picking up the broken rungs. I should be able to glue them back. Again.

"How'd you hurt your wrist?"

Something else to look at, to distract myself with, so I don't have to meet his searching eyes. I took the tensor bandage off earlier, to allow my skin to breathe and to give my fingers a chance to stretch. My wrist is back down to normal size now and the coloring is more yellowish green, not nearly as ominous looking. "When we tumbled into the ditch, I guess. I didn't feel it until after." Maybe I should put the bandage back on now, though. My thoughts are so frazzled, I may forget and bump it against something. Where did I put that—

"Catherine."

I inhale sharply at the sound of my name on his tongue. I've always hated my name. It's so ordinary. Even the spelling is unimaginative. When I was eleven, I went through a phase where I spelled it "Kathryn," because I wanted to be different. It threw everyone for a loop and pissed my mother off something fierce. Teachers kept asking me to spell my name correctly and I refused, earning me a trip to the principal's office.

Hearing Brett say my ordinary, unimaginative name in his deep, gravelly voice for the first time makes me hear a simple beauty in it I've never experienced before.

"Yes?"

"Can you please sit down?"

Gathering my nerve, I slide into the chair opposite him, taking a sizable gulp of my wine, hoping that'll help combat the tension.

And then I meet his gaze.

He has what I would call "soul-searching" eyes. They meet yours, but they don't just look at you. They look *into* you, delving deeper, beyond the layers and guises, to uncover who you are at your core.

Or maybe it's just me he's trying to read.

After a long moment, he matches my earlier move, bringing the rim of his glass to his full pink lips, downing half the cheerful orange liquid in a few big gulps.

I may never wash that glass again.

"I'm sorry I invaded your house like this. I just . . ." Even beneath the mangy beard, I can see Brett's strong, angular jaw tense. "I needed to talk to you before they got hold of you."

They. The media, I'm assuming.

"Do you think they'll get bored sitting out there?"

He smiles sadly. "They're too much, even for me, and I've grown up with it. I can't imagine what all this is like for you. I get why you'd want to avoid it."

I shrug. His worry for me—and how plain it is on his banged-up face—is endearing. "There never was any way to avoid it forever. I guess it's kind of good that it's finally out in the open. I've been dreading it for a week now."

He nods slowly. "So, that was your boyfriend who spoke on the news?"

"Oh, God. No!" I roll my eyes. "And if you hear that I've been arrested for killing him tomorrow, don't be surprised."

Brett's face lights up with his laugh, a beautiful and deep melodic sound that breaks apart the thick cloud of tension, and I start giggling along with him. Thank God Brenna sleeps like the dead, at least for the first few hours. "Who is he, then?"

"My boss's nephew. I agreed to go on a blind date with him that night, and it was the worst date I've ever been on in my life."

Brett searches my features, a hint of a smirk touching his lips. Aside from the quick appraisal of my house, I don't think those eyes have left my face this entire time. It's unnerving. "I'm guessing it wasn't so bad, in his opinion?"

"He doesn't seem to have clued in yet, no."

"And he thought he'd take full advantage of the situation by promoting his dealership."

"I'm glad it was that obvious." I down the rest of my wine and consider going for a refill, but I don't want this guy thinking I'm a drunk, so I stay put. "So you said in your news thing this afternoon that you're going to make a full recovery. That's great."

For the first time since I sat down, he averts his gaze from me to wander over my kitchen cupboards, an odd, hard expression flickering ever so quickly. He takes another big gulp of his SunnyD, his sharp Adam's apple bobbing with his swallow, before setting the glass down carefully.

"So . . ." His eyes drift from my face, over my shirt. "You like cats?"

I instinctively fold my arms over my chest, feeling all the more self-conscious in my underwhelming A-cup size. "Only the angry kind."

He chuckles, shaking his head. "How on earth did you pull me out of that car? You're so small." He lifts his hands up, palm out. "Don't take that the wrong way. I'm sure you're really strong and all, I just can't see how you did it. I mean, I was imagining a"—his voice cuts off, his brow furrows deeply—"a different sort of woman. But you're so small and I'm . . . well, look at me."

I've barely stopped looking at you. God, and I'm blushing again. "You must have come to at the last minute and stood."

His head is already shaking. "I have a broken tibia and a shattered ankle, my shoulder was dislocated, *and* I had a major concussion. I wasn't capable of pulling myself out of a bucket seat."

"Well, then . . ." I let my words drift. I guess that means I, Catherine Wright, pulled a man double my size out of a burning car.

"Well, then . . ." he matches, ensnaring me with his intense eyes. They hide unreadable thoughts I'm suddenly desperate to know.

The spell is broken when Keith hollers at someone outside. "Hey! You want to be arrested for trespassing? No? You've got three seconds to . . . Oh, you want to take pictures of me? Sure. Okay . . ." His shouts fade as he no doubt charges for whoever's testing him, the porch steps creaking under his weight.

"You know they won't leave you alone, right?"

I sigh. "Until they get their story, yeah, I know."

His fingertip absently traces the wood grain of my table. "What are you gonna do?"

Just the idea of having a TV camera pointed at me makes me tense up. "I figured Brenna and I would hole up in here for a while, until I figure things out." But for how long? We can't stay here forever. When will it be safe to send her to school? If they hound me at my doorstep, will they have the audacity to track my daughter, too?

Brett's face softens at the mention of Brenna, and he glances behind him, toward the bedroom doors. "That's your daughter's name? Brenna?"

I smile and nod.

"She's sleeping?"

"Obliviously."

"How old?"

"Five. Six in July."

"You must have been really young when you had her."

"Eighteen."

His mouth opens, but then he hesitates. "What you did for me, it's a pretty amazing story. People will want to hear it. From you. I wish I could make it all go away, but I've been dealing with these people long enough to know I can't. If you want my advice, it's best to just get it over with."

I groan. "That's what Keith said."

"Then he's a smart guy. You should listen to him."

"He has his moments. But don't tell him I said that."

Brett's chair creaks in protest as he leans back against it. "No pressure at all, but if you want, we can set up an exclusive interview with someone reputable. Give them your story, let people hear it, and they'll move on to the next thing fast enough. Honestly, waiting will only make it worse. They're already looking for anything they can on you." A frown flickers over his brow.

"Yeah, I saw the news." He doesn't have to explain further. "It was a long time ago. I thought I was in love. I didn't think . . ." I fumble over my words. "I was just a stupid teenager who—"

He reaches across to grasp my hand around the stem of my glass.

My tongue stops working under that touch. Does he feel what I'm feeling, too? Is his heart racing right now? Or is it just me?

"I don't care about any of that, and you don't have to explain yourself." He lets go and reaches into his pocket with a slight grimace. He pulls out and slides over a folded piece of paper that he obviously prepared before coming here. "Here's my number. Think about doing the interview and let me know. And you can call me anytime, day or night. Anything you need. Absolutely anything, I'm serious."

I reach for the paper, our fingertips sliding against each other again. A strange current courses through me, making me keenly aware of every square inch of my skin. The paper's still warm from sitting in his back pocket. I collect it in my fist, reveling in his body heat.

Brett shrugs. "And who knows? We could probably get a bidding war started. Someone may cut you a big check for this."

"What?" I blurt out.

I think he mistakes my shock for excitement, because he smiles. "They say they don't pay for news stories, but that's bullshit. Everyone wants to hear from the woman who saved me. You may as well cash in on it."

I can't keep the scowl from showing. "I don't want to cash in on this. That's not why I helped you. I'm not one of those people." Is that what Brett thinks I am? Someone who looks for ways to make money from tragedy? Someone like my mother?

Or is it because I'm on welfare. Have they reported that yet? It's not like I *want* to be on food stamps and getting checks for rent, but I don't have much choice, with a child and only my GED, which I *finally* got three years ago.

His eyes widen with apology. "I didn't mean it like that, I swear. People do it all the time. I just figured . . ." His eyes flicker across my living room before snapping back to me, as if he just realized what he was doing.

Yes, I could use the money. But I won't cash in on a tragic car accident to get it.

"I'm sorry. It was a dumb thing to suggest. I don't know why I did. I guess I'm just used to . . ." He finishes off under his breath with, "those kind of people," and then sighs. "Either way, it's still a good idea to do an interview. My publicist can set it all up for you. And I can be there with you, if you want."

Would that be better or worse for my nerves, having Brett in the room with me? With a shaky sigh, I nod. "I'll think about it, but the TV thing isn't me. I don't like having a spotlight on me. I don't want *that* life."

His lips twist. "You mean *my* life?"

"I'm just saying that it's not for me. I need things to be simple for me and for Brenna." My gut tells me that he and Keith are right. I just need to get this over with and move on, and hopefully not humiliate myself, or my daughter, in the process.

Speaking of Brenna . . .

I glance at the analog clock on my ancient avocado green stove—the landlord refuses to replace that relic, fixing it himself every time it tries to die—to check how long I have before she's likely to wake. A few hours yet. But if she finds Brett here, I'll never get her back to sleep.

Unfortunately, Brett takes that as a signal that I want him to leave. "I should probably get back to Philly." My table groans in protest as he uses it for support to stand.

"No. I didn't mean to . . ." I let my words drift. What am I going to do, beg him to stay? "You didn't drive yourself here, did you?"

He chuckles, slowly easing himself onto his crutches. "No. I have a driver. He's waiting outside with Officer Singer." He heads for the door.

I move past him, intent on opening it for him.

"Wait."

The single word is uttered in a soft whisper and yet somehow makes me jump.

Brett hobbles toward me, his face twitching with pain, until he's mere inches away. Towering over me, forcing my head back. "I'm sorry, I don't know what I was expecting when I got here, but it wasn't you and I was nervous."

"*You* were nervous?" I can't stop the weak giggle from escaping my lips.

His eyes roam my face. "It's not every day that someone saves your life. And then I saw you and . . ." The softest sigh escapes his lips. "I haven't actually said 'Thank you' yet."

I train my eye on his Adam's apple. *He saw me and what?* "There's no need."

"Of course there is. I've been lying in a hospital bed for the past week, thinking of what I'd say when I finally met you, and here I am now and even though I'm talking, I feel completely speechless." He reaches up to toy with a wayward stand of my hair. I've all but forgotten my disheveled appearance at this point. "And in awe."

"*You're* in awe?" I snort, and then my cheeks burn bright with embarrassment and I avert my gaze to the floor, because I just snorted in front of Brett Madden.

"I would be dead if it weren't for you."

"Anyone would have done the same."

"No. That's not true. A lot of people would not have done the same. A lot of people would have taken one look at the car and not bothered. Or they would have seen the first flame and run." His large hand gently and completely wraps around my biceps, his touch both soothing and inducing heart palpitations. "You're half my size, you have a child, and you did the impossible, and because you did that, I'm standing here right now."

I almost left you there.

I can't shake my guilt. I avert my gaze to study the old floor. And his navy blue Nike sneakers. Or rather, his sneaker, since the other foot is in a cast. "I'm just glad it worked out."

His hand settles under my chin, pushing against it until I lift my head.

With a deep, shaky breath, I meet Brett's eyes, rimmed with dark bruising yet still beautiful. And glistening with moisture now.

A strange, unexpected bubble of warmth swells inside my chest at this very vulnerable side of him.

Hooking his free arm around my shoulders, he awkwardly pulls me in tight against him, resting his chin on top of my head.

Despite my apprehension, I can't help myself. I melt, my cheek against his firm chest, my arms slipping around his trim waist, until I hear the sharp inhale and I assume I'm hurting him. I begin to pull away but his arm only tightens around me, squeezing me against him. I can feel every contour of him. He must feel the same of me.

I silently pray that my hair doesn't smell like the batch of battered fish that Leroy burned in the kitchen this afternoon. I didn't have the foresight to shower right after work.

Brett doesn't seem to be in a rush to let go, so I close my eyes and let myself enjoy the warmth of him, losing myself in the fantasy that this is more than just the embrace of a grateful man.

A knock sounds on the door a moment before it creaks open. I immediately pull away just as Keith and a giant, burly guy step through. I'm guessing that's the driver, though I'd peg him as the bodyguard.

"Your mother just called me," the man says in a deep baritone.

Brett sighs. "I'm going to assume she's the reason why my phone's been vibrating nonstop in my pocket?"

It has? He never glanced at it, not once.

A slight smile touches the driver's face. "She doesn't sound too happy. Says you were supposed to take your pills two hours ago."

"Yeah. I was in a rush to get here and I forgot. I'm starting to regret that." He winces in pain as he turns to peer down at me. "I'm serious about setting up the interview. Let's get them off your back, Catherine."

There's my name on his tongue again. My body hums with excitement as I offer him a tight smile. "We'll see."

He does another brief visual sweep around my house. "Until then, you should think about staying with family."

There's no way I'm bringing this to my parents' doorstep. And I refuse to be driven from my home by those assholes. "We'll be fine here. The drapes are all drawn. They're not going to break in." I look to Keith for confirmation. "Right?"

"No, I can't see them doing that. But I'll stay here tonight and I've got the guys keeping an eye out. She'll be fine as long as she stays put," Keith says.

Brett nods, sizes him up with a curious gaze before turning to his bodyguard. "How fast can V.S.S. get a body out here?"

I frown. A body? Does he mean a bodyguard?

"Two hours," the hulkish man answers in that rumbling voice. "I'll call it in now, if you want."

"Yeah. Please."

"Is this *really* necessary?"

"Why don't you take a stroll outside and see for yourself?" Keith dares me, and the look on his face tells me that's the last thing I want to do.

"Just for a few days, until the attention dies down," Brett offers, his voice soft. Almost pleading. "I'd feel a lot better. So would my family."

I picture the front of my little cottage adorned with a giant armed man in a suit, and I nearly laugh. But his concern for me keeps the amusement at bay. "So what *exactly* will this 'body' do?"

"Keep people who aren't supposed to be here off the property and away from your door."

"Think of Brenna, Cath," Keith reminds me, going straight for my weak spot.

"If you think it's necessary." I hesitate. "Thank you." God only knows what one of those guys will cost.

"He'll come to the door and introduce himself within the next two hours. We'll send Officer Singer his name beforehand so you know who to expect."

"Okay."

Brett hesitates. "Could I have your number?" It's a simple request, and yet there's something timid and boyish in the way he asks.

Just as there's something altogether giddy and girlish in the way my heart flutters when I nod and reach for the pad of paper on the side table. I manage to scrawl my number using my injured right hand—it's sloppy but legible—and then gingerly hand it to him, feeling Keith's eyes on me the entire time.

I'm so wrapped up in Brett's presence that I don't hear the bare feet padding on the floor until it's too late.

"Mommy?" Brenna's standing in the short hallway in her bubble gum–pink pajamas, her sleepy eyes blinking as she tries to focus on the strange men in our house. "It's noisy out here."

"Get back to bed. I'll be there in a sec," I whisper, trying to shoo her before she fully wakes.

"What happened to his leg?" She points at Brett's cast, ignoring me completely.

"He broke it," Brett answers with a grin, watching her little face scrunch up.

"How?"

"In a car accident."

She frowns. "There's been an awful lot of car accidents around here lately."

I can't help but chuckle. She's too sleepy to connect the dots.

"'Kay. Come on, Squirt." Keith spins her at the shoulders. "Say good night, Brenna."

"Good night, Brenna," she mimics, giggling all the way to my room because she thinks she's being clever.

When I turn back, Brett's looking at me strangely.

"What?"

He shakes his head. "Nothing. Have a good night."

Should we be saying good-bye instead? Will I see him again?

With one last glance over his shoulder at me, Brett struggles out the front door on his crutches. I turn the dead bolt and then scurry to the window to watch him ease down the steps with great difficulty. I've never been on crutches, but they don't look easy to navigate on the best of days.

Lights flash from Rawley's parking lot as he makes his way to the car. Photographers who have snuck back on foot. A few minutes later, the SUV drives off.

"So?"

Keith's voice startles me. I hadn't expected him out so fast, but of course Brenna went straight back to sleep for him. "So?"

"You just sat across the table from Brett Madden. How do you feel?"

I couldn't have begun to describe what I feel right now, even if I wanted to. But I don't, especially not to Keith. I pick up the remote to flip on the news, curious to see what they're saying.

The front of my tiny white clapboard cottage rental is on the screen, with Keith standing in my doorway and Brett hobbling up the front steps on crutches, and a caption below that reads, "Brett Madden visits Catherine Wright at her home."

A fresh wave of shock rolls through me. I won't be sleeping tonight.

Keith yanks the remote out of my hand and, turning it off, tosses it to the coffee table. "Gin rummy?"

"Fine, but I'm an invalid, remember."

He fishes the deck of cards out from the side table drawer. "Easy to beat. Just how I like it."

■ ■ ■

I inhale the scent of Brenna's shampoo—strawberries and cream—as she sleeps soundly with her back to me, her hot little body overheating mine. But I still don't pry myself from her, content to have her close to me in the darkness while I lie awake and ponder Brett's surprise visit tonight. It has sufficiently distracted me from the fact that my dirty laundry is now being aired across national television.

For the first time since the accident, all I can think of is him.

Of his beautiful aqua-blue eyes and his warm, genuine smile.

Of how relieved I am that he's going to be fine.

Of how much I enjoyed my brief time with him, as shocking and overwhelming as it was.

Of how it felt having his strong arm wrapped around my body.

Of what it would feel like to have him hold me close, not because I'm the woman who saved him but simply because he wanted to.

When I finally drift off to sleep, I'm reveling in that hopeless fantasy.

Chapter 11

...

"So when's he coming back?" Keith asks, his back to me as he peers through the blinds, a cup of coffee against his lips.

"When is *who* coming back?" Brenna chirps, adding with exasperation, her tiny hands grasping her playing cards, "I'm *ready!*"

"Uncle Jack. Next Sunday, after his trip to Cancún." My phone conversation with my brother lasted twenty minutes—the longest I've ever had with him, as we mainly communicate through texts. "How's the guy doing out there?"

"Seems fine." Keith takes in the rigid military man standing outside next to my front porch. He's the second shift and he looks eerily similar to Hawk, the deep-voiced man who arrived last night, dressed casually in a golf T-shirt and dark wash jeans and wearing a gun. "You sure you even need me here?"

"I'm not sure of anything anymore," I grumble, picking up my cards for another round of go fish.

My phone buzzes again. Brenna's annoyed groan is louder than mine.

Keith chuckles. "Misty?"

"Probably." I powered my phone back on today and found twenty-seven text messages from her. Once the expected "It's tomorrow! CALL ME" and "I can't believe you didn't tell me!" and "You're all over the news!" lines were out of the way, the influx of questions and inappropriate comments started, because I'm pretty sure she'd have spontaneously combusted if she couldn't get them out in one form or another.

Is he as hot in person as he is on TV?

Are you going to see him again? Can you call me so I can come over?

What was he wearing?

What did he smell like?

Did you get to touch him?

Did he touch you?

I hate you so much! Can you ask him to come to Diamonds?

Do you think he'd be okay with me hugging him?

I won't lie, when I read that last one—Keith's favorite—I pictured a cute big-breasted Misty with her arms wrapped around Brett's chest and a spark of jealousy flared.

Then, because I hadn't answered her messages, she started flooding my phone with pictures of him. I don't know where she found them, but suddenly, I had photos of Brett in tuxedos and swim trunks and everything in between. Of him alone, and of him arm in arm with plenty of beautiful women.

Women I could never compete with.

Keith turns and flashes those dimples at me. "Oh, come on! Read it out loud. I need some entertainment while I'm cooped up in here with you. Let me guess . . . she wants to know what color his boxers were."

"I wouldn't put that past her."

Brenna's face pinches. "Why would she want to know that?"

With a sigh, I reach for my phone.

How are you doing?

It's not from Misty. It's not even from this area code. Could it be . . . Nervous flutters explode in my stomach.

"What's wrong?" Keith asks, turning to see my frown.

"Nothing. Be back in a sec." I duck into my room to fish out the lined piece of paper, my thumb sliding over his neat scrawl.

The numbers match.

Brett Madden is texting me.

I sit, perched on the edge of my bed, staring at the four simple, innocuous words, and I'm at a loss for a response. What so many women would give to have Brett Madden texting them.

And all I had to do was pull him out of a burning car.

What do I say? That things suck? That I'm a prisoner in my own home? That the news is dragging my skeletons out of the closet and parading them down the street? Between the inappropriate questions, Misty also informed me that Raven News had run an in-depth five-minute clip on Scott Philips—on his family, his college education, and his years teaching. Thankfully, they haven't interviewed him yet. I don't think I want to hear what he has to say about me.

I don't want to make Brett feel bad, though.

I'll live.

As soon as I hit Send, I cringe. Seth Grabner didn't live. Brett almost didn't. Will he see that as a callous response?

"Ugh . . ." I'm such an idiot. I wish I could retract that.

I quickly punch out, *How are you?*

I bite my thumbnail and wait until three dots begin dancing on my screen.

I'll live (thanks to you). Are the police still on guard?

I smile.

If by "on guard" you mean washing my dishes and playing go fish with Brenna, then yes. It's like Fort Knox around here.

V.S.S. reported that it's under control.

So he's keeping tabs . . .

Their guns are awfully persuasive.

I hope you offered them SunnyD.

I stifle my giggle.

I only offer that to my favorite guests.

And now it seems like I'm flirting.

Sounds more exciting than my life. I have a doc visit this afternoon, but I'm laying low otherwise.

How is your leg?

Based on what he said about his injuries yesterday, he must be in a lot of pain.

My mom is spoon-feeding me drugs because she doesn't trust that I'll take them. If I suddenly stop responding, it's because I've passed out.

I can't help myself.

I have to ask, what's it like having a movie star for a mother?

She's just Mom to me.

I guess so.

Since we're asking questions . . . Did you and Officer Singer date at some point?

I frown. Why is he asking me that?

No.

Never?

Nope. He's one of my best friends. Why?

It just seemed like there was more to it than a cop doing his job.

Well, we did kiss behind the gym when we were twelve.

That must be it.

I can't believe I just told you that.

And why are we even talking about Keith?

BTW, my other best friend is in love with you.

I roll my eyes at myself. Yes, that's much better.

There's no response from Brett for a moment. I wonder if he passed out. Where is he right now? On his couch?

In his bed?

Thoughts of him sprawled out on a mattress are interrupted by three dots.

Oh?

It's a single word, and I'm not sure how to take it. Does he like hearing about women obsessing over him, or does it annoy him?

Yes, she flooded my phone with all kinds of pictures of you.

There's another long pause, and then, *Did you see this one?*

An image follows quickly, of Brett in a French maid's outfit at least two sizes too small, his muscular, hairy legs on full display, a wide, goofy grin on his face, a beer in hand. From the other costumes around him, I'm guessing it's a Halloween party.

It's a terrible, unflattering picture. I burst out laughing.

Oddly enough, this one was not included.

I think my publicist suppressed it. Not sure why.

For the life of me, I can't figure it out either.

I'm going to regret sending that to you when I'm not high on Percocets.

It's saved for future blackmail.

Brett Madden clearly has a sense of humor. And he can laugh at himself.

And I'm not sure, but I think he might be flirting. Or he's just heavily medicated.

I'm still giggling as I watch the three dots bounce, wondering if I'm going to get another ridiculous picture.

I was so out of it yesterday that I forgot to ask you how much you had to pay for your truck. I owe you.

And just like that, my bubble is flattened.

You don't owe me anything.

I owe you everything, actually. Starting with a new vehicle, and help with all the shifts you're missing.

Tension creeps into my shoulders. Is this why he texted me to begin with? Is this the only reason?

That's very generous of you, but I'll manage. I always have.

Even as I type the words, I can hear my mother yelling at me for being stupid and stubborn. How do I explain that it just doesn't feel right to accept money from him? That just picturing the entire transaction—him handing over a check, me accepting and cashing it—makes me uncomfortable in my skin.

I wait five minutes for a response, but it doesn't come.

"Mommy! I want to play!"

I sigh, setting my phone on my bed, hoping I didn't piss him off. "Coming . . ."

■ ■ ■

"Brett Madden was *here*, in your house, and you didn't think to call *me*?" Misty glares at me, not bothering to veil her hurt. "Or even tell me about the accident?"

"I guess I wasn't thinking straight . . . I'm sorry." As much as I wasn't ready to deal with Misty's exuberance, when she showed up on my front porch with a box of cupcakes from the Sweet Stop—bribery, so she could grill me about Brett in person—I found myself sighing with gratitude. Misty has stuck by me through everything. She was there when it felt like everyone else had turned on me. She was there in the delivery room with me when I had Brenna, alone and terrified and screaming in pain. Whenever I've needed help, she's showed up.

Though I'm not sure how much she's helping me now. With a folder on her phone dedicated to pictures of Brett Madden, she isn't exactly unbiased, swept up in the romance of the story.

"You should tell him you want to see him again. I'll bet he'd drop everything and come."

"I'm not going to do that! He's at home, resting. He barely survived a car crash."

"But he did, thanks to *you*."

"That doesn't mean he's at my beck and call."

"But wouldn't it be nice." Misty licks the buttercream frosting off her fingertips while she lounges in the La-Z-Boy, her legs folded up beneath her. "He owes you everything."

I roll my eyes at her.

"So . . . now what?"

"Now . . . we wait for the reporters to give up or get bored and leave me alone." A few more days, perhaps? I mean, I know Brett and his family are a big deal, but there are way more important things to be reporting on than this.

The steps outside creak, and a moment later, Keith lets himself in with his key, his arms laden with grocery bags.

"How is it out there?"

He shoots me a "don't ask" look as he unceremoniously drops the bags on the table. Three apples tumble out, but he rounds them up with his quick reflexes before they roll to the ground and bruise.

"I didn't think it was *that* bad when I drove in."

I take in Misty's heavy eye makeup and the favorite black blouse she's wearing. Even her blonde curls are smooth and springy today, care of a long morning routine that she doesn't bother with too often. I'm guessing she was hoping to be caught on camera.

Keith's smirk says he's guessing the same. "Surprised you're not warming the chair that Madden sat in."

"Oh, don't worry. I spent some time there." She waggles her eyebrows suggestively, making Keith grin and me groan. She's always flirting with him and he's always lapping it up, though everyone knows she thinks he's too boyish and he thinks she's too flighty.

He nods toward the TV. "You're actually watching the game. I'm impressed."

"Too bad they're losing." Tonight will be the second loss. Two more and the Flyers are done for the season. I feel terrible for Brett.

Keith frowns, looking around. "Where is she?"

"In her room, coloring. Brenna!" I holler. "Keith is here!"

Her bed creaks as she slides off and comes running out. But instead of focusing on Keith, her eyes land on the box of cupcakes.

"As if you haven't already had one." Keith lifts it out of her reach.

"I haven't!"

"Really?" He swipes a finger over the streak of chocolate icing marring her cheek. Evidence.

She giggles as she jumps and waves her hands, trying to reach the box even though it's impossibly high.

"Man . . . these look good." He peers in at the three that are left. "Which one will I have . . ."

"Not the double chocolate!"

"This one looks *amazing*." He lifts the double chocolate one out and opens his mouth wide, pretending to take a bite.

Brenna stops jumping and her bottom lip puffs out.

"Keith, you're so mean!" Misty hollers.

He grins, putting it back. "Fine. Red velvet it is."

"No! I'm saving that one for Vince." Brenna darts to the blinds, prying them apart with her little fingers. "Is he back yet?"

"Not until tomorrow morning. Vince does days and Hawk does nights."

"Can Vince drive me to school tomorrow?"

I smile, hearing the hopefulness in her voice. She's been obsessed with the stony-faced security guy since he snuck in to use our bathroom earlier today. I don't know how much experience Vince, who looks to be in his late twenties, has had with small children, but he didn't seem to know how to deal with Brenna's verbal assault as she trailed behind him to the door, firing off question after question. "I don't know if you're going to school tomorrow yet. We may have to wait until things calm down a bit."

"What about Hawk? Don't you think he might want one of these?" Keith asks, finally settling on a vanilla.

"Mommy won't let me go outside, so I'm waiting until he has to pee." She observes the night shift guard who took over for Vince at six P.M. and will be relieved by him at six A.M. I can't imagine standing outside someone's house for twelve hours through the night.

"Who do you think is cuter? Vince or Hawk?" Keith teases, wiping the cake crumbs from the corner of his mouth.

Brenna spears him with a glare, her nose wrinkling up in disgust, making us all laugh.

"Okay. Enough spying. Say your good nights and get ready for bed."

Brenna does a lap around the room, doling out hugs that she reserves for family and close friends, and then trots toward her room.

Misty smiles after her. "So when do you think you're going to come back to work?"

"Not anytime soon," Keith answers at the same time that I say, "a few more days."

He glares at me.

"What? I can't just sit in here forever. I need to make money!"

Misty heaves herself off the La-Z-Boy and collects her purse. "Well, you'll definitely make enough of that. The place is crawling with people. Lou is running ragged, trying to cover."

Guilt hits me, that the older woman is having to wait tables on account of me. Lou is as loyal as they come, yet I can't help but wonder what her breaking point might be, if she's finally going to decide that enough is enough and replace me. This is business, after all.

Then what will I do for a job?

"I'll definitely be back in a few days," I reiterate.

"Good. I miss you being there." Misty pauses at the door. "Hey, I noticed Hawk isn't wearing a wedding ring. Do you think he's dating anyone?"

Leave it to Misty to notice something like a wedding ring in the thirty seconds it took to confirm her identity and allow her up my stairs. Granted, Hawk is decent looking. "Don't know. He's not exactly big on conversation."

"Why don't you bring him one of these and find out." Keith holds the box out for her.

She grins, snatching one up. "Good idea, Officer Singer. I'm sure he could use one, for the long night ahead."

I shake my head, taking a silent bet with myself that, if he *is* single, she'll be leaving here with his phone number. It doesn't matter how many failed relationships she's had, she'll charge full steam ahead into a new one.

I wish I was fearless like her.

The sound of cards shuffling breaks my thoughts. "I picked up my cribbage board on the way. Have you ever played?" Keith asks.

I stifle my groan.

Chapter 12

. . .

"Why couldn't Vince drive me to school?" Brenna whines from the backseat of Keith's Ford F-150.

"Because *I'm* driving you." Keith's eyes scan for the newspeople as we coast down my driveway.

"But I wanted Vince to drive me."

"What am I, chopped liver?"

"Why would you be chopped liver?"

Keith heaves a sigh. "Never mind. Vince is waiting at your house for when I drive your mom back, which will be very soon." To me, he says, "For the record, you're an idiot and this is a bad idea."

"If I don't work, I won't be able to pay bills next month. Plus, I can't sit in that house playing cards anymore. I'll go crazy!" It's been five days since my name was released. The more reputable, bigger news stations have moved on. They can't sit there forever. It's now the smaller state stations and the freelance guys—the ones with long spy lenses, who sleep in their cars and who don't get paid unless they deliver a candid photo—who linger. And there are enough of them to make my stomach tighten.

"And you really think you're going to be able to work?"

"I have to try."

"Why are they pointing cameras at us?" Brenna asks as we turn onto the street.

"Keep your head down, sweetie." The windows are tinted, but I don't trust that completely.

Brenna is tucked in behind me as we pull onto Main Street, on our way to drop her off at the day care attached to the school. The principal called. Apparently having a dozen reporters and photographers camped outside your house isn't a good enough reason to keep your five-year-old home for more than two days. Seeing as I'm getting charged for before-school day care today anyway, we may as well drop her off now.

Keith promised that even the most aggressive reporters know little kids at school are off-limits, but he also lined up the guys on shift to patrol the area for lurkers.

Even with my warning, Brenna cranes her neck. "Are those the people who stand in front of the camera and tell the news?"

"Get down!" I follow my anger with a frustrated sigh. I've yelled at her more these past few days than in her entire life, and I feel terrible. "Some of them, yes."

"Have they been out here all night?"

"Some of them have." To Keith I grumble, "It's six A.M. You'd think they have somewhere else to be." They're causing quite the buzz around town from what Keith said. Business at Rawley's and the sandwich shop across the street has doubled with all the coffee runs and sudden interest in playing pool.

"What do they want?" Brenna chirps.

I close my eyes and take a deep breath, biting back the irritation that threatens to erupt. It's been an endless stream of questions, and I'm at the end of my rope despite telling myself over and over again that she's only five and can't help herself.

"They want to talk to your mom, Squirt."

"Because you helped that man with the broken leg?"

I heave a sigh. "Something like that."

Keith peers into his rearview mirror, watching her, smiling. "Your mom did something super brave. Isn't that cool?"

"Yeah. But what do they want?"

"They want your mom to tell them what happened that night."

"Why?"

"Because that's their job. They want her to go out there and say hi."

"Can we go say hi after school?"

"No, baby. We can't." There's no way I'm letting my kid's face end up on national television. "Listen, Brenna, if anyone tries to talk to you about me or about the accident, I want you to go straight to the office and tell Mr. Archibald. Okay?" She has the same principal as I did when I was in elementary school. He was old even back then.

"Okay, Mommy." She's so easy, so agreeable, like none of this is really a big deal.

Maybe it's not. Maybe I'm making things harder than I need to.

■ ■ ■

March 2010

Heads begin to turn as I move through the main hallway before class, my backpack slung over my shoulder, shedding snowflakes with each step.

"That's her," I hear someone whisper as I pass.

I keep my head ducked until I make it to my locker. There're only two minutes before the bell rings for homeroom—I intentionally waited outside as long as I could—and yet no one seems to be in any rush to get to class.

I hide within my winter jacket as I fumble with my lock, the shake in my hand making it extra hard to work the dial.

Another whisper carries, this one not so quiet. "I heard he turned her down. She's making it all up to get back at him."

I grit my teeth and ignore it. Finally, my lock pops free. When I open the door, a folded sheet of paper falls out, landing conveniently in my hand. My stomach churns as I open it up to read the female scrawl: As if Philips would touch a nasty ass like you. Stop lying, slut.

■ ■ ■

"What did you expect? Even if that Mayberry asshat hadn't told everyone that you work here, they would have figured it out by now."

I stare out at Diamonds' parking lot. There isn't a single spot available. "It's six thirty in the morning! I've never seen it so busy."

"You've got every retired, unemployed, and shift worker within a twenty-mile radius here. Plus the star chasers. Plus them." He nods toward the row of news vans parked and waiting, people leaning against the sides with phones against their ears, or cigarettes hanging from their mouths. In some cases, both.

I sigh. "Awesome. And *this* is how people will see me." I throw my hands at my Diamonds uniform, a '50s diner-style sherbet-orange-and-white dress. I clearly didn't think this through.

"You know, for someone who likes to avoid chaos and attention, you sure picked a good time to go out of character."

"I'm trying to *avoid* being homeless," I remind him.

"*I* warned you . . . *Lou* warned you . . . Hell, even Misty warned you."

He did. And they did. But . . . "They'll figure out that I'm not going to talk to them and give up. They *have* to, eventually, but I can't hide in my house until they do. I have to get back to my life." Even with the money the regulars threw in, I'll be dipping into my savings if I don't get back, and soon.

"I can lend you some cash."

"I'm not taking your money."

"Your parents?"

I glare at him. "They just spent a small bundle on my SUV." And I intend on paying every cent back. Brett's text floats through my thoughts. I briefly concede that I must be an idiot for refusing his money so quickly. It's followed by a wave of disappointment that I haven't heard from him since Saturday.

Keith throws his hands up in the air in a sign of "I give up" and then, gunning the engine slightly, pulls his truck around to the back entrance. When he cuts the engine and unfastens his seat belt, I frown at him.

"You know you don't have to do this, right?" He's been cooped up in our house with us, sleeping in Brenna's twin bed at night, running errands and helping me keep occupied while ensuring I stay away from the TV. Lucky for me, I've already used up my meager data plan so I can't troll the Internet.

He starts his stretch of night shifts tonight, though. And he has court, so he won't be around this afternoon, either. Truth be told, I'm a little nervous.

"What don't I have to do? Eat breakfast?" He slides out and comes around to meet me in front of the truck. "No offense, but the fake Froot Loops won't exactly sustain me until lunch."

I give him a friendly elbow on our walk to the back door, side by side. "Thank you. For everything. You're a good friend." I punch in the security code—besides Lou and Leroy, I'm the only one who knows what it is—and lead Keith into the kitchen.

The familiarity of Diamonds hits me immediately—the low buzz of customers' voices, the steady hum of TVs broadcasting news and sports, the printer churning out order after order, bacon sizzling on the grill, a smell that makes my mouth water. I can't believe I'm saying this, but I've missed it.

"Look what the cat dragged in!" Leroy smiles wide at me over his shoulder as he flips a stack of pancakes onto a plate in one fluid motion. He could do that in his sleep, he's been at Diamonds so long.

I stick my tongue out at him but follow it with a smile, realizing how much I've missed him, too. He's easygoing, friendly, and has the biggest heart I've ever come across. I couldn't imagine Lou married to anyone else, even though it hasn't been easy for them.

No one would ever mistake Balsam or any of the surrounding towns as "multicultural," so it goes without saying that mixed-race relationships are rare. Rumor has it that their romance caused quite the stir around these parts. It took a year for me to find the guts to ask Lou about it. She told me everything. They secretly started dating back when Lou was still in high school, when her father hired Leroy to help in the kitchen. That was forty-two years ago, and people were even less willing to accept it then. Plenty of the locals expressed their displeasure through nasty gossip. Some regulars stopped coming. Business at Diamonds, already a well-established diner, took a hit. But Lou's father ignored the bigots and went about his business, loving his daughter and supporting her and the man she loved. Soon enough, the old generation of simple minds were replaced by more progressive ones—or at least people who didn't care who married who as long as they got their Diamonds burger just how they liked it.

Once Lou's dad was sure it was serious, he promoted Leroy to run the kitchen and taught him everything he knew. Though he also warned Lou more than once that life would be easier for her if she chose a different man.

Lou has never been one to take the easy way out.

A lot of people in this area never really warmed to Lou and Leroy. It didn't help when their only son—she was too busy running the diner to think about having more than one child—grew up to be a less-than-stellar human being, robbing Diamonds with a mask and a gun because Leroy and Lou wouldn't give him money. He'll be in prison for a while longer for that one.

The day she hired me, I was convinced it was about wanting to help a pregnant eighteen-year-old. But the more I got to know her and about her, the more I started to see that it was about taking pity on someone who had been ostracized by the people around here, much like she had.

Leroy slides a plate under the hot lamp and slams his hand down on the server bell. "Mornin', Officer Singer."

"Mornin', Chef Green."

Leroy started calling Keith "Officer Singer" the day Keith got accepted to the police academy, and in turn Keith tacked on "Chef," even though Leroy is technically nothing more than a seasoned line cook. I'd never say that out loud, though. He makes the best banquet burger in the state.

Leroy grabs a new order from the printer. "Didn't think we'd be seeing you again for a while, little lady."

"Why wouldn't you see me again? I still have bills to pay."

He shrugs.

I wrap my apron around my waist and fasten it at my back. "How's it been this morning?"

"Been a zoo all week. Great for business, but everyone's bustin' their asses."

"Sounds like Lou needs me, then."

Leroy starts chuckling in that deep-belly way of his.

"What? Why is that so funny?"

Whatever he's thinking, he only answers with a headshake. "Does Lou know you're comin' in today?"

I tie my long blonde hair back into a ponytail. "I always work Wednesdays."

"Thought so."

"I tried to warn her, but she wants to learn the hard way." Keith eyes the fresh batch of pancakes sizzling on the grill. He knows if he hovers long enough, Leroy will toss a plate his way.

"It's going to be fine." Taking a deep breath, I push through the door.

A dozen eyes are on me in an instant, and they quickly multiply, heads swiveling from booths and tables, mid-order to mid-bite, whispers of "that's her" carrying over the clanging dishes and ringing bells to reach my ears.

And soon that familiar buzz of conversation has died down, and my face is burning bright as literally every single person in Diamonds has stopped what they're doing to simply stare at me.

I don't even notice the cameras pointing, snapping pictures of me standing there in my uniform, shell-shocked, until Keith hooks my arm and pulls me back with a quiet "Not a good idea."

"You've got that right." Lou appears out of nowhere, to both shield and herd me through the door. "Come on, now."

I'm back in the safety of the kitchen before I can breathe again.

It's not like last time, I remind myself. It's not like it was after Scott.

So then why am I feeling this same dread?

Leroy tosses another platter of pancakes onto the pickup counter, shooting me a sympathetic smile. "Told you. A zoo."

"And you're the white lion they all came to see," Lou mutters, wiping a thin sheen of sweat from her brow with her forearm. "What were you thinkin' coming in here?"

I yank at the straps of my apron. I can't tell what I feel like doing right now—crying or puking. It's a toss-up, really. "That I need to work? That I want my life back?" My voice cracks with frustration as tears begin rolling down my cheeks. It's not even a fantastic life, but it's mine and I worked hard to carve it out of the mess I made for myself years ago. If *this* is what I'm going to face every time I step out, I won't be able to work. And if I can't make money . . .

She sighs, reaching up to pat my shoulder. "It'll get better, Cath. Eventually it'll all go back to normal."

"When? Because I don't have time for 'eventually'!" I sob.

Her brow twists with concern. She opens her mouth to answer, but her words are cut off by a loud clatter. We turn in time to see Leroy pick up the fallen plate of pancakes from the floor and toss it in the trash.

"I'm sorry!" That's my fault. Lou wasn't exaggerating all those years ago—Leroy honestly can't handle seeing women cry. Misty makes him drop a pan once a month because she's *always* breaking into tears about something when she's hormonal.

"Hush." Lou grabs a napkin and wipes at my cheeks. "We'll figure it all out."

"I'll tell you when it'll go back to normal." Keith yanks a slice of crispy bacon from a warming tray, earning Leroy's disapproving frown. Very few things annoy him. Poaching bacon during the busy breakfast shift is one of those things. "After you do that interview Brett Madden offered to set up."

"That means being on camera in front of *millions* of people." Just the idea makes me nauseous. I don't think they comprehend this.

"I'm sorry to say this, but he's right. They're all lookin' to be the first to talk to Catherine Wright. The faster they hear your version, the sooner they'll move on to being a nuisance to someone else."

"Can't we just kick the reporters out?"

"If I thought it would help, I would. But it's all the damn customers, too! I guess I could threaten to boot them out if they take pictures of you."

"No, don't do that." The last thing I want is for this to negatively impact Diamonds. I sigh. "I guess I'll head home now." Another day without work. And I need to put in twenty hours a week if I want to keep collecting my subsidies. How long before they cut me off?

"Here, dolly. It's your favorite, and looks like you could use a good meal." Leroy sinks two Styrofoam take-out containers into Keith's hands, weighed down with what I'm sure are his famous blueberry pancakes.

I doubt I can stomach a single one.

Lou gives my forearm a pat. "Remember, you did a good thing for that man. I just wish things were easier for you because of it."

"I guess it could always be worse," I mutter, heading for the back door.

Five reporters and as many cameramen are waiting for me right outside, shoving their microphones in my face, shouting at me. The clicks and flashes of cameras make me wince and flinch, capturing every unflattering impression of me that they can.

"Are you currently collecting welfare?"

"Are you still in contact with your former art teacher and lover?"

"Reports suggest Scott Philips has been romantically involved with a seventeen-year-old student in Memphis. What do you have to say about that?"

"Who's the father of your child?"

"Did you save Brett Madden knowing how much he was worth?"

"Was Seth Grabner swerving to avoid your car when he drove into the tree?"

"Is it true that you're suing Brett Madden?"

"*What?*" I explode, spinning around to try to find the ones who asked those last questions. "No! No! And no! Stop making things up!"

Keith's arm ropes around my shoulder protectively as he pushes past them to his truck, ushering me into the passenger side and shutting the door. They trail him, firing off questions his way, too—specifically, who he is and who he is to me—but he smoothly ignores them, rounding the truck and climbing in, inches from slamming his door on a microphone.

"Did I know how much he was worth? Did I cause the accident? Am I going to sue him?" I shriek, a fresh wave of tears welling in my eyes, spilling down my cheeks. "What kind of disgusting people are they?"

"They're idiots, Cath."

"I know that. But do people believe them?"

The truck jerks to a stop several times as Keith struggles to back out around the reporters without running them over. "Other idiots probably do."

I'm so frazzled, it takes me a moment to focus. "Did I hear one of them say that Scott is with a student?"

Keith's lips press together.

"Seriously?" Is he that stupid to try it again?

"I don't know if it's true or not. One of the guys told me about it last night. I guess some hockey fans following the story recognized their art teacher. He's been working down at that private school for five years without anyone knowing about what happened up here."

"Is he going to get away with it again, if it's true?"

Keith shrugs. "I'll let you know when I hear more."

I sink down in my seat as we speed out of Diamonds' parking lot. "You know what? I don't even want to know. I have enough problems." My stomach is churning. "I can't have them making up all this shit. What if it gets back to Brenna?"

"Until they hear your side, they're going to latch on to any bullshit shred of a story they can and run with it." He gives me a look as he turns onto the main road. He doesn't have to say it.

Give them the goddamn interview.

■ ■ ■

It takes me thirty minutes of staring at Brett's number on my phone to collect my nerve and hit Call. I hold the phone to my ear, clearing my throat several times.

He picks up between the third and fourth rings, and answers with a groggy "Yup?"

My eyes shoot to my alarm clock and widen with panic when I see the bright numbers. It's only seven thirty in the morning. Shit. I completely forgot. I'm a second away from hitting End, when I hear, "Catherine?"

I wince. "Yeah. I'm sorry. I went to work today and it was a total circus so I came home, thinking I could call you. I forgot how early it is." I'm rambling. "I'll call back later."

"No! It's okay. Seriously. Just give me a minute."

"Okay." I hold my breath and listen to Brett on the other end, to his groan and quiet curse. A pill bottle rattles. He must be in a lot of pain first thing in the morning, with his meds having worn off in the night. I try my best not to picture him lying in bed, but I fail miserably and end up playing a silent guessing game of "What does Brett sleep in?" while he, I assume, takes his medication.

That game has my cheeks heating up. I've seen the pictures Misty sent me and I have a pretty active imagination, deprived of the real thing for too long.

His muffled sigh fills my ear, like he's settling back into his pillow, and it sends a warm shiver down my spine. "How many monkeys were there and did they dance?"

"What?" I frown, replaying his words. Is he delusional? What kind of meds do they have him on?

"You said you're at a circus."

"No . . . I mean I went to work. And it was . . . I—"

His throaty chuckle cuts off my words. "Sorry, bad joke."

"Oh!" I finally clue in. I'm usually quick to the draw on comebacks. Why does he make me so flustered?

"I'm sorry I never responded to your last text. I ended up passing out. I've been in a bit of a fog these last few days. These painkillers are strong."

I swallow a sigh of relief. "So you weren't ignoring me. You were just high."

"Basically." He sighs. "Makes it easier to watch my team lose."

"I'm sorry." They lost again last night. I've learned enough about hockey to know that one more loss and the Flyers are out of the playoffs.

"So, I take it there were a bunch of reporters ordering the diner's breakfast special this morning?"

I guess he doesn't want to talk about his team. "And every local who didn't have somewhere else to be."

"Heroes draw big crowds. Especially pretty ones."

"I'm not . . ." I roll my eyes, but I'm also fighting a smile. *Brett Madden thinks I'm pretty.* "Please don't call me that."

"What? Pretty?"

"No. A hero."

"So I can call you pretty?"

"Yes. I mean no! I mean . . ."

"All right. It's early. I shouldn't be teasing you yet." I can hear the smile in his voice. Is he always such a flirt? Or is he just trying to make me comfortable?

There's no time for either right now. "Can we do that interview you were talking about? Something really simple and quick and small to get them off my back."

"When?"

"I don't know. *Soon?*" I wander over to my bedroom blinds and peek through. A tall, brambly hedge divides my backyard from the one behind it. You'd think no one's getting through that, and yet I could swear I saw the glint of a camera lens in the sunlight more than once. Maybe I'm just paranoid. "I'd really like to get this over with so I don't have a hundred people videotaping me serving fries and filling ketchup bottles in my hideous uniform."

"I'll get right on it." The grogginess in his voice has cleared. "You're home now?"

"Yeah. I lasted at Diamonds all of twenty seconds."

"Okay. Give me a few hours. We'll get this set up and make it as easy as possible, I promise."

The guy barely survived a car wreck less than two weeks ago. He's got broken bones that have left him in agony. I just woke him up, and now I've got him arranging a freaking interview, when he should be lying in bed and watching a Netflix marathon and not moving. "I'm sorry to be saddling you with all this so early. I just—"

"Don't apologize." There's a sharpness to his tone that catches me off guard, but he follows it up with a soft "Don't ever apologize for any of this. I want to help you in any way that I can."

I smile. There's a sincerity about Brett Madden that I have to believe is impossible to fake. Plus, talking to him makes me feel like everything is going to work out.

Still, him calling me a "hero" makes my stomach churn. Would he call me that if he knew I almost left him? I hesitate. "Brett?"

"Yeah?"

"I need to tell you something."

"Shoot."

I open my mouth. No, not over the phone. I'll wait until I see him again. "Thank you."

He chuckles. "Yeah, okay. I'll call you back. Do me a favor and don't answer any numbers you don't recognize."

"Don't worry. I've already learned that lesson."

"Talk to you soon."

I end the call and then let my body flop backward onto my bed, closing my eyes. Soon. Things will be back to normal soon.

Who am I kidding?

I have a feeling nothing will ever be normal again.

■ ■ ■

I must have dozed off, because I'm startled awake by my phone's ringer. As soon as I see Brett's name, I perk up. "Hello?"

His smooth voice fills my ear and instantly warms me. "We're all set."

"What?" I frown at the clock. It's eight thirty-seven. It's only been an hour since we talked.

"The interview. It's all set."

I pull myself up. "Really? Already? Oh, okay." I pause, wondering what the right next question should be. "When? Where?"

"So, here's the thing. I know you said you wanted something really simple."

Unease slips into my stomach, churning it, as I wait for Brett to elaborate.

"But Kate Wethers of *The Weekly* called my publicist this morning and—"

"*The Weekly*? That's . . . that's not small. That's not simple." I'm already shaking my head before the firm "no" manages its way out. That's pretty much *the* journalistic news broadcast. They report on major stories, like wars and political corruption. Lou always has it on the TV at the diner on Friday nights, until the regulars start bitching about wanting to watch sports. Why the hell would they want to report on me?

"I know. I was originally thinking *People* or *Us Weekly*, because this is more their thing—"

"*People*? *Us Weekly*?" My head is still shaking. *No, no, no. Small and simple, I said. I did say that, didn't I?*

"Okay, hold on, Catherine. Just hear me out before you refuse. Promise?"

I heave a sigh. "Fine," but it's not going to matter. He's not going to change my mind.

"Okay, so Kate Wethers thinks this is the kind of heartwarming, happy-ending story that the world needs right now. She's smart, and she's fair, and she hates shitty journalism, which is what she sees when she reviews the media surrounding this story. All the crap about that high school teacher—"

"I can't talk about that with her, on national television!"

"Why not?"

"Because I recanted my statement."

"Are you saying that nothing happened between you two?"

I hesitate. I don't want to lie to Brett. "I'm not saying that," I finally admit.

"You just didn't want him to go to jail, did you?"

"Right."

"I didn't think so," he says softly. "And I think you should talk about it. Just a bit. Just enough to let viewers see that a thirty-year-old teacher with a lot of ties to the community manipulated a seventeen-year-old high school girl and then tried to cover his ass. It wasn't right, what happened to you. I mean, hell! The local newspaper made him look like a victim!"

I swallow. "How much did you read?"

"Honestly? All of it. Every article I could find online."

I close my eyes as my embarrassment takes over. "I was a different person back then. I don't want you to think that I'm . . . like *that* anymore." How do I make him understand without saying the actual words?

"I don't care if you nailed the entire football team, if that's what you're getting at, Cath," Brett says bluntly. "It doesn't change what I think of you."

What exactly *does* he think of me?

"Kate wants to set things right. She wants you walking out of this interview able to hold your head high, because that's what you deserve. Are you with me so far?"

"Yeah. I think so," I answer reluctantly.

"The great thing is that they're based here in Philly. The team can be at your place by three."

"Whoa. Wait. *Today*? *Here*?"

"Yeah, they want to come to your house to film. It gives the entire story a much more personal, everyday human touch. You'll also be more comfortable, in familiar surroundings. Trust me, I've done plenty of interviews, so I'm speaking from experience. Plus, I told them you likely wouldn't be willing to leave your daughter. So if you two could spare a few hours—"

"You mean me and Brenna? No. There's *no way* she's going to be a part of this interview."

"But they think—"

"I'm not exposing my child to this. I don't want her on camera, or pictured, or even named. In fact, she's not even going to be here." I don't know where she'll go, because Keith has court this afternoon. But I don't care. "This is nonnegotiable."

A long pause meets my words. "You're right. I'll have Simone communicate that to them. But you're willing to do it otherwise?"

I wander out of my bedroom and into my main room to survey the shabby curtains, the worn floors, the cupboard doors that don't quite hang right. If this is what they want—to show the world the life of the single mom and diner waitress who saved their superman from certain death—and if it gets the rest of the circus off my back . . .

But. "There are things I won't talk about."

"Like?"

"Like my relationship with my parents. We're finally at a point where we're talking again, and I don't want to ruin that with this inter-view. They're the only family Brenna knows."

"Okay. Anything else?"

"Brenna's father. That's off-limits."

Brett hesitates. "So he's not in her life at all?"

"No."

"Got it. I'll make sure they know those two things. And I'll be there the whole time, too, just to make sure. If that's okay?"

"Of course it's okay!" *Too eager, Cath.* "Yes. I mean, yeah. I'm glad. I mean, you should be a part of this." I'm rambling again. Because mixed in with my dread over this interview is excitement. I'm going to see Brett again. Today.

"Good." I hear the smile in his voice. "See you this afternoon, then."

We hang up and I begin surveying my house, wondering if I can actually make it, and myself, presentable in time. *And* figure out what to do with Brenna.

Maybe Vince would babysit an almost six-year-old.

Chapter 13

• • •

"You didn't have to do all this," I tell my mother as she fusses over the fresh bouquet of plum-colored tulips that she brought, now sitting on a side table.

With Keith in court and Brenna's regular babysitter in school, I was desperate. *Almost* desperate enough to ask Vince. But I decided to try my mother first, fully expecting her to say no because taking Brenna at three would require missing work, and her boss is the type to dock pay for each hour lost.

Surprisingly, she not only agreed, she left work at noon to hit up the Belmont Target for some décor items to "spruce up" my place. If I wasn't so frazzled about this interview, I might be insulted.

"Don't be ridiculous. You needed help."

"Thank you. I was afraid I'd have to leave her with Vince."

"I'm sure she wouldn't have minded."

"It's not her I was worried about."

"Hand me the scissors, please?"

My mom came not only with flowers but also with thick, warm gray wool curtains, her reasoning being that the current blinds and sheers don't offer enough privacy against all these reporters. She can "almost" see into my living room from the outside, even with them closed. I don't believe her, but on the off chance that she's right, I'm not going to argue.

"There." She steps back and eyes the living room, where we assume the filming will take place. "It's not my style, but it doesn't look bad with these added touches."

That's Hildy Wright's way of offering a compliment. I've learned that I can't take offense to it. And I have to admit, her added touches work well with my eclectic "décor."

That doesn't mean I want her here when Brett arrives, which is any moment now. I'll have maybe thirty minutes alone with him, at most, before the news crew gets here.

It's my only chance to talk to him, to tell him *exactly* what happened that night.

"You should probably head over to get Brenna. I called the office to let them know you'd be picking her up."

She checks her watch with a frown. "It's a five-minute drive, Cath. What am I going to do? Linger in the parking lot, twiddling my thumbs?" She grabs Brenna's coloring kit and stuffs it into the end drawer, right on top of my sketchbook.

It's obvious that she's stalling. "Fine. I'll be in the bathroom."

"I could probably get your father to take off work and mind Brenna at home, so I could be here with you."

"No, that's okay." That may have come out a tad too fast, but there's no way in hell I'm doing this interview with my mother in the same room.

She nods. I can tell that's not the answer she was hoping for, but this isn't about her.

I turn toward the hall.

"Wait."

She just stands there for a moment, her fingers tapping against her thigh. "I suppose you'll be talking about Mr. Philips?"

I was wondering when she'd finally ask. "Kate Wethers will likely bring it up."

She swallows hard. "I need to say something."

Here we go.

What is she going to do? Give me a script? "Don't worry, Mom. I won't say anything disparaging about you. I told them that our relationship was off-limits."

She sighs. "I was going to tell you that your father and I are one hundred percent on board with your decision to do this interview. And I hope you say whatever you feel you need to say to be able to hold your head up high. Just keep in mind that you recanted your statement, which means you have to be careful. Knowing that family, they'd launch a defamation suit against you. I . . ." She purses her lips. "If I could go back and do it all again, I still would have reported that man. But I'd like to think I would have done other things differently. I know you and

I will never be best friends, but I hope one day you'll see my intentions for what they were."

I think that's as close to an apology as I'll ever get from her.

She turns to peek out the window. "I noticed that the toilet paper roll was near empty but I don't know where you keep your extras. You should change it so your guests aren't put out."

"Right." I leave her to do a quick scan of my tiny bathroom—and, yes, to replace the roll. And then I do a scan of myself in the mirror, of the silky powder-pink three-quarter-sleeve blouse and dark blue jeans I decided on after wrestling into everything in my closet, some things twice, wishing I still had my little black dress, a real miracle find for a secondhand store. I've run my flatiron through my hair and I'm wearing more makeup than I normally do, but I figured that the camera will dull it anyway.

All in all, I look a thousand times better than I did when Brett showed up at my door five days ago. Am I really ready for this, though? The tightness in my chest would suggest otherwise. In truth, I feel the overwhelming urge to call him and cancel the whole thing.

"A black Escalade just pulled up!" my mom hollers from the front window.

Too late now.

My stomach does a flip as I hit the light switch and approach, to watch my mother smoothing her hands over her dress and running a finger through her hair as she watches through a crack in the blinds.

"Wow." She peers over her shoulder at me with a look. "He's . . . *Wow.*"

"Yeah. I've noticed," I say, tugging on the front of my blouse again.

She turns her focus back to the driveway. And suddenly her mouth drops open. "Holy shit!"

My eyes nearly pop out of my head. My mother never swears. *Never.* "What?"

"Did you know she was coming?"

"*She?*"

The porch steps creak, and my mom drops her voice to a whispered hiss. "His mother!"

Meryl Price is here?

I simply stare at the door, frozen in place as a knock sounds.

Thankfully, my mother has her wits about her, heading to flip the dead bolt and open the door. "Come in, come in!" She ushers them through, her voice more high-pitched than normal, her fingers that dangle at her thigh trembling slightly. I don't think I've ever seen her flustered.

Holding my breath and my bladder, I quietly watch as a giant bulldozer of a man—seriously, he had to have been a linebacker in a previous life—dressed in all black, his jacket open to reveal the handgun holstered at his side, steps in and offers a nod to me as he passes by, sticking his head into each of the bedrooms and the bathroom, an earpiece tucked into his ear. I hear him say, "All clear," to no one that I can see. There wasn't this security rigor on Brett's first visit. It must be because of *her*.

Brett eases in on his crutches, immediately searching me out. The bruising around his eyes has improved some. He's dressed in a black crewneck shirt that hugs his chest in a flattering way, and charcoal pants that hug the rest of him in an even more flattering way, the one leg rolled up to allow for the cast.

He's removed the bandage across his forehead and I can now clearly see the angry red seven-inch scar just below his hairline. His hair is styled like it was at that charity event, in thick waves combed off his face, and even though he still has a full face of scruff, it looks like it's been tidied up.

Brett simply stares at me for a long moment, that same awestruck look still in his eyes. I wonder if it's a reflection of the awe that's surely in mine. Despite everything, a bubble of excitement erupts inside me.

I'm so happy to see him again.

"Hi, I'm Hildy Wright, Catherine's mother." My mom's voice pulls his attention away.

He offers her a handshake and that genuine smile. "It's a pleasure to meet you." God, he's so charming, even when he's not doing anything out of the ordinary. I can practically see my mother melting into a puddle. Hobbling to the side, he gestures a hand behind him. "Mom?"

The epitome of glamour strolls through the door.

Meryl Price.

In my home.

She's wearing a figure-hugging ivory dress, and that figure is as hourglass perfect in real life as it is on the screen. As is her silky shoulder-length hair, the color of corn silk, and her flawless face. The only jewelry she wears is a rather modest diamond wedding ring. I wonder if she even has to try to look that good and, if so, how long it takes. My mother came straight from work, so she's still wearing her office attire—a navy blue pencil dress and simple but classy pumps, some costume jewelry that pulls the whole look together. Her shoulder-length blonde hair is curled at the ends and her makeup is light. She's always been naturally striking, and yet next to Meryl Price, her hair and complexion look dull, her dress faded and ill-fitting.

Meryl Price offers my mother—for once, speechless—a small, warm smile and handshake, before quickly moving on, searching me out just as her son did moments ago.

And when her gaze locks on me, her impeccably made eyes immediately well up with tears. By the tightness in her jaw, she's trying to keep them at bay as she strolls toward me, her matching ivory heels clicking against my worn floor. I'm sure this linoleum has never been graced by such expensive shoes before. "Catherine," she utters breezily.

I'm terrified of saying something stupid, and so I say nothing, simply offering my uninjured hand when she reaches for me. She ignores it, pulling me into a hug, her glossy hair caressing my cheek, her exotic floral perfume filling my nostrils. Her slender arms, as defined as mine are though she's in her early fifties, squeeze me tightly.

"I don't know how to adequately thank you for saving my son's life." I open my mouth to downplay it, but she cuts me off. "You have a child, too. So you must be able to appreciate how grateful I am."

That gives me pause. What if our roles were reversed? What if it had been my child trapped inside a car wreck and this woman wrapping her arms around me had risked her life to pull Brenna out?

I would never have been able to find the right words.

It's odd that I never looked at it from that angle before, but Meryl Price is right. Brett, that giant man leaning against his crutches for support, broken and bruised, will always be her child.

I'm finally able to return her squeeze, a new, wordless understanding passing between us.

We part just as Brett's driver walks through the door, carrying another elaborate floral arrangement. A short, curvy woman with a jet-black bob storms in after him, her arms laden with several sizable containers of what appear to be catering trays, her eyes scanning my house. "Over there for now, Donovan." She juts her chin at my coffee table on her way past, heading for my kitchen table to unload her arms. "I'm Simone, Brett's publicist."

"Hi." I frown at the trays.

"Brett mentioned how much you liked the last bouquet of flowers. And I know how draining these types of things can be, so we brought food with us to make things easier for you," Meryl says, patting my forearm. "I hope you don't mind."

She has a graceful way of speaking. I think she could convince me of just about anything.

"No, of course not."

Simone pops off the lids and the waft of freshly baked bread catches my nose, reminding me that I haven't actually eaten today. There's easily enough food here for fifteen people.

"Catherine, perhaps they'd like something to drink?" my mom hints.

"No need. We brought that, too," Simone chirps, and Donovan reappears just then carrying a Starbucks-branded carafe.

"You're really . . . prepared." And considerate.

"That's why I keep her around." Brett throws a wink at Simone.

"You're lucky that you're still in pain or I'd smack you, the hoops you ask me to jump through," Simone fake-complains on her way past him to stand in front of my couch, hands on hips, assessing the area. It takes her all of three seconds to notice. "You have no family photos."

"No, I put them all away." I glance to Brett, looking for support.

"It's fine, Simone. *The Weekly* already agreed to it."

But Simone frowns. It doesn't seem to be fine with her. "They agreed to not having the child here. But we need *something*. A couple framed photos on the side table. You must have one of those?"

"I have a bunch, but they're in a drawer where I put them." I can't help the irritation from creeping into my voice. *The child?*

She heaves a sigh. "Look, I know you want to protect your daughter. But part of this is building a more positive media image for yourself. I'm sure you've already heard some of the less than flattering things that have been said about you—"

"Many times." I quickly cut her off in case she felt the need to begin listing them.

"Well, the best way to—"

"I will *not* put my child's face on national television for publicity efforts." I'm struggling to keep the emotion out of my voice.

"But—"

"No."

"You heard her, Simone," Brett says, and that serious no-nonsense tone is back. His eyes flicker to me and I silently thank him with a small smile. "Besides, I think people will fall in love with her just as she is."

Simone's mouth clamps shut. She glares at Brett, clearly unhappy about my stance and his support of it. But she also knew what it was before coming here. She must have thought she could sway me.

My mother seems to have found her tongue and her nerve. "For what it's worth, I think my daughter is doing the right thing by keeping Brenna away from the spotlight, and if Kate Wethers wants this interview to go ahead, you had better let her people know not to try to go against Cath's wishes." She reaches for her purse. "I have to pick up Brenna. It was so nice to meet you." She smiles first at Brett, and then Meryl.

But Meryl rushes over to take her hand graciously. "We'll see each other again. I'm sure of it."

My mom purses her lips and nods. She's trying to keep her cool. I wonder if she's going to call her girlfriends the second she's out the door and shriek like a thirteen-year-old girl at a One Direction concert. I almost wish I could be there to witness that.

"Keep an eye out for any reporters tailing you home from Brenna's school," I call out after her as she makes her way out the door.

With that, she's gone, and Simone's lips are puckered as she looks for another angle. "Do you have *any* family pictures you'd be willing to put up? You, and your parents, your brother and sister . . ." Simone pushes. "We really need something. A personal, family-oriented touch."

The woman is relentless, but I have to believe she knows what she's talking about.

"I have a few old ones in a shoe box. I could dig them out."

Simone's phone starts ringing. "Great, let's do that," she says, seemingly appeased, answering her phone with a clipped "Simone Castagan." Donovan trails her as she heads out the front door to take the call.

Leaving Brett, his mother, and me alone.

Meryl starts emptying a plastic bag of paper cups and lids and creamers—and I lose myself staring at her for a long moment, because for just that moment she appears to be any other ordinary mom and human—before I remember myself. "Here, let me get some real cups, at least." I rush for the cupboard, searching for my best mugs, the ones that aren't chipped or cracked or covered in tacky slogans. Basically, anything that doesn't say, "garage sale find."

"You have a very nice place."

I barely keep the snort down. I live in a hovel compared to what they're accustomed to, and I know because I found pictures of their Malibu house online. She's just being polite. "That's kind of you to say."

"I mean it. It's so quaint and . . . cozy. You've made a lovely home for your daughter."

When I turn back, I see her eyes wandering over the space. She has such an honest way about her that I almost believe her. But then I remind myself that she's an award-winning actress.

"May I?" she asks, suddenly moving in beside me and gesturing to the soap, her diamond ring sparkling, even under my dull lights.

"Yes. Of course. Make yourself at home." I silently thank my mom for insisting I run an SOS pad over the sink.

"And Brett, darling, please sit. You shouldn't be on your feet," she adds over her shoulder in that airy voice.

"I'm fine, Mom."

"No, you're pale, and the doctor told you to stay off your feet. Sit." She softly chastises him, wandering over to drag a rickety chair out for him.

He *is* sort of pale. But still drop-dead gorgeous.

He offers me a sheepish look before easing himself in, grimacing in pain.

Guilt overwhelms me. I shouldn't have pushed him to get this done right away. He shouldn't be here. "I'm sorry, we should have waited a few weeks to do this, until you're better."

"I'll be fine."

"Did you take your pills?" Meryl asks.

"I will after the interview. They make me sleepy. You know that," he says in an overly patient manner, as if he's anything but.

"You should get some food in you." Meryl peels back a lid and pulls out a plate and cutlery from the plastic bag. I'm guessing they're disposable, but they're nicer than the porcelain dishes I have in the cupboard. "Egg salad, right?"

Brett's face pinches, and she shakes her head at herself, chuckling. "It's your sister who loves egg. I always get you two mixed up. Here, ham and cheese. And some carrots on the side." She plates everything for him and sets it in front of him, like a doting mother would do for her small child.

When he looks up, when he sees me pressing my lips together to try to hide my smile, his face breaks into a wide grin. "You're thinking about how you do this for your five-year-old, aren't you?"

I can't help it, I burst out laughing.

Meryl winks at me, then kicks off her fancy heels and demands, "Eat! Before I have to hand-feed you like I *would* a five-year-old."

Something about watching them interact—the all-powerful and glamorous Meryl Price treating her son like a regular overbearing, worrying mother would; the sexy, strong Brett Madden scrunching his nose at eggs—puts me at ease for the first time since before the accident.

■ ■ ■

"Let's have you sit back all the way . . ." Rodney peers through the lens of the camera that's angled on my ugly floral couch. It's one of two cameras, the other poised to record Kate Wethers, who will sit in one of my rickety kitchen chairs to the left of us. The one that's been glued back together several times. I swear, they chose the worst one intentionally.

The crew arrived in a Suburban with a THE WEEKLY decal on the side forty-five minutes ago and have since turned my living room into a stage.

I follow Rodney's instructions, scooting all the way until my back hits the couch.

"Okay, good. And I want you to turn your body into Brett."

Turn *into* Brett? I'm practically *on top* of Brett. This love seat feels more like an armchair now that he's sharing it with me. They've insisted that they want us beside each other for the interview, though.

"More. Let's have your knees touching."

I offer him a nervous smile as I nudge his right knee with mine. If the close contact bothers him, he doesn't let on. He leans back in my couch, the picture of calm, as if he's done hundreds of these interviews before. He probably has.

"Yeah, that's perfect. Jess? I need the screen adjusted a half inch my way."

His assistant scurries to shift the shiny silver screen as directed. Brett explained that it helps angle the light to avoid unflattering shadows and glares. "Good?"

Rodney gives two thumbs-up. "Just like the studio. Aside from the mikes, we're all set. Katie, how much longer do you need?"

Kate Wethers, the prime-time news celebrity and striking brunette who I've seen gracing the television screen for years, stands beside my kitchen table and chats with Meryl as if they're old friends—and maybe they are. Or maybe it's just that Meryl is so easy to talk to.

"Give me ten." She waves over the makeup girl, though I don't know what more she needs done, given that she looks camera-ready.

I've already been dusted and rouged. Brett just laughed and shook his head when she tried to minimize his bruising.

Ten minutes.

Even with Brett next to me—where I can feel his presence, his warmth, his support—I don't know if I can do this. Especially because I never had a chance to talk to him privately. We haven't had a moment alone, what with Meryl here, and then the rest of them, and now the sweat is beginning to trickle down my back at the prospect of him touting words like "hero" and "incredible" and "I owe her everything," and of the look on his face when he hears the *entire* story.

"Hey." He gently nudges me with his elbow. "You need a quick breather before we start?"

"Yes." It comes out in an exhaled sigh. "But am I allowed to move?"

He chuckles. "You can do whatever you want."

"Okay. Actually . . ." I hesitate, swallowing against my growing fear. "Can I talk to you for a minute? Somewhere that's not right here?" I hope I can be a little more articulate in the actual interview. Thank God it's not going to be aired live.

A curious frown wrinkles his forehead. "Of course."

We weave around all the equipment and people, Brett struggling to edge by. There aren't many options for privacy around here. Outside is off-limits and I'm not about to lead him into the bathroom for a deep conversation, so it's basically either Brenna's bedroom or mine.

The second we step into mine and he shuts the door, I know I chose the wrong one for my current level of anxiety. I've never had a man—besides Keith, when he was hanging a corner shelf on the wall or helping with Brenna—in my bedroom. And to have Brett here . . .

His eyes flitter around the cramped rectangular space, dimly lit by my bedside lamp, to land on the picture of Brenna that sits on my dresser beside my freshly washed and folded and very unsexy white cotton panties and bras. I see his eyes skim over them momentarily before reaching for the picture frame.

He studies her face. "She has your jawline. And your mouth. And the shape of your eyes. She's pretty much your mini-me."

"Not quite but . . . almost."

"She's beautiful." He sets the frame down. "You're really worried about how all this will impact her, aren't you?"

"It's stirred up stuff I don't want her hearing about yet. The sooner this is all over, the better."

"Right. I hope so. Do you mind if I sit?" He's already heading for my bed, that same pained expression on his face that's there every time he moves.

"Your leg's really hurting you, isn't it?"

"Nah. It's getting better."

"Liar," I whisper, edging over to take a seat next to him. It's probably better that I don't face him straight on for this.

"You're really nervous, aren't you?"

"Nah," I mimic.

"Liar." He smiles. "It's going to be fine, trust me. Kate's one of the good ones, and Simone made sure she knows what's off-limits. Don't worry. She told me herself, she wants you walking away from this looking like the hero that you are."

There he goes, using that word again. "See, that's the thing." I catch myself picking at my fingernail, so I clench my fists to stop. "The other day, when I told you what happened that night? I kind of left something out of the story. Something important." My chest feels two sizes too small for my lungs to work properly. Brett says nothing, waiting for me. "When I first got there, your head was hanging forward and there was all this blood," I close my eyes and the image appears. "I put my hand on your chest and I could feel your heart beating, so I knew you were alive. So I tried to get you to wake up. Then, when the car caught fire, I started yelling and trying to pull you out. It was impossible. You were so heavy, and your boot was stuck on something. You moaned but you didn't wake up." A prickly knot sprouts in my throat, sparking tears in my eyes. I swallow against it. "The fire was getting so hot, and so much closer, and the smell from the fire and your friend . . ."

Brett inhales sharply.

"I gave up on getting you out. I backed away, knowing that you were alive. The other night, you said that most people would have left you there. I'm one of them. I *did* leave you there."

"No, you didn't."

"I did! I was just about to turn and head for the ditch to get away from the fire when you finally lifted your head. That's the only reason I came back. But I did leave you there." Suddenly the sickening weight on my lungs lessens, and with each inhale, breathing becomes easier.

An odd bittersweet relief overwhelms me. Relief that Brett now knows the full truth.

But what does he think?

My heart pounds in my ears for ten long beats before he speaks. "You're kidding me, right?"

I frown, seeing the mixture of amusement and sympathy on his face.

"Cath. You didn't leave me there."

"But I—"

"You didn't leave me there," he repeats. "And even if you hadn't gotten me out, and I hadn't survived, you *still* didn't leave me there." His eyes narrow with understanding. "Is this why you've been hiding?"

"I guess it hasn't helped. This, and just being in the limelight again. I had a rough time after that stuff in high school. A lot of people around here saying and doing things to me and to my family. I really didn't want to relive it, and I don't want Brenna dragged into it either. She'll hear about it one day. I just wanted it to be on my terms."

In a somewhat tentative move, he reaches over to rope an arm around my body. He pulls me closer to him, until my shoulder is pressed against his side. His other hand finds my chin, lifting it until I'm forced to peer into his eyes. "I won't let that happen. And besides, I don't think there'll be a single bad thing that anyone can say about you after they watch this interview."

I feel my cheeks flushing at being so close to him. "You may be a little bit biased."

His sad smile dissolves into a dazzling one. "You're right, I'm completely biased. You could do just about anything and I'd still have you sitting high on a pedestal."

My chest swells with a sudden and overwhelming wave of affection for this man.

I must be starving for human connection because, just like the other night, I can't help but sink into him, resting my head against his strong chest, trying to get closer, wishing that time would stand still.

"You ready to go out there and face the world together?"

"Or we could just stay right here?" I joke.

"That sounds like an even better idea," he says softly, as his gaze drifts over my bed and then back to my face, his eyes dropping to my mouth and lingering.

As if he might want to kiss me.

Foolish wishes for a foolish girl.

I remember feeling this same way long ago, sitting in a hard plastic chair at the front of the class, lost in a teenage girl's impossible daydream, in which my art teacher might lust for me as I did for him. Where he might pick me over all the other, prettier girls in school.

That impossible daydream turned out to be not so impossible after all.

Then again, it also turned into a nightmare.

A sudden rapping against the door makes me pull away. Brett's arm slides off me, leaving me cold.

"Brett? Catherine? Are you ready?" It's Meryl.

"Just a sec," he calls out to his mom.

"What do I say when I get to that part in the story?" The moment of peace is gone and my nerves are kicking in again.

He uses my bed's footboard to stand and adjust himself on his crutches. "What do you want to say?"

"I don't know. What would you do?"

He shuffles his way toward the door, stopping just before it. He reaches out for me, his large hand beckoning.

My breath catches as I eye it. Hesitantly, I step forward, sliding my hand into his, feeling miniature by comparison. He's shockingly gentle, though, closing his fingers over mine. Pulling me toward the door and closer to him, he reaches up to push a stray stand of hair off my face. I meet his eyes.

His mint-laced breath skates across my face as he hovers over me for five long heartbeats, something unreadable in his expression. "I've always been big on the truth."

"The truth." I exhale a shaky breath, his proximity making me a little dizzy. "I can do that."

Chapter 14

. . .

March 2010

"Mr. Philips is waiting for you." Mrs. Lagasse's narrow face is even tighter as she scowls at me from behind her secretary's desk.

I don't bother smiling back—the woman has never been friendly to me. I stroll past her and down the hall to the principal's office at the end, my stomach in knots.

"Close the door behind you," Mr. Philips instructs somewhat absently, his focus remaining on his computer screen for a long moment after I've pushed his office door shut and taken the chair across from him.

Finally, he turns to settle his naturally cold, hard gaze on me. It's nothing like his son's. "Miss Wright, I wish we were meeting under more pleasant circumstances."

And which circumstances would those be? I've sat across from him at this desk on more than one occasion and it has never been pleasant. Though, I'll agree, this time feels a hundred times worse. "How is he?" I blurt out before I can stop myself.

Mr. Philips's lips press together as he seems to consider his response. What must he think about Scott and me being together? "Hurt," he finally says. "He doesn't understand why you would go to the police with this . . . matter." The way he says it makes me think he knows the truth—that Scott and I are together. Or, were together.

The lump that's been lodged in my throat for the past nine days flares, hearing that I've hurt Scott. "I didn't want to, I swear. I would do anything to get out of it. Please tell him that."

Mr. Philips settles back into his chair, his fingertips meeting each other in front of him. "Then recant your statement."

"What?"

He smirks, as if he knows I have no idea what that means. "Tell them you're withdrawing your statement. Tell them you made it all up. They don't have enough to pursue the charges without your testimony."

"But . . . Won't I get in trouble?" And what about the texts? My mother's account?

"No." He says it so simply. "Do you want Scott to go to jail? Do you want his reputation ruined?"

"No! Of course not."

"Then recant. They'll let you go."

"But . . . lie to the police?"

"People do it all the time. They won't pursue it." Mr. Philips leans forward. "You don't have to cooperate with them, Catherine. You're the 'victim.'" I don't miss his sneer at that word. "They won't force a victim to testify, and if you refuse to testify, then this whole mess will go away. Isn't that what you want?"

I nod furiously.

■ ■ ■

I coil my fingers together as everyone takes their places, Brett easing around the furniture with careful maneuvers. I just watched him wash pills down with a bottle of water, unable to delay it any longer. He's putting up a strong front, but there is pain in his eyes. Even though he encouraged me, I'm feeling guilty for pushing this interview on him so soon.

Meryl rubs his arm affectionately as he passes her to edge around the coffee table. Just as he's turning to sit, he knocks his cast against the corner of the table, his face contorting in pain, his eyes closing.

Instinctively, I reach for him, grabbing his hand, hot and rough and so tense. "Are you okay?"

Keeping his back to everyone else, his chest puffs out with a deep inhale. With a long, slow exhale, his grimace fades and that relaxed, perfect smile appears again. "Yeah, I'm good."

And I'm left holding his hand with a room of people watching us.

I quickly drop it and resume my old-lady hand-wringing in my lap as Jess clips on my microphone. If we don't get this over with, I'll be rocking back and forth soon enough.

My love seat cushion sinks as Brett settles in next to me, and I feel myself naturally tilting into his big body, as much as I try to hold myself up straight. Rodney spent so much time repositioning me, I'm afraid to throw off my angle by adjusting.

"You good?" Brett whispers.

"Yup." My tight one-word answer, delivered in a high-pitched squeak, betrays me.

He leans in, ever so faintly catching my ear with his mouth. "Just remember to take a deep breath before you answer each question. It'll help, I promise. And if there's something you don't want to answer, just nod toward Simone and she'll shut it down. Or take my hand."

As if I'm going to take Brett Madden's hand on a prime-time television broadcast.

"'Kay?"

I give him a nod as Kate, in a smart blouse and pencil skirt, saunters in to take her seat, adjusting her microphone. She looks like she might roll out of bed ready to be on camera. I doubt that's the case, but I wish I was as at ease with this whole production as she is.

Rodney starts the countdown. "Five . . . four . . . three . . . two . . ."

You could hear a pin drop on my floor, the two heartbeats of silence are so acute. And then . . .

"I'm Kate Wethers and we have a special exclusive interview for you tonight. We are in Balsam, Pennsylvania, with Brett Madden, Philadelphia Flyers captain and son of actress Meryl Price, and Catherine Wright, the heroic woman who saved his life by pulling him from a burning car . . ." Kate speaks smoothly and eloquently, and without error, as if she's practiced her speech for days and could recite it in her sleep, her sharp green eyes—lined with crow's-feet to suggest she's older than the early forties that I first pegged her at—locked on the camera. She introduces the accident—in case there's a single person in the U.S. who isn't already aware—and the aftermath, ending with the dramatic revelation that the mysterious person who saved the two-hundred-and-twenty-pound Brett is, shockingly, a petite five-foot-four woman.

With that, she turns to face Brett and me. I feel the camera zooming in on my face, but I don't look at it, keeping my eyes locked on Kate and trying not to bare my teeth like a feral animal when I force a smile. Brett, Meryl, and Simone promised that Kate is kind and classy, and wouldn't try to twist my words or come in from left field and leave my mouth gaping open.

I just want this over with.

Brett and Kate share pleasantries, Kate expressing how happy she is that he is recovering, Brett congratulating her on a prestigious journalism award she recently won. Not a cord of tension pulses through him. I wish I could be that relaxed.

"And this is the lovely young lady the world has to thank for allowing us to continue enjoying Brett Madden's smile, charm, and talent. Catherine Wright, how are you doing?"

Speak! Speak! Speak! "A little out of sorts, honestly." I clear my throat several times, flashing a nervous smile at Brett, who nods encouragingly at me.

"So, Catherine. Or is it Cath? I've heard both in the brief time I've been here."

"Either. Just not Cathy, please."

She chuckles and then turns her attention back to Brett. "So, that fateful Friday night, you and Seth Grabner were on your way to celebrate clinching a spot in the Eastern Conference finals, were you not?"

"That's right. Sid Durrand has a place up in the Poconos and he was hosting the team there."

"And it was Seth's car that you were in?"

Brett smiles. "He was *dying* to get his Corvette out on the road again after storing it all winter." His smile falls off. "I meant . . . He really wanted to drive it."

"And you've already been clear that there was no alcohol involved in the accident."

"That's right."

She turns to me. "Cath, why don't you tell us what everyone wants to hear in your own words: the night you saved Brett Madden's life."

"Well . . ." I remind myself to take a deep breath, just like Brett coached me. "I was on my way home from an unsuccessful blind date . . ."—even though Gord sold me out the way he did, and he deserves to have his ego taken down ten notches, I won't be outright cruel—". . . and I was taking Old Cannery Road. There was this red sports car. It was—" I bite back my words. I told the police that I thought the driver was speeding, but there's no need to condemn him now. "It was foggy. Really foggy," I say instead, which is not a lie. It's surprising, how much I remember about that night, and with how much clarity I can recall it, right down to the panic and feeling of helplessness.

"So you found Seth Grabner first?"

I nod. "Yeah, he was . . . It wasn't good." I feel Brett tense beside me, and I quickly move on. "Then I found Brett in the passenger side. He was still breathing, but unconscious."

"Was the car burning at this point?"

"No. I could smell something odd, but it didn't catch fire until about twenty or so seconds later." I shake my head. "Or, honestly, I don't know how long after. Anyway, when it did, I knew I had to get him out of there. I had already unbuckled his seat belt, and I was trying to pull him out. I managed to get his right leg out of the car, but his left boot was stuck under something."

"You tried to pull this two-hundred-and-twenty-pound man beside you out of the car." She gestures at Brett right next to me, to emphasize his size, which I'm sure is already clear with me sitting so slight next to him.

Something about the way she says it makes me giggle. Maybe at the absurdity of me even trying in the first place. "Yeah, he's as heavy as he looks."

Next to me, Brett chuckles softly.

She leans in, her voice dropping a notch, as if she's somehow more engaged in the story. It's a subtle but clever move on her part. "So then what happened, Catherine?"

I avert my gaze from her and look into a camera lens, but then remember that they told me not to do that, so I drop my eyes to the coffee table, struggling to control my racing heart. "I kept shouting and screaming, but he wouldn't respond, and it was *so* hot, I felt like my skin was going to melt off. So I started to back away. For just a few seconds, I gave up," I finally admit in a shaky whisper. "Nothing I was doing was working."

Silence fills the room.

"You were crying," Brett suddenly says, almost to himself. "You kept saying that you were sorry, and you were crying."

I turn to regard the frown zagging across his forehead. "You heard me?"

His blue eyes search my features. "I guess I did. I just didn't remember it until now."

For a few moments, Kate, the camera, the crew . . . they vanish.

Kate's voice pulls me back quickly, though. "That must have been an absolutely terrifying and impossible decision for you." Her brow furrows with sympathy. "You're a twenty-four-year-old woman, a single mom with a five-year-old child waiting for you at home, you had already put yourself in harm's way. *And*, by basic logic, a woman of your size can't possibly have the strength to lift an unconscious man of Brett Madden's size out of a bucket seat." She waits a few beats, maybe to let those words sink in, before going on. "But you didn't really give up, did you? Because otherwise he wouldn't be sitting next to you."

Relief swells inside me, and for the first time since she's started talking, my smile feels genuine. "He coughed and lifted his head. I saw him do it, so I ran back and started screaming at him to pull his leg free, hoping he'd hear me. And somehow he did, and I had both of his legs out of the car, so I wrapped my arms around his waist and started pulling."

Kate holds her hand up. "Let's stop right there for a moment, because I want to make sure viewers understand this." She turns to look at the camera. "Brett Madden was not in a pickup truck, or an SUV, or one of those vehicles you need to climb into. He was in a '67 Corvette. Now, I don't know about you guys, but the last time I was in a Corvette, I could barely haul myself out of it, it was so low to the ground." She has a light comedic flair that makes her stand out from other prime-time newscasters, even when she's reporting on difficult topics.

"My dad said something along those lines," I agree with a giggle.

She turns back to me. "How on *earth* did you get him out?"

I shrug. "Honestly, I don't know. One moment I was tugging on him, and the next we were tumbling backward into the ditch. I figure he came to and gathered some last-minute strength."

Kate focuses on Brett. "Is that what happened? Can you explain it?"

"No, I can't explain it. With my injuries, the likelihood that I suddenly lifted myself out is close to nil."

"So, you're saying . . ."

"I don't know how she did it, but . . ." He turns to meet my eyes with such intensity, I feel a furious blush burn my cheeks. I drop my focus to my hands. "I owe Catherine my life."

A deafening silence lingers in the air. An intentional pause from

Kate, I suspect, before she goes on. "So, by all accounts, you shouldn't be sitting here right now."

His leg presses against mine in a discreet—to everyone but me—move. "No. I should never have made it out of that car alive."

"And what does it feel like to know that? Has it changed your perspective?"

He uses the trick he taught me and inhales deeply. "To be honest, I don't think I've come to terms with it yet. I was so used to rolling out of bed in the morning with nothing but an upcoming game or practice to focus on. That's where I put *all* my energy. The game was everything to me. Now I open my eyes and I replay that one night in my head, and I tell myself that the pain in my leg is nothing, that I should be six feet in the ground, so I don't have a right to be upset if . . ." His voice drifts and he swallows. "I've been given a second chance to live that one of my best friends didn't get. I need to make the most of it."

Kate Wethers's face fills with sympathy, and I can't tell if it's staged or sincere. "So, you and Seth Grabner were quite close off the ice, too, then."

Another hard swallow. "I've made a lot of good friends over the years. But Seth was one of those guys I instantly knew would be around long after we retired. Losing him . . . there's a giant hole in my life." Brett's voice has turned husky. It's all I can do not to reach out and take his hand, to try to offer him some sort of comfort. I settle on pressing my thigh against his, a returned sign of affection.

"I think your team would say there are two giant holes on the ice, not having you and Seth Grabner on there with them. By the time we air this interview, the Flyers will have played game four of the Eastern Conference Finals and may be out of the play-offs. What has it been like, sitting on the sidelines and watching them struggle?"

"A hundred times more painful than this." He haphazardly waves toward his casted leg. "I want to be out there, helping them. They've all worked hard and they deserve to win."

Kate's brow pinches just a touch. "While alcohol wasn't a factor in the accident, the police report says that speed was. This has caused quite a stir with sports fans and the media who feel that the accident was preventable and that the nearly one hundred and twenty-five million dollars tied up in contracts to you two should have guaranteed more responsibility on your part. How do you feel about that?"

Brett dips his head forward, pausing a moment. He must have expected that question to come up, as difficult as it is. "There are many things I wish I could go back and change about that night, but I can't. I'm truly sorry if we let people down."

Anger flares inside me. He almost died. One of his best friends did die, and all people seem to care about is winning a stupid trophy.

And he's actually apologizing for not being able to give it to them.

I feel the overwhelming urge to defend him, my mouth going so far as to open, ready to blast fans.

And then Kate turns to the camera. "We'll be right back in a few minutes to talk more with Brett Madden and Catherine Wright about this incredible story." There's a pause, and then Kate calls out, "I could really use a water, please, Margaret?" Her assistant scurries over with a bottle of Evian.

I force myself to take a few breaths and calm down. "Are you okay?" I ask, sensing his mood shifting.

"Yeah." The couch sinks under Brett's weight as he leans closer to me. "You're doing great."

"Oh, right."

"He's right. You are," Kate interrupts through sips. "And we're half-way through. When we jump back on, we're going to talk more about you, Cath. About your current life, about your daughter. I know"—she holds up her hand before I have a chance to object—"we'll keep it brief and vague." Her knowing eyes meet mine. "And we'll talk a bit about your past, too."

I nod wordlessly.

She waves to Rodney, and he begins the countdown again.

"And five . . . four . . . three . . . two . . ."

Kate does her little opening spiel again, and then turns to me. "Catherine, you didn't exactly walk away from the accident unscathed, did you?"

"No." I hold up my wrist, the bruising more pronounced under the lighting. "When Brett and I fell into the ditch, I must have sprained my wrist. It's a lot better, though. Another week and I should be back to normal."

"But your car wasn't so fortunate."

I smile sheepishly. "No. Because of the fog, I pulled up right behind the Corvette, hoping that my headlights would help me see. And then it caught fire and spread to mine before the fire department could put it out."

"So you've lost your car."

I shrug. "Yeah, but my parents lent me the money to buy a new one, so I can get to and from work. I really appreciate it." I add that last piece more for them than anyone else.

"You're a waitress at a local diner, is that right?" Kate makes it sound like she's not entirely sure, which I know is not the case. I'd bet that her research team handed her a full dossier on me for the drive over.

"Yes."

She frowns. "Hard to work as a waitress with a sprained wrist, isn't it?"

I nod. "I've had to take some time off."

"Do you have any concerns about losing your job because of this?"

I smile. "No. Luckily, I have an amazing boss, so I think I'll be okay."

"*When* you can actually work again. But what are you going to do until then? I mean, you're a single parent to a little girl. You have bills to pay."

"Money is the last thing Cath needs to worry about," Brett cuts in, adding, "as stubborn as she's being about accepting help from me."

I roll my eyes before I can stop myself.

Kate's soft chuckle fills my little house. "Brett is one of the highest paid NHL players and a son of Hollywood royalty. Surely you'll let him at least buy you a new car, Catherine."

I turn to shoot a questioning frown his way, whispering, "Did you put her up to that?"

Forgetting that I'm wearing a microphone, so they likely caught that.

Brett's hands go up in surrender. "See? I'm not the only one who thinks it's completely ridiculous that you wouldn't let me help."

"Tell me, Catherine, is there a specific reason you won't accept Brett's offer?"

I shrug. "I don't know. It just doesn't feel right. It'd be like me profiting from the accident."

"So, if he replaced your old car with an identical—"

"Loud, rusty, falling-apart Grand Prix with no horn and two hundred thousand miles on it, then yes, I suppose that would be fine." I smile, realizing how absurd that sounds. "I'm happy I was there and able to get him out." My throat begins to swell with the very thought of *not* sitting here next to him, his leg pressed against mine, feeling his warmth. Of how tragic it would have been for the world to lose a person like him.

"But you can understand why he feels he owes you, right?"

"I guess I just feel like, in a way, *I'm* the lucky one here, for being in the right place at the right time to help him, and to get to know him after. If he's going to be in my life, I want that all to be because he *wants* to, not because he feels obligated."

Oh, my God. The moment I pause, I desperately wish I could take everything I just said back. I've made myself sound like a woman who's crushing on Brett Madden.

Even if I am, I don't want anyone knowing about it. Especially not him.

A tiny smile of satisfaction flickers across Kate's face, and then, thankfully, she's whisking the conversation off in another direction. "Catherine, tell me something," Kate leans forward, until she's perched at the very end of my rickety wooden chair. If she's uncomfortable, no one would ever know. "You wouldn't allow the police to release your name after the accident. You kept your identity hidden for a week, even from the Madden family, who were desperate to meet the woman who saved Brett's life. Why?"

I'm sensing this is the segue into talking about Scott Philips. "I didn't want all the media attention that I knew it would bring."

Her eyes narrow. "And did that have anything to do with what happened in 2010, with your high school teacher?"

I swallow, and remind myself that I've already been through this and I came out on the other side. And avoiding it won't make it go away now. "Yes."

She leans back in the chair. It creaks, and I panic momentarily, imagining it breaking apart and Kate Wethers falling flat on her ass in my living room. I wonder if they'd edit that part out. "For viewers who are unaware, seven years ago you claimed that you were involved in an intimate relationship with your art teacher, Scott Philips. You were seventeen and he was thirty. He was arrested on charges of corruption of a minor, but the charges were dropped not two weeks later when you recanted your statement. The district attorney claimed that there was not enough evidence to take this case to court, even though the police report showed evidence of text conversations between you two, as well as an eyewitness report of Scott Philips waiting in his car outside your home in the middle of the night."

Kate pauses for a few seconds. I'm noticing that she does that when she's about to ask a question where I have to talk a lot.

"Can you tell us a bit about this teacher in your own words?"

"Wow." I can't help the nervous giggle. "I haven't talked about him in a really long time." I feel a nudge against my leg. Brett, trying to get my attention.

"You okay?" he mouths, worry in his eyes.

No. I smile and nod.

"Just, anything. What was he like as a teacher, for starters?"

"He never felt like a teacher to me. Not like all the other ones. He was more like an older friend, someone I could talk about music and books and art with. Everyone called him Scott in class. He was attractive and flirty."

Kate's eyebrows raise. "Flirty?"

"He had this smirk that girls in school talked about. A lot of girls liked him."

"And he liked you."

I drop my gaze to my hands. What can I say that won't get me into trouble? "I thought so."

"You exchanged texts, did you not?" She adds, as if to reassure me, "The police had proof of them. One of Scott Philips telling you how beautiful you were."

I nod. Scott claimed that the text telling me I was beautiful was innocent in intention but extremely poor judgment on his part. I seemed like a girl with low self-esteem. He was only trying to boost it.

"And then your mother followed you as you were sneaking out one night and witnessed you climbing into a car driven by him. She was the one who filed the report with the police."

Another nod. Scott claimed that he was on his way home from a friend's house and saw me walking down the street, so he pulled over.

His friend corroborated it, though much later on it became common knowledge that that friend was in Philly that night. Ironically, at a Flyers game.

"How did you feel when she did that? Were you angry with her?"

Brett's hand slides against my thigh ever so subtly, and I know he's checking to see if I'm okay with this, if I want Simone to intervene.

But I remember what my mother told me about saying what I need to. "I was crushed. I didn't see it the way she saw it. I only saw a man I loved and wanted to be with. I hated her for a very long time because of it."

"You say you loved him. Did he ever make you feel like he might have reciprocated those feelings?" She seems to be choosing her words carefully.

This is where it gets dicey. What do I say? Yes, he told me that he loved me on more than one occasion and I'm tired of denying it, of allowing the lie that he and his family cultivated to go on. Of allowing Scott Philips to get away with it. But to admit that means opening doors I had no intention of ever opening again.

I choose my response just as carefully. "When I gave my statement to the police, I was terrified. I didn't know I had any choice but to tell them *everything*. It was spring break, and a week later when school started, I was called into my principal's office. He's the one who told me that I was considered a victim and that, if I recanted, the charges against Scott would be dropped. I didn't want Scott to go to jail, so I recanted my statement."

Kate Wethers's expression tells me that I was right, that I don't need to answer her question directly to tell her everything she needs to know. "Your principal was Scott Philips's father, was he not?"

"Yes."

"Did he know you loved his son?"

"It seemed like it, but I can't speak for him."

"So, to summarize . . . Scott Philips was charged and released on bail, and his father—the principal—calls you, the seventeen-year-old victim, into his office and persuades you to recant your statement so the charges against his son can be dropped."

I hesitate. I never told my mother about that meeting with Mr. Philips. She assumed someone had talked to me, convinced me to recant, but I never told her who. I didn't want to give them more ammo to use against Scott. At the time, I was thankful for the out his father had given me. "Basically. Yes."

"Why would you agree?"

"Because I loved Scott."

She nods softly. "And did anyone else witness this meeting?"

"The secretary saw me go in, but she wasn't actually in the room."

Kate heaves a deep breath, the first time she's done that this entire interview. "So, fast-forward a bit. The charges are dropped and Scott Philips returns to teaching in your school. Did you talk to him?"

I shake my head. "He never came back to teach my class."

"And the local newspaper published an article on him not long after, basically painting you as this vixen who used her irresistible wiles to try and lure this thirty-year-old *man* into temptation with sexy clothes and relentless flirting. Of course they didn't name you, but I would assume that everyone knew who you were?"

"I think that's safe to assume, yes."

She pauses and looks at me searchingly. "Did you feel like you were guilty of trying to *seduce* Scott Philips?"

I flush at the word. I'm still ashamed for the way I acted with him, though it wasn't as people made it sound. "You mean . . . did I wear tight jeans to class? Yes, I guess I did. Were my T-shirts fitted? Yeah, probably. Though I don't honestly know how much that could have helped . . ." I look down at my A-cup chest as if to make a point.

Did I just draw attention to my underwhelming breasts on national television?

Heat crawls up the back of my neck as I giggle nervously. "Oh, God. Please edit that part out."

"No, *please* keep that part in," Brett counters with a chuckle, earning my gentle elbow against his ribs. But his playful sense of humor brings with it a sense of relief for me. I can get through this with him by my side.

"Did you ever talk to Scott Philips again?"

I hesitate. "I went to his house to see him, once. He told me to leave. So I left." I sigh. "I was seventeen and in love and foolish. I made a lot of bad choices."

"I don't know any teenagers who don't make a lot of bad choices, to be honest. Most of them just get away without it being the talk of the town. It sounds like a lot of people were less than impressed with *you* for the entire ordeal. What was life like for you in 2010?"

"Not easy. Not for me or my family."

"Not everyone made it so hard for you though, did they?"

I smile. "My boss, Lou from Diamonds, didn't. Her husband's great, too. They're like family to my daughter and me. And the man who rented this house to me, he's been very nice. He's only raised the rent once since we moved in, and barely."

Her face softens. "You became pregnant with your daughter a few months after this incident, correct?"

"Seven months later." I swallow. "That's right."

"And you had moved out of your family's home by then."

"I was . . . Things were hard for everyone at that point. I thought my life was ruined."

"I'll bet." A knowing look flashes through her eyes. "Listen, I've driven past plenty of schools where the girls have their kilts rolled up to where they're more like booty shorts. Should they do that? No. But that's not a pass or an excuse for teachers to flirt with their students, or take it farther. What you wore to school or how you felt about Scott Philips, or even what you may have said to him, is irrelevant. We shouldn't even be talking about it now." She turns to the camera. "I know people at home are probably wondering what happened to Scott Philips. My sources confirmed that he has been teaching art class at a private high school in Memphis, Tennessee, for the last six years. The parents of students at that school were unaware of his past until now, thanks to Catherine Wright's story breaking late last week."

Kate's smooth, melodic voice is so soothing despite the topic that, for a brief moment, I nearly forget that we're being filmed. But then she turns to me, breaking the spell. "Cath, do you think Scott Philips should be allowed to continue teaching?"

I know she wants me to publicly condemn him, to punish him on this open stage.

"I guess it depends on the parents of the students he's teaching."

"Do you regret recanting your statement?"

Had I not . . . Scott and I would have been done either way. But how much worse would it have been, dealing with a trial and lawyers? I nearly shudder at the thought. "All I know is that no one can run from their mistakes forever. But I would really just like to move on from mine."

Genuine sympathy shines in her eyes. "I agree that it's time everyone focus on the incredible side of this story, that you risked your own life saving this man beside you. From my brief conversation with Brett's mother, I know that the Madden-Price family can't sing high enough praises for your bravery. Did you know whose life you were trying to save that night, Catherine?"

I shake my head.

"No idea at all?"

"None."

"And when did you find out that the man you had saved was a superstar?"

"When Keith—I mean, Officer Singer—was driving me home and I saw all the news vans on the road. I thought it was a bit strange, that much attention for an accident."

"And? Were you shocked?"

"Yeah. But, I mean . . ." I look to Brett, smile sheepishly. "I don't watch hockey, so I still didn't know who you were anyway."

Brett's eyes twinkle as he laughs along with Kate.

"I bet that'll change as soon as Brett's back on the ice, right?" She winks at me and then smiles at Brett.

I feel him stiffen, but he hides any evidence of discomfort from the camera with a charming grin. "I'll have her passing me the puck in no time."

He's going to teach me how to play? As in, he's going to be around once this all blows over? Or is that just a line, part of this act for the public?

"So what's next for you, Catherine?"

"Uh . . ." I shrug, somewhat caught off guard by this question, still stuck on the idea of Brett being a part of my life. "I don't really know. I plan on going back to work as soon as I can, and raising my daughter. You know, driving her to and from school without reporters camped outside my door. That'd be nice."

Kate smiles. "You've been raising your daughter on your own this entire time, have you not?"

"Yes."

"And what has her father had to say about your recent bravery?"

"Nothing, he's . . . He's not a part of our lives." It's a roundabout way of bringing up Brenna's father and I didn't expect it, making me stumble over my words.

"Has she ever met him?"

"No."

"Does he know about her?"

This is off-limits and she knows it. It's my own fault for answering in the first place. I seek out Simone from behind the center camera.

"No more about the child," Simone states abruptly.

"You tried going into work a few days ago. How was that?" Kate asks, so smoothly changing topics, as if she were testing the waters to see how far she could get before I or Simone pulled the plug. Her sources must have fed her the local rumors about Matt.

It takes me more than a few heartbeats to regroup. Brett leans into my side ever so slightly, to remind me that he's there. "A disaster," I admit. "There were a lot of people, taking pictures of me. And reporters asking me terrible, inappropriate questions. I had to leave right away. I can't work like that, and if I can't work, then I can't pay my bills. So I'd appreciate it if people would give me some room to breathe. That's why I agreed to this interview. We figured that we'd give everyone the story once, and then I could go back to my regular, quiet life. It's the only interview I'm willing to do."

"Kind of hard for people not to want to meet you, what with your heroic efforts and all."

"I'm just thankful that Brett's alive." I glance over to find him watching me with an odd, sad smile.

"Well, I think I can say, on behalf of all Americans, hockey fans, and women everywhere"—she winks playfully at Brett—"thank you for your incredible bravery, and for risking your life. Your daughter has quite the role model to look up to. Brett, when will we see you on the ice again?"

"As soon as my doctor gives the okay."

"And your fans look forward to that day." Turning to the camera, Kate ends with "This is Kate Wethers, bringing you an exclusive interview with Catherine Wright and Brett Madden from Balsam, Pennsylvania."

Catherine *and* Brett.

"And we're out." Rodney cuts a switch and the red light shuts off. "I wouldn't touch that."

"I agree. You were both great," Kate purrs, already out of her chair and collecting her jacket as if in a sudden rush. She reaches out to shake my hand, her grip firm and smooth. "Thank you for giving me the opportunity to meet you. I hope I helped give you some closure."

"You did. Thank you."

Her eyes flicker between the two of us, and a secretive smile touches her lips. "People are going to eat this story up."

"When is it airing?" Brett asks.

"Friday night, eight P.M. Eastern."

"*This* Friday?" As in, two nights from now? I guess that's better than waiting idly for weeks. Still . . . Now that the interview is over, my anxiety over being filmed is quickly shifting to the reality of countless strangers watching me on television. I hope I didn't sound stupid.

The living room studio is dismantled in fifteen minutes, and the team is packed and out the door in twenty.

Meryl, who has been virtually invisible through the entire filming session, now checks her phone and stands. "I'm sorry to rush out the door, but I have a plane to catch."

"You're filming a movie in Australia." I remember Keith mentioning something about that.

"Yes. And now that Brett's out of the hospital and on the mend, I can't ask them to hold off production any longer. So, unfortunately, I have to go." She reaches out to take my good hand in hers, a broad smile filling her lips. "You were wonderful. People are going to love you." There's something about her breathless voice that's completely soothing.

"I don't know about that. But do you think it will stop them from camping out by my driveway?"

She chuckles, leaning in to give me another warm hug. "With a little bit of time, things will be back to the way you want them." Her gaze flickers to her son. A long, knowing look passes between the two of them. I wonder if it has anything to do with the whispered conversation they shared in the kitchen while the crew was packing up, too quiet for me to hear, but the air around them seemed charged. "I'll be waiting in the car for you."

Simone fills the space Meryl just vacated in front of me. "Here's my info." She thrusts a small white business card into my hand. "Lay low until after the interview airs, and don't answer any question about Brett or the accident without running it by me first. In fact, don't talk to reporters, period. They have a way of twisting your words to tell their own story. Got it?"

"Yup."

"What are you not going to do?"

Why do I suddenly feel like my five-year-old child? "Talk to reporters?"

"At all."

"Right."

"I'll issue a public statement that you've given *The Weekly* an exclusive interview and you won't be giving any more. We'll see if they listen." She turns toward the door but then stalls. "Oh, and stay off all social media. No matter how curious you are, *do not* read comments, *do not* look for reactions. Nothing. Understand?"

"That will be easy. I'm out of data for the month."

Finally satisfied, she slings her purse over her shoulder and is on her phone, heading out the door behind Meryl.

I fumble with Simone's card, tucked between my fingers.

Brett nods toward it. "Put that number into your phone and make sure you use it whenever you think you might need to. Even if it's really simple. She *wants* you to call her, trust me. It's easier than sorting out anything afterward."

Simone on speed dial. "Can't wait."

Brett chuckles. "I know she can be a bit brash, but she's really good at her job."

"Seems like it." I take a deep breath, glancing around my space. I can't believe it held that many people and didn't burst at the seams. "It's so quiet in here now."

"It's nice." He peers down at me with soft eyes. "Breathing better?"

My shoulders lift with exaggeration as I inhale and exhale deeply. I am, actually. "I'm so glad that's over."

He smiles. "It gets easier."

"I'll take your word for it. That's the only one I'm ever doing."

He stares down at me with those intense blue eyes of his, something unreadable passing through his gaze.

"What?"

He hesitates. "I'll make sure you get your life back, if that's what you want. But it won't be overnight."

"Thank you, for all your help. I'm sure you want to get back to your life now, too." A life that doesn't belong anywhere near Balsam, Pennsylvania.

"Right." He pauses. "My dad and I are hitching a ride to Toronto with my mom on her jet tonight. My grandparents live up there, so we figured we'd hang out with them for a week."

"So you'll be home in a week?" A twinge of disappointment stirs in me.

"Actually, I think I'm going back to California with him for the summer. If I can't travel with my team, I may as well be with my family."

"Oh, that's . . ." Toronto, tonight . . . California, for the summer . . . That's so far away. And so soon. It's not like he needs to tell me these things, but he didn't even mention it this morning, when he was arranging the interview. "Did you know you were going before you set this up?"

"No. It was a last-minute decision." He opens his mouth as if to say more, but halts.

Silence lingers as I search for an answer that won't show my growing dismay. "I'm sure it'd be good to put some distance between you and *all this*." And me.

"Yeah, I guess." A frown flickers over his brow. "It'll give me a chance to clear my head. My mom is convinced I haven't been thinking straight. Maybe I haven't."

"I'm not sure I have, either." *I've been too busy fantasizing about you.* But . . . Brett is going to be gone for the *whole* summer? That's three or four *months*. My spirit sinks doing the math.

"It'll help things for you, if I stay away. Though I kind of feel like I'm abandoning you." Tender blue eyes settle on me, and I sense a question behind his words.

I wrap my arms around my body to help shield off the sudden chill I feel. So quickly, so unintentionally, Brett invaded my life. And just as quickly, he'll be gone, leaving me in turmoil. I can't be angry with him for it, though. He's right. The best thing he could do to help my life settle is to get far away. But I wish it weren't the case. "Don't worry. Hawk and Vince are great."

He nods. "Keep them until things are calm again."

This has become too awkward. I'm not sure what else to say except, "I guess this is good-bye?"

He shifts on his crutches. And grimaces.

"You really should get off your feet."

"That's what my doctor keeps saying."

"Well, you want to heal as fast as possible, don't you?"

"Yeah. It's just hard, being cooped up. I'm not used to it."

"I know exactly what you mean." I chuckle. "Well, minus the broken bones."

He reaches for my injured wrist, gingerly taking it in his hand, his thumb rubbing over the bruised part. "Still hurting?"

"Hardly." *Not right now.*

Brett's phone vibrates in his pocket, so loud that I can actually hear it. "That's my mother. We really do have to catch a plane." I expect him to hobble past me with a simple farewell, but instead he adjusts his weight on his crutches and hooks an arm around me, pulling me into his chest, just like he did the first night we met. Only now my hair doesn't smell like burned fish batter and I'm not in loose sweats. And, oddly enough, though we've had barely any time together, I feel like I know him.

"I'm sorry for disrupting your life. You've already been through enough."

I close my eyes and let myself sink into him, thinking how very not sorry I am. Not about this part, anyway.

"Call me if you need *anything.*"

"I'll be fine." What if I simply want to hear his voice?

How did this go so quickly from Brett being the man I pulled out of a burning car to him being the man I wished was actually part of my life? Whose mouth on mine I wished I had license to tip my head back and feel?

Heat crawls up my face at the very idea that Brett might be able to sense what's going through my head. He's showing affection to the woman who saved his life. And I want to show an entirely different kind of affection right now.

He pulls away far enough to lean down and plant a lingering kiss on my cheek, just an inch away from my mouth.

I close my eyes, wishing that he'd shift to the right just a touch.

And then he does.

For only a second his lips are on mine and then they're gone with a sigh, long before I can shake my shock and unfreeze. Did he mean to do that?

He maneuvers toward the door on his crutches and glances back at me once, to smile.

I want to beg him not to go.

To run to him and throw my arms around him so he can kiss me again, for real this time.

I want him to fall deeply and madly in love with me.

But I press my lips together and root my feet to the ground before I manage to humiliate myself.

And then Brett Madden is gone.

Chapter 15

■ ■ ■

"You 'told,' not 'telled,'" I correct Brenna, testing my right hand as I unload the dish rack of mugs. I should be back to carrying plates of food without too much difficulty by Saturday, which is good because that's when I'm scheduled to return to work.

"I *told* Owen that he shouldn't say mean things about Brett because it was an accident and accidents happen, and hockey is just a game. But he said that his daddy said it was Brett's fault if they don't win."

I roll my eyes, but quietly pray to God that the Flyers do somehow miraculously win the next four games, which is what my dad said would need to happen for them to make it to the final round. Apparently it's a long shot, especially without their two best players.

"Who is this Owen kid, anyway?"

"Owen Mooter. He's in grade one."

"Mooter?"

"Yeah. He's new."

"I figured." I'd remember that name around town. "Don't listen to Owen *Mooter*. He's just repeating what his dad said, and his dad is an idiot." I quickly add, "But don't tell Owen Mooter that I said that. And don't call anyone an idiot. It's not nice, and I don't want another call from Mr. Archibald." I've already heard from the principal more in the last three days than I have in the entire school year. Once, to tell me to get Brenna back to school. Then to ask if I'd have Brett come talk to the kids at the school assembly. And again today, hoping to get play-off tickets for him and his son.

"Okay, Mommy."

"People will stop asking you questions soon. I promise." I shouldn't make that promise. With the interview airing tomorrow night, it might make things worse.

"I don't care if they ask me questions."

I sigh. But I do, if those questions veer into other topics. "Did you pick out a book?"

"I can't decide between these two."

It's a nightly occurrence, the great dilemma of which book we should read, as Brenna stalls the inevitable bedtime. "So read one to yourself right now, and I'll be in to read the other one. Hurry up, Brenna. It's almost nine thirty. You should have been in bed an hour ago." Everything is off around here these days.

But instead of turning around and heading into her room, she wanders over to the front window. The slats of the blinds are now permanently bent where her little fingers pry them open to peek outside.

"Leave Hawk alone, please."

"I don't see any people behind Rawley's."

"Good." Between having Kate Wethers's crew roll in here last night—signaling that I'd granted an interview with a national broadcast—and the public statement that Simone issued on my behalf that I will not be granting any more, Keith says the swarm of vultures has thinned somewhat.

"Start reading. I'll be there in a sec."

"Okay, Mommy," Brenna says in her cute singsong voice, skipping back to her room. It makes me smile as I open the kitchen cupboard to stack the clean dishes, and wonder how much longer she'll be so agreeable.

I frown at the white envelope lying on top of the dinner plates. I don't remember putting it there.

My stomach tightens with wariness the moment I feel the weight of it, sensing the thick wad inside. I tear it open and my jaw drops. "What the . . ." I fan it with my thumb. Twenties and fifties and hundreds.

There are thousands of dollars in here.

Along with a note and two hockey tickets. I immediately recognize Brett's writing.

Catherine,
I know you don't want my money. That's why you need to take this.
                                                        —Brett

Heat flushes to my cheeks. He must have snuck the envelope into the cabinet yesterday. Either way . . . he's right, I'm not okay with accepting a secret stash of cash from him.

I fumble for my phone. Scrolling through my list of contacts, I stall for all of three seconds before I hit Call. Despite my immediate anger, I also feel more than a hint of excitement that I have an excuse to call him.

My heart sinks just slightly when it goes to voice mail.

"Hi, it's me, Catherine." How many Catherines does he know? "Catherine Wright," I clarify, and then roll my eyes at myself. "I just found the envelope tucked in my cupboard. I wish you hadn't done that. Thank you, but . . . you really shouldn't have." Maybe I should have given this some thought before calling. "This is way too much. I get that you want to cover the income I've lost, but I've only been off two weeks. I wouldn't earn this much in four months. And I didn't do what I did for money. Even after I found out who you were, I still didn't want your money. I've told you all this already. It's like . . ." I'm struggling to articulate what I want to say. I did a better job with Kate Wethers, even when I sounded like a love-struck girl. "It's like you're handing me a reward for saving your life. Like you put a price on your life and apparently it's worth . . . I don't know, what is this?" I thumb through it again. "Five thousand? Six? You're worth way more than six thousand dollars." I gasp the second the words leave my mouth and register in my brain. "Wait! That came out wrong. That doesn't mean I want *more* money. I don't want *any* of it." I groan. "God, I hate leaving voice messages."

I turn to find Brenna standing in her bedroom doorway in her Olaf pajamas, staring at me with wide, curious eyes. I must sound like a crazy person right now, ranting at someone on the phone for *giving* us money, when for her entire life, she's heard me talking about things we can't afford.

I take a deep breath, and when it sails out my lungs, some of my steam goes with it. "I appreciate the gesture. But I just can't accept it. I need you to take it back. Good night."

I hang up, wishing there was a way to delete my voice mail and start over. I briefly consider calling back and leaving another, more civil message, but I'm afraid it'll only make this entire situation more embarrassing.

Then it occurs to me: Was he screening my call? Has he been waiting for me to find the envelope?

I frown. "What day is it, again?"

"Thursday."

I dart over to turn on the TV and search out the Flyers game. My stress over the money temporarily vanishes as I see the score. "They're going to win!" There's only thirty seconds left in the game and the Flyers are ahead by two goals. Brett is guaranteed to be watching the game right now and on the edge of his seat. No wonder he didn't answer.

I sigh with relief as the seconds count down and the buzzer goes, and the Flyers collide into each other in a sweaty heap of joy. At least Brett will be in a good mood when he listens to my ranting, rambling message, and then dismisses my request entirely, as I assume he's going to.

"Come on, Brenna. Let's go read that book."

Chapter 16

. . .

I still can't hear a knock on my door without tensing up, it seems. Not even when I'm expecting someone. Like my parents, who are coming here to watch the *Weekly* broadcast with me.

Mom called earlier today, adamant that I bring Brenna to their house to watch the interview together. I refused. I haven't left the house since Wednesday, except to ride with Vince to take Brenna to school, and I have no intention of doing so until it's all over.

So she told me they were coming here and hung up before I could tell her not to. That I'd rather send Brenna to her room, turn all the lights out, and watch it alone, almost as terrified today as the day I told the police and the DA that I was recanting my statement.

I rush to the door, not because I'm eager but because I don't know who might be lurking with cameras in Rawley's parking lot and I don't want to subject my parents to that.

My plan is to hide behind the door and shut it the second they cross the threshold, but when I see Jack and Emma trailing them, I forget about potential spies in the bushes.

"Uncle Jack!" Brenna shrieks, tearing across our living room to throw herself into his arms.

"Jack?" I can't help but stare up at him. He left for college last fall and didn't come home for Christmas because the flights were too expensive and a seventeen-hour drive in the winter wasn't smart. In that time, he's packed at least thirty pounds of muscle onto his six-foot frame and grown his short dirty blond hair out into a shaggy style.

"Got any food?" He chuckles, patting his hard stomach before wrapping his arm around my neck and pulling me into a hug.

"What the hell have you been eating in Minnesota?"

"That's what I asked him," Emma jokes, pushing the door closed behind her.

Her round blue eyes settle on me as she tucks a strand of hair—cut to her shoulders now—behind her ear. I've always envied her for that auburn shade. It's so much richer than my ash-blonde. She inherited other things I have coveted, too—a C-cup, long legs, and a brain that can solve complex math equations effortlessly. "Hey, Cath."

"Hey . . . I thought you had an exam today."

She shrugs. "Yeah, I finished it and jumped in the car to get here in time."

"Wow, that's . . ." That's a three-hour drive. That's something I'd never expect Emma to do on my expense. We used to be a lot closer when we were younger, but we drifted, and then I became the older fuck-up sister who put our family through hell and she became the angel child who could do no wrong. I know I embarrass her. She told me as much.

Wait a minute. I turn to Jack, who's holding a squirming and giggling Brenna under one arm like a football. "Weren't you supposed to be in Cancún until Sunday?" He was definitely there. He has the burned nose and golden tan to prove it.

"Managed to get an earlier flight back. Just walked through the door a half hour ago."

"Yeah, cutting it close." Dad throws a playful punch at Jack on his way to claim the La-Z-Boy. "Your mother said you had leftovers?"

I head straight for my fridge to pull out the containers I packed. "Sandwiches and salads. Beer, too. Want one?" Keith stocked the fridge for himself, but I'm sure he won't mind.

"Yes, please," Jack calls out.

"Have you somehow aged by two years since you went away?" Mom shakes her head at me, taking one for my father.

Jack groans and settles himself into the love seat. "Why did I agree to come home this summer?"

"Because you missed me!" Brenna grins wide as she climbs onto his lap. She'll be all Uncle Jack this and Uncle Jack that for the next week.

He tickles her ribs. "Not as much as you missed me."

Not as much as *I* missed him, I realize, watching the two of them now.

"How old are these?" Emma asks, through a bite of a sandwich, wiping her mouth of croissant flakes.

I can't read her expression. Is she about to comment on how they're not fresh? "They're from the interview on Wednesday. They should still be fine, though."

"They're *really* good." Emma takes another big bite, her finger picking up a loose twig of rosemary as I let myself relax. "They're fancy."

"Well, *Meryl Price* was eating them so . . ."

"I still can't believe you guys met her. What's she like?"

"It was only for a minute but she seemed gracious." Mom hands Jack a plate that she made for him.

I roll my eyes at him, mouthing "giant baby."

He grins in response as half a sandwich disappears into his mouth with one bite.

Mom carries one of my kitchen chairs over to settle next to my father. Emma does the same, finding another open space, leaving me a spot on the love seat next to my brother. It's strange to have my family in my home. My sparkling-clean home. It's the cleanest it's probably ever been. I spent the past two days scouring every inch, trying to keep my mind and nerves occupied.

My family has never all been here at once. Emma's never been, period. But they're here now, in an unspoken show of solidarity, Jack going as far as to cut his vacation short by two days. It's suddenly overwhelming.

I thought I was nervous on the day of filming. Now that I'm about to watch myself on TV—knowing that *millions* of people are also going to be watching this—I'm considering setting a bowl beside me just in case I need to puke in it.

"Why did I ever agree to this?" I grumble, sliding into my spot on the love seat.

"Because of all those reporters hounding you," my dad reminds me through a sip of his beer. "I only saw two guys hanging around on the bench tonight when we drove in. He was right."

"Who was right?" Brenna chirps.

"Brett, sweetie." I smooth her matted hair and plant a kiss on top of her head. "Remember? The man with the broken leg."

"I forget what he looks like."

Rivetingly handsome. "You're going to see. He'll be on TV, too."

"When can he come here again?"

"Better be soon, because I can't believe *you* met him before I did," Jack growls through a mouthful, throwing me a piercing glare.

"He's in Canada right now."

"Well, when he's back."

"I don't think he'll be coming around again anytime soon." He hasn't responded to my ranting voice message from last night either. I don't know if that's his way of refusing to acknowledge my refusal, or if he's figuring it's been two weeks since the accident, he's paid up, and the interview's done, so it's an acceptable time to cut ties.

Footfalls on my porch steps sound and I instinctively hold my breath.

A moment later, the door creaks open and Keith steps in.

"Hey!" my dad hollers, holding up his bottle of beer in the air as if to toast him. "Thought you were gonna miss it."

I frown at Keith's uniform. "You don't start until eleven."

"I'm covering a few hours for someone. Jetting over as soon as this is done." He reaches over to clasp hands with Jack. "Dang, you're gonna get too big to skate fast."

Jack gives him a mock glare. "No way."

"Hey, Squirt."

Brenna only smiles.

"What? No hello for me now that *he's* here?"

She answers with that maniacal laugh of hers, which makes me shake my head.

"Quiet! It's on!" Mom exclaims, ending all conversation.

Oh, God. My stomach rolls as I slide an arm around Brenna to pull her close to me, suddenly wishing that everyone would just leave so I can die of embarrassment alone.

My phone dings with an incoming text and I glance at it, assuming it's Lou or Misty, both at Diamonds tonight.

It's a text from Brett.

Are you watching?

A flutter of excitement competes with my anxiety.

With a full entourage. You?

With my dad and grandparents. Granny's making popcorn. I think she assumes this is one of my mom's movies.

I'll admit it gives me some comfort to know he's watching with me, even if he's a thousand miles away.

Just wanted to check in. I'll let you go.

I want to respond, to tell him to not let me go, that he can check in with me anytime he wants, but Kate Wethers and her co-anchor, Rick Daly, a broad-shouldered man of about forty with caramel skin and a wide, charming smile, fill the TV screen, distracting me.

Her strong but smooth voice fills my house once again. "Most of you have heard about the recent tragic car crash that claimed the life of Philadelphia Flyers right wing Seth Grabner and nearly claimed that of Brett Madden, captain of the Flyers and son of Academy Award–winning actress Meryl Price. Thanks to the determination of a good Samaritan, Brett's life was saved. On Wednesday night, I traveled to Balsam, Pennsylvania, to speak with this good Samaritan, Catherine Wright, a twenty-four-year-old single mother and waitress, who just happened to be at the right place at the right time. For Brett Madden, that is. As you can imagine, there has been a lot of excitement in the media for this story, amplified by the fact that Catherine remained in hiding for an entire week from everyone, including the man whom she saved. Tonight we are bringing you an exclusive interview as Catherine speaks out for the first time since the tragedy."

"Mommy, you're squeezing me too tight!" Brenna complains, and in her next breath, she squeals, "That's our living room!"

There I am, dressed in my dusty-rose blouse and sitting stiffly on my floral couch next to Brett, who's leaning back, his elbow propped on the armrest. Even with a broken leg and in pain, he looks at ease next to me.

I wore the wrong blouse. Under those lights, the pink matches the pink base color in the couch. I match my couch. Why did no one tell me to go change? And there sit Brett and Kate, looking sleek and stylish in their solid dark colors.

Maybe no one will notice.

"You match the couch!" Brenna exclaims, earning my groan and Jack's chuckle.

"You look really great, Cath," Keith offers to soften the reality.

I guess I do look okay, other than my bad clothing choice. "They did my makeup," I mumble, unable to keep my eyes from Brett, remembering the feel of his arm occasionally brushing against mine in this very spot. The makeup girl did manage to catch him with some powder around his eyes and it helped a bit, but Brett looks pretty banged up. And yet still handsome, play-off scruff, bruises, red angry scar, and all.

"That's the guy I met."

I wrap my arm around Brenna and pull her to me tight, shushing her with "Yes. Let's watch."

"How did he break his leg?"

"His car hit a tree. Now hush."

"Did it hurt?"

"Yes. Shhh!"

Shivers run down my spine as I listen to myself recount details from the night, my voice sounding so foreign. The camera has zoomed in on my face, and I struggle not to silently criticize my nose, and my expressions, and anything else I can self-consciously pick apart about myself.

Anyone can see that I'm nervous. They've edited the interview well, though, the frames zooming in and out on each of our faces when we're speaking, catching plenty of close-ups of Brett as he listens to me talk.

In fact, the two of us share the screen a lot.

I didn't realize how focused Brett was on me while I was talking, not until I see it now. His eyes hardly ever left my profile, his jaw tightening, his chest rising with deep breaths, his eyes blinking back emotion of his own, his hand on his lap tensing, fingers stretching as if he's about to reach for me more than once.

And once or twice, the camera captures a close-up of his aqua blue eyes when I turn to look at him. That fascinated way he looked at me—I didn't imagine it. The camera has caught it, plain as day.

It also captures the times those eyes drop to my mouth. I feel my face heating as my entire family watches and listens quietly. Somehow, with only angles and edits, *The Weekly* has made this look like a highly intimate interview.

They didn't edit out any of the dialogue either. Not even the part where I disparage myself and look down at my chest. That earned Jack's belt of laughter, even as my cheeks burned bright. The only thing I noticed that they did take out was the part where Simone told them to move on, but the part about Brenna's father not being a part of our lives . . . even that's still there.

Thankfully, Keith sensed the topic switching to Scott Philips and scooped up Brenna before I had a chance to, carrying her to her bedroom with a promise to show her something cool on his phone. She'll hear about her mother's sordid past sooner than I'd like, but not tonight.

The fifteen-minute on-site segment is over in a flash, and then the show is back to Kate and Rick in their newsroom. "What an incredible story!" Rick exclaims. "Can you imagine driving home on some lonely dark road and coming across a wreck like that? I mean, I'd like to think I'd do the same thing that Catherine Wright did."

"We'd all like to think we'd be that brave, but honestly? I don't know how many people would be. Especially when you're a petite woman? You saw the two of them sitting next to each other. That wasn't a trick of the camera. She's half his size!"

She's right about the size, but I'm beginning to think there may have been some tricks of the camera. Putting us side by side on a snug couch, having my knee rest against his, all the close-ups . . .

I can't help but think they're trying to suggest something.

"She seems like a real sweetheart. Honestly, I had no idea what kind of person you'd be facing when you went off for that interview."

"A brave young woman who is working and raising her daughter in the best way she can is who I was facing." Kate's shaking her head. "Nothing makes my blood boil as much as hearing how, at seventeen, she was victimized not only by a teacher but also by the school principal and her community."

"We only have her word, though, Kate. And she recanted her statement," Rick warns.

"Because she was in love with him. I believe that she was telling the truth in the first place. The statement she gave to the police, she didn't know she had any other choice. She was seventeen and terrified. And we *do* have more than just her word, Rick. Our sources had no trouble tracking down the school secretary, Mrs. Lagasse. She remembers Catherine Wright being called down to the office that day. She wondered what the girl could have done wrong within the first hour of classes resuming after spring break. And then news spread that Catherine recanted the very next day, and she questioned what was said behind those closed doors."

My and Rick Daly's eyebrows pop up in unison. That bitter old secretary remembered that day?

"Plus, there's the arrest report. Tell me, Rick, what was a flirty thirty-year-old teacher doing texting his student, telling her she's beautiful? That wasn't the only text he ever sent her, either. He sent her many others that the police recovered."

"No smoking gun, though."

"No. He was careful. And how about the night Catherine Wright's mother followed her out and found him waiting in his car outside. He claims he was just 'in the neighborhood.'"

Rick shakes his head. "It definitely raises questions."

"Our culture sensationalizes this fantasy of students and their older, attractive teachers falling in love," Kate says. "Girls develop crushes on their teachers all the time. I know I did! His name was Mr. Smith and he was twenty-seven years old. He taught me science my sophomore year. Mr. Smith, if you're watching"—Kate holds her hands up to the camera in a calming gesture—"don't be creeped out, but you were a hottie when I was fifteen. My point is, a lot of girls develop crushes on their teachers. And what do teenage girls do when they have crushes? They giggle, they flirt, they raise their hands to answer questions, they ask for extra help after class. Their hormones are raging, their curiosity is at its peak. But there is no valid excuse for a teacher to take that to the next level, if that is in fact what happened here. I guess we'll never be able to let the justice system determine that, though. Not after Catherine Wright was influenced to recant her statement by her school principal—Scott's father—and then the DA decided not to pursue the charges. The district attorney who was part of the same college fraternity as Scott Philips's father, by the way. That took my little team of investigators only two hours to uncover. That makes me want to ask more questions. You too, Rick?"

Rick heaves a sigh. "And now Scott Philips is teaching at a Memphis private school?"

"For now. Since this story aired and his identity and past have been made known, we've received reports of a similar situation with another female student. Hopefully the Memphis police department will investigate." She shakes her head. "This is a case of a privileged *man* taking advantage of a teenage *girl*, probably because he figured he wouldn't be punished. His father was the principal, his uncle was the superintendent, his mother owns a successful real estate brokerage here in town. Her family *founded* Balsam. And you all heard how Catherine was treated, how her family was treated. The job losses, bricks through windows, the name-calling, the spitting—"

Rick sounds genuinely surprised. "Girls, spitting at each other?"

"I've seen that happen, too. And in this case, it was bad enough that Catherine dropped out of school just to get away from it all, making her life even harder. Thank God there are good people in that community, like the owner of that diner, which I'm definitely going to be eating at the next chance I get." Kate levels the camera with a hard gaze. "Was Catherine capable of saying no to her teacher? Sure. She wasn't a *child*. But she was in love, and when you're a teenage girl in love, you aren't capable of truly appreciating the consequences to your life. This is not a woman who should ever have been villainized, and I can certainly tell you that after the way she risked her life, she should be honored and celebrated as the hero she is. Brett Madden has a guardian angel and her name is Catherine Wright."

I release a lung's worth of air. Kate Wethers has just earned a fan for life.

"I don't know, Kate. I'm thinking he has more than a guardian angel there." Rick flashes the camera with a newsworthy smile and an eyebrow waggle. "I think we *all* just saw the way they were looking at each other."

"Oh, believe me . . . I felt it the moment I walked into that house. She's a pretty young lady and, well . . . *Brett Madden* . . ." She shoots the camera a knowing look.

"Yeah, tell me about it. Handsome and talented? I think that the rest of the male population got the short end of the stick," Rick gripes.

Are they actually saying this on air? Is this *actually* happening on a reputable show like *The Weekly*? My cheeks begin to burn.

"Let me just say that if we see the two of them walking down the street hand in hand soon, I won't be the least bit surprised. *I'm* definitely hopeful."

My mouth drops open as I feel five sets of eyes—Brenna's still in her room, laughing at something on Keith's phone, thank God—shift to me. I can't believe Kate Wethers just insinuated that Brett and I might become a couple. On a national broadcast!

What must Brett think? He must be cringing.

This is humiliating.

"It sure would be one heck of a way to end that story." Rick chuckles. "Young, single mom saves life of hockey star and celebrity son and then wins his heart? It sounds like a fairy tale."

Kate turns to the camera. "America? What do you think? How many of you would love to see a budding romance between Brett Madden and his rescuer, Catherine Wright?"

I squeeze my eyes shut. *Oh, my God. She did not just ask that.*

"Thank you for that inspiring interview, Kate. It's not our usual story, but it honestly made me smile, watching it. I think we all needed that, especially in light of what's happening in the rest of the world right now. We'll be back to discuss the recent bombings in the Middle East and what they may mean for our country."

For ten long seconds, the only voices in my tiny house are coming from the car ad on TV and Brenna's prattling from her room.

"That was a really good interview, Cath," my dad finally offers, clearing his throat. "And he seems like a decent enough guy."

My face is burning. "Yeah. He is." Who is probably regretting ever stepping foot on my front porch right now.

Brenna comes trotting out and over to us, diving onto the couch, oblivious of the lingering awkwardness. "Is the show over?"

I pat her head. "Yes. Say good night and go brush your teeth for me, please?"

"Can Uncle Jack read me a book tonight?"

"Yeah, Uncle Jack can read you a book tonight," Jack answers, tickling her. She breaks free of his grip to skip around the room, doling out her usual hugs, then takes off for the bathroom.

"I gotta head to work," Keith says, standing by the door, jangling his keys in his fingers, his face holding an odd expression.

"Are you driving past Brown Street?" Emma asks, oblivious.

Keith shrugs. "I can. Why? You need a ride?"

She's already pulling on her jacket. "I'm heading over to Rhonda's for a few hours. See you guys in the morning. Cath, see you soon?"

"Sure. How long are you in town?"

"Just until tomorrow." She hesitates. "Did Mom and Dad tell you?"

"Tell me what?" I look to my dad, who's tipping his beer back to finish his bottle.

She takes a deep breath, her excited smile telling me this is good news. "I got into Yale!"

"Wow. That's . . . amazing." First Columbia for undergrad, now Yale for law school. "Congratulations." I'm happy for her, though my smile does feel a little bit forced. As much as I love seeing my siblings, my ego takes a hit every time they succeed. Here they are, Jack on a sports scholarship, Emma going to Ivy League schools, and I'm still at Diamonds, serving fries and pancakes, with no end in sight.

"Cha-ching." Jack stretches as he stands.

"Don't worry about that. We'll figure it out," my mother briskly answers, collecting the dirty dishes from the coffee table.

Emma shoots Jack a dirty look. "Anyway, I have an internship that starts on Monday and I'm moving in with a friend this weekend, so I'm driving back in the morning."

So, she clearly came home just for me. "Thanks for being here." This will probably be the only time I see her before fall. She doesn't come back to Balsam often anymore. My mother complains about it nonstop.

She nods and then, after a moment's hesitation, reaches out to wrap her arms around my shoulders in a slightly awkward hug, whispering in my ear, "We're always here for you, Cath, if you'll let us."

She releases me and I shift my gaze to Keith, who's waiting by the door. "I'll call you tomorrow?"

"Not too early."

"Right." My phone chirps in my pocket. My heart skips a beat at the thought that it could be Brett, but the second chirp, and the third, and the fourth, in quick, almost inhuman succession, tell me that it's Misty and she was watching the broadcast at Diamonds. And she's freaking out.

I can't deal with that right now. I quickly type out, "tomorrow," followed by a heart.

My dad eases out of the La-Z-Boy. "Well, Hildy? I guess we should be heading home now, too."

"Yeah, you've gotta start putting in those overtime shifts to pay for our little lawyer," Jack mutters, earning a glare from my mother this time.

"Not any more than the overtime shifts I had to put in for our little hockey player, you ungrateful little—" Dad cuts off and glances over to see Brenna standing in the doorway with her book. He ends with "—darling son."

Jack throws him a wink and a full-dimpled smile, before chasing Brenna into her room, calling out over his shoulder, "I'm going to Billy's after. Don't wait up."

My mom has always been big on not sending her kids out in the world with a massive student debt, so I'm guessing they expect to pay for at least part of Yale. I don't know what "figuring it out" would mean, though, short of taking out a second mortgage on their house. I wonder if Dad knew about this before they offered to buy my SUV? Even if he did, I can't in good conscience let him work himself into an early grave for me, not when I do have the money.

"Wait a minute." I run to my room and fish out the envelope from the loose floorboard where I hid it. Turns out my ballpark estimate of six thousand dollars was *way* off. I count out $7,750—the "deal" Gord gave us—and tuck the rest away, but not before snagging the tickets.

My parents are already at the door when I emerge. "Brett left an envelope of cash in my cupboard. I was going to make him take it back, but I have a feeling that's going to be impossible." I hold out the money. "This is for the Escape. So now we're square."

Dad shares a glance with my mom. "Cath, that wasn't a loan. We wanted—"

"And I appreciate it. Really, I do. It means a lot to me that you helped me when I needed it. But you have Yale to pay for now, and I *can* pay this back, so take it. Please. I know you don't have money just lying around. You'd have to work a lot of hours for this and you're not getting any younger."

He purses his lips, hesitating for another brief minute before he quietly accepts it.

"Also . . . Brett left these. I figured you'd want to go."

My dad's eyes widen as he studies them. "Tickets to game six?"

"If it happens, right?" They have to win tomorrow's game first.

"These are some *good* seats." He pauses. "Does Jack know?"

"I haven't said anything yet."

My dad grins. "Don't. Let me break it to him."

What that means exactly, I can't be sure, but it will no doubt involve some level of torture-in-jest.

"When do you plan on going back to work?" my mom asks, coiling a silk scarf around her neck.

"Tomorrow."

Surprise touches her face. "You should wait a few more days."

"I'm good. I'll probably pick up a Sunday night dinner shift, too." I don't normally work Sundays, but I need to be busy right now, not sitting around here, stewing over this interview, driving myself insane.

"Can you not afford to wait? How much did Brett leave you?"

I brush the inappropriate question off with "More than enough."

"Well, then—"

"If you could take Brenna tomorrow . . ."

My mom heaves a sigh, but thankfully doesn't push any harder. "We could take her right now, so you're not dragging her over so early."

"That's okay." I don't think I want to be alone tonight, anyway.

"Don't forget, if you ever want a Friday night free . . . you know, if you want to go out for any reason. On a date or something." Dad's gaze drifts to the television.

"That was all camera tricks."

My mother opens her mouth, hesitating for only a moment. "You saved his life, Cath. It makes sense that he would feel something deep for you because of that."

"I know."

"He's still in shock over it all. It'll be a while before his emotions settle to something more . . . normal."

Until he's thinking straight again. He used those exact words. No wonder he bolted for Toronto last minute. I'm beginning to think that whispered conversation between Meryl Price and him, over by my sink, was about this very issue. She saw the looks, and she panicked. Maybe she saw Kate Wethers's mind churning. It's one thing to appreciate the woman who saved her son's life. It's entirely another to allow a poor single mother to become the female lead in this conjured fairy tale.

"You two live very different lives that wouldn't mesh well. I'd advise you to—"

"I know my reality, Mom." I don't mean to snap, but it comes out as such, anyway. Why does she insist on "advising" on everything? As if I'm not capable of thinking for myself?

Dad clears his throat and gives her a high-browed stare. A warning, I think.

I watch them leave, her caution lingering in my mind and souring my mood as I wash the dishes to distract myself, Jack's deep voice carrying from Brenna's room.

I know Brett's still in shock. I know he lives a very different life. I know I wouldn't fit anywhere in it.

I know all of this.

And yet hearing my mother say it out loud felt like a pinprick to this subconscious hope that's been flourishing, as I've allowed myself to get lost in thoughts of his body's warmth against mine, the strength of his arms wrapped around mine. Of that fleeting kiss.

Kate Wethers may very well be right. Maybe Brett does feel something for me beyond gratitude. But my mother is also right. It won't last. The shock will wear off and his body will heal, and he'll be back to chasing pucks and enjoying the perks of his celebrity status.

That's just how life is. A person can tell you he loves you one day and tell you that you need to move on the next. He can be everything to you, and then a mere memory.

I've already learned that the hard way.

"Night, little monster." Jack pulls Brenna's bedroom door mostly shut behind him. "She's gotten so big."

"So have you, you gym rat." I eye him as he strolls toward the kitchen counter, collecting Dad's empty beer bottle on his way by. He'll always be my little brother, but he looks like a man now. The baby face is gone, replaced by a hard jawline and stubble.

He chuckles, giving my shoulder a playful push. "I'm not the one pulling guys out of burning cars, Sis."

I roll my eyes.

"But seriously, can you call me the next time he's here? I wanna get on the ice with him."

"I don't think he's going to be 'on the ice' anytime soon. Definitely not while you're here."

Jack yawns and stretches his arms over his head again. The sleeve of his T-shirt falls down and I catch something black on his biceps.

"No way!" Pushing the sleeve up farther, I take in the number eighteen tattooed on his skin. "Mom is gonna freak out!" I can't help but laugh. Of all the things I did do that my parents hated, getting a tattoo was not one of them. "When'd you get that done?"

He grins. "January, right after Madden broke two NHL records in the same game."

"Wait a minute, you had Brett's number tattooed onto your body? Obsessed much?"

Jack shrugs. "I told you, he's my idol."

"Oh, my God. Wait until I tell him. Actually, no, I'm not sure if I want to. That's a little bit weird."

"No, it's not."

"Yeah, it is."

"Whatever. I'm headin' out. Let me know if you need help with Brenna. I'm done work every day at five."

"For the record, I still think you're nuts for taking that job at Hansen's." He's going to be working with my mom all day, every day.

"For the record, I agree with you, and I'll probably want to slit my wrists by the end of next week, but there's not exactly a lot of choices for summer gigs around here."

"They never called you for that bartending job at the resort?"

"Nope. So it's basically Target, with Mom, or Diamonds."

"You could bus my tables."

"No, thanks. But maybe you can get me a job guarding your house. I'm as big as that goon out there."

"But he has a gun."

"I could have a gun."

"No, *you* could not have a gun." My brother loses his house keys at least three times a week.

"You're probably right. Oh, and I might crash here next Friday night."

"So Mom doesn't have to see you stumbling in from somewhere?"

"Something like that. See you later." A thick arm ropes around my neck, and he pulls me into a hug, his throat growing a little husky as he whispers, "Proud of you, Sis."

I sigh. "You just want tickets to the game."

"Lower level, if possible, but I'm not too picky." His face splits into a wide grin.

The urge to tell him that Dad has them in his back pocket is overwhelming. Instead, I smile at his broad back as he strolls to the door, his navy boxer briefs exposed at his waist. "Pull up your pants!"

I get a middle finger in answer. "Oh, and just so you know, Dad wouldn't mind at all if you were bangin' Madden."

"Oh, my God. Good night!" I hiss, throwing the dish towel at his head, missing him completely. He ducks out the door with a laugh.

I wander over to retrieve the rag, shaking my head and feeling the flush in my cheeks as I push reality aside and allow myself to dream again, even for just another moment.

Me and Brett.

Brett and me.

My fingers lift to graze my lips, remembering the feel of his on them. He kissed me on Wednesday night. It was fleeting, but it was still a kiss.

And the way he was looking at me through that entire interview . . .

I don't know how much time I lost in that daydream, but I went deep enough that I jump when a knock lands on my door. It's followed by a second, and a quick third, and an "I know you're in there, Cath!"

I should have known that Misty wouldn't be brushed off so easily this time.

The moment I open the door, she pushes past me, her orange Diamonds uniform carrying with it the faint waft of coffee grinds and fried food. Hawk is standing at the bottom of the steps, offering me an apologetic shrug, even as his eyes trail after her.

"Coming straight from work?"

She tosses her purse on the couch. "Have you talked to him since the interview?"

"No."

"So call him."

"I can't call him right now!" The fact that he hasn't messaged yet speaks volumes. He must be feeling the exact same way I do: awkward.

"I knew you would be like this!" Misty's eyes, already enormous, look like they're about to pop out of their sockets. "You have Brett freaking Madden drooling *all* over you on national television and you're going to pretend like it's nothing."

"It's just a story. It's not real!" Even still, my heart leaps at her words.

"I can almost hear your mother's voice when you say that." She rolls her eyes at me. "I know what I just saw on TV and that was a guy who is infatuated with you."

"Maybe . . . For now."

Her groan of exasperation is loud enough to wake Brenna, I'm afraid.

"Why are you so angry with me?" As ditzy and bubbly as Misty can be, in the rare moment that she has a bone to pick, she doesn't mince words. I'm almost afraid to hear what might come out of her mouth.

"Because I *know* you, Cath. You won't give this a chance, even if you want to. You push away every guy who ever shows any interest."

"*What* guys?"

"Exactly! You don't even notice them! And now Brett Madden is majorly into you and you've basically scared him away."

"What?" I can't help but laugh. "No, I haven't."

She folds her arms over her ample chest in that condescending way. "Do you realize how many times you said that you just want everything to go back to normal during that interview?"

"Because I do?"

"'Normal' doesn't include Brett. It will *never* include him. You basically told him you don't want him in your life. Is that what you really want?"

No, that tiny voice screams inside my head. I think back to our good-bye two nights ago. *I'll make sure you get your life back, if that's what you want.* He did say that, and that questioning look that came along with it . . . Is that what he meant?

But he also said that he needed to clear his head, that he wasn't thinking straight.

Staying far away is for the best.

I sigh. Explaining this to Misty will be impossible, though. There's no point even trying. "I need to be smart."

She shakes her head. "If this is being smart, then you need to be stupid. Be an absolute idiotic moron. Be like me."

■ ■ ■

I'm flipping through my sketchbook when my phone chirps. I scramble for it, holding my breath against hope that it's not Misty, messaging me with yet more grief. As if I didn't get an earful from her already tonight.

My heart skips a beat when I see Brett's name.

They promised us they'd spin a positive story, but I didn't see that coming.

I chew my thumbnail, trying to decide how I should respond. It's been two hours since the interview aired, and he's only messaging now. Does he sound bothered by what they said? Finally I decide on:

Yeah. They definitely spun a story.

I anxiously watch the three dots dance on my screen, telling me Brett's typing.

Simone thinks it'll blow over fast enough, but she's already working on killing it.

An unexpected wave of disappointment floods me. Obviously, that's what he wants. To kill the idea that the two of us would ever be together. And why does it even bother me so much that Kate Wethers insinuated something might happen between Brett and me? Is it because it's not true?

Or because I wish it was?

I can't think of any answer except *Okay*, so I type that out.

We'll fix this, trust me.

With a heavy sigh, I set my phone aside.

Tomorrow.

Tomorrow, I go back to work at Diamonds.

Tomorrow, I face whatever shit storm this is going to produce.

Because I've been here before and the only way to get past it is to just try to forget and move on.

Chapter 17

．．．

"Fries or salad with that?" I stand with my pen to pad, poised, waiting for Beverly to make up her mind.

"Oh, I think I'll have . . ." Her crooked finger is on the side salad options that come with the burger, as if she's seriously considering them. She does this every time she comes in with her husband for dinner on Sunday night. "Fries," she finally whispers, as if afraid to admit she wants the unhealthier option.

I pretend to add it to the order, though I've already penciled it in. "Coming right up."

"Thank you, dear. Oh, and I saw you on the news." Every wrinkle on the woman's eighty-something-year-old face lifts with her grin. "You were so wonderful for saving that young man."

I offer her a small nod and smile, the one I've perfected in the last two days of being back to work, along with the standard "I just did what anyone would have done." If I had a dollar for every time I've said that, I'd have enough to pay rent this month and maybe next.

"Are things back to normal for you?"

I hold that fake smile, ever aware of Hawk's presence three tables over. He and Vince have taken up residence at Table 7 with bottomless cups of coffee, looking as out of place as one would imagine bodyguards on duty for a waitress might look, even in their golf shirts and khaki pants. "They are." Aside from the round of applause that I earned the moment I stepped out of the kitchen yesterday morning—unsettling me for a good hour—and the countless questions about Brett that I answer with Simone's scripted response sent via text of "We've become friends who shared a traumatic experience but nothing more," I guess it hasn't been *too* bad. Especially since the photographers who hovered on the sidewalk yesterday were not there when I arrived tonight.

Lou banned them from stepping foot inside Diamonds but wasn't able to stop them from snapping pictures of me through the window, in uniform and pouring coffee. I did my best to give them only my back, and some of the regulars even tried running interference, standing in their way and going outside to admonish them for harassing me. Though it didn't help much, their efforts were appreciated.

It shouldn't be a surprise that those pictures made it to the Internet within hours. Still, it took everything in me to keep my face smooth when Misty shoved her phone in my face to show me an article with the headline "Brett Madden's Guardian Angel." At least they used a flattering candid shot of me in my diner uniform.

It was a million times better than the other articles she insisted on showing me: "Meryl Price Threatens to Disown Brett if He Doesn't Break It Off with Catherine," "Madden Rewriting His Will to Leave Everything to Catherine," and, my personal favorite from a bottom-feeding tabloid, "Welfare Mom Carrying Madden Baby."

Lou finally threatened to put Misty on straight midnight shifts if she mentioned one more word about "all that nonsense."

"Have you met his mother?" Beverly asks.

I sense ears perking up all around me. Another question that's been asked more times than I can count. "Yes, I have. She's very nice." Another standard line, though entirely true.

"And where is he now?" She glances around, as if he may be hiding in a corner.

"Canada, visiting his grandparents."

"Will he be back soon?" She looks genuinely concerned.

"I think he'll be in California for the summer."

"Well, I'll root for you two, anyway."

I can't even bring myself to quote the standard line. "I'll put your order in now." I wander over to the computer at the end of the counter.

Misty turns from the screen to show me her pout.

"Don't start with me again."

"You should tell him how you feel!"

"It doesn't matter how I feel. Besides, I don't even know how I feel."

"Be careful, your pants are about to catch fire."

"I'm wearing a dress."

"What are you two talking about?" Lou's stern voice from behind us has Misty clamping her mouth shut and darting away before she can get herself into more trouble with the boss.

I start punching in my order as Lou sidles up beside me. "No one botherin' you?"

"Besides Misty?" Lou's expression has me backpedaling. "Just kidding. Everyone's been fine. Nice, in fact."

"Hmm . . . You're holding it together well."

I can't help the nervous chuckle. "You think so?"

"You just keep your head high."

"I'm trying. And I'm sorry about all this."

"Nothin' to be sorry about." She pauses, her eyes surveying the area around us, and I sense she has another reason for this check-in. "I know you don't like talkin' about him, but I thought I should mention, so no one catches you off guard . . ." She drops her voice. "That thing about Scott Philips bein' involved with one of his students? Sounds like they're treatin' it seriously down in Memphis. There's going to be a police investigation."

I stifle the frown that threatens to emerge, just hearing that name. I'm so sick of his looming shadow, returning to haunt me after all these years. "Yeah, Keith already told me."

She drops her voice so low that I have to lean in to hear her. "Did Keith also tell you that when Scott left Philly to teach in Balsam, it may not have been his choice? There may have been an incident with a sixteen-year-old student."

"No . . . I never heard that."

"The girl wouldn't speak so nothin' ever came of it, but things are rising to the surface now, with all this noise. As they always do. Not that I wish any of this upon others, but it would definitely shine a light on that bastard for everyone."

And then maybe they wouldn't doubt me anymore.

"*Also* . . . Mr. Philips will be retiring immediately from his job as principal of Balsam High. He was supposed to be there for one more year." Lou waggles her eyebrows knowingly.

I wonder if the school board had a talk with Mrs. Lagasse. "Something good came of all this craziness, then."

She nods once, a flicker of satisfaction dancing across her face. "Hopefully not the only thing." She winks and is moving toward the door before I can ask her exactly what she means.

I turn in time to see her shaking hands with an older man of maybe fifty, his dress pants and button-down shirt marginally out of place for Diamonds. A woman who I presume is his wife stands next to him in a modest churchy-looking peacock-blue suit, her short sandy blonde hair set in perfect waves, her curious eyes roving around the diner.

I don't remember ever serving them here, but they look familiar. Lou exchanges a few words with them before pointing in my direction. I'm too slow to avoid the eye contact, the man's green irises locking on me right away.

"Cath, come on over here for a minute!" Lou hollers, waving me over.

I meet them at Table 22—a booth by the window, in my section—and force a polite smile.

"Have you met Mayor Frank Polson and his wife, Clarisse?"

"No, I haven't." *That's* why I recognize him. Not that I'm political—I've never actually voted and I hope to hell he doesn't ask me if I have—but the man's face has been pictured in enough ribbon-cutting ceremonies and pancake breakfasts over the years that I *should* have known who he was.

From what I remember overhearing around the diner, Frank Polson isn't an educated man, but he is a resourceful one, having worked his way up from laborer to management at the major pulp factory, making countless connections within neighboring communities with each passing year.

He won the mayoral election in 2012 by a landslide and became the first person with no blood ties to the founding Balsam family to hold that position. Last year, he was reelected to a second term.

He extends a weathered hand. "Catherine Wright, it's a pleasure to meet you."

I take it gingerly, followed by his wife's. "I'm sorry about all the chaos around town; I'm sure the locals are getting annoyed by now. It should die down soon."

He pauses to consider me quietly. "There's no need to apologize. You've made our community awfully proud. You're a hero."

I swallow my surprise. "Do you need a few minutes with the menus before you order? I can come back."

"Yes, please. It's been a while since we've been here." He has the decency to look at least a little bit embarrassed at that admission. "And thank you, by the way, for agreeing to come to the ceremony."

I feel the deep frown settle over my forehead. "Ceremony?"

"We've never actually awarded a Key to the City."

"A *what*?"

"Yes, we're all excited to see Cath recognized for her bravery." Lou's stern glare stills my tongue. "We'll let you look at our menu and then Cath'll be back in a few minutes. I'd recommend the fish and chips special. We just got some wonderful haddock in. Customers have been raving." Nudging me away, she leads me out of earshot.

"Did you know about this?"

"Keith may have phoned to tell me that the mayor was coming in."

Keith . . . Of course his fingers are in this pot. I'm shaking my head. "I don't need a *key* to Balsam. I don't even know what it is!"

"It's just a symbol to show that you're an important resident of Balsam. Don't worry, it'll be a small, private affair. Nothing flashy, nothing too painful. Lord knows you'll have a coronary otherwise."

I open my mouth to argue more.

"I don't insist on much, Cath. I'm insisting on this."

"Why?"

"Because this is a good thing, and you deserve good things in your life, whether you'll accept that or not."

I brush that away. "Or maybe this is just the town's way of quickly saving face after how bad *The Weekly* made it look?"

"The mayor may have mentioned that he's ashamed of how this community treated one of its own in a time of need," Lou says carefully. "But who cares if part of this is about the town saving face? You live here, Cath. Your roots are here. They will *always* be here, and I think you'll be much happier if you can find a way to make peace with the place. There's nothin' worse than hating your home."

"I guess."

"Call this Balsam's way of finally makin' amends." She drops her voice. "Lord knows Mayor Polson isn't a fan of the Balsams, even though he played the right game during elections."

I huff a sigh. "So, when is this *ceremony* anyway?"

"Two Sundays from now. In the afternoon." She strolls away, throwing over her shoulder, "And don't even try tellin' me you have to work that day."

■ ■ ■

"Can we call the boat 'Stella'?"

"I thought the dog's name is going to be Stella."

Brenna peers up at me with those rich brown eyes, her little body tucked into her sheets. "But I really like the name."

"Okay. We'll name the boat Stella. Where should the name go?"

Brenna's index finger draws a line on the hull of the sketch. "Is that a good place?"

"Sure, it is."

She smiles down at the page, and I can see her imagining herself standing on skis and clutching a rope while the boat tows her around Jasper Lake.

"I'll add it in tonight. But you need to go to sleep."

"Why couldn't Jack babysit me tonight?"

"Because Jack and Grandpa went to the hockey game." The Flyers managed a miracle by winning last Saturday's game, bringing the series back to Philly tonight. I thought Jack was going to start crying in the voice mail he left for me, after Dad finally revealed the tickets.

"Brett's hockey team?"

"Yes."

"Did they win?"

I smile. "They did." I'm so relieved for Brett. Just one more victory and they'll be in the play-offs, even without their two best players.

"How long are the workers going to stay?"

I struggle to follow her scattered train of thought. "The workers?"

"Vince and Hawk and . . . that other guy, who was giving them a vacation."

"Oh. Right." We've avoided using the word "bodyguard" or "security" around her, not wanting to make her think that there is any danger. "I don't know. A few more days, maybe? *Good night*, Brenna." I give her a knowing look that says to stop with the questions.

I'm almost out the door when she calls out in her innocent little voice, "Do you know who my daddy is?"

I inhale sharply. She's asked me about her dad before. She's asked me where he is.

She's never asked me this, though. "Of course I do. Why would you ask that?"

"Because Jerry Baldwin in fourth grade said that for someone who doesn't even know who my daddy is, you sure hit the jackpot. What's a jackpot?"

If a kid is saying that, it's because he's repeating what he heard at home, from his asshole parents. "It's kind of like saying that someone won a big prize."

"So you won a big prize?"

How do I answer this? "I think that boy meant we were lucky that we met Brett, because he's such a nice guy." I'm hoping that focusing on Brett will steer her away from her other question.

"Oh." I can see her pondering that. "Will he come back soon to visit us?"

I force a smile. "I don't know. I hope so."

The words are meant to appease her, but I realize that I'm speaking the truth.

Chapter 18

...

I push through the back door of Diamonds on Wednesday night with a sigh of relief. I'm unsupervised for the first time since returning to work. Hawk agreed to stay at my house with Brenna and her sixteen-year-old babysitter.

That relief is short-lived, though, when I discover Misty hovering inside, waiting to pounce. "Has he called you?"

I force a casual tone. "Not since last Friday. He's with his family. He's moving on."

"And have you texted him?"

She glares at me with exasperation when I don't answer.

"What! If he really wanted to talk to me, he would have reached out." I don't want it to look like I'm expecting something. Like I'm sitting here waiting, pining for Brett. I made a vow years ago that I'd never let myself look that pathetic again, and I intend to keep it.

Misty's on my heels as I skirt past her and toss my purse on the shelf by Lou's office. "Just send him a message to say good luck with the game tonight. Simple, easy. It's what a *normal* person would do."

"So now I'm not normal?"

She gives me a pointed stare. "If my life depended on your skill with flirting, then hand me a shovel because I may as well dig my own grave."

I sigh, equally frustrated with Misty and with myself. I wasn't *always* like this. I remember a time when I had no problems walking up to a guy at a party and in no uncertain terms letting him know that I wanted him.

Clearly, the scars Scott left me with run much deeper than I'd like to admit.

"Come on, *please*? Just do it and see where it leads. Give me at least a shred of hope before I start dropping cats off on your doorstep."

Misty can be as relentless as a gnat and, though she worked the day shift and is only here for another hour, she'll bug the hell out of me until Lou catches wind and tears her a new one. Besides, truth be told, I've been thinking that tonight's game is as good an excuse to reach out to Brett as I'm going to get.

She's right. It's harmless and innocent. Unpresumptuous. Right?

"Fine." Steeling my nerve, I pull my phone from my pocket and punch out a quick message, my stomach swirling with each word:

Good luck tonight.

Then shove my phone into my pocket. "There. Happy now?"

"Happy about what?" Leroy asks, his deep voice startling me from behind as he steps out of the walk-in fridge.

"Nothing!" we chirp in unison.

"Uh-huh." He chuckles, shuffling past with a tray of freshly made burger patties, his eyes on Misty. "Don't think I wanna know what that Cheshire Cat's grin is all about, but it's too busy out there to be fawning over hockey players."

Misty huffs and takes two steps toward the door before stopping. "Do you know how many people want you two to get together? You should see all the stuff online."

"No, thanks." I fumble with the apron ties around my waist. "Why do people even care? They don't know us. What happens between us has no impact on them."

"Because it's like a fairy tale!"

A fairy tale.

The poor, lonely waitress with a past, the jaded single mother with scars, who scrubs ketchup off tables and serves fries to truck drivers, ensnares the rich, gorgeous, kind prince. I guess it's kind of like Cinderella. Though Cinderella got herself beautiful glass slippers on her night of magic. Mine involved shabby black heels, which were left for dead in a ditch.

I open my mouth to warn Misty that we need to get out front when my phone vibrates in my pocket. I smother the excitement. "Who else is working tonight?"

"Rose and Caitlyn."

Two thirty-something-year-old ladies who know how to manage their sections. Good.

"You should get out there before Lou finds you. I'll be another second." I wait until the door to the diner stops swinging behind her before I pull out my phone, my heart pounding against my bones.

Can I call you?

I exhale and try to calm my racing heart. Maybe Misty was right, all I needed to do was reach out.

I'm just starting my shift now. After?

I should be home and settled before ten.

Sure. Let me know when you're free.

The kitchen door flies open. "Is Cath here—oh, thank heavens." Lou's face is flushed. "I don't know where these people keep crawlin' in from, but they're *all* asking if you're workin' tonight. It's gonna be another busy one." She frowns. "Where's your security guy?"

I tuck my phone into my pocket. "At home, with Brenna."

Lou's brows raise.

"I'm fine. Leroy'll protect me."

His face splits into a wide grin as he deftly swings his cast iron frying pan by the handle. "Are you tellin' me I get to deliver an ass whoppin' tonight?"

"The only ass gettin' whopped around here will be yours if you don't get Table Twenty-nine's food up in the next three minutes!" Lou scolds.

Loading my arms with a rack of clean glasses, I march out onto the floor, my spirits soaring as I count down the hours until I hear Brett's voice again.

■ ■ ■

July 2010

I pedal languidly in the early-morning heat, just fast enough to keep my bike upright as I coast down quiet Main Street, eyeing the strip of colorful storefronts and cafés. Places where owners greet tourists with wide smiles and welcoming gestures.

Owners whose eyes flashed with surprise when they saw my name at the top of my résumé, who forced polite smiles and "We'll let you know" about jobs they immediately decided they would never consider me for. I never got so much as a phone call from anyone.

I don't even try to push aside the bitterness that edges my thoughts lately. It's going to be a long-ass summer of killing days at the park, at the library, at Jasper's public beach. Anywhere but home. But at least it's summer.

At last I'm away from the whispers and sneers that trail me through the claustrophobic halls and classrooms of Balsam High. I wonder if people will be bored of talking about me and Scott by the time I have to go back.

I stop to avoid the car door that's thrown open ahead of me, an elderly man stepping out without bothering to check his side view mirror. A small part of me wonders what would have happened if I'd been pedaling a little faster, if I'd been knocked to the left, into the traffic that coasts past. Would anyone truly care? How fast would they come running?

I'm still waiting for the man to move when the door to Balsam's little French café—aptly named Le Petit Café—opens.

My breath catches in my chest as Scott steps out, a brown paper bag in one hand, a tray holding two paper coffee cups in the other, a smile on his face. He uses his foot to hold the door open for a blonde woman.

She's pretty. She's older. She's polished.

She's his ex-girlfriend.

And when she offers to take the tray of coffees from him, it frees his hand to take hers.

My stomach plummets as I watch them walking side by side, hand in hand, away from me.

■ ■ ■

"Hey, Cath! Your guy's at the game!" Chip calls out from his barstool, pointing the remote at the flat-screen as he turns up the volume. The arena is filled with a sea of white and blue as thousands of Maple Leaf fans pour into their seats. The place isn't without a healthy smattering of orange-and-black jerseys, though.

"He's not my guy," I correct him, even as my heart skips a beat and my eyes glue themselves to the TV screen, waiting for a glimpse of Brett's handsome face. I guess the doctor's orders of rest don't apply to game seven.

Ever aware of the prying eyes around me, I try to hide my smile as the TV cameras zoom in on him in the box, looking sharp in a char-coal suit and tie, his navy shirt drawing out his piercing eyes, talking to another man. The bruises are nothing more than faded yellow-tinged marks now, and his hair is styled in that tousled sexy way that I love.

Brett glances up and, realizing that he's on camera, offers a small, reserved wave to the crowd. A loud roar of cheers and hollers erupts and I can't contain my grin.

However, I can't miss the low undercurrent of jeers as well. Nor do I miss the flash to the crowd, to see that it's not fans wearing Leaf jerseys doing it.

"Are Flyers fans booing him?"

"Yup," Chip confirms through a sip of his Coke.

"Why?"

"Because we were pretty much guaranteed the Cup and now it's a crap shoot."

"But they've made it to game seven!"

"This series should've been done three games ago. People are blaming Madden and Grabner for it."

"They're blaming a dead guy? Are you *kidding* me?"

He shrugs. "They're blaming the guy who was driving his Corvette too fast down a winding road in the fog. That accident was completely avoidable. *And* because they were on their way to a "work function," we're gonna be paying out Madden's monstrous contract as if he got hurt on the ice, even if he never puts on skates again."

I've always liked Chip, a simple, easygoing twenty-nine-year-old who works at the same paint factory that my father used to work at and comes here several times a week for dinner. But now I glare at him.

He lifts his hands up. "Hey! Don't shoot the messenger. I'm just telling it like it is." He nods at the TV. The camera keeps panning back and forth between the ice and Brett, sitting quietly, waiting for the game to begin. My heart skips every single time I catch a glimpse of him. "Grabner was rated one of the top right-wingers in the world. And Madden is a god on the ice. He leads the league in points this year by a wide margin. Losing the two of them crippled us, accident or not."

I shake my head. "People are assholes."

Chip lifts his bottle of Bud in a mock cheer. "Here, here."

"What time does the game start?"

He glances at his watch. "About twenty minutes?"

I'm here until at least eight thirty. Maybe I can catch the end of it at home. That'd give me a chance to admire Brett in private . . .

My fingers fly over the monitor to punch in orders, my attention pulling too frequently to the TV.

I freeze as a tall blonde bombshell with tanned skin appears in the box next to Brett, the fitted T-shirt she's wearing accentuating her incredibly fit body and her perfect round breasts.

I don't need anyone to tell me that that's Courtney Woods. I've seen enough pictures of her, and of them together.

I take a deep breath.

Okay . . . they dated. They're obviously still friends. She's there for moral support. It *is* a huge night for him.

She slides into the seat next to Brett and sets a pint down in front of him with a smile.

And then she presses into his side and reaches for his hand, weaving her fingers through his.

My stomach drops as he turns to look at her for a long moment. He leans in toward her, and I'm saved from having to watch them kiss as the camera flips over to the commentators.

I learned how to steel my expression long ago. I do it now, focusing on the screen in front of me, feeling the curious eyes piercing me from every direction.

I guess I know what Brett wanted to talk to me about.

■ ■ ■

"What are you doing here?"

"That's how you greet your favorite brother?" Jack is sprawled out on my love seat, can of beer in hand, Brenna tucked under his arm. Brenna, who should be in bed.

"You're her favorite brother?" Brenna chirps.

"Of course I am." He scoffs.

Her face scrunches up. "Mommy has other brothers?"

"Where's Victoria?" I interrupt, Jack's humor lost on her.

"I sent her home. Figured I'd save you some money."

"And she just left?" She's normally more responsible than that.

"I don't think she *wanted* to." Jack grins, the kind of grin that tells me my sixteen-year-old babysitter was blushing furiously when he strolled in. Probably explains the poor judgment. Still, I'll need to talk to her about leaving without calling me to check in.

And none of this explains why Jack is sitting on my couch. "Why aren't you watching the game with your friends?"

He shrugs nonchalantly. "Didn't feel like it." That's bullshit. Jack *always* feels like hanging out with his friends, and on a do-or-die hockey night like tonight especially.

"We saw Brett on TV!" Brenna exclaims.

I nearly flinch as my eyes drift to the screen. I have no desire to catch another glimpse of him with his face in *her* ear. Or worse. "How bad is it?" Toronto was up by three points when I left Diamonds.

"Five—one. We're done for," Jack complains bitterly. Though I'm beginning to think that wary look he's giving me right now has nothing to do with the score of the game.

I sigh, in no mood to talk about Brett and Courtney with anyone. It was all I could do to finish my shift, taking orders and smiling at customers and answering their curious "Did you know?" questions with "Of course I did," before I could escape to Lou's office to do my closing. Wishing more than ever before that Diamonds was smaller and the process was simpler, that we all just used one register and weren't responsible for balancing cash and card receipts. Because a basic thing like counting money suddenly seemed an impossible feat, my head already swimming with disappointment.

And an odd sense of humiliation, as if Brett had somehow publicly slighted me, even though he's done nothing wrong.

Misty has sent five texts, begging me to call her. Thankfully, she left at six, because dealing with her reaction in front of everyone would have made it ten times worse.

"Come on, Brenna. You should already be in bed."

Jack leans in to whisper something in her ear. I have no idea what it is, but, miraculously, she doesn't put up a fight. Nor does she plague me with her usual twenty-questions routine. In fact, she doesn't say a word as she gives him a big hug and then trails me to her room and crawls under her blankets.

"Mommy?"

My hand stalls on her lamp switch. *So close to getting away without interrogation.* "Yes?"

"Why are you sad?"

I force a smile, to hide the fact that I am. "Who says I'm sad?"

"Uncle Jack." She pauses to study my face with a small frown. "And your eyes."

"My eyes?"

"Yeah. You have sad eyes."

"It's just been a bad day."

"Oh . . ." She pauses. "But then why do you have sad eyes so much?"

The observation is a razor-sharp prick, coming from my child. I can't even hold my fake smile. "Why do you say that?"

"That's what Grandpa said."

I frown. "When did he say that?" It's not like my dad to say things like that.

"When I was at their house. He was showing me pictures of you when you were little and I said that your eyes looked really bright back then, and they don't anymore, and he said it's because you have sad eyes now."

"He actually called them that?" I swallow the lump forming in my throat. I can't deny that I haven't heard a comment here or there, mostly from the Gord Mayberrys of the world—insensitive customers with cheesy "Why so glum?" lines.

Her head bobs. "He said they're always like that now, and I said not *always* because they looked different when you were on TV that day. And when you laugh."

Which isn't often enough, probably.

The knot in my throat swells by double, pricking me, making it hard to swallow.

I shut the light off before she can see the tears. Sensing her little arms in the air, I bend down to let her wrap them around my neck, the feel of her muscles tightening, her way of trying to console me, offering a moment's reprieve.

"I'm sorry you had a bad day."

"It's okay. Everyone has bad days, but tomorrow will be better." I have to believe that. "Night, babe. I love you."

Thankfully, Jack is cursing the TV when I emerge and I use the chance to duck into my room to change.

But I don't change. Instead, I crawl onto my bed and pull out my phone. Jack always leaves his hotspot open for me. He has no issues spending a hundred bucks a month on a data plan.

I click on the link Misty texted me.

Brett Madden reunites with MMA fighter Courtney Woods.

I read the article, my heart sinking with each word. According to ESPN, Courtney arrived in Toronto this afternoon and was seen pulling up to the gates of the Madden family residence in King City, a rural community north of the city known for its rolling hills, prestigious horse farms, and wealthy estates. Paparazzi snapped a shot of the tall blonde at the airport, and an inside source has confirmed that they've reconciled after breaking up last fall, after a nearly year-long relationship. His recent near-death accident sparked the reunion.

And there, at the very bottom of the article, I'm mentioned. Specifically, that despite wishful rumors of Brett and me being linked romantically, we remain nothing more than friends who shared a traumatic event.

I frown at the number of comments to the article below. That many people have something to say about this reunion?

What exactly are they saying?

Despite my promise to Simone and my better judgment—my day can't possibly get any worse—my curiosity finally gets the better of me.

■ ■ ■

"Cath?"

I cover my mouth with my hands, trying to smother my sobs. After a moment, I manage to call out, "I'll be out in a sec."

"You okay?"

"Yeah. Fine."

The door to my bedroom, where I've been hiding out for the past half hour, creaks open and Jack pokes his head in. I turn away from him, but it's too late to hide my tear-streaked cheeks and my puffy red eyes. Pushing the door shut behind him, he quietly sits down beside me, my bed creaking under our combined weight. "What's going on?"

I hold up my phone, my bottom lip wavering. "Why are people so mean?"

He puts his arm around my shoulders and pulls me against him in time for me to start sobbing uncontrollably against his shoulder. "What the hell are you doing?"

"I've stayed away from it up until now, but I was curious. I just wanted to see what people were saying, so I clicked on the comments . . ."

A lot of people have *a lot* to say.

And most of it was about me.

So many of them call me brave and kind, label me an angel, proclaim that I was touched by God's will to manage what I did. They thank me over and over again, for risking my life to save such an incredible man. A man they've never met but obviously dream about meeting one day. A man they idolize. Many of them are praying for me and wishing me only happiness after what *that teacher* did to me. They don't think it was right, the way I was treated, the way Scott Philips got away with it. They're disgusted by it. *So* many people wholeheartedly agree with Kate Wethers—Brett and I would make a beautiful couple and they want to see it happen, because it would make for such a happy end to the story.

But all those kind words and well wishes quickly fade into oblivion, next to the other comments that have been floating around since the interview aired.

The ones that label me ugly and stupid, a white trash whore who'll be serving fries for the rest of my life. That I need a nose job and a boob job, that my eyes are too big, that I'm too skinny. That I should be cut off welfare, that *I'm* the problem with America today. That I deserve what happened with Philips because I must be a slut if I got pregnant so young. That I'm lying about everything that happened the night of the accident because I just want the attention. That they hope Brett gave me a pity fuck before he returned to Courtney. That even if Brett and I had gotten together, he'd have ditched me the second his leg was working and he was back on the ice, banging hot puck bunnies.

Those are just words. Then there are the pictures, the memes. Still shots that people actually pulled from *The Weekly* interview, of me sitting on my couch next to Brett, my face contorted in midspeech, and hurtful little captions to go along with them. I guess they're meant to be funny.

They only made me cry harder.

People actually took time out of their lives to make these.

Jack groans. "You *never* read the comments! Those people are fucking trolls. Losers with sad, small lives and nothing better to do than spew crap and hate. It's all bullshit."

"And yet it hurts so much when it's about you." When almost everything they've said, I've thought at some point or another. "This feels like seven years ago all over again. Except *worse*. I can't handle this."

"Yeah, you can. You're the strongest person I know."

Me, strong? "No I'm not."

"Yeah, *you are*. You're way stronger than Emma, or Mom."

"Mom's a rock."

"No, Mom just doesn't take risks, she always plays the safe card."

I simply shake my head.

"I still remember when you walked out of the house with your backpack slung over your shoulder. It was like you'd been sitting in your room waiting until the stroke of midnight."

"I was."

"You set out to survive on your own, with no job and no money, and you did. The day you moved out, Mom and Dad had a huge fight. She guaranteed that you'd come running back within two weeks with your tail between your legs. But, stubborn ass that you are, you didn't so much as call. And then, when she found out you were pregnant, she actually brought a contractor in to give an estimate on a basement renovation, for when you came running home with the baby because there's no way you'd be able to hack it. You never did. You handled everything life threw at you and you did it all on your own."

"With the help of a few people," I correct, though I offer him a small smile, appreciating the words. I flop back on my bed, suddenly exhausted. I feel like I could sleep for the next week.

"You *can* handle this, Cath."

I stare up at the ceiling. It's in desperate need of a fresh coat of paint. Jack leans back beside me, the accompanying creak making me think we're about to break the frame, which was a garage sale purchase. It hasn't had to bear the weight of a man lying on it since before the day Keith loaded it into his truck and brought it here for me six years ago, sad as that may be.

"Did you want what Wethers said to be true?" he asks softly, a rare seriousness in his tone.

Yes. Clearly I did, if this stings so much.

"He just feels indebted to me," I say instead. Not answering the question.

"Maybe."

"Misty thinks I'm an idiot for not throwing myself at him when I had the chance."

"Misty's good at throwing herself at guys." He pauses. "Has Singer said anything?"

"No. Nothing about that, anyway. He's texted a million times to see if I needed anything."

"I ran into him the other day when I was jogging. He wasn't really himself. I think he finally realized he doesn't have a hope in hell with Madden as competition."

"There *is* no competition." I hold up my phone to show Jack the side-by-side graphic meme someone created: a svelte, glamorous Courtney Woods next to a still of me from the interview, in my pink blouse, looking like a meek extension of my ugly-ass garage sale couch. "And talk about not being able to compete."

He sighs. "Here, can I show you a little trick?" He takes my phone and closes out the page. "What do ya know? Just like that, none of it exists anymore."

"Funny."

"Let them be miserable while you're working on bangin' my idol."

"Jack!" I'm shaking my head at him, but a smile tugs at my mouth. "That's never gonna happen."

He pulls himself back to a sitting position, hauling me up to sit next to him. "Seriously, can't you just find someone normal? First you fall in love with your art teacher and you almost send him to jail. Then you get knocked up by a drug dealer who can't help you out because he *does* go to jail. Then you have to go and pull Brett Madden out of a burning car and make him fall all over you like a lovesick puppy on national TV. Why can't you just find . . . I don't know, a banker, or a plumber?"

I'm giggling because, as harsh as that reality is, it's coming from Jack, who I know doesn't judge me at all. "Or a used-car salesman?"

"Now you're on the right track. I need a car."

I wipe the remaining tears from my face. "Thanks, Jack. For being here. For knowing when to come." I never would have asked.

He sighs. "Just keep your head up. And promise you won't ever look at that shit again. That was dumb. I'm going to cut off my hotspot when I come here if I catch you doing it again."

"I won't. I promise. I'm done. I'm moving on." I toss my phone to my bed stand, the weight of it suddenly unbearable. "I take it the game's finished?"

He nods, his dour expression telling me that the Flyers won't be playing again until next season.

■ ■ ■

"Twenty eighteen's our year, right?" Jack grumbles to Hawk as they ease down my porch steps, Jack dressed to jog home.

"Hope so," comes the bodyguard's deep response. The radio in his SUV buzzes with low voices, the commentators dissecting the game, highlighting all the ways that the Flyers screwed up and lost their chance at playing for the Cup. I've heard "Madden" said at least twice in the past twenty seconds, even though Brett wasn't playing. It's not hard to figure out where the brunt of the blame is going to fall, regardless.

But it's almost a relief to me that I won't have to face Brett sitting in a box with Courtney Woods beside him again anytime soon. I'm sure there are already more than enough stills of them splashed all over the Internet.

Maybe now everyone can move on.

Including me.

"You should go home, Hawk," I tell him.

The fierce-looking man frowns a little. "I'm supposed to—"

"I'm good. Look, they're all gone. There's no one around anymore."

"But Mr. Madden insisted—"

"That you stay until I feel safe. I feel safe now, so you can go." I cap it off with a smile.

After a long pause, he offers a curt nod and heads for his truck. To phone in to headquarters and get permission to leave, no doubt.

"You gonna be fine to get home?"

Jack is leaning over to fix his loose shoelace. "I've only had three beers."

"Keith is going to notice that they're gone."

"Good. Tell him to buy better stuff when he restocks." With a wink, Jack is off, running down the lane.

"Stay on the sidewalk!" I holler after him.

My phone is ringing from my bedroom as I step back inside, and it's a piercing sound, carrying through the silent house. While Brenna's a deep sleeper, I still run for it, afraid it might wake her.

My heart stutters when I see Brett's name on the screen.

I already know why he's calling. To tell me what I've seen with my own two eyes. What *everyone* has seen. What people—complete strangers who don't know me, will never know me—are now gossiping about. And as trivial as Jack made it all sound, every little reminder makes me nauseous.

I don't know what to say to him.

And so I simply sit there, the volume muted, staring at his name as I wait for it to go to voice mail. It takes me almost a minute to collect my nerve and listen to the message, a sad smile touching my lips as his voice fills my ear. "Hey, Cath, it's Brett. I figured you'd be done work by now but maybe not? I was at the game tonight and just got home. It's the first time I have a moment's privacy. Anyway . . ." He heaves a sigh. "I wanted to warn you that there was going to be some stuff floating around in the media about me and my ex getting back together . . ."

Just the way he says it feels like a punch to the gut.

". . . Simone thinks that's the best way to deflect the *Weekly* spin. Courtney was up for it, so she flew in from LA today to lend some weight to the story that Simone pitched."

Simone pitched it. So she's the reliable source. Makes sense. That was her tagline they used.

He pauses. "Did you watch tonight's game, by any chance?" I don't miss the touch of wariness in his voice. "Anyway . . . it's all for show. We're not back together."

I close my eyes, the familiar burn in my stomach flaring painfully.

"So . . . yeah. I just wanted you to know that. And I was hoping I'd get to talk to you in person, but . . . anyway . . ." He sounds so sedate, so unsure of himself. I imagine that has to do with his team's loss tonight. Though, it'd be hard for any of those guys to muster up a smile right now. "So, yeah . . . Good night . . . . Or good morning . . . I don't know. Talk to you soon?"

As far as bumbling voice mails go, Brett just beat out my "take your money back" one from last week. I wish I could laugh about it.

I wish I could just take his words at face value.

I wish I could believe him.

I crawl into bed and close my eyes. I press my phone against my ear and get lost in Brett's message—not in his words, but in his voice: a deep, melodic song that I can somehow feel right down to my very core.

Each time I hit Replay—seven times in total—I hope something will click, something will change. Something will tell me that I can accept his explanation and find the guts to talk to him.

But I can't.

Because his words are words I've heard before. This explanation is one that I've heard before. This kind of false hope has consumed me before. And the probability of facing heartbreak again . . .

I set my phone on my nightstand, Brett's message unanswered.

I promised myself I'd be smarter.

■ ■ ■

July 2010

I walk swiftly toward his house, my bike cast aside at the park across the street, where I've been sitting for three hours.

Waiting, for the familiar rumble of Scott's motorcycle.

Gathering my nerve to speak to him for the first time in four months.

His house is on a quiet street, in a quiet neighborhood, in the oldest part of Balsam. It was his grandmother's bungalow, willed to him when she passed away. It's small and charming and, best of all, its front door is set back a little to offer privacy.

I reach his porch as he's sliding a key into his front door, the creak of the wooden steps announcing my approach.

He pushes aside a wave of golden-brown hair, mussed from wearing a helmet. "You can't show up on my doorstep like this. You know that."

"Why won't you even look at me anymore?" My voice trembles with barely contained emotion, my face no doubt a splotchy, mascara-streaked mess.

He hesitates. "You know why."

"I saw you coming out of the café today."

"Cath . . ." He leaves his door open a crack and turns to face me, those warm hazel eyes softening. He glances around us, checking for prying eyes. "She's a kindergarten teacher and we dated for years. If she's willing to give

me another shot, it says something about my character." He shrugs. "I need to help my reputation right now."

His *reputation isn't what's suffering. "Are you sleeping with her?" A fresh wave of tears threatens.*

"Please don't cry, Cath. I'm sorry." His throat bobs with a hard swallow. "Do you still love me?"

His gaze slowly drifts down over my frame—the midday summer heat making my tank top and jean shorts cling to my body—before lifting to meet my eyes again. "You know how I feel about you. I will always feel that way about you."

I take a deep breath, brush my tears from my cheek. "I miss you so much."

He hesitates, his eyes flickering to the house next door again, the only vantage point with a clear view of us, thanks to a crop of trees in front. "I miss you, too. But we shouldn't have allowed that to happen."

Chapter 19

■ ■ ■

"Seriously, I didn't need a police escort to go shopping," I insist to Keith, barely avoiding the town worker as she waters flowers. It's the first days of June, and the tulips that graced the planters have been replaced by bright bursts of petunias, marigolds, and lime-green coleus, flowers that will adorn Main Street in the coming summer months. And then, like clockwork, they'll be replaced by indigo and golden mums and orange pumpkins to mark autumn and, after that, thick evergreen boughs, red ribbon, and twinkling white lights. Really, there isn't a season where this stretch isn't tended to with the utmost care. The valley could be suffering the worst drought in Pennsylvania's history and I'll bet this worker would still be out here every Saturday morning, watering, keeping Balsam beautiful and the tourists coming in.

And, truth be told, we may actually be facing a drought soon enough, as we've gone from unseasonably cool to stifling hot in a week's time, the weather forecasts calling for highs of midnineties by this afternoon.

"Then you shouldn't have tried that lame 'I have nothing to wear' excuse on Lou." Keith taps the rim of Brenna's baseball cap, pushing it lower over her face. This is the first time she's been anywhere with me besides a car ride to school, and I'm not entirely sure there won't be a photographer lurking, given that today is this Key to the City ceremony they're forcing me to attend.

I roll my eyes. Keith showed up on my doorstep with coffee and donuts at a quarter to ten, exactly fifteen minutes before Threads, a boutique clothing shop and the only one in Balsam, was to open. Apparently Lou called him last night to ensure I got out and bought something for myself. She didn't call Misty, I'll note, which would have been the more obvious choice. I think Lou still worries about my safety.

There's absolutely no need. I've gotten plenty of curious looks, but no one has said anything to me beyond a hello.

I hold Brenna's hand extra tight as we head for Keith's truck, trekking carefully over the cobblestone street that marks the center square of Balsam. My other hand grips a shopping bag holding a dress that I hope is appropriate for this afternoon's event. No one seems willing to tell me much about it at all, except that I'm to be ready at three thirty and we're going to Lander's Mill, a museum on the outskirts of town.

"Can we get ice cream? Please!" Brenna begins tugging my arm toward the Sweet Stop. "Please, please, please, please, *please!*"

Normally I'd say no, that it's too early in the day for ice cream and the five bucks they charge for a double cone is robbery. But I just treated myself to a dress that cost me more than I've ever spent on an outfit. And she's such a good kid, never complaining about all the things we can't afford.

She squeals as I lead her toward the door.

"I'll wait out here. Nothing too messy, Squirt, or you'll be cleaning my seats!" Keith calls after her.

She's not listening, already pulling me in past the red-and-white-striped awning.

We pass a table of giggling teenagers who immediately silence. I hear hushed whispers of "That's her!" and heat crawls up my neck. It's a ridiculous reaction for a twenty-four year-old woman in the presence of girls who can't be more than sixteen, but it somehow brings me right back to high school.

"Okay, Brenna, hurry up and pick please."

"Um . . ." She lifts onto her tiptoes to see inside the ice cream chiller.

"Face off the glass," I quietly scold, offering an apologetic smile to the teenage boy behind the counter who waits for our order with a lackluster expression. Poor kid has to wear a silly white cone for a hat; I'll bet he's not happy with that.

"Cotton candy . . . pineapple orange . . . chocolate chip . . ."

I struggle not to roll my eyes as Brenna reads each label, just as she does every time she's choosing an ice cream flavor at Diamonds, where we have a whopping five options. In the end, I know she'll pick Dutch chocolate, because she always picks Dutch chocolate.

At least there isn't a line.

I let my gaze wander over the various counters—over the decadent handmade chocolates and French *macarons*, over the blocks of fudge and cupcakes—and I inhale, relishing the scents of icing sugar and freshly brewed coffee. I haven't been in here in years. My parents used to bring us once a year on our birthday, as a special treat. I always looked forward to it.

"Catherine?"

I spin on my heels at the voice.

"It's me! Krystal? Remember? From English class?"

"Hi." Yeah, I remember Krystal from English class.

■ ■ ■

October 2010

The push isn't hard, but I'm drunk and caught off guard. I stumble into Dixon Teller, who merely shrugs me off. Assuming it was an innocent bump, I wipe the spilled beer from my jacket and get set to move on.

"Why are you even here?"

I guess it wasn't an innocent bump.

I turn to meet the voice.

Krystal. Quite possibly my biggest enemy. She sneers as I pass in the hallway, loudly whispers behind me in class. It's like she's made it her mission to make my life hell. More than it already is.

Cold green kohl-lined eyes spear me with hatred. "No one invited you. No one likes you. No one wants to touch you. You're a whore." And then, as if to emphasize her point, her mouth twists. And she spits. The beer-tinged gob lands on my cheek.

Something inside me finally snaps.

I drop my cup and lunge for her, my fingers grasping for her neck, her hair, intent on inflicting pain.

Strong arms rope around me and pull me back before I can find purchase. DJ's friend Matt, a nice enough guy who smells faintly of weed and cigarettes, is hauling me away, kicking and screaming.

■ ■ ■

The last seven years have been kind to Krystal. She looks more grown up now, the heavy black liner and red lipstick replaced by subtle taupe shadows and pink gloss, her sun-bleached hair now a shiny golden blonde.

"It's been a while, hasn't it?" She makes it sound as if we're old friends, catching up.

What am I going to do, or say, standing in the middle of an ice cream shop with my daughter next to me?

I smile politely. "It sure has."

Another young man wearing a pointy white cone hat appears behind the counter for her. "Yes, hi, I'm here to pick up an order? Maxwell," she tells him. While the guy disappears into the back, Krystal turns her attention back to me. "I'm in town for my mother's birthday."

I glance back at Brenna, who has made it to the far left of the chiller now, her tongue poking out the side of her mouth in that unconscious way she does as she reads the labels. At least the guy waits on her with a hint of amusement now. "So . . . what have you been up to?" Not that I care.

"I'm living in Philadelphia. I just got my first teaching job. High school English. Go figure, right?"

"Right." Glad to know she's molding young minds.

"Oh! And can you believe it?" She lifts her manicured hand to show off the sparkly diamond on her ring finger.

"Congratulations."

"Yes!" She holds her hand in front of her to admire her own ring. "He's a lawyer, on track to be partner."

"Mommy, I've decided. Dutch chocolate, please," Brenna tells the guy.

"Is this your daughter?" Krystal asks, peering down at her. But Brenna's too busy watching the guy to make sure the scoops are full so she doesn't turn.

"Sorry, she takes her ice cream seriously."

"Well, she has her priorities straight, then." Krystal chuckles. "So, I watched that interview. I said to Justin, 'I went to school with her!'"

And what else did you tell him? All I can do is smile, but I know it doesn't reach my eyes.

It doesn't dissuade her from talking, though. "And ho-ly. Brett Madden." She whistles softly. "He's gorgeous."

I guess I can't fault the world for noticing his looks before anything else. I'm no better. But he's so much more than just a handsome face. "He's a really nice guy," I acknowledge, smothering my sadness.

I never did respond to his message. He's called twice since, once to see if I really didn't need Hawk and Vince anymore. A second time "just to touch base." The first call I genuinely missed, the second I left unanswered. Both times, I fell asleep listening to the voice mails.

I haven't been able to bring myself to call him back yet. So much for being brave.

I reach into my purse to get my wallet.

"Oh no, please. Put the little girl's ice cream cone on my bill."

"I can't—"

"Yes! Please. It's done. It's done, right?" She looks expectantly at the guy.

I don't want to argue and cause a scene, so I mumble a thanks and grab a handful of napkins instead. "Well, it was great seeing—"

"I was really hoping you two would . . . you know . . ." She sighs dreamily. "What a fairy-tale ending to an incredible story."

I feel heat crawl into my cheeks as other customers perk up. "They must have been looking to boost ratings or something, spinning it that way."

"Sure didn't look like it." She waggles her eyebrows. "Wouldn't that be amazing?"

Brenna tugs on my sleeve to get my attention. "Can we go now? I have to pee."

For once, I'm thankful for Brenna's impatience and tiny bladder. "Yeah, it would have been." I put my arm around her, pulling her close to me. "It was good seeing you, Krystal. Good luck with the wedding."

"Yeah, okay." She opens her mouth as if to say something but hesitates. I use that chance to shuttle Brenna out the door, toward Keith.

But a few moments later, she comes running out. "Hey, wait!" She looks tentatively from me to Keith, to Brenna, who's already sporting streaks of chocolate on her nose and chin, and then back to me, her face full of uncertainty.

"Come on, Brenna." Keith leads her to his truck and out of earshot.

Krystal's lips press tight. "I just . . ." She takes a deep breath. "I just wanted to say that I'm sorry for how horrible I was to you in high school. I'm mortified by it, actually."

"That's . . ." I stop myself before I brush it off with "that's okay." Before I brush it off as no big deal because I just want to avoid all of this and move on. Instead, I find myself asking the question I've thought of asking so many times. "What did I ever do to you?"

She sighs and looks down. "I heard you fooled around with Darin the weekend after he broke up with me."

"Darin?" I frown.

"Darin Metcalfe. He was the quarterback. We dated for two years."

"Oh." Right. I did fool around with him. It was at that crazy house party that got shut down by the cops. I was drunk and he was hot, so when he started flirting with me . . .

She hesitates, as if considering her next words. "And Mr. Philips was a flirt. I mean, he smiled a lot at me. I guess I thought he and I might . . . well, I guess I was jealous. Turns out I dodged a real bullet there." She offers me a sympathetic smile. "Not that that's any excuse for how I treated you. Anyway, I've thought about you sometimes, hoping I'd get a chance to apologize one day, and that you might forgive me. That's . . ." She clasps her hands together in front of her, her gaze flickering away before meeting mine again. "That's all I wanted to say."

I'm speechless. If someone had said I'd run into Krystal Maxwell and get a stumbling, nervous apology from her, I would have laughed in their face.

Is this because of the interview? Now that I know Brett Madden, does she just want to be on the right side of my fence?

Or is it just because she actually does feel bad and truly is sorry?

Can I simply forgive her?

She turns to head back into the store.

"Hey."

She peers back at me with bright blue eyes, nothing but sincerity in them.

"Thank you for saying that. It means a lot to me."

Her face breaks out in a wide, genuine-looking smile, and she heaves a sigh, like she was holding her breath. "Maybe I'll see you around."

"Maybe."

She disappears into the store, the group of teenagers sitting at the table watching us intently. I climb into Keith's truck.

"You look like you've been slapped." He nods toward the spot where Krystal and I stood moments ago, dropping his voice. "What was that about?"

"Some closure, I think."

For both of us.

■ ■ ■

"Hey, I've been here before!" Brenna squeals with excitement as we turn into the long winding driveway of Lander's Mill.

Keith casts a slight wave at the police officers standing at the entrance, busy in conversation with the reporters parked on the road, trying to gain access.

"Yeah?" Keith engages Brenna as I quietly steel myself for what is to come.

"Yeah. They used to cut down trees here and make furniture out of them!"

"Well, not right here. But you're right, this building was made using the original mill." The real Lander's Mill—some twenty miles north, still within Balsam County—thrived in this area for more than a century before shutting down in the 1980s. The large barnlike structure ahead of us, of weathered pine and factory windows, was constructed from salvaged materials. It was dismantled and transported here as part of a deal between local officials and developers, after the developers bought the land under the defunct business, with the intent to tear down and parcel off estate properties. Local officials fought them for years, deeming it a historical landmark and refusing to approve the necessary zoning paperwork, all while the original buildings fell further into disrepair and were finally condemned.

And then a smart businessman stepped in and offered a solution: If the developers were willing to foot the bill to salvage and help build this main structure, and the town officials were willing to provide a grant to fund the operation of a museum, he would invest in the Lander's Mill we're now facing—a piece of history, as well as a picturesque event facility. It's been voted the Best Wedding Venue in the region by *Cosmopolitan*.

And it's a place where there are currently too many cars for my anxiety level.

"Stop fidgeting," Keith mutters, pulling his pickup truck into a spot marked RESERVED.

"Easy for you to say." I smooth the silky material over my thighs. "Are you positive this is okay?"

"It's fine," he assures me, his gaze flashing to my outfit—a flowing, floral maxidress—before sliding from his seat.

I sigh as my toes hit the gravel drive and I hold the door open for Brenna.

She scampers out, the hem of the dress my mom bought her last week, just for this ceremony, swaying like a bell cup around her lithe frame, nothing but excitement oozing from her. "Is Uncle Jack here yet?"

"Probably." There are *a lot* of people—some I recognize as local business owners, others are strangers—milling around, throwing curious glances my way. A lot more than I'd have expected for "a quiet, small ceremony."

I finally spot my mom's blue Subaru, right next to Lou's black-and-tan Chevy pickup. My mom had tried insisting that we arrive together as a family, but Keith helped me avoid that mess, knowing I wouldn't be able to handle the added anxiety that comes with Hildy Wright. And Jack assured me he'd herd her inside so I don't have to deal with her "helpful" suggestions before the ceremony.

Keith stops beside me, his gaze following mine. "Notice the news vans on the road?"

I spear him with a knowing look. As if I wouldn't.

"Notice that there aren't any *here*?"

"How'd you manage that?"

"It's a private event, invitation only. I told Polson that this is the only way you'd agree to it. He was okay with it, actually. He wants our local papers writing the story."

To make sure it reflects well on Balsam, that cynical voice inside my head whispers. "That's . . . Thanks."

"It *does* mean you may have to smile for one or two of them. Maybe even answer a question."

"Fine." After *The Weekly*'s interview, I think I can handle that much.

Brenna tugs on my arm. "Come on! Let's go!" I pull on the stylish ruby-red jacket that I borrowed from Misty—in case the spaghetti straps of this dress felt inappropriate—and brace myself as we head for the heavy wood doors.

We step into the anteroom, which tastefully displays artifacts from the original mill while also serving as a welcoming entranceway to the larger event room. The faint waft of cut wood and age still permeates the air.

And a familiar cologne.

I gasp at the sight of stunning aqua-blue eyes.

Chapter 20

■ ■ ■

I hold those eyes for a long moment, before noticing anything else. Like the fact that his face is clean shaven, his jawline even more sharp and masculine than I imagined it to be. He's obviously been spending some time outside because his skin has a slight glow to it, the kind you get with forgoing sunscreen on a hot spring day. Other than his leg still being in a cast and the thin pink line across his forehead, he looks perfectly normal. Well, more like breathtakingly handsome. The pre-accident Brett.

"Good, I'm glad you made it! You look lovely, dear." Clarisse Polson's voice is soft and soothing, her thin hand cool against my sweaty palm as she pounces on me. "A few more minutes until everyone is ready. We'll have you seated on the dais and . . ." She talks quickly, walking me through the basic steps for the ceremony, not giving me a chance to adjust to the shock of seeing Brett here. "Frank is just chitchatting out front, but I'll let him know you're here. We'll start in a few minutes."

I do my best to acknowledge her words with a smile and nod, and then my gaze quickly shifts back to the man leaning against his crutches.

What is Brett doing here?

I search out my dear friend and find him darting through the door to the main room rather quickly.

Of course Keith knew Brett would be here.

". . . and this is what they used to chop the trees," Brenna says, her childish voice carrying over the low buzz of voices from the other side of the wall as she points out the axe, followed by the two-person saw mounted along the wall above it. "And *this* is what they used to cut the wood into smaller pieces back in the really olden days. But they used those machines in the picture in the olden days that weren't *really* olden. And *this* is . . ." I think Brenna could rival Clarisse on pouncing speed.

She wasted no time marching up to Brett and—possibly without so much as a hello, knowing her—beginning to walk him through all the displays, regurgitating everything she remembers from her field trip.

Brett patiently hobbles alongside her and lets her babble away, a small genuine smile touching his lips as he gives her his undivided attention. He's wearing a tailored charcoal suit today, the pant leg cut to accommodate his cast, the gold tie against a crisp white shirt a sharp, stylish look.

I can't peel my eyes off him.

"You have a future historian there." A deep voice pulls my gaze to my right. The man I saw on television the day Brett addressed media for the first time after the accident stands before me, also in a suit. They really dressed for the occasion.

"Hi, Catherine. I'm Richard, Brett's father." For a moment I think he's going to hug me as his wife did. He doesn't, but he does seize my hand in both of his, holding it tight. "It's a pleasure to finally meet you."

"It's nice to meet you, too," I manage to get out. He looks so much like Brett, only older, his build smaller.

"I would have come for the *Weekly* interview, but we thought it might be too overwhelming for you."

"It *was* a bit overwhelming," I admit with a laugh, making him smile. He has the same devilish twinkle in his eye and strong jaw as Brett. I can see why Meryl fell for him.

I like him immediately.

Two men close in next to him. One, I recognize as the Flyers coach. The stony face I watched on TV has softened somewhat, though he still looks like the type of guy who spends his days yelling at grown men with ease. Even in this heat, he wears that same black Flyers jacket that he wore during the postgame interview—a jacket you'd wear at a rink rather than at an event where everyone else is in suits—but something tells me this isn't any more his thing than it is mine.

"Catherine, this is Coach Adam Roth," Richard introduces us. I get a firm handshake and a gruff "Hello" by way of greeting, before Richard's attention shifts to the looming man next to him, having well over a foot in height and I don't dare guess how much weight on me. "And this is Sid Durrand, the Flyers owner."

Just looking at this guy, in his well-cut suit and his sparkling watch,

the lights from above catching the embedded diamonds, I can see
that he has money. More than Richard, though? Possibly not, and yet
I note that Richard doesn't ooze his wealth. In fact, I have to remind
myself that this man is married to *the* Meryl Price. Not because I don't
think he's handsome or distinguished enough. He is both, in a Robert
Redford *The Horse Whisperer* kind of way. But he has a quiet air of so-
phistication about him that I feel from Brett, too.

"They said you were tiny, but I didn't believe it," Sid says with a
wide smile and a thick Kentucky accent. He shakes my hand so hard
that I'm afraid he might reinjure my wrist, and I struggle not to wince
from the sizable rings digging into my flesh. "It's a pleasure to meet
you. Brett hasn't shut up about you."

I feel my cheeks flush as I steal a glance over to the other side of
the room. Brett's back is to me and Brenna is still blabbing away, but
there's no way he missed Sid's booming voice.

Clarisse pokes her head in. "All right, we're about to start. We have
seats waiting at the front for you, Richard—and your daughter, Cath.
If she could come with me?"

"Brenna?" I call out.

". . . And a long time ago, this man fell into the wood chipper and
it chopped his legs up into little bits."

"Brenna!"

"Yes, Mommy?"

They both turn in time to catch my grimace.

"Can you go with Brett's dad and Mrs. Polson?"

She wanders over to take in the three looming males.

"I'm the one you're looking for. Hi, my name is Richard." He
reaches out to shake her hand. She eyes it warily, but finally accepts it.

He doesn't seem at all offended. In fact, his warm smile grows
wider. "So what happened to the man who fell into the chipper?" he
asks, leading her out the door.

All caution disappears. "Oh, they pulled him out before it could
chop up the rest of him and then he got fake legs and . . ." Her voice
fades as she disappears into the main room.

"Goodness. I think we might have to talk to the museum hosts
about what they're teaching these kids!" Clarisse laughs nervously.

I sense a wall of strength next to me. Trying to calm my heart rate through a few short breaths, I finally turn to meet Brett's gaze. There's so much emotion swirling within his eyes—some of it I've seen before, some of it I can't even guess at—and I find myself struggling to manage a simple "Hi." It comes out throatily.

"Hey."

"I thought you'd be in—"

"Okay, everyone. If you'll follow me, please. Brett and Catherine, if you could come in last."

Brett and Catherine.

We're ushered into the main room, where at least a hundred sets of eyes latch on to us.

"I'm right here if you need me." The low whisper comes just as we're waiting in line to take our seats in front of everyone. Brett knows I'm nervous. He knows I'd rather be anywhere besides heading for a small stage to collect an award.

I glance over my shoulder and see that same expression on his face as he wore during the interview—of worry, of awe, of . . . what everyone is so desperate to label adoration. It's only been two and a half weeks since I saw him last, and yet it feels like I've been waiting an eternity.

All I can manage is a small smile and nod before facing the crowd, focusing on the familiar faces in the front row. My parents, Emma and Jack, Lou, and Leroy? Who's running the kitchen? Misty's blonde curls bob as she ducks in to stand at the back, the Diamonds orange-and-white uniform somehow flattering her. Jack has a wide grin plastered across his face—for me or his idol behind me, I can't say.

"Okay, this way!" Clarisse directs in a whisper, waving us forward. I sense Brett's hand skate across the small of my back in the faintest of touches, reminding me to breathe.

■ ■ ■

"Please tell me that's the last one?" I plead behind my fake smile. Keith nods toward the photographer as he passes us, his camera lens already in pieces. "It's the last one. I should charge you a management fee."

"You certainly seem to be orchestrating things for me. Especially behind my back." I glare knowingly at him, but smooth it over quickly as Coach Roth and Sid Durrand pass by, nodding their final farewells to me. They were both great sports during the event, serving mostly as photo ops for local media. Though Sid did say a few words of thanks to me on behalf of the NHL that turned my face red. Actually, I'm certain my face was red throughout the entire ceremony.

"Admit it, that wasn't so bad."

"It was better than I expected," I grudgingly admit. It only lasted twenty minutes, and no one so much as hinted at the idea of me giving a speech, thankfully. Even Brett's words were brief, but from the heart, expressing his appreciation for me being at the right place at the right time, for him. But he didn't gush, he didn't say anything that made me overtly uncomfortable.

"See? It won't always be a complete circus around him. Don't use that as your excuse for pushing him away."

I stare at him, taken aback. Keith hasn't uttered a single word about the romantic spin Wethers put on this story, and I wasn't about to ask him for his opinion, not when I suspect his own feelings for me. But I've seen it weighing on him, the worry evident in his eyes. I've sensed him biting off words before letting them escape. I've assumed he was against the idea entirely.

"I better grab some of those tiny sandwiches before Jack eats them all."

I follow his sight line to the small crowd milling around the patio, an elaborate three-level stone construct. Sure enough, my brother is hovering over one of the waiters who carries a silver platter, filling his hands with appetizers two at a time while he gawks openly at Misty a few feet away. Wearing that same stupid love-struck grin he had on when he was fourteen and met her for the first time.

Misty's eyes aren't on him, though. She's too busy trying to make her way over to Brett and me now that the interviews are over. But by the looks of it, she won't have a chance. Lou has one hand on her shoulder and a scolding expression on her face, while Misty is smiling and arguing politely. I know them too well, even from a hundred feet away. Lou's insisting that Brett and I have a chance to talk, and Misty is determined to undermine her. Then Lou points to the parking lot where Leroy is waiting and Misty's hopeful face falls. As usual, Lou has won. I'm guessing Misty is his ride and they need to get back to Diamonds for the Sunday dinner rush.

"You can talk to them tomorrow," Keith says, taking off at a swift pace before I can take a step.

Leaving me alone with Brett for the first time today.

Breathing in deeply, I wander over to the gazebo, a white lattice structure crawling with clematis vines, the backdrop for countless wedding photos, I'm sure. Today, we used the space as a quiet location for a few pictures and brief interviews with three of the local newspapers and a Philadelphia paper.

"Thought you were never doing an interview again?" Brett teases, his gaze drifting over my frame as I gingerly climb the steps, hiking my dress a few inches to avoid tripping over the hem.

"I thought so, too, but Puppet Master Keith decided differently."

Brett chuckles and gazes out at Jasper Lake, allowing me the chance to study his handsome profile. He's seated on a bench and leaning against one of the thick posts, his suit jacket removed and draped casually over the rail. It's the perfect position to show off his fit body, and the faintest sheen of sweat that glistens from his forehead adds to his allure. "I'm glad they chose this location. It's nice. Peaceful."

"I haven't been here since I was six, but it hasn't changed much. I've never been to an event in there, though." I ease myself down on the bench next to him, trying not to be obvious as I inhale the lingering scent of his cologne that I adore.

Brett's eyes shift to my lap, to the ornate key within my grasp.

"Need a big gold key?" I joke, holding it out in the air. I guess it's the thought that counts, but I'm still trying to figure out what it *really* means to me—beyond being just a decorative ornament. My name is engraved in the side, in beautiful cursive font, along with the date.

"My mother's going to be jealous. She's always wanted one of those."

I can't help but laugh. "Your mother has a star on the Hollywood Walk of Fame. And, what is it . . . *three* Oscars now?"

He grins. "But not a big gold key."

"Tell her it takes time and a lot of hard work."

His responding chuckle somehow makes me giddy. "She said she's really sorry she couldn't make it. She was trying, but they added another week of filming and she couldn't take off again. Plus, she didn't want this turning out to be about her, which it inevitably would have had she shown up."

I *had* noticed the curious glances and wondered if half of those in attendance had accepted the invitation with the hope that Meryl Price might be there. "That's kind of her, even to consider it."

"My sister was going to come, too. She had a ticket booked. But she got a callback for a second audition that she can't miss."

"For what?"

"I can't remember." He frowns. "Some new HBO series, I think? Anyway, I know she's really hoping to get this one."

"HBO. Wow. That's . . . big." Not quite as big as my shift at Diamonds tomorrow morning.

Brett's gaze travels over the small crowd. "I'm glad your family came."

"Yeah, me, too. Surprised, really. But they all came. Even my sister. And of course Misty, and my boss and her husband . . ." It was a front row of broad smiles. There was a time when I didn't believe that I had so many people to support me.

He hesitates. Brett must have figured out that my past with my family is a minefield. I sense the questions brewing. "When Keith called to ask me if I'd come, we talked a bit."

"Oh, yeah?" Of course Keith would have been the one to call him. "About what?"

"About you and your family." Brett watches me warily. "About what happened between you guys."

"Things were different. *I* wasn't easy." I instantly feel defensive, although I'm not entirely sure whether it's on behalf of me or my family.

"I'm not judging you, Cath. Or them," Brett quickly says, his voice soft. "I just wanted to know what happened, that's all. Maybe it'll help me understand you a little bit more."

There's a long pause, long enough to allow tension to grow.

"So your brother plays for Minnesota?"

"Yeah." I smile. "He also has a crush on you." *So does my best friend.*

And I'm . . . I take a deep breath and, pushing aside my own feelings, tell Brett about Jack—how much he loves hockey, his scholarship, the tattoo on his bicep. Brett lets me ramble on about my little brother without interruption, without any glint of awkwardness in his eyes, simply smiling, his eyes roaming my features until I find myself flushing from the intensity of his gaze.

"I guess he'll find some use for those season tickets Sid gave you, then?"

I chuckle, remembering the dumbstruck expressions on both Jack's and my dad's faces when Sid Durrand announced that the Flyers would be awarding me two lower-level season tickets for the next twenty-five years as a small token of their appreciation. "I'm going to be getting a lot of free babysitting thanks to those. Not that Jack won't get the most use out of them anyway, seeing as I'd feel like a fraud if I said I was a hockey fan. I didn't even know who you were until a month ago." *And now you've become a permanent fixture in my thoughts, despite every attempt to distance myself.*

"I'm just glad you didn't refuse to accept them."

Which reminds me . . . "I paid my parents back for the Escape."

"Good. That's why I left the money." No mention of my rambling voice message to him.

"You left *way* too much. I'm going to give it—"

"No."

"But I—"

"No, Cath." He counters the sudden sharpness of that one word with a dimpled smile. "Don't bother arguing with me. I've got a lot of spare time on my hands to fight you and I promise you, I'll win one way or another." Brett adjusts his position on the bench.

I catch the wince that he tries to cover.

I let the topic of money slide. For now. "How's your leg?"

"Itchy as hell, but I think staying off it for the past two weeks helped a lot."

"You mean your doctor was right? Who knew?"

He treats me to that grin of his, though I can see a hint of sadness in his eyes.

I hesitate. "When do you think you'll be playing again?"

"Depends on how my ankle heals. I'll be in this cast for a few weeks at least, until they think it's safe to swap it for a walking cast. Then it'll be another few months of that with a ton of physical therapy."

"So, a while."

He nods quietly. "They're taking another X-ray tomorrow, so they may be able to give me a better idea."

"Nervous?"

"A little." He pauses. "But with my team done for the year, I'm not being hounded for updates from the public. At least there's that."

"I'm sorry they lost." *And I'm so sorry I never returned your call to at least tell you that.* I had so proficiently convinced myself that avoiding contact would help squash my rising feelings for him. Two seconds into seeing him today, I realized that those feelings haven't gone anywhere and I'm not only an idiot, I'm also an asshole.

"Yeah, I'm sorry, too," he offers after a long drawn-out moment, his gaze drifting to the lake again.

"It wasn't your fault."

His jaw tenses. "It's one thing to get injured taking a hit in a game. But how *this* happened?" He shakes his head. "People are right. That city has paid me so much fucking money and this is what they get in return."

"No, Brett. People aren't right. Not those people." I could argue more but I doubt he'll believe me.

I sense his mood shifting, so I switch to a lighter topic. "I'm sure California will be nice for the summer. Are you heading there after this, or going back to Canada?"

He's quiet for a moment, as if considering his words. "I guess that depends on you." He turns to regard me with an intensity I haven't felt since that night of the interview, when we sat on my bed and I confessed my deep, dark secret about nearly leaving him in the car that night. When he embraced me and I found myself wishing we could stay in my room forever. "Kate Wethers may have put a spin on that interview, but can we stop pretending that there's no truth to it. At least . . ." His eyes drift over my features, settling on my mouth. "You can't look at me like *that* and tell me there isn't."

My cheeks burn, and I avert my eyes to the lake. I didn't realize my adoration was *so* blatantly obvious.

"Why didn't you call me back?" He asks the question so softly, and without even a hint of malice, and yet I still flinch.

"I'm sorry, I—" I falter. Searching for a good answer but coming up short.

"Was it because of Courtney?"

Yes. And no. If I admit that that is part of it—a big part of it—then I'm basically admitting to having feelings for him. Though it sounds like he's already figured that out.

"It's because of a lot of things."

"Like?"

"There's just . . . lots of reasons." I stumble over my words.

Silence hangs between us. Somewhere in the distance I can hear Brenna giggling, and I'm grateful that she hasn't insisted on interrupting us just yet.

"Is it because of the cameras and the reporters? Because it isn't so bad anymore, is it?"

"For now. What if they come back?"

He shrugs. "Then we figure it out together. It's manageable."

"I can't sit inside my house with a bodyguard outside."

"Then you don't."

"And what? Wear a disguise?"

He chuckles. "I actually know some people who do that. I've never tried it. Well, unless you count my hockey gear. No one recognizes me in that, especially if I'm wearing an unmarked jersey. It's kind of nice. But really, it's not as bad as you think it is."

"Can you just walk out of your building right now without being noticed?"

"Right now, no. Not with everything that's been going on. They're hoping they'll catch a picture of me and Courtney, or me and you. Magazines pay big bucks for those. But normally . . . it's fine. I might sign an autograph here and there, but otherwise I can walk around without being recognized at all. At least, I could before the accident." He pauses. "It's honestly not that bad." His voice is soft, pleading.

"It's not just the media, Brett." I wish it were.

"Then what else? You have to tell me."

"Why?"

"What do you mean, why?" He chuckles. "Because I'm crazy about you and you won't even answer my calls. I need to know how to fix that so you'll give me a chance. *Please.*"

I'm suddenly light-headed and wondering if I heard him right.

His gaze shifts to focus intently on his hands, folded in his lap.

"I've never had trouble making friends or finding girlfriends. But it's always been harder figuring out exactly why they're there. They say they don't care who my mom is, or who I am. But everyone's secretly angling for attention or money, or both. You, though . . . you *really* aren't looking for either. Who I am seems to be working against me with you."

"I don't mean to—"

"It's okay, Cath. I like that about you." He turns to study my face. "And, God, you're so . . . You took me completely by surprise, that first night I met you. I thought you were the most beautiful woman I've ever met."

I recall the oversized sweats and my hair in a messy pile on top of my head. "I've seen the women you date, Brett. Now you're lying to me."

"Trust me, those women don't look like that when they're not layered with makeup and in front of a camera." His gaze skates over my features—over a mouth that I've thought was too wide more than once, and eyes that seem too catlike, and a nose that is too pointed at certain angles. "They're not like you."

You're beautiful, too, I want to say, but I can't manage the words.

He grins sheepishly. "When I went home that night, I told my parents that I was madly in love with the woman who saved my life."

Oh, my God. My heart's beating in my throat.

"Of course they convinced me that I was completely overwhelmed and that I needed to get some rest."

"I'm sure they were right," I mumble.

"I thought so too, honestly." He swallows hard. "But then you had to go and be not just brave and beautiful but also humble, and funny, and honest. And I couldn't stop thinking about what it'd be like to be with you." His hand stalls midair, catching himself as he's reaching for a loose strand of my hair. "So I need you to tell me what I need to do for you to give me that chance." His jaw tenses as he locks eyes with me. "Please."

"I just don't fit in your life." It's barely a whisper. I'm struggling to think straight.

He runs his hands back through his mane of wavy hair, the color of sand after a heavy rainfall. "That's just money, Cath. That's not who I am. Please tell me you don't think I'm that shallow. It's insulting."

I'm taken aback, his plea sparking an unexpected wave of shame. Never had I looked at it that way, that acknowledging our different social classes would disparage anyone but me. "I don't think you're shallow. I just think you're caught up and the feelings you have for me won't last. And I'll be the one hurt when you finally figure that out." There. I've said it as plainly as I can.

I don't know what I expected from Brett in response, but a broad smile of satisfaction isn't it.

"You should go to California for the summer, like you planned," I continue, trying to sound sure of myself.

He laughs bitterly. "That was never *my* plan. My mom is the one who made me promise to leave, the night of the interview. She saw the way I looked at you, and she knew right away what was going on. So she convinced me that I needed to distance myself and be a hundred percent sure my head was clear before I acted on it."

Maybe that celebrity rag that reported Brett's mom threatening to disown him wasn't so far off after all.

It's as if he can read my mind. "It's not because she disapproves of you, Cath. She thinks the world of you. She just didn't want either of us to get hurt because we weren't thinking straight."

"My mom basically said the same thing." Though from her point of view, the only possible outcome was that *I* would get hurt. That would be her worst-case scenario, and the best way to avoid that scenario was to be practical and never risk it in the first place. As Jack said, she plays it safe and doesn't take risks.

"Maybe they know something. Maybe we should listen to them." As much as I hate to admit it.

"And what? Sit around for the summer, trying to convince myself that what I'm feeling for you is *just* gratitude?" His stunning eyes settle on me. "Life is too short to do what other people think you should do. That's what *I* know." His gaze dips to my mouth. "Then again, I've never let fear hold me back."

Then you've never been crushed before. That's where Brett and I differ. What he calls fear is what I call being smart, being responsible, and thinking about Brenna.

"You don't believe me, do you? That this isn't just gratitude."

"No," I answer bluntly.

His lips press together, as if he's searching for a way to convince me. And all I can do is stare at that mouth, so soft and lush and appealing. Thoughts of it grazing mine that night send blood rushing through my body.

"What would make you trust me? What do you want to know? Ask me whatever you want, and I'll tell you. I'm an open book."

That's quite the open invitation.

I want to know *everything*. Every trivial detail. His favorite music, his favorite color, his favorite TV show. Does he still talk to his child-hood friends? How close are he and his sister? Does he sleep on his stomach or on his back? Does he cook, or does he have someone do that for him?

Has he ever had a broken heart?

"Why did you and Courtney break up?" *What kind of friends are you? The kind that occasionally screw? Where did she sleep while she was visiting you in Toronto?* I will the silent, painful questions to stop so I can actually listen to his answer.

"Because she lied to me."

That's not the answer I expected. "About what?"

"About something that she didn't trust me to handle properly. I can't tell you exact details, but the details aren't important anyway. She didn't trust me with the truth."

"And you're big on truth." I remember his advice to me the day of the interview.

A soft, secretive smile touches his lips, as if he's also remembering the moment in my bedroom.

I choose my next words carefully. "Was it . . . Did she have a choice about lying?"

"Everyone has a choice."

"But I mean, was there a good reason for her to lie?"

"Is there ever? Especially when it's to someone you say you love?"

"I guess not." I hesitate. "Did you love her?"

His lips twist in thought. "I probably would have, given enough time."

"But you're still friends." Perhaps friends who might reconcile for real?

Again, it's like he can read my mind. "We wouldn't have lasted as more, to be honest. It took the accident for me to figure it out."

Unexpected relief fills me. "Why not?"

"We want different things in life. She loves the cameras and the attention, and being splashed on magazine covers everywhere. She wants fame. She's the type of person you'd expect to see on a reality TV show."

I shudder, and he laughs.

"Yeah, that has never been my thing either, and I think I would have gotten sick of it eventually. I want simpler things in life. I want . . ." His eyes drift to his casted leg, stretched out in front of him. "I want to play again, to have a family . . . I don't know. A normal, quiet life, I guess. Or as normal and quiet as it will ever be, anyway. And I want someone in my life who wants those things, too."

Someone like me, I will myself to hear.

"So . . . what now? With Courtney, I mean? She's okay with pretending?" I don't hide the doubt in my voice. How on earth would any woman who loved Brett and lost him be willing to pretend for the sake of another woman?

Brett's face turns grim. "I wasn't expecting her to be all over me at the game. I should have anticipated it, because that's Courtney. She knew the cameras were on us and I wouldn't be able to react. She backed off after I told her to stop, but I know what it looked like." He adds softly, "I know what it must have looked like to you."

My jealously flares as I imagine that blonde, beautiful woman pressing herself against him.

"She told Simone she was okay with it, but it seems she was hoping it would lead to something real. So I made her leave the next day and agree not to say a word about us, one way or another. Let people believe we're together for a few more weeks, at least. But I won't let anything like that ever happen again, I promise." Brett frowns. "You still don't believe me, though. I can tell."

"The last time a guy told me that a relationship with his ex was just for show . . . he ended up marrying her."

"The teacher?" Brett asks softly.

After a moment, I nod.

"I'm not him, Cath."

"I know you aren't. I just . . . I'm scared, and trying to be smart."

Slowly, tentatively, he reaches over to take the key from my waiting palm, his fingertips skating over mine in a slow, intimate way.

My heart races inside my chest as I watch him turn the key over and over within his grasp. Finally he focuses on my face again, his eyes settling on my mouth. "Do you have any idea how badly I want to kiss you right now?"

I inhale sharply as my cheeks flush.

He chuckles. "Don't worry. I won't try, not in front of all these people. And not until you tell me it's what you want."

I let out a shaky breath.

The weight of the gold key settles back in my palm at the same time that Brett's giant hand folds over mine, his fingers weaving through, the tips settling on my lap. "We can take it as slow as you want."

There's so much strength in his grasp, and I feel that overwhelming urge to let go of every worry, every fear, every inhibition. "I'm not sure that slow is possible." I can't even think straight when I'm near him, when he's touching me. All I can do is *feel*.

And all I *want* to feel is him.

With Brett . . . I wouldn't fall in love, I'd plummet.

A sheepish smile touches his lips, his fingers curling tight around mine, squeezing just enough but not so hard that the key between us will hurt my palm. "Yeah, I'm not sure it is either. But I'm okay with that. And I'm okay with waiting until you are, too. Just . . . please stop trying to push me away. I *want* to be in your life, and not because I feel obligated."

An echo of what I said in that interview.

How is this happening to me?

These kinds of things don't happen to me.

Suddenly I'm aware of our surroundings—as always, we're out in the open. On display for everyone to watch. And I feel people stealing glances, out of simple curiosity, or hope, or even envy. I can't think of the last time anyone envied me, and yet how couldn't they now, as I sit here next to Brett, who, against all odds, is convinced that he wants *me*?

"Noooo!" Brenna's wild giggles carry to us, pulling my attention away. She's trying to outrun Jack and Keith as they both chase after her at a slow jog, her short legs moving impossibly fast as she tears around a tree. My parents, Emma, Lou, and Brett's dad are standing together off to the side, laughing as she outmaneuvers the grown men, diving between Jack's long legs and scrambling to her feet, to keep going, her pristine dress covered in grass stains that I doubt I'll be able to get out.

Only half the crowd remains. I don't doubt they're lingering for a chance to speak to Brett.

"We should probably go over there, so you can greet your many fans."

He sighs, then grabs his crutches and climbs to his feet. "Hey, isn't that . . ." He frowns, off into the distance.

I know exactly who he's looking at. I spotted Gord Mayberry's oafish lumbering gait an hour ago, as we were escorted to the gazebo with the newspaper reporters. It was clear he was heading our way before Lou and Keith steered him away. "Yup. They invited the county's business owners and Mayberry's is a big dealership." It hasn't gone unnoticed that Scott Philips's mother, a prominent Realtor, isn't here. Whether she wasn't invited or she chose not to come, I'm sure I'll hear about it later.

Brett smirks. "So how did he take the breakup?"

I can't help but laugh. "Right, the breakup. I don't think he's quite figured it out yet."

"Didn't he watch the interview?"

"Yeah, he did." We walk toward the patio slowly, Brett picking his way carefully on the stone path. "He assumed that when I said 'unsuccessful blind date' I meant something else." Somehow, Gord seems to think that there's still hope for us. He's shown up at Diamonds twice since. I shake my head. "Lou keeps apologizing for setting us up." I'll never understand why she did in the first place.

"Funny. Here I am thinking I should thank her for it," Brett says with a laugh.

Because if it weren't for that date, I wouldn't have been driving along Old Cannery Road that night.

The realization suddenly makes me look at that idiot in a different light. A smile pulls at the corners of my mouth. "So should I, I guess."

Chapter 21

...

"He actually said that? He used those exact words?"

I knew I shouldn't have been so honest with her. I guess I need to talk it out with someone, though, and Misty's the only one I can do that with. "More or less."

Misty growls her frustration. "I swear to God, Cath, I love you, but you're going to drive me *insane*! Why are you not with him right now?"

"We need more time to talk. People wanted to meet him, and then Brenna was starving because of course she wouldn't eat the food there, and then he had to get back to Philly . . ." Saying our good-byes with family lingering close by hindered what I *really* wanted to say to him— that I want more than anything to be carefree like Misty and throw my heart into the ring.

I just . . . it's not so easy for me to let go of control like that. Because that is what I'd be doing—letting go of control. Putting my heart in harm's way.

But I did promise to answer the phone the next time he called.

"Yeah, meeting him would have been nice." Misty scratches at a ketchup stain on the hem of her uniform, still bitter that Leroy dragged her back to Diamonds immediately after the ceremony ended. She drove straight here after her shift to interrogate me, not bothering to text or call in advance. I think, maybe, she was hoping he'd be here.

"I'll introduce you next time."

"Which is when, exactly?" I feel her eyes boring into my back as I take my time dunking a glass into sudsy water.

"I don't know yet."

I catch her rolling her eyes in the window's reflection. "You know that no relationship is ever guaranteed."

"I know."

"Nothing good in life will ever come to you if you don't take some risks."

"I *know*."

"The best things in life *always* come from taking risks."

"Have you been reading those inspirational messages again?"

"It's a great calendar: 365 quotes for 365 days." She winks. "I'll get you one for Christmas."

"Listen, don't tell *anyone* about this. It's all up in the air."

Misty releases a dreamy sigh, the rare, more serious side of her evaporating with her giggles. "Do you know how incredibly jealous I am of you right now? God, just think! What I would give to be able to kiss that man." She pauses. "I've never been with a guy with a broken leg. Do you think you'll have to wait to—"

"How are you doing in there, Brenna?" I holler extra loud, my cheeks flushing just thinking about what the first time with Brett would be like.

A splash sounds in the bathroom. "Yup! Almost done."

"'Kay. Two more minutes." Brenna would turn blue from cold if I let her, just so she could practice holding her breath underwater all night.

"Oh, I almost forgot. You'll never guess who sent me a friend request on Facebook."

"You're right, I won't." I barely remember Facebook. I had an account in high school. But once the hateful messages started coming through, telling me what a skank and slut and liar I was, and how I deserved to die for trying to ruin Scott's life, I deleted it. I haven't so much as opened it since.

"DJ Harvey."

The plate slips from my grasp and tumbles into the sink. "Isn't he in jail?"

"No, he got out six months ago. He cut a deal so his sentence wasn't as bad." She says it so casually, as if she's forgotten that he's a scumbag, that not only was he dealing drugs while they were together, but also, after she dumped him, she found out he had been screwing around on her for most of the five months that they were together.

A bubble of discomfort rises inside me. Good ol' social media. No one's ever truly out of reach anymore. "So . . . are you actually talking to him again?"

"No. I mean, I accepted his request because I was curious. He apologized to me." She says it with surprise, and shrugs. "That was kind of nice to hear."

"I guess." Just like it was nice to have Krystal's apology. As horrible as she was, that was years ago. Maybe everyone deserves a second chance. But what Krystal did and what DJ did aren't exactly on the same level. "What does he want?"

"Nothing. He saw the news and remembered that you and I lived together. It made him start thinking about me."

My eyes dart to the bathroom. "Don't bring up that night with him. Or Brenna."

"Relax! He doesn't even talk to Matt anymore. Matt tried to pin everything on him. DJ hates his guts now."

"Still . . . if you keep talking to DJ, don't mention her or that night."

"Please. If that night ever comes up, it'll be me asking him who he screwed while I wasn't looking, besides Jacqueline Forester," she mutters, studying her nails.

While I'm helping Brenna dry off and dress from her bath, I hear the door creak open and Keith's low murmur of greeting. Thankfully, the running sink drowns out the sound of Misty and him casually flirting back and forth.

"Do you ever stop jumping around?" Keith says as Brenna skips out of the bathroom in a fresh pair of pajamas. He's dressed in uniform for his shift tonight.

"Nope! Why are you here? We've already seen you, like, *all* day long."

"Just thought I'd check in before I go to work. Is that okay?

"I guess."

He watches her do laps around him. "Did you have fun today?"

"Yup."

"Do you like Brett, Brenna?" Misty asks casually, feigning innocence.

"Yeah. He's nice."

Misty throws a mischievous grin my way. "Your mom thinks so, too."

"Yeah. She smiled a lot today. Her eyes weren't sad."

Again with the sad eyes. She says it so innocently, and yet I can't help but flinch. Is that how my child will remember me? I check my watch. "Why don't you pick out a book to read with Uncle Jack. He said he'd come by and say good night." We are conveniently on his jog home from the gym. Though, to be honest, I think he'd detour if we weren't.

Her eyes light up. "Can Uncle Jack sleep here? *Please?*"

It's endearing, how much she loves him. "I'm not sure you two would fit in your bed."

"Well . . ." Her face twists with thought. "We could sleep in your bed, and you could take my bed."

Always the problem solver. I can already tell that I'm going to have a harder time with her as she gets older. "Uncle Jack has to get up early for work and he needs his sleep. He isn't used to having little girls in his bed with him." Both Misty and Keith snort, earning my warning glare. "Okay. Go on, now." I send her off with a playful pat against her bum.

"So? All good around here?" Keith helps himself to a glass of milk, frowning at the single beer in my fridge. Jack left him one, at least.

"Yup, we were just talking about how Brett Madden basically professed his undying love to Cath today." My warning glare doesn't shut Misty up. "So how does a guy do it when he's wearing a cast, anyway? I mean, it'd be hard to be on top, wouldn't it? I guess he'd have to just be on the bottom, and be careful not to bang his leg on anything, right?"

I dare a glance at Keith to find him taking his time with his milk, his glass tipping slowly back. Questions like that are par for the course with Misty, but when it's pretty clear she's talking about Brett and *me* having sex . . .

"I wouldn't know. I've never broken my leg," he answers calmly, placing the glass in the sink.

There's a long, lingering moment, where the mood in my house shifts. Misty finally gets a clue and makes a face.

Keith fishes his keys from his pocket. "I have some paperwork left that I should finish before Kerby skins my ass. Call if you need me, Cath." His expression has smoothed over to that unreadable cop face, the one he uses to hide whatever's going on inside his head. Or his heart.

Misty cringes as he walks out the door. "Shit. I'm sorry. I thought you already filled him in."

I give her a flat look.

"Right. Why would you rush to talk to your best guy friend who's secretly in love with you about another man. Yeah. I'm a little slow sometimes, okay?"

I dart out the door. "Hey, Keith! Wait up!"

He's almost at his car. His feet slow, but it's a long moment before he turns to face me. "What's up, Wright?"

He rarely uses my last name, and when he does, he's usually doing his best to create distance between us.

I don't even know how to approach this. We've never actually addressed any feelings that Keith might have for me.

I finally decide on "I know you're the one who called Brett about coming today. I just wanted to say thanks."

Keith's unreadable gaze shifts to a spot behind me. "It's no big deal, really." And yet I can clearly hear the lie in his voice, I can feel the tension swirling around him. "It's all good. See you later." He turns back toward his car.

"Keith."

"Whatever makes you happy, makes me happy, Cath. *Always*. You know that."

I fight against the prickly ball forming in my throat and the tears forming in my eyes. "You're the best friend I could ever ask for."

He turns back to face me again, his jaw tightening as he nods. "So . . . you and Madden? Is it real?"

"I don't know what it is," I answer honestly. Real for now?

"But you want it to be."

"I don't know." That's a lie. "Yes."

Keith chuckles, dropping his focus to the stones under his boot. "Well, I've never seen you look at a guy like you look at him."

"It's just . . . I'm scared. He's so convinced that this isn't just because I saved his life. What if he's wrong? What if he decides I'm not what he wants?"

Keith offers me a sympathetic smile. "You mean *when* he decides, right? Because you just keep doing everything you can to convince yourself that he will."

I forget sometimes just how well Keith knows me—my fears and my insecurities. "How could he not?"

His gaze roves over my face. He doesn't say anything for a long moment, and then he reaches up to skate his thumb over my cheek-bone, catching the tears as they start to roll.

He lets his hand fall away. "You know what, maybe he will and maybe he won't, but if you don't even try, you'll only have yourself to blame." He hesitates. "You think I'm upset because I can't handle you falling for another guy? Yeah, I'll admit it's hard for me, but that's not what this is about. How many excuses have you come up with already? Let me see . . . Madden's a celebrity and you're a waitress so it'll never work, right? I'm sure Hildy has had something cynical to say that hasn't helped your confidence." He counts on his fingers. "What else? Pho-tographers are a pain in the ass, that's another strike against Madden. Another reason to avoid taking a chance to be happy. With a really decent guy, by the way."

"And you don't think those are valid reasons?"

"I think they're worth considering, sure. But . . ." He takes a step forward. "You keep saying you just want to move on, but I'm beginning to think you don't want to move on at all." He hesitates. "Do you still have a thing for Philips?"

"No!" My anger flares. I can't believe he'd even suggest that.

"Well, then what is it? So it didn't work out and he's a huge asshole, and you got hurt. Get over it already. Everyone else has!" He purses his lips to stop from saying more. I'm glad, because I don't think I want to hear any more hard truths from my best friend right now.

The sound of gravel crunching up the driveway cuts our conver-sation short. It's Jack, on his way home after the gym. I quickly brush away the rest of my tears.

"Singer!" Jack hollers. Sweat runs down his cheek. He's oblivious of the conversation he's just interrupted. "Did you catch the score for the Phillies game?"

"Four-all about ten minutes ago. Did you sprint here all the way from the gym?"

He leans over, his hands resting on his knees. "Uh-huh."

Keith shakes his head as he climbs into his car. "If I catch you drinking my beer again, I'll have your ass charged."

"When are you gonna take me out with you?" Jack asks, smoothly ignoring his reprimand.

"So you can see how little the police actually work? Hell, no."

Keith's chuckle is hollow. "I'll do a couple laps around here later, Cath."

"Thanks." I avert my gaze, the pain of being utterly dissected by my best friend too raw. I quietly watch his taillights as the car rolls down the driveway.

Jack frowns. "What's going on?"

"Nothing."

I'm expecting him to pester me, but then he sees the red Honda in the driveway. "Whose car?"

"Misty's."

His eyes light up.

"No. Jack."

"But—"

"Stick to girls your own age."

"Yeah, yeah . . ." he mutters, climbing the stairs on my front porch. The moment we walk in, my words are forgotten.

"Hey, Misty." That same goofy grin on his face as earlier has appeared again.

"Hey, Jack! I'm sorry I couldn't talk earlier." Her eyes widen as she takes him in, and I see that spark in them that flashes when she's assessing an attractive guy. "How did you get so *huge*?"

I roll my eyes, while his grin grows wider. "My coach is a hard-ass for body conditioning."

"That's not a bad thing." She smiles, her playful confidence unwavering, even in her Diamonds uniform.

"Brenna's waiting for you." I usher him out of my living room with a push, my fingertips coming back damp. "Ugh, gross. Don't get in her bed like that."

"Yeah, yeah . . ." He winks at Misty, that cocky swagger of his emphasized as he disappears.

"Jeez, your brother is—"

"Nineteen."

"Yeah, but—"

"Nineteen."

Misty presses her lips together with frustration. Finally she mutters something that sounds like "fine," as she climbs out of the La-Z-Boy, grabbing her keys and purse. "What happened with Keith?"

"Nothing. He's just worried about me." I'm not about to get into that conversation.

"He's *always* worried about you."

"He's a good friend."

"So am I. See you on Wednesday." She disappears out the door, but not before hissing, "After you've called Brett!"

I sigh.

■ ■ ■

Brenna lies under her covers, one arm around her stuffed dog, a book in hand, a deep perplexed frown on her face. "So why did they give you a key if it doesn't open anything?"

I push her curls off her forehead. "It's just a symbol. It's their way of saying that the town thanks me for saving Brett's life."

"Oh." Seemingly satisfied with that answer—until she sees it again, no doubt—she curls onto her side. "Is Brett going away again?"

"I don't know. We'll see." It depends on me, apparently.

"Does he live far away?"

"A couple of hours. Not so far away." A lot closer than California.

"When will we see him again?"

"I don't know." Misty, Keith, Jack on his way out . . . now Brenna. Good grief, I wouldn't be able to push thoughts of Brett aside even if I wanted to.

"Maybe if you told him you wanted to see him again, he'd come over."

I stifle the urge to correct her and smile instead. "Night, Brenna."

I reach for her lamp to shut it off.

"Mommy?"

I sigh. It was a long day and my patience is wearing thin. "Yes, Brenna."

"Who hurt you?"

So innocently, she moves from Brett to *that*. It takes a moment for me to recover. "What do you mean?"

"Uncle Jack said that someone hurt you a long time ago."

"When did he tell you that?"

"When he was babysitting." She peers up at me. "Who was it?"

Dammit, Jack. "Just someone I knew a long time ago."

"A friend?"

"Sort of."

"Was it a boy or a girl?"

"A boy." *A man.* I *was the girl.*

"How did he hurt you?"

I hesitate. It's too soon to have this conversation; she's too young. "He made me believe things that weren't true."

"He lied to you?"

"Yeah."

"Did you love him?"

"Yeah."

"So that's why you made Brett leave?"

"I didn't *make* Brett leave."

"Uncle Jack says you made him leave."

I struggle to keep my tone casual. "What else did Uncle Jack say?"

She shrugs. "That you really like Brett but you're scared. Actually, he called you a chicken."

What an ass. "What else?"

"Hmm . . ." She looks up as if searching through her thoughts. "That you're blind. But he didn't mean *actually* blind, like you can't see. I can't remember what he meant."

"That I can't see something that's right in front of me?"

"Yeah. That."

I wonder if Jack realizes just how adept his niece has become at regurgitating conversations. "Anything else?" Just so I have all my facts straight before I kill him.

"I don't think so." She pauses, and then states with absolute certainty, "I don't ever want to fall in love with a boy."

I smile. "Yes, you do. Or, you *will* when you're older."

"But what if he hurts me?"

"Then you just try again."

"But *you're* not trying again." There's a hint of accusation in her tone. At least, that's what *I* hear.

"That's . . . different."

"Why?"

I struggle for an answer. "It's not something I can explain right now. Maybe when you're older."

"Is it because you're scared?"

"Yeah." Is it wrong to admit that to your child? I only remember my mother being all-powerful when I was young. She could solve every problem, she knew everything. She was never scared, as far as I was aware. Of course, she must have been. She just never admitted it.

A look of resignation flickers across Brenna's face. "If you're scared, then I'm going to be *really* scared."

A heavy weight settles on my shoulders. "It's okay to be scared." I brush her mop of golden curls off her forehead. "But you won't let that stop you, because you'll be brave."

She scrunches up her face in thought. "Then can't you be brave, too?"

I tried.

It's not worth it.

It's not that easy.

But I haven't tried. Brett *is* worth trying for. And it may not be that easy, but I'm always telling her that the best things in life aren't easy.

What kind of role model have I become for my impressionable young daughter?

"I guess I can be." I sigh. "I just have to figure out how."

She seems to ponder that. "Well, Uncle Jack said that Brett really likes you. So you should just tell Brett that you like him, too."

I smile. "That sounds easy enough."

"And he's nice so you don't have to be scared of him." Her face breaks out in a bright, hopeful grin. "Uncle Jack says he *really* likes it when girls tell him they like him."

I burst out laughing, partly at her innocence, partly at the obnoxious look I can imagine being on my brother's face when he said that. "Night, Brenna." I shut off the light and duck out. And find myself staring at my living room wall as I replay that conversation from every angle, wondering if I said the right things. If I should have handled it differently.

Wondering what kind of example I'm offering my daughter.

A mother who has perpetually sad eyes.

A mother who hides behind her fear.

A mother who has forgotten how to let herself love.

A mother who everyone keeps touting as brave but who isn't, really. Not at all.

And with that, the last threads of uncertainty that held me back today, while sitting with Brett, snap.

My hands are trembling as I type out a message:

My 5 yo said I should tell you I like you.

I can't keep my fingernails from my teeth as I wait for a response. It comes almost immediately.

I like hearing that.

I breathe a sigh of relief and let out a small giggle.

She said you would.

She's smart. Takes after her mom.

Is that what I am? I take a deep breath . . .

I wanted you to kiss me today.

And I let myself plummet.

Chapter 22

■ ■ ■

Have you been to Philly lately?

I'm half smiling, half frowning at Brett's cryptic text as I punch in a food order.

Not in years, why?

Watch the game with me this Saturday?

My heart does a flip.

What game?

Have you heard of a sport called hockey?

I roll my eyes.

But your team isn't playing.

We're cheering for Toronto now.

I smile with understanding. Of course. His dad is Canadian, after all.

Where?

Well, seeing as you're too embarrassed to be seen in public with me, I guess my place.

I struggle not to giggle as I deliver three coffees to Table Twelve, replaying the text conversation that ensued after I finally found the nerve to reach out last night. Brett has a playful sense of humor, and I was treated to it into the early hours.

My phone vibrates in my pocket as I'm waiting for my food.

Is that a no?

Sorry, some of us have to work.

I follow it up with a smiley face and:

I'd love to. Let me see if I can find a sitter.

Bring Brenna. My dad will be here.

Are you sure? She talks a lot.

I think I can handle one chatty little five-year-old girl.

I remember Jack and sigh.

What about a chatty, giant nineteen-year-old boy who will kill me if I don't let him tag along?

Bring him. Donovan will pick you guys up.

He wants to send a car all the way to Balsam for us? I shake my head with a chuckle.

We peasants can drive ourselves.

He knows how to get in and out of the building without people noticing.

I sigh, somehow having let the situation slip my mind. The media has moved on to the next juicy piece of gossip, thankfully, but that doesn't mean a tip or picture wouldn't pull them back to Balsam. Plus, I get the sense that Brett thinks I'll bolt like a skittish cat the second I see a camera pointed at me again.

Leroy bangs on the bell that announces a ready food order, and I jump. Five plates sit on the ledge in front of me. I hadn't even noticed him putting them there.

"Better not let Lou catch you with your head in the clouds." Leroy gives me a knowing smile. I haven't said a word about Brett, but I guess it wouldn't be that hard for them to figure it out. I'm relieved that Misty isn't working. I haven't decided how I'll handle telling her that we're talking, or if I will. After the way she blabbed to Keith last night, I'm just not sure she can keep something like this to herself.

Fine. Gotta get to work. Let me know how your doctor's appointment goes.

I drop my phone into my pocket and plant my feet firmly back in reality.

■ ■ ■

It's almost ten when I hear the front steps creak. I assume it's Jack or Keith.

Until a knock sounds.

Through the blinds, I spy a single figure leaning against crutches, waiting.

A wild rush of butterflies flutters in my stomach. I haven't heard from Brett since lunchtime, before his appointment. And now he's standing on my doorstep.

Wrapping myself in a blanket—not for warmth but rather to cover the threadbare nightshirt I'm wearing—I throw open the door. "Hey, what are you doing here?"

Brett stares down at me through glossy, intense eyes for a long moment before giving his head a slight shake. "I had to see you." He's not smiling.

I peer past him to the front yard. Donovan's SUV is parked out there, blocking the view for any possible lurkers behind Rawley's. But, just to be safe, I usher him inside, the faint scent of beer trailing. "Is everything okay?"

He hesitates for a moment, and then reaches up to twirl a wayward strand of my hair, damp from my shower. The rest of it is piled on top of my head. Finally, the smallest smile curls his lips. "I was always partial to Piglet."

It takes me a moment, but then I let out a small giggle, realizing that I've wrapped myself in a Winnie the Pooh fleece blanket. Of course Brett, even in a pair of jeans and a plain gray T-shirt—fitted just enough to settle over the curves of his broad, sculpted chest—looks like he could be on his way home from a cover shoot.

"I didn't wake you, did I?"

"No, I couldn't sleep." *I was worried when I hadn't heard from you*, I don't add, afraid that would make me sound clingy. I hesitate. "How was the doctor's appointment?"

The hard line of his jaw tenses. "Okay." He reaches up, tentatively, to unfasten my hair clip, releasing the long, damp tendrils to tumble and settle against my bare neck. A shiver runs through me as his finger skates over my skin, as his eyes flicker to my lips. I sense him leaning forward and I inhale sharply.

He freezes, then shifts away.

And I'm left dizzy with anticipation. It takes a few moments to calm my breathing. "Come and sit."

"Good idea." He hobbles over and practically falls into the love seat, pushing his crutches to the side with a quiet "I hate these fucking things." They land on the floor with a noisy clatter.

I wince, my eyes darting to my bedroom, where Brenna sleeps.

"Shit." He closes his eyes and drops his head back. "I'm sorry."

Yeah. Brett's been drinking, and by the looks of it, drinking a lot.

"It's okay," I assure him, but I edge over to close the bedroom door all the way.

"You wouldn't happen to have a beer or anything, would you?"

"As a matter of fact, I have the perfect thing for you." I head to the kitchen to grab a tall glass of water. I do have that last can of Keith's beer in the fridge, but I'm not about to hand it to Brett right now.

"Here."

He smiles as he reaches for the glass, his hand grasping my fingers in the process.

"I'm just going to change into—"

"No. Don't." His gaze skates over my bare legs as he releases a soft exhale, tugging on the blanket to guide me down.

I settle onto the couch next to him, squeezing myself in next to his splayed legs, and quietly watch him drink, the sharp jut of his Adam's apple bobbing with each swallow. The tension radiating off him.

"What happened today?"

He doesn't answer, but the sheen coating his eyes, the way he blinks several times, answers me.

"You know you can tell me anything, right? I would never say a word to anyone."

His muscular chest lifts and drops with a deep breath. "My career could be over."

"But . . ." I frown as the shock of his admission settles over me, as I study the cast on his leg. "Hockey players break bones all the time. Isn't there that one guy who broke his back?" I'm racking my brain to remember what Jack and my dad were arguing about the other night. "I can't remember his name, but he played again."

"The official statement is that they are remaining hopeful but my doctor isn't happy with how it's healing so far."

"What does that even mean? It's only been a month."

"It was a bad break. Several breaks, actually." Brett stares ahead vacantly. "He said that I should prepare myself for the possibility that I won't be able to play like I used to. Maybe not at all. I *could* be walking with a limp for the rest of my life." His voice is full of raw emotion. "I figured I'd be playing for another ten years, but here I am, twenty-six and fucking finished. If I can't play hockey, I don't know what the hell else I'm going to do with my life." His hand lies limp in his lap. "I keep telling people how I'm thankful to be alive and there's more to life than just this game, but right now . . . I feel like my life is over."

My heart throbs for him.

He sounds so lost.

"Does anyone else know?"

"My parents. And now you."

I struggle to find the right thing to say. I don't want to simply dismiss the doctor's words as premature because that won't ease his worry. Sure, I could point out that he's in a good place financially. But I don't think this is about money at all. It's that his entire reality, everything that he has worked so hard for, could be taken from him.

I finally settle on "We're not going to give up hope just yet."

He grunts softly but says nothing, and I feel like I've said the wrong thing. But what *do* you say to a world-class athlete who has worked his entire life to get to where he is, only to have it all end so abruptly? I guess the same thing you say to a doctor who loses use of his hands, or an artist who loses her eyesight.

"I'm so sorry, Brett. If I could fix it for you, I would."

I get a solemn nod in return.

I take the glass from him and settle it on the coffee table, and then I pull his hand into mine, flipping it over so I can draw my finger along the creases. I used to do this same thing with Scott's hands. I remember Scott's hands being smooth and delicate, marred only by the occasional leftover oil paint.

Brett's hands are rough and calloused. His left index finger is slightly bent, as if he broke it and it didn't set properly. They look like hands that have worked hard to help him get to where he is today.

Suddenly, he grasps my hand, turning it to study the lead smeared over my fingers with a frown.

"It's pencil."

"From what?" His gaze drifts to my sketchbook, sitting open on the coffee table. "What is that?"

"Nothing. Just . . . something for Brenna." I lift the cover with my toe, shutting it.

When I turn back, I find Brett staring hard at me. "What?"

"You look incredible tonight."

I can't help the unattractive snort or the grin that follows. "You must be *incredibly* drunk then."

Finally, he smiles. The first real smile that I've seen since he arrived, a dazzling smile that has the power to turn me into a giggling teenager if I allow it to.

A long moment of silence hangs in my little house, as he studies me, as I sense thoughts racing through his mind that he doesn't give voice to.

Finally, he points toward the coffee table. "Tell me about that."

"It's nothing, really. Just a sketchbook."

Leaning forward, he collects the book in his lap and begins flipping through the pages. "The Gingerbread House . . . ?" He studies the old sales listing I kept and tucked into the inside cover. "Seriously, what is this?"

Heat crawls up the back of my neck. "Just a daydream that Brenna and I have had for a while." I tell him about the house down on Jasper Lane with the twinkling Christmas lights. "It's kind of silly, but it got me drawing again after so many years, so that's something."

"That's what you want to do? Own an inn?"

I'm struggling to focus on anything besides his left hand, settled on my thigh, his palm hot against my bare skin, his fingertips splayed, his reach wide. I silently thank God for small miracles—namely, the miracle that I shaved my legs tonight. "It wasn't even about an inn when I first started this. It was a way for me to bring it to life for Brenna. I wanted to show her how to dream. But then the idea grew on me. I think it'd make an amazing little place for tourists to stay." Despite my complicated history with Balsam, my adoration for Jasper Lane has remained unblemished. If I lived there, I feel like I could have an entirely different life.

"Tourism's big around here in the summer, isn't it?" I'm waiting for a hint of mockery in his tone, but there's nothing so far.

"Not just the summer. The local wineries and the festivals draw a good crowd in the fall. And then there's the winter, with the ski hills. I've overheard customers at Diamonds complaining that rooms can be hard to come by, even when you call a year in advance, especially over Christmas. Balsam is really pretty at the holidays."

He pauses on the full sketch I did from memory of what the house looks like in December, the windows trimmed with big wreaths and crimson bows and tiny white lights. I even used vibrant emerald and ruby-red pencil crayons to add a dash of color. "This is amazing. You're really talented."

"Thanks."

"Did you ever think of going to school for this?"

"For a while, yeah." *Until I dropped out.* Shame bubbles inside me. Still possibly my biggest regret is walking down the steps of my high school that last day, knowing I wouldn't be back. "It's hard to get into college with a GED, though." I keep my eyes on my sketchbook and silently pray that he doesn't judge me too harshly for that.

I feel Brett's gaze flicker to me. "He was your art teacher, wasn't he?" I nod.

"And that's why you stopped drawing for all those years?"

Another nod.

Brett slowly flips through the pages, pausing on the small den that I've filled with little tables, adorned with tiny English teacups and white porcelain plates. "Breakfast room?" He reads the title.

"It faces east."

"The morning sun." His finger draws over the yellow-tinged rays that pour through the window.

"It'd be nice, wouldn't it?"

He keeps flipping, stalling over the conservatory off the back that I've sketched, filled with lush green plants and a seating area for reading in the afternoon.

"I added that in."

"And this?"

"There's a two-bedroom in-law suite on the left-hand side. That's where Brenna and I would live." I flip over the page to show the husky sitting in its doghouse. "With Stella, of course."

"Of course." Brett smiles as he keeps going through page after page, of bedrooms and front foyers, and parlors that I've spent hours designing, nothing but intrigue displayed on his face.

"This one's my favorite."

He stops on the two-page sketch of the room on the third floor.

"I love all the slanted ceilings, and there's this giant skylight here. And you can see the lake from the window. I don't know if I'd actually want to rent that part. I think I'd keep it for Brenna and me. There's a separate staircase at the back of the house that takes you all the way up."

He slides his finger over all the built-in bookcases I've drawn. "So, when were you thinking of buying this place?"

I laugh. "I doubt the new owners have any plans for selling it." Last I heard, a wealthy older couple with a large family from the city bought it.

He reaches the last page, closing the cover gently before setting it back down on the coffee table. "It's good to have dreams. Without dreams, we wouldn't have goals. And without goals . . . what's the point of living?" His head falls back, and it stays there, as he stares at my ceiling, his thoughts clearly somewhere far away. There's an air of melancholy hanging over him that I wish I could dissolve for him.

I turn and rest my head next to him, admiring the sharp curve of his throat and the sculpt of his lips for a long moment. Every inch of him is perfect. "I was a high school dropout, sleeping on a couch in my friend's apartment with no job, when I found out I was pregnant. I thought my life was over. I regret a lot of things, but I can't imagine my life without Brenna. She's the good that came from all of it." As much as I love his hand exactly where it is on my thigh, now I lift it to my mouth, pressing my lips against the back of it. Desperate to console him in any way that I can. "Things have a way of working out. They *will* work out for you, Brett. Even if the doctor is right, and you can't play anymore. Something good will come from the bad. It always does. That's how life balances itself out. That's how people keep going."

"*You* came from it." His head rolls to the side, to face me, his glazed eyes drifting over my features, his mouth so close that with just a slight lean, his lips would be grazing mine. "My feelings have never been just about you saving my life. Not since the moment I met you." The words are a beat deep within my chest, his voice having dropped so low. "When I'm looking for a way to say thank you, I send flowers, I give a hug. I don't drive myself crazy thinking about—" His words cut off with a sharp inhale, his hand within mine tensing slightly. Closing his eyes, he slowly breathes out. Finally, he meets my gaze again, his eyes raw and heated, his breaths ragged. "*This* has never been about gratitude, Catherine."

I'm having a hard time breathing.

"Tell me you believe me."

"I believe—"

He steals my last word with his mouth. My brain struggles to process what's happening. There's no mistaking it for simple friendly affection this time. Brett Madden is kissing me. Or *trying* to kiss me, because I'm frozen.

And when the shock finally wears off, I accept that I want this—and Brett—more than I've ever wanted *anyone* before.

He begins to pull away. "I'm sorry. I shouldn't have—"

I press forward, stealing his words as swiftly as he took mine, my fingers reaching for his cheek, the lightest coating of stubble tickling my skin. And just as I was frozen a moment ago, he now is, too. For a fleeting second I'm afraid I've missed my chance, I've screwed things up.

And then he moves in quickly, his hand grasping the back of my head, his tongue slipping along my lips, coaxing my mouth open. Darting in to lick me with expert strokes, the flavor of beer teasing my taste buds. I sense an urgency in him, as if he *needs* this. And maybe he does after the sobering news he received today. That he thought to come here, that he *needed* to come here . . .

I silently allow myself to accept that this man truly wants me, for however long that may be.

I've lost my grip on my blanket, now pooling half on the floor, my ratty nightshirt climbing high on my hip as I press against Brett's warm body. That body that I've been dying to touch. My hand begins to drift and explore, shyly at first, from his cheek to his neck, my fingers trailing along his hard curves as he kisses me deeply and with complete abandon. His breath hitches as I reach his chest, pressing my palm against where his heart now beats frantically.

I remember the feel of high school boys, their skin still soft, their bodies still developing.

I remember Scott Philips', a man's body, with definition and a coating of hair over his chest.

Brett feels altogether different, unreal. A sculpture of honed muscle and hard work flexing beneath my fingertips.

He breaks free just long enough to give me *that* look . . . that heated gaze that sends a thrill through my body and wipes all thoughts clear from my head. I don't actually say the word "okay," but he must be able to sense it because in one surprisingly quick movement, Brett has hooked a hand under my knee and is hoisting me with little effort onto his lap to straddle him.

"Your leg," I whisper against his mouth, afraid I'll hurt him.

"Fuck my leg," he growls, pulling me close against him, stretching my thighs wide, until my chest is flush against his and his arms are wound around me, and I can feel him hard against me. God, it's been *so long* since I felt that.

And every day of every year of being without has been worth it, for this very moment with Brett.

His hands stretch across my back, fingers splayed, holding me tight, making me feel slight within their impressive span. I can't help the intentional way I grind my hips, the deep throb beginning to stir within me. That earns a soft curse from his lips. A simple, common curse that is so sensual coming from him, his voice vibrating deep within me, making me moan against his mouth.

He tugs at my nightshirt, the hem bunched within his fists. "This is the softest thing I've ever felt," he murmurs against my lips.

"I should have thrown it out about three years ago," I whisper.

So smoothly, his fingers slip beneath my nightshirt just as his lips slide from mine, trailing along the hard line of my jaw, my breath trembling as I feel the first strokes of heat skating across my neck. "Don't. I'm enjoying what I can see through it."

I inhale sharply as his calloused hands skate upward in one smooth, agonizingly slow stroke, tickling my rib cage and memorizing the flat plane of my stomach.

I swallow against my self-conscious worry that my breasts aren't enough for him—I've seen the kinds of girls he dates—but still I tense the moment his thumbs draw over them, slowly outlining their subtle shape.

He must notice my wariness because his hands pause where they are, as if to allow me to get used to his touch. "You're perfect. You know that, right?" When I don't answer, he pulls back, just far enough to meet my eyes, his nose nuzzling against mine affectionately. "I wouldn't want to change one single thing about you. Ever."

My heart pounds in my chest. He must be able to feel it with his hand against me, the pad of his thumb now moving again, sliding softly back and forth over my nipple.

I catch his lips and we're locked again, his hands drifting, circling around to my back, gaining a strong hold of my body so he can pull me tighter. I let my own hands explore again, more confidently this time, down that strong, thick neck that leads to an even more impressive collarbone peeking through his shirt. I fist his shirt as he fisted mine, wishing it were off, wishing I could feel his warm skin against mine.

I break free of his mouth and lean back far enough to push his shirt up, exposing the ridges of his hard stomach and chest, heaving and caving with each labored breath. "Oh, my God. You're . . ." I take in his golden skin, speckled with goose bumps, his nipples peaked. He is the most perfect human being I've ever seen, and he wants *me.*

His grip on my hips tightens as my eyes follow that small trail of dark hair from his belly button, downward, imagining my fingers slipping below his belt. Even if I couldn't already feel him against me, the ridge in his jeans is blatantly obvious.

I press my hips into him again, a moan escaping me with the delicious friction.

"Cath." Warning shines in his eyes, his breathing shaky.

I grind against him again, the ache deep inside me so consuming, I no longer care that we're on my couch in my living room, or that this may have gotten out of hand.

"Dammit . . ." His fingers coil around the sides of my panties, tugging on them threateningly.

"Mommy?"

The one word, spoken in a sleepy voice, is like a cold bucket of ice water dumped over both of us.

Brett's fingers loosen their grip a split second before I scuttle off his lap, his shirt falling to cover him just as Brenna staggers from her room, rubbing balled-up fists over her eyes.

"Shit," I whisper between ragged breaths, hoping she's still too drowsy to process what she might have seen. Hoping I can get her back to sleep before she fully wakes. "I'll be back in a minute." I climb off the couch.

"Brett?" She asks sleepily.

I sigh. *Great.*

"Hey, Brenna." He seems to have sobered up almost immediately.

"What're you doing here?"

"Visiting your mom. I had a rough day and I wanted to see her."

"Back to sleep, Brenna." With my hands on her shoulders, I try to gently steer her toward her room.

She wriggles free, wandering over to the couch, the bottoms of her pajamas slightly too large and sagging in that adorable way. She studies his cast. "Does your leg still hurt?"

He frowns, following her gaze. "Not as much as it used to. I'm trying not to think about it, though."

"Why? Does it make you sad?"

He nods.

"You should think about things that make you happy. That's what I do when I'm sad."

It's jarring, hearing words I've said over and over again repeated in her child's voice.

Brett regards her for a long moment, an unreadable expression on his face. "What do you think about?"

She doesn't miss a beat. "My dog, Stella. I don't have her yet, but I will one day."

A smile slowly stretches across Brett's face. "A dog named Stella would make me happy, too. What else?"

I should be stopping this, getting her back to bed—God knows it'll take forever now that her brain is firing—but it's impossible not to simply stand back and watch the way Brett is with her, so genuine and natural.

"Umm . . . Uncle Jack . . . ," she picks through her thoughts, "ice cream, books, my dolls, waffles . . ."

Brett's trying hard not to laugh. "In that order?"

"Yeah. Oh," she giggles, "I almost forgot, my mom."

"Yeah, she makes me happy, too." His gaze flickers to me, a secretive glint in them. "But you should get back to bed. It's late."

"Say good night, Brenna."

She sways with a touch of hesitation before climbing onto the couch and wrapping her arms around his neck. "Good night."

Brett stalls, unable to hide the momentary surprise from his brow. But when he curls an arm around her body, cocooning her against him, I'm pretty sure my heart is about to explode in my chest.

It takes me a moment to gather myself and usher her back to bed. Thankfully, she doesn't argue when I tell her I can't leave Brett alone. She simply rolls onto her side and closes her eyes.

I emerge to find Brett on his feet, maneuvering around the coffee table on his crutches. He's heading toward the door. "So, when do kids actually start sleeping through the night?"

I sigh, trying to hide my disappointment that he's leaving. "When you parent them properly. I've created a monster. But I've never minded it. Until now." I step closer to smooth my hand over the top of his T-shirt, offset just a touch. "It's probably a good thing, though, that she got up when she did."

"I didn't come here, looking for *that*, I swear. I don't want you to think that."

"I don't think that at all." But what must Brett think of me? That I would so easily climb onto his lap, so quickly press against him. "I'm not usually so . . . It's been a really long time for me," I blurt out. Since I've been with a man. Since I've trusted a man.

He says nothing for a long moment, simply stroking my hair off my face with a gentle touch. "How long?"

"Since Brenna's father."

His brows lift in mild surprise.

"What?"

"No. It's not bad." He takes a deep breath. "I shouldn't have come, not when I've been drinking."

My hand drifts to his chest to rub against his curves. "I'm glad you came." And more than anything right now, I wish he could stay. But that's not an option, not with Brenna.

He seizes my fingers, holding them over his heart, letting me savor the strong, steady thrum. "I should go."

"Okay." My body still hums with the thrill of being pressed against him.

He leans down to kiss me, his soft, wet lips coaxing mine to move with them in a languid, intimate dance. Slowly, he pulls away, just enough to settle his forehead against mine, our noses grazing each other. "I *really* should go."

My giggle is playful as I take a step back.

"And don't you dare get rid of that." His gaze drifts over my worn nightshirt, stalling on my chest before dipping farther down to study my thighs.

I blush furiously. "You *really* should go."

His face splits into a grin.

"Here, let me get the door for you." With my hand on the door-knob, I hesitate. I don't want to remind him of it, but I'm sure he hasn't forgotten. "I'm sorry about the news today. But nothing's for sure yet."

His jaw tenses with his nod.

Leaning in, he leaves one last, lingering kiss on my lips. "Night, Cath."

"Night."

I watch from the window as the taillights of the SUV disappear down the lane.

And I can't keep myself from smiling.

Chapter 23

∎ ∎ ∎

"Did I ever tell you that you're my favorite sister?" Jack grins at me from his side of the black SUV before letting his gaze drift out the window to the city that approaches. "But don't tell Emma. I'll probably need a free lawyer one day."

"Why does he have a gun, anyway?" Brenna asks loudly, and it takes me a second to realize she's talking about Donovan. She's been glued to the Disney movie on the little TV screen since we left home, headphones channeling the audio.

"For safety. He's also a bodyguard," Jack says.

"What?" she yells, then grins and pulls her headphones off. "What did you say?"

He repeats himself, adding, "The other guys had guns, too, remember?"

"They were bodyguards? I thought they were just workers."

"They worked at being bodyguards."

"Oh." I can tell she wants to ask more, but, quickly distracted by the movie, she slides her headphones on again and goes back to watching.

"You gotta admit, this is pretty sweet." Jack's trying to play it cool, but his long jean-clad leg is bobbing with excitement.

It *is* nice, I silently admit, to be picked up and taken all the way to downtown Philadelphia in a nice, clean, roomy SUV, not having to worry about the city congestion or parking or navigating the one-way streets. I've been to Philadelphia maybe a handful of times and not usually right downtown. That's where Brett lives, in a condo along the Delaware River, about a ten-minute drive from the arena according to Donovan.

I'm dying to see his place. A home can tell you a lot about a person. My home would tell you that I don't have a lot of money but I take pride in finding the possibilities in the unexpected. A rickety library cart for a side table. A worn and weathered door frame that I turned into a standing mirror. A paint-splattered wooden ladder that Keith helped me mount horizontally onto the wall to use for books.

Many times over the past weeks, I've wondered what Brett's world looks like. Where he lives, where he sleeps, where he likes to unwind. Soon, I'll know.

"Why is he wearing a suit?" Brenna suddenly hollers.

I meet Donovan's eyes in the rearview mirror for just a flash before he shifts them back to the highway and the sea of taillights, but I don't catch a reaction, one way or another.

I lift one side of her headphones. "I guess he likes wearing suits. Stop yelling, please."

"You should have heard Dad today, when I told him. I think he was bitter he didn't get an invite, too," Jack says.

"He's getting season tickets for the next twenty-five years. Plus, I couldn't very well bring Dad and not Mom." And there's no way in hell I'm subjecting Brett to that, yet.

"Just think, if you and Madden ever get hitched, you could probably get tickets to any Cup game you want."

I shoot a glare at my brother, acutely aware that Donovan can hear us, even though he's pretending not to listen. I would die if he went and told Brett that I was talking marriage on the way over. "You've been reading too many fairy tales with Brenna. No one's marrying anyone."

The radio fills the silence for a dragging moment.

"But imagine if you *did* marry—*ow!*" Jack rubs the spot behind his ear where I just flicked him. After a few seconds he mumbles softly, "Still my favorite sister."

"Right." I sigh, letting my gaze drift out over the sea of buildings that we're approaching. This was supposed to be my life. Living in a big city, going to college, having a cool job. Seven years later, I'm still in Balsam with no life goals beyond paying my bills each month and making sure Brenna is cared for. I'm beginning to fear that I'll turn a corner one day and find half my life gone—Brenna grown up and moving out, and me, still in that little cottage rental behind the pool hall and serving greasy breakfasts and Leroy's famous burgers. I can only regret so much, though, because this city world I dreamed for myself didn't include Brenna.

I frown at the horizon ahead of us. "Are they calling for rain later?"

"There's a big storm system moving in," Donovan replies, his voice a deep rumble. "Supposed to last into the night."

I eye the dark clouds. "I'm glad you'll be driving, then."

Brenna leans over. "Mommy?"

"Yes?"

She glances at Donovan and then back to me, to whisper, "Why doesn't he have a neck?" Only it's not a whisper because of those damn headphones.

Jack covers his bark of laughter with a strangled choking sound.

My face burns as I shoot her that look—the one that says, "Don't ask questions like that"—and she ducks her head. When I finally dare glance ahead, I see Donovan smiling.

■ ■ ■

We pull up beside a service elevator in the underground parking garage of Brett's building. A man with a handlebar mustache and a kind smile is waiting there with a special key. He introduces himself as the manager and spends the next twenty-four floors talking odds of the Leafs winning the cup with Jack, who of course knows every stat on every player. I glean what I can so I don't seem completely clueless—Toronto and LA are playing, they're tied two games apiece, and Toronto hasn't won a Cup in fifty years—and then I let my attention drift to my surroundings.

Brett's building is basically what I expected—new and luxurious. Outside, it's one of those all-glass high-rises, towering over the surrounding buildings with the river in easy sight. Inside, it's sleek and modern, with long, well-lit hallways lined with extra-tall mahogany doors on either side.

As we reach the end of the hall, Donovan rings a doorbell.

"You're squeezing my hand too tight!" Brenna whines.

"Sorry." I take a deep breath to try and calm the butterflies thrashing in my stomach.

The door opens to a smiling Richard. He shifts back, giving us room to step into the simple all-white foyer. "We'll give you a call later," he says to Donovan, dismissing him.

Someone shuffling sounds from inside.

"Just stay put! I'll bring them in," Richard hollers, winking at

Brenna and taking Jack's hand in a firm handshake. "Good to see you again, Jack. You know, last we talked I didn't realize you played for the Gophers."

"Yes, sir." Jack's cheeks flush. I know what he's thinking—for Richard to know that, Brett must have said so, which means his idol was talking about Jack.

"Go on in, both of you. Brett's just over there, resting on the couch." He smiles at me. "I'm so glad to see you again, Catherine. Meryl will be happy to hear that you're here." There's a flicker of something in his eyes. I can't read it entirely, but I'm fairly certain it's positive. At least I hope it is. I didn't quite realize until just now how much it matters that Brett's parents approve of this thing between Brett and me.

I drop my voice. "How is he?" Brett and I have talked every day, mostly via text, but our conversations have been light. Flirty. I haven't broached the subject beyond the ambiguous "How are you feeling, today," to which he hasn't elaborated beyond "alive." As if that's all he has to hold on to, in all of this.

Richard shrugs. "He's trying. It doesn't help being cooped up. I've tried to keep his mind busy with our charity stuff, and I managed to get him out a few times. You know, to lift weights at the gym, or just enjoy the good weather by the river, but . . . I'm glad you're here." Ushering me in with a hand laid ever so gently on my shoulder, he leads me around the corner.

My breath catches at the sight of Brett, stretched out on a brown leather sectional, his leg propped up on pillows on top of a rectangular coffee table.

His intense gaze locks on me and he says nothing for three . . . four . . . five seconds before giving his head a small shake. "I'm sorry I didn't get up to meet you at the door. Or get dressed." He gestures at his long, lean body clad in a soft black Flyers T-shirt and black track pants.

And here I was, just thinking how appealing he looks, his hair falling back in a natural wave, his jawline hard and shapely, his blue eyes genuine and bright. The scar across his forehead is impossible to miss and yet I barely notice it. "It's okay. You have a pretty good excuse."

This man wants me.

And the last time I saw him, he was kissing me with abandon, leaving my lips tender for days, and the rest of my body envious. I'm desperate to feel the press of his mouth against me once again. But I stay where I am, whether it's because of the audience, my impressionable daughter, or I'm suddenly feeling shy around him.

"My mom bought that for today." Brenna points at the short black jumpsuit I grabbed at Threads just yesterday, after having admired it on the mannequin while shopping last weekend. The silk material is soft against my skin; the style loose but flattering—a one-piece slip on, cinched at the waist by a silk tie, the top sleeveless with a deep-V cut into both front and back, the shorts showing off a lot of thigh but not too much. It's classy and stylish, something my wardrobe sorely lacks.

I feel my face redden as Brett does a lightning-quick scan, stalling over my bare legs, before turning back to give Brenna his attention. He smiles. "She looks very nice."

"Yeah. She does," Brenna says in that casual way of hers. "Did you know that my uncle plays hockey, too?"

"I did. We met last week, remember?" Brett reaches forward to shake hands with my brother, who's desperately trying to play it cool.

Brenna wanders over to a glass case in the corner of the room that houses Brett's plaques and trophies, her backpack still slung over her shoulders. Brett's eyes are on her the entire time, an unreadable look in them. "Did you win all these?"

"I did."

She nods slowly to herself, and then her rich brown eyes roam over the rest of the living room. I let mine roam along with hers.

Brett's condo is nothing like I imagined.

"Modest" would be the word I might use for it. It's a corner unit and double the size of my house, easily, but I assumed it would be bigger. Also, it's sparse. The glass case is really the only personal touch I see. The place is simple and clean. The main area is open with a high ceiling over the living room. A loft overlooks us, with an industrial-looking set of metal stairs leading up. Everything is light—white walls with only two pictures hanging on them, soft gray curtains to block out an impressive view of the river, should they be pulled closed. To be honest, it looks like Brett just moved in. Or that living here is only temporary.

Richard heads into the adjoining sizable kitchen—with white marble countertops and stainless steel appliances—and opens the fridge. "I'm gonna order pizza in a minute. Can I offer anyone drinks? Water, beer, wine . . . I was sent out for some SunnyD for the little lady."

Brenna's face squishes up. "The orange stuff? That's for my mom."

Oh, Brenna. My face barely had time to cool down.

The sound of Brett's laugh carrying through the place *almost* makes up for my embarrassment.

"Where's your bathroom?" *So I can drown myself in the toilet.*

Brett points to the hall on the far side. "First door."

"Get your coloring kit out of your backpack," I instruct Brenna on my way past her, adding in a whisper, "and stop telling him all my secrets."

Brett's chuckle follows me all the way to a small but clean bathroom. The décor is as generic as the rest of the condo. Not that I wouldn't take Brett's place in a heartbeat. I would just put some personality into it.

Then again, he *is* a guy, I remind myself. A guy who travels a lot and is probably not sitting in Philly all summer in the off-season.

I do a quick check of myself, thankful that Lou let me take off a few hours early from work today. The beachy waves that Misty taught me how to put in my hair with the curling iron are holding well, as is the subtle smoky eye makeup I worked on for almost a half hour.

Brenna's little voice chirps from the living room. "I've seen you on the TV."

"Well, I *am* on TV, sometimes."

"No, but like *all* the time. We have this thing. If you press the red button, it'll tape what you're watching onto these big black tapes."

Oh, no.

"A DVR?" I hear Brett ask.

"Yeah. I mean, no."

"Sounds more like a VCR," Richard offers.

"People still use those?"

"In case you haven't noticed, my sister is ghetto," I hear Jack mutter.

I leave the bathroom in a rush.

"My mom taped a lot of shows with you on them. She watches them *every single* night after I go to—"

"Brenna!" I exclaim rather loudly, cutting her off, my cheeks burning bright. I spear Jack with a glare for not putting a muzzle on her sooner, but he grins wider, tipping his bottle of beer in the air toward me. Bastard. He knows I won't pull a Hildy Wright and take it away.

Brenna looks up from her spot on the couch next to Brett, her coloring kit scattered on the coffee table. "Yeah, Mommy?"

I sigh. She's just so innocent, I can't be angry with her. "Make sure you don't accidentally bump Brett's leg, okay? You'll hurt him."

"I *know*."

I can avoid Brett's gaze for only so long before I feel compelled to meet it.

"The drive over was fine?" he asks casually, as if my daughter didn't just basically make me look like a crazy woman who sits in her living room and watches tapes of him late into the night.

I clear my throat. "Yeah, it was great. But did you know there's a big storm coming in? I feel bad for making Donovan drive in it tonight."

"We'll wait it out. Come, sit." He points at the tall glass of SunnyD sitting on the coffee table, right beside him, a knowing grin touching his lips.

I settle in, wondering exactly how much space I should leave between us.

"Hey, Jack and Brenna, come and help me pick out a few pizzas here," Richard calls out.

Brenna's on her feet and running toward the kitchen before Jack even has a chance to finish his sip.

"Brenna likes broccoli and sardines," he teases, earning her shriek of disgust and my laugh. It's all so comfortable, so easy. And, I think, as Brett lifts an arm up and over my shoulders, intentional on Richard's part.

Brett pulls me into his chest in a hug. "I'm glad you came," he whispers, his lips grazing my cheek.

I inhale the scent of his cologne and sigh, my blood stirring instantly. My fingers toy with the hem of his soft cotton T-shirt, desperate to slide under, to graze the chiseled plane of his stomach again. "I missed you." I thought it would be hard for me to admit that out loud, but the words just slip out.

He pulls away just a touch and his aqua-blue eyes drift downward toward my mouth. I lean in, desperate for a kiss.

"One with chicken, Cath?" Jack hollers, startling me.

I sit back and clear my throat. And silently curse my brother. "If you'll eat some, too."

"You know I will." Jack will eat anything.

Brett shifts to his original spot and settles his hand on his thigh, his pinky stretched just far enough to drag along my bare skin, teasing me mercilessly.

"He's having a great year, huh?" Jack wanders over, tipping his bottle to the TV screen, where they're showing highlights of Toronto's team captain.

"Incredible year. He stole three goals from me at my last game against them." Brett turns the volume up.

They start talking about points and assists, and plus-minus scores, things I don't understand and am not going to pretend to. I'm glad I brought Jack, though. It makes this feel that much more low-key. I sit and quietly listen, observing as Brenna colors her book, and Richard fills bowls with chips and popcorn and other snacks, and everyone waits for the game to start. No cameras, no media, no stress. No talk of heroes and saving lives.

And I let myself imagine us doing this all the time.

■ ■ ■

"No, no, no . . ."

"Pass it!"

"Get it out of there!"

Brett, Richard, and Jack are all yelling at the TV as the little clock in the corner counts down the last seconds of the third period. Much like they've been doing for the past two and a half hours. I was afraid I wouldn't know what to talk about during the game, that conversation would be stalled, but there's been very little conversation at all. Just a lot of hollering and cheering.

And yet it's easily been one of the best nights of my life.

When the clock expires, Toronto has squeaked by with a one-point win. There's a pile of sweaty hockey players crashing into each other on the ice, Richard is on his feet, congratulating them all through the TV, Jack is twirling a sluggish but giggling Brenna around in the air, and Brett is quietly contemplative, an odd mix of resignation and happiness on his face.

I give his thigh a gentle squeeze. "Next year, it'll be yours."

He answers that with a tight smile before seemingly shrugging it off, draping his arm casually over the back of the couch behind me. "I still can't believe this is the first hockey game you've watched from beginning to end. That's appalling, actually."

I merely shrug, earning his headshake and chuckle.

Brenna frees herself from Jack's grip and crawls onto the couch beside me. "I'm tired."

I can't help the small sigh of frustration that escapes. I don't want the night to end. It's only nine thirty, but we have a long drive and Brenna's been curled up on the couch in her pajamas for the past half hour, the built-up excitement of coming here tonight having finally worn her down.

"You and me both, kid." Richard stretches his arms over his head. His gaze drifts to the wall of window, where rain is drizzling against the glass. The storm doesn't seem to be in any rush, though; the bursts of lightning are slowly becoming brighter, the rumbles of thunder only now beginning to grow deeper and more frequent. Heavy rain warnings have scrolled across the bottom of the screen repeatedly, advising motorists in the Philadelphia area to stay off the roads for the evening. "Looks like you're stuck for a while, at least. Why don't you take my spot right over here where there's lots of room?"

Richard stretches a gray knit blanket over Brenna, who has slithered over and settled in comfortably. He gives the top of her head a playful rub to mess her hair. "You know, there's a free room upstairs, if you'd rather just stay the night." Kind gray eyes peer to me. "Probably a better idea than dragging her home so late tonight."

Stay overnight? Here? With Brett? My heart begins to race. And his dad, Brenna, and Jack, I remind myself. "Thank you. I guess we'll see how the storm is." I climb to my feet. "But just in case we go, I should say goodbye now." Brett said that Richard was flying home to California on Thursday.

I'm about to offer my hand when Richard pulls me into a tight hug that lasts a good five seconds. Oddly enough, it feels natural. "We will see you again, and soon," he assures me. "Need anything before I turn in, Brett?"

Brett declines with a thanks.

Giving Jack a firm handshake, Richard disappears down the hall.

"Hey, Cath?" Jack is pulling on his jacket, his eyes on his phone. I'm still amazed by how much he's grown. "I'm actually going to head out. I've got a friend from school who wants to meet up."

"Out in that storm?"

"It's just a few blocks away."

I shouldn't be surprised. I half expected him to ditch us at some point. When you're nineteen years old and single, why go back to a sleepy town when you're in the city on a Saturday night? "Okay. But what about getting home?"

He shrugs nonchalantly. "She said she'd drive me tomorrow."

"*She*. Uh-huh." I roll my eyes. "Just don't forget to text Mom to let her know not to expect you."

He groans. "Nine months of freedom and now I'm back to doing that."

Brett chuckles. "Don't miss those days."

"Tell me about it. Listen, it was amazing hanging out with you." Jack leans in and clasps hands with Brett. "If you're gonna be around this summer and on the ice, I'd love to get out with you."

"Definitely." Brett smiles, but I sense him stiffen. My chest pangs for him.

"Talk to you tomorrow, Cath?"

"Call me if you get into trouble. But don't get into trouble."

He leans down to kiss the top of my head. "Night, favorite sis."

"Be *safe*," I tell him, watching him gently ruffle Brenna's hair and then saunter out the door.

And now it's just the three of us.

Brett turns the volume down on the TV until it's just a low murmur. He watches Brenna closely. "Will that bother her? Should I turn it off?"

"That kid can curl up in a booth at Diamonds and fall asleep within minutes. The noise actually puts her to sleep." A crack of thunder sounds and her little body jolts slightly. "Though *that* might wake her up if it gets worse."

Brett's warm hand drags lazily over my bare thigh, one of many fleeting touches and gentle nudges he's stolen tonight, when attention wasn't on us.

Does he realize what he's doing to me?

My heart feels like it's about to explode in my chest.

"Sounds like my dad. He'll be out cold and snoring within thirty seconds of his head hitting the pillow. My mom's convinced he's narcoleptic."

I steady my shaky breathing, trying to shift my focus from climbing onto Brett's lap right here—with my daughter five feet away—to Richard. "I like your dad a lot. He just seems so . . . *normal*."

Brett's eyebrows quirk. "And that surprises you?"

"Yes. I mean, no! I mean . . ." Ugh, I sound like an idiot. "I feel like I might run into him at the grocery store on a Tuesday afternoon and, if I did, we could talk about . . . I don't know . . ." A crack of thunder sounds. "The weather. Or the news, or . . . you know, *normal* stuff."

Brett squeezes my thigh, his skin hot against mine. "I knew what you meant. I just like seeing you get flustered."

"That's not funny," I mock-protest, even though I'm smiling. I poke him in the ribs, my finger digging into hard muscle. He doesn't even flinch, grabbing my hand and holding it for two . . . three . . . four seconds before his eyes flicker to Brenna.

With a heavy sigh, he lets go. "My dad's the best. He kept me and Michelle grounded while we were growing up. Not saying that my mom's not great, too. It's just that her life is insane. She gets recognized everywhere. She can't go out without her bodyguard."

"How does she deal with it?"

"A lot better than my dad does. He hates the cameras. He hates Hollywood. But they don't bother with him anymore, because he doesn't give them anything worth reporting about. He actually wants to move east again. He's been working on my mom for a while now. She was holding out, but since the accident . . ." He shrugs. "He thinks she'll give in soon. Plus, Michelle got that role so she's moving to Miami. My mom and her are really close. They do everything together."

What must that be like, I wonder, a spark of envy flaring inside. "You guys lived in Canada for a while, didn't you?"

"Yeah." He sighs, smiling. "Feels like so long ago. But it was the best thing they could ever have done for us. I got the coaching and the competition that I couldn't get anywhere else. At least, not in California."

Another crack of thunder sounds. The rain is pelting against the glass in sheets now, the wind picking up. Yet inside Brett's condo, curled against his side, listening to the dull rasp of his voice as my daughter snores softly nearby, I couldn't feel more at ease. "How long were you there for?"

"Until I was fifteen and my sister was fourteen. Then we moved to New York. It was just him a lot of the time, with my mom off filming somewhere. He took me to every practice, every game. He built a rink in our backyard every winter, just so I could practice more." Brett shakes his head. "My dad sacrificed everything for all of us. For my mom, so she could have her career and I'd have a shot at the NHL, and my sister could chase after what she wanted, which turns out to be acting, too."

"He sounds like an incredible father." I think mine would have been, too, had circumstances been different. I see the closeness between him and Jack. And there's definitely a shift in my relationship with him in recent years. I actually feel like I'm starting to have one.

"He is." Brett's brow tightens. "It kills me that, after all that, that he has to sit here and watch another team in the play-offs."

"Meanwhile, all he's thinking about is how happy he is that he gets to sit and watch a game with you." Every time I think of Brett not surviving that accident, an uncomfortable burn blossoms in my chest. It's unbearable to even imagine.

Brett sighs. "I know you're right. I have to just shut up and get over it. I'm sure Seth would rather be alive and sitting on this couch right now." His jaw tenses.

Somehow, in all the hype around Brett and me, Seth Grabner's death became a quiet, accepted loss for the media, fading to only a line mention within weeks. Instead, they've chosen to focus on the miraculous part of the story—how Brett survived in the first place. Seth's story is finished, over. A tragedy but an unfortunate death due to his own carelessness, I've heard many times over.

Even I'm guilty of settling my focus almost immediately on Brett—and myself, selfishly.

I rest my hand over where his sits on my lap. "You were good friends, weren't you?"

A sad smile curls his lips. "When we first met, he was playing for Tampa and I was playing for the Bruins. He would ride my ass on the ice. Every pass, every block, every goal, he was on me, ready to fuck it"—Brett glances at Brenna—"to take my chance away. No one's ever pressed me like him." He chuckles softly. "I wanted to punch the bastard in the face. And then the Flyers brought me on and, a year later, him. We were in sync from the first day on the ice. I can't imagine playing without him now." He picks at the label of his beer bottle, the one he's nursed through the entire night. "His girlfriend came by yesterday."

"That must have been hard."

"She pretty much sat here and cried on me the entire time." His throat bobs with a hard swallow.

"Were they together long?"

He shrugs. "Four months? Maybe five? I don't know. But he wasn't the type to stick to one girl for more than a few weeks, so I knew she meant something to him."

What about you? I don't say the words out loud, but I can't help think them. Sure, he was with Courtney for a year, but there was plenty of time when he wasn't tied down, and a guy like him—with his looks and his money and his social status—must have had his pick of the prettiest puck bunnies throwing themselves at him after games. I've learned all about those, thanks to my brother, who for some reason thinks it's completely normal to phone up his older sister and fill her in on his college escapades.

I don't see Brett being the type to bring home a random girl for the night, but I could be way off. It may feel like I know him, but I don't yet, not really.

I desperately want to, though.

Beside us, Brenna lets out a small snore. Brett shifts his gaze to her for a long moment. Into the lingering silence, he finally says, so softly, "Can I ask you something?"

My stomach tightens with anxiety. "Yeah."

I feel his eyes on my profile. "Does she ever ask about her dad?"

Somehow, I just knew it would have to do with Brenna's father. "Sometimes."

"And what do you tell her?"

I hesitate. "What am I supposed to tell her?"

Brett frowns, shakes his head. "Sorry, I just . . . I was thinking how hard it must have been for you, to be alone and raising a kid so young."

"It's always just been her and me. That's what she knows. That's what *I* know." I study her peaceful face. "And I try to give her double the love to make up for anything she may be missing."

"Could you get child support from him, at least? Is he still in prison?"

"I'd have to give him rights to her, and there's no way I'm doing that." Just the thought of having to share Brenna makes me uneasy.

Brett's becoming adept at reading me. "You really don't like talking about it, do you?"

"No."

The first real uncomfortable silence hangs over us, and suddenly I find myself itching for escape. "The storm doesn't seem as bad as they made it out to be. We should probably think about going."

"I don't want you to leave." I turn to meet earnest blue eyes. "Take my room. Don will drive you tomorrow."

"Where will you sleep, then?"

"I've been in a spare room since I came home. The stairs are a pain in the ass."

My gaze wanders from the metal staircase that would be a nightmare with crutches, to Brenna's sleeping body, to the steady pour of rain against the windowpane—the storm is probably just as bad as they made it out to be—back to Brett, who's patiently waiting for my answer.

"Look at her. She's so warm and comfortable. You're not going to make her sit on a cold leather backseat for hours in a storm, being jolted and bumped, risking her life. She'll wake up confused and afraid. She might not fall back asleep again for hours."

Brenna is the easiest car-to-bed transport ever, but I'm not about to tell Brett that because I like that he's making it so easy for me to say yes for smart, responsible, nonhormonal reasons. I glance down at my outfit. "I didn't really come prepared."

"Borrow one of my shirts."

Sleeping in Brett's bed and wearing his clothes. *With my daughter*, I remind myself. But still. Not how I saw tonight going.

A million times better, actually.

"Okay?"

Those dimples settle deeply into his cheeks with his smile. "Okay."

I nod, suddenly overwhelmed by the very idea of an entire night with him.

"Let me call Don. Can you manage bringing her upstairs? I would but—"

"Don't be silly." I chuckle, even as I'm hit with the mental image of my daughter in Brett's arms and my heart stutters.

"There should be some extra toothbrushes and clean towels in the bathroom. And don't worry, my dad changed the sheets."

Is it wrong that I'm disappointed, hearing that?

I feel Brett's eyes on me as I scoop up Brenna's tiny, hot body. It used to be so easy to move her, but I'm finding it's getting more and more difficult. My arms are straining by the time I reach the top of the staircase.

Brett's bedroom is on the small side, and as sleek and neat as the rest of his place, with a view of Philadelphia from two sides, though the curtains are already drawn. I don't spend too much time there, just long enough to tuck her into the king-size bed and make sure she isn't going to stir. A loud crack of thunder sounds as I'm sneaking down the staircase, and I cross my fingers that she doesn't wake in a panic.

Brett's not in the living room, so I take the time to clean up, collecting and loading the dirty dishes into the dishwasher, and then head for the bathroom.

A low voice from the cracked bedroom door catches my ear, stalling my steps.

"No . . . I don't care . . . No . . ." Brett's voice carries that rare edge. "Give them whatever they want to keep them quiet. I don't want this getting back to her."

Unease settles into my spine as I replay his words. That can't be Donovan that he's speaking to. Who needs to be kept quiet? About what? And what doesn't he want getting back to "her"?

"No, they're not getting a fucking dime of this . . . I don't care . . . Just let me know when it's done, okay? I've gotta go."

I close the bathroom door quickly, before he catches me eavesdropping.

When I step out a few minutes later, Brett is just emerging from his bedroom. He smiles at me.

I hesitate. "Is everything okay?"

"Everything's great. Will she be comfortable up there?" There's no hint of that edge in his voice anymore.

"Yeah, she's out cold for now. The storm may wake her up, though, if it gets any louder." Maybe that conversation had nothing to do with me. But if it didn't, then who did it have to do with? "Are you sure everything's okay?"

He brushes a loose strand of hair from my forehead. "As far as you and I are concerned, everything is perfect."

Another loud crack of thunder answers, and I hold my breath, pausing to listen for a long moment, my eyes on the ceiling above us.

I have to laugh when I realize Brett's doing the same thing.

"Come here, I have to show you something." He retreats into his room. I follow with a stir of excitement in the pit of my stomach as I take in the half-made bed. As with every other part of Brett's condo, this room is sleek but void of personality—white paint, white bedding, nothing but a flat-screen TV hanging on the wall.

"Just curious, how long have you lived in this . . ." My question gets lost in my throat, as Brett swings himself forward on his crutches until his broad body is looming over me, trapping me between the wall and his dominating frame.

"In this condo? About three years. Ever since I signed with the Flyers." He leans forward to drag his lips over mine. "I've been dying to do this since you walked through the door," he whispers, his long, thick lashes tickling my skin as he blinks. "I wake up every morning thinking about you." My head thumps softly against the wall as I close my eyes, reveling in the feel of his mouth against my ear. "I go to bed at night thinking about you." Blood rushes through my veins with the adrenaline his words create. "Please tell me it's not just me."

"It's not," I manage to get out in a whispered moan, thankful that where I'm hesitant to voice my attraction to him, Brett seems to have no fears at all.

I let my gaze drift out the window behind us, the image of Brett's back reflecting on the glass. A twinge of worry pricks the responsible side of me. "Can people see in here?" The lights are on, the curtains aren't drawn, and this side of the condo faces another building. Sure, it's storming, but—

Brett slaps his hand against the light switch in answer, throwing us into darkness as he closes his mouth over mine again. This time he grasps my waist and pulls my body closer, swallowing me up in his arms as he balances on his crutches, his tongue slipping across the seam of my lips, taunting me, urging me to open for him. I do, and he sighs against me, settling into that slow, hypnotic way he has of kissing.

Heat is thrumming through my veins in seconds, waking my limbs, making my skin itch for his touch. Making my fingers tug at his T-shirt, wanting it off.

Wanting his pants off, too.

Wanting *my* clothing off.

Wanting to feel every inch of his hot skin against mine.

Lightning skitters across the sky frequently, sending bright flashes into the room. A tease, really, to give me the briefest glimpse of his broad shoulder or the curve of his hard jaw.

"Are you okay with me bringing you in here?" he whispers against my mouth.

"Yes."

"How far do you want this to go, tonight?"

I hesitate. Would he think less of me if I told him the thoughts that are swirling inside my head right now? If I asked him whether he has protection in that nightstand drawer? If we have to worry about being overheard?

As usual, he somehow senses what I'm thinking. "I'm fine with *anything* you say, Cath. You just have to tell me, so it doesn't go too far. You'll tell me, right?"

"Yeah."

"Good." He breaks free of me to ease himself back the three feet to the edge of his bed. Leaning his crutches haphazardly against the nightstand, out of the way, he holds a hand out, beckoning me.

I'm careful not to bump his cast in the dark as I step forward. I settle my hands on his shoulders, though I can't keep them from wandering, drawing lines along the hard ridge of his collarbone with my fingertips, marveling at how his muscles surround it. I let my fingers slip under his shirt, careful not to stretch the cotton.

Warm hands cup the outsides of my thighs, sliding up and down soothingly, slowly. On the third pass, his fingertips slip under the loose material, all the way to the edge of my lace panties beneath. I never really considered how easy the access under this jumpsuit is, and now that he's gently gripping the curve of my backside, a deep throb settles in my core.

"You are the most stunning woman I've ever met."

I shake my head at him and smile, a wordless dismissal of his flattery. He's literally seen me at my worst—unshowered, smelling of burned and greasy diner food, in ratty threadbare clothes. He's delusional.

He grins. "I'm glad you're oblivious. I think that's part of your charm." An especially long wave of lightning explodes in the sky, filling the room, enough to catch his adoring eyes as they peer up at me. "I have *never* wanted anyone as much as I want you. Not even a fraction."

My heart swells with his words, raw and emotional and undoing me with their sincerity.

"I . . ." I falter. I remember a time when I didn't care if a guy knew I wanted him. When the idea of flirting wasn't met with apprehension, when the thought of being abandoned and heartbroken never entered my mind. When I didn't know what it would feel like to be shamed for my having expressed desire in the first place.

But that's all years in the past and this is Brett, a guy who I have to believe would never allow me to feel shame for a second. I can be smart and still live, still allow myself to trust.

And chase after what I want.

I can let myself love again.

"Take this off," I ask, too shyly, but I balance the meek request by tugging at his shirt.

Without hesitation, his hands leave my body to reach over his head and smoothly peel off the soft cotton, tossing it aside. Lightning flashes and I stifle a groan at the brief glimpse of those curves and ridges.

His responding chuckle is dark and playful. "There's a switch over there, on the wall. Hit that and then you can turn on the lamp."

I do, and a panel of curtains slides across the windows, closing off the chaos outside. The lamp casts a pleasant dim glow.

Brett grins, his eyes twinkling as he watches me blatantly gawk at him. "Better?"

I manage a nod, and then I'm giggling at myself, at how dumb-struck and shy I become around him.

"Get over here." He guides me onto the bed next to him, gently easing me down, struggling to twist his body toward me while keeping his casted leg away. While the angle has his stomach muscles tensing in a way that makes my jaw temporarily drop, it can't be comfortable.

"Stop, you're going to hurt yourself. Lie back." I press against his bare chest, taking in his hot skin against my palms as I push him back onto his elbows. The sheer size of him, sprawled out across the queen-size bed, is overwhelming.

"How on earth did I ever get you out of that car?" I let my hand drop, intent on settling it on his stomach. Only he's sliding himself up the mattress.

And my hand lands about eight inches lower.

I jump, pulling away quickly, but not before I've managed a solid feel of him through his track pants. "I didn't mean to touch *that*." My cheeks flame.

He falls back against the bed, his breathing more labored than before. An intimate chuckles escapes his lips. "What *were* you trying to touch, then?"

"Your stomach." My eyes flicker to the washboard ridges, but then they veer farther down, to where the sharp cut of his hips angles south, and his track pants highlight his hard length.

"Can you please stop rushing me? I'd like to take things slow."

My giggle is soft, at first. An embarrassed sound, but it quickly grows and strengthens, until I'm laughing from deep within my belly, unable to contain myself.

"What's so funny now?"

"My friend Misty was wondering how this would work, with you in a cast." Clumsy, I would say. All elbows and knees, and nothing at all like the sensual scene from a movie.

"Well, if you'd stop trying to take advantage of me, maybe we could find out."

"Oh, shut up." I reach out to poke his rib cage but he's ready for it, grabbing hold of my wrist. He easily pulls me over and onto him, until I can feel his heart beating wildly against my chest.

I study the beautiful face below me as he pushes my loose hair off my face and seems to study mine. Despite the butterflies in the pit of my stomach, I feel comfortable with him.

"Let me show you how it'll work." Brett grasps the back of my head and pulls me down, his arms coiling around to hold me against him as he kisses me deeply, the mood around us suddenly shifting.

The storm outside has passed without waking Brenna, the rumbles now distant and soft, the rain a light drizzle against the glass. It's no longer masking the sounds of our urgent lips, growing pink and swollen from friction, or our shallow breaths, or our low moans, each of us waiting for the other to make that daring next move.

It's Brett who finally breaks, his fingers fumbling with the silk tie that cinches the material around my waist, tugging it loose. He pulls free of my lips long enough to look up at me, asking permission as his hands settle on my shoulders, the straps within his grasp.

I give him a single nod.

And then he's sliding the top of my outfit down, exposing the skimpy black lace bra from Target that I splurged on this past week. His mouth trails downward, landing on my collarbone as he pushes me onto my back to wriggle the loose-fitting outfit to my hips. He doesn't stop there, though, using his one hand to pull it down past my thighs, past my knees. I lift my legs, allowing it to slip past my ankles and off.

It's as if Brett's reached his threshold of slow and steady, though, because he's immediately reaching behind me to unfasten my bra with ease. I know that if I told him to stop, he would. But I don't say a word, letting him maneuver himself until he's propped on one elbow and taking a peaked nipple into his mouth. I gasp at the first feel of his tongue against me.

I still can't believe this is happening.

Wrapping my arms around Brett's head, I stroke my fingers through his thick mane of hair and close my eyes, trying to soak in the feel of him adoring my body. Trying to remain calm.

Until the hand that idled briefly on my stomach begins to slide down. I tense and his hand freezes, his fingertips resting at the edge of the waistband of my panties. He lifts his head to peer at me, his lips parted and wet, his breath skating across my chest, gooseflesh prickling.

His blue eyes dark and glossy.

"I'm just nervous," I admit, letting him see my shy smile as I toy with a strand of his hair.

"So am I." He leans over to kiss me gently on the lips again.

And then his hand slips into my panties.

Our sharp inhales are simultaneous, at the first slide of his finger, at the glaring proof of how much I want this, and him. He doesn't say a word, though, sighing softly as he touches me, as I feel his calloused hand so smoothly, so masterfully work at a languid rhythm, my body relaxing and opening up to him and, soon, beginning to tilt in search of relief.

And still those blue eyes remain locked on mine, and instead of feeling self-conscious, I don't mind at all, grazing the fine stubble on his cheek with my thumb as my breathing grows ragged and my throat begins to burn and, finally . . . he watches me as my body tenses and pulses beneath his touch, his own breaths shaky.

He falls onto his back; the strain of holding himself propped on one elbow must be wearing. "God, you are so fucking beautiful. Your body . . . the way you come . . ." His hooded gaze roves over my slender frame, naked expect for the skimpy pair of black panties. "I want to do that every single night."

"Uh-huh." Doubtful that any guy would be *that* keen.

"You don't believe me?"

"*Every* single night?"

A sly grin unfolds across his lips. "Well, in one form or another. Wouldn't want you to get bored."

"As if I could ever get bored." My eyes drift over his heaving chest and his splayed legs and . . . that sizable ridge. To have *that* every single night. He's so vibrant, so alive, so . . . mine. Deep inside, I hear that little voice insist that *I* saved him. Every inch of him.

My hand aches with the need to feel him again.

I roll onto my side and smooth my hand over his stomach, as I meant to before.

And then I reach lower to grasp him, this time intentionally.

He's impossibly hard.

He simply watches me as I gather the nerve to push my fingers beneath the waistband, first of his pants, and then his briefs, to fill my hand with him, delighting in the smooth, velvety soft skin.

A soft curse slips from his lips with the first swipe of my thumb over his tip, his fingers reaching up to toy absently with strands of my hair as I slowly begin to stroke him. But the elastic makes it difficult.

"Help me take these off," he says, tugging at one side. Freeing my hand, I sit up and seize both sides of his pants, waiting for him to lift his hips, the anticipation of seeing Brett naked for the first time almost too much to handle.

"Mommy!"

"Shit," I hiss at the sound of Brenna calling me, her voice laced with fear. I look at Brett, sprawled out on the bed. "I'm sorry. I'll only be a minute."

"Put this on." He hands me his T-shirt and I yank it over my head. The hem reaches midthigh.

"Mama!" It's louder, more urgent.

"I'm so sorry."

"Don't be."

"I'll be back." Stealing one last quick kiss, I rush for the stairs, not wanting her to try them half-asleep. Or wake up Richard. I find her huddled in a ball on the landing, a sulky, sleepy look on her face. Scooping her up, I bring her back to bed and tuck her in to the warm, silky sheets. She reaches for me, though, her eyes closed but her little fingers grasping the air, and I know that I won't be free to simply walk out.

I lie down next to her, and she slithers over to curl into my chest. "You smell like Brett's perfume," she murmurs.

I smile, not correcting her, and quietly wait for her shallow breathing. It's twenty minutes before I can peel myself away without her stirring.

Ducking into Brett's bathroom, I gingerly search his drawers for the spare toothbrush, while taking inventory of all his personal things—his brand of deodorant, the razors he shaves with, the small glass bottle of cologne, half-full.

My heart skips a beat when I spot the opened box of condoms in the bottom left drawer. A peek inside shows me that there are only a few left. While I don't want to think about Brett having sex with other women, I'm wondering if maybe I should bring one down with me.

I contemplate that as brush my teeth and then, reminding myself that we're better safe than sorry—and it's already been well proven that I can't take birth control pills reliably—I tuck one into the palm of my hand and tiptoe back to Brett's room.

He readied himself for bed while I was dealing with Brenna. His track pants now dangle from the bottom corner bedpost, his body is covered to his waist by a sheet.

And he's sound asleep.

So I simply sit on the edge of his bed and admire his peaceful, beautiful face for a long moment.

And think again how close he was to dying that night.

How close I was to never getting the chance to know him, to feel *this*.

Whatever *this* is, that's growing between us. It's intense and fast-moving, that much I know. And I expected no less, no in between with him, no casualness, not after what we've been through together.

It *does* feel magical. It *does* feel like a fairy tale. That a man like Brett—so charming, so talented, so breathtakingly handsome, so seemingly perfect in every way—would become infatuated with an ordinary woman like me.

No wonder people want the happily ever after between us.

I want the happily ever after.

Even if I'm having a hard time allowing myself to believe it can exist.

I resist the urge to rest my palm on his chest—not wanting to wake him now that he's managed to drift off—and I shut off the lamp.

And decide, right then and there, that I'm going to take full advantage of every second with him, for as long as this crazy spell fate has cast over us lasts.

Chapter 24

. . .

It takes me three seconds to remember that I'm in Brett's bed.

And another two to realize Brenna's not beside me.

It's seven A.M. She likes watching cartoons as soon as she gets up. At home, she can turn on the TV by herself, but Brett's setup is more complicated than ours. She'll try, of course, because she's stubborn. She'll start pushing buttons until something works or the screen is full of noisy static and she wakes up both Brett and Richard and—

I throw the sheet off my body and head downstairs to retrieve her before my imagination becomes reality.

I hear nothing at first, which makes me more than a little nervous. She's usually pretty good about not getting into things, but she is still only five. From the bottom of the steps, I see Brett's bedroom door open a crack.

". . . but all he does is change his clothes and put on glasses. How come people can't recognize him?"

I give the door a push and it creaks open.

Brenna's sitting cross-legged at the foot of Brett's bed, watching a Superman cartoon on the flat-screen affixed to the wall. Meanwhile, Brett is lying in bed, his casted leg free of sheets and propped up on a pillow, his muscular thigh on display.

"Hey," he says in a soft, throaty voice.

"Morning." I do my best not to ogle his bare chest.

But fail miserably.

I'm not the only one staring, though. Brett's eyes dart to my bare legs before meeting my face. "She asks a lot of questions first thing in the morning, doesn't she?" He says it with a smile, but I can't help but feel bad.

"Brenna, please tell me you didn't wake up Brett."

"I was already awake," he assures me.

"Then why were your eyes closed?" Brenna's attention is still glued to the TV.

"I'm trying to help you out here, kid. Work with me." He chuckles. "She came in about fifteen minutes ago to ask me how to use the TV in the living room. It's too complicated to explain, so I told her she could watch in here until my painkillers kick in and I can attempt to get up."

A quick glance at his nightstand and I see the small bottle of pills.

He pats the spot next to him in bed. "We're watching Superman."

After a moment of hesitation, I settle down next to him, smoothing out the hem of his shirt. "How did you sleep?"

"Well. And not well." His lips, looking as red and chapped as mine feel, curl with a smile.

"I know what you mean." I lay in bed for another hour last night, staring at the ceiling.

He steals a glance Brenna's way to make sure she's zoned out on the TV in front of her, and then he nods, and mouths, "Come here." With my own glance at Brenna, I finally lean in to give him a somewhat chaste but still decidedly intimate good morning kiss.

He grins. "What's that look for?"

"Nothing." This still doesn't feel real.

I'm still waiting to wake up.

Or for Brett to wake up.

Brenna starts laughing and I automatically pull back. But she's not watching us; her eyes are glued to the cartoon.

Still . . . we can't do this right now. I distract myself by scanning Brett's room, hoping to notice what I was too preoccupied to notice last night, to learn something about him that hasn't already been covered by the news. "You like to read?"

He follows my gaze to the paperback sitting on the nightstand. "I go through phases, but yeah."

"What is that . . ." I frown as I take in the cover. "A dragon?"

"Yeah."

"Really?" I can't keep the incredulity out of my voice.

He chuckles. "You say that like it's a bad thing."

"No, I just can't picture you into those kinds of books." I've never actually read one, but I remember the socially awkward guys from high school sitting around a lunch table, planning out their weekend of

Dungeons and Dragons role-playing. That was more than enough for me to cast judgment at the time.

He drops his voice to a whisper, though I can guarantee Brenna isn't listening. "If it makes you feel more at ease, I have a few *Sports Illustrated*s and *Playboy*s in the nightstand."

"For the articles, right?"

A wry smirk twists his lips. "Not even a little bit."

"You're supposed to lie about that."

He reaches up to push the few wayward strands of hair off my forehead, a somber expression replacing his amusement. "I'm not going to lie to you."

"Not even about looking at pictures of half-naked women?" Any of whom he could probably have in real life, given who he is.

"About *anything*." He locks eyes with me, not wavering for a moment. I've never met a guy so determined to maintain honesty. It's almost unnerving.

I'm the first to break away from that steady gaze. "So, what else do you do when you're not on the ice or reading about dragons?"

A little frown curves his brow as he thinks about that question for a bit. "Well, I golf in the summers. Hang out with my friends, mostly, drinking beer and trying to beat each other at one video game or another. Fly down to see my family whenever I can, help teach kids how to skate. But hockey has pretty much been my life for . . . my life. I'd roll out of bed and throw on my skates before the sun was even up and be out on the rink in the backyard with my friends before school. After school, my dad would sit in the net for hours, letting me shoot pucks on him. We had this big asphalt pad—like a tennis court except specifically for me—so I could play ball hockey when it was too warm for ice. I've wanted to play professionally for as long as I can remember. It's all I've ever wanted to do."

"Wow, that's . . . dedication."

He smiles, but it's tinged with sadness. "It's a ton of sacrifice. People don't realize how hard I've worked to get to this level. Weekends driving to arenas hours away from home for tournaments. Six A.M. weekday practices. Planning vacations around my game schedule." He chuckles softly. "Man, my sister would get so pissed off when we couldn't go somewhere because I had hockey."

I remember Jack spending a lot of time playing road hockey down the street, and my dad leaving with him for hours on weekends to go to games somewhere. But they weren't nearly as dedicated as Brett and his dad were. Maybe that's because my dad didn't have the luxury of not working and our yard wasn't big enough for a rink. We certainly didn't plan family vacations around a hockey schedule. We barely took family vacations to begin with.

From the sounds of it, Brett has lived, breathed, and slept this sport his entire life.

Which makes his injury all the more devastating. My heart aches for him. I settle a soft kiss against his collarbone but say nothing.

He smiles, though, maybe seeing the sympathy in my eyes. "You know what you said last night? That my dad would rather sit on the couch and watch a game with me than not have me around at all . . . you're right. And you risked your life for me. I owe it to you to focus on the bigger picture here."

"You don't owe me anything. Just focus on getting better." I smooth the pad of my thumb over his shoulder soothingly, my fingers itching to touch his chest. "We're going to stay optimistic."

"I'm trying." He turns to study me, vulnerability and fear in his eyes. "I've never given much thought to life after hockey. Does that make me an idiot?"

"No, it makes you passionate about your dreams and living in the moment."

He grunts. "Or just a privileged asshole who's never had to worry about my future."

"Or maybe that," I tease, but soften it with another stolen kiss against his collarbone, my lips lingering a moment longer this time. "You've never thought about retirement?" Even the greatest players have to hang up their skates eventually.

"Not really. Well, I figured I'd be coaching. And teaching my own kids how to play, of course. But beyond that . . ."

My stomach flutters at the thought of Brett with kids of his own. Of him being a father. I'm betting he'll make a great father one day.

I realize he's smiling at me.

"What?"

"You're really easy to talk to."

The sound of pots and pans clanging finally pulls Brenna's attention from the cartoon. She inhales. "What's that smell? Are those waffles?"

"Not just waffles. The best waffles in the world."

"Better than Leroy's?" Brenna's eyes widen as she stands on the bed.

"Oh, yeah. Definitely better than Leroy's." Brett nods, his face serious.

She hops off and skips out the door toward the kitchen.

"Who's Leroy?"

I chuckle. "The cook at Diamonds, and when she tells him you said that, you're going to be blacklisted from the diner."

"Before I've even been?"

"He takes his cooking seriously."

"Huh." Brett wastes no time sliding his arm beneath me to drag me over and onto his warm, bare chest. His fingers weave through my hair to get a grip on my head, and then he's kissing me. Not in the chaste way, like earlier. He kisses me as if he's two seconds from pulling my T-shirt off my body, his free hand balling the cotton in a fist until it's sliding up to settle around my waist and my panties are pressed against his hip.

Soft footfalls running down the hardwood are the only warning we get, but we manage to break the kiss just before Brenna's in the doorway. "He's making whipped cream, too!" she announces with an excited shriek.

"He'll let you lick the beaters if you help him. But you better go, quick!" Brett's heart is hammering against my chest.

Brenna narrows her gaze at us, me draped over him. "What are you doing?"

"Your mom was helping me take my medicine."

"You had to take more?"

"Yup."

"Oh." She opens her mouth to ask something else, but the sound of whirling beaters distracts her and she trots away.

"Good recovery," I tell him.

"I'm impressed with myself, actually."

"She'll be back in about thirty seconds."

He groans, his arms relaxing their grip on me. "I guess it's time to get up, then."

288

K.A. TUCKER

With great reluctance, I peel myself off Brett and out of bed, readying his crutches for him.

He eases himself up slowly and with a pinched face, then adjusts his boxer briefs at the groin where they cling and show enough to get my blood racing.

He grins playfully. "I can't believe you left me like that last night."

"It could have been a lot worse." I could have been almost all the way through . . . My lips part at the thought of Brett orgasming.

He curses softly, following my train of thought. A mischievous twinkle sparks in his eyes as they rove over me. "Can I have my shirt back?" He grasps the hem and begins lifting it.

"Hey!" I step out of his reach, giggling as I playfully swat his hand away, earning his soft chuckle.

"I'm gonna grab a quick shower. Could you bring me down one from upstairs and leave it on the bed? I'm out of clean clothes."

"Of course." I marvel at the way the muscles in his back and shoulders strain with each step toward the adjoining bathroom, unable to imagine what it would feel like to have that body crash into me on an ice rink, pads or not. "Do you need my help in there?"

He stalls and, after a moment, begins to laugh, low and soft and full of meaning. Turning around, he gives me a full length of him—the hard lines of his stomach, the way his hips cut into a V, the way his briefs stretch with a full erection inside them. "It's probably better that you stay out here."

I imagine a naked Brett standing in the shower, and I feel myself blush furiously.

His laughter follows me out the door as I rush up the stairs, shaking my head the entire way. Maybe one of these days, Brett won't be able to fluster me so easily.

■ ■ ■

I sip my orange juice and quietly watch Richard putter around the kitchen, preparing breakfast. I tried helping earlier but he shooed me out.

"So, I heard you were a stagehand when you met Meryl?"

"That's right." Richard dries his hands on the tea towel and then shifts his attention back to the waffle iron. "Started out working on small sets. You know, for TV commercials, ad campaigns, things like that. Not exactly exciting, but it was a foot in the door. And then a friend of a friend hooked me up with a production company, and that was it. I was in. For almost three years." He smiles fondly. "Loved it."

"But you left it behind for Meryl."

"And the kids. Yeah." He sighs, testing the edges of the cooking batter with a fork, frowning slightly. "I thought I'd go back at some point. But Meryl's roles kept getting bigger, we kept getting busier. I figured one parent in the movie industry was enough." His gaze flickers over to the living room, where Brenna sits quietly on the couch, her eyes glued to a cartoon, a beater in her hand. "How's that coming over there, Brenna?"

"Not finished yet."

He chuckles. "Michelle was like that. I always joked that she'd lick the chrome plating right off."

I study a fleck of orange pulp sitting on the rim of my glass for a moment, deciding how to ask my bigger question. "How did you learn to handle the crazy parts? You know, the cameras and the newspapers, the gossip."

He doesn't answer right away. "I wouldn't say I ever learned how to deal with them. More like I learned how to ignore them. I knew that if I let them get to me, Meryl and I wouldn't last." For just a moment, his gray eyes flicker over to me, where I sit perched on a barstool, and then he's stooping to place the waffle onto the oven plate with the others. "You having a hard time with things?"

I feel like he already knows the answer to that, but he's asking in that way fathers do, pretending to be clueless to get their kids to open up. "It's been nice and quiet lately, but, yeah. It was overwhelming for me right after the accident."

"That was in the height of the story. It'll get better."

Will it, once they find out that Brett and I are together? I push that worry aside. "Were they ever cruel to you?"

"We had our share of it, more so when Meryl was younger. Mostly rumors of affairs. A handsome costar that Meryl was filming a movie in Thailand with, a bodyguard . . . But if there is one thing that I can count on with my wife, it's her unwavering belief in always being honest. I knew that if she even thought something might happen, she'd sit down and have a frank talk with me about it. It's one of the things I love most about her. It's one of the things that has kept us sane. We've really pushed the importance of honesty with our kids, too."

I've noticed.

Richard is pulling bowls out of the fridge, getting last-minute preparations ready. "You have to remember, Brett has grown up knowing that world. Sure, we sheltered him from much of it, but the idea of a security detail and people being interested in our lives isn't out of the ordinary for him. I've had to remind him that it is for you. Plus, the way you two met was bound to stir up a commotion from day one. At least Meryl and I could date in relative peace. You two have it harder."

I try to hide my smile. What has Brett told him? I know they're close, but the thought of him having a conversation with his father about us dating makes me feel warm inside.

Richard opens his mouth, but stalls for a moment, his eyes flashing to the hallway. "Just remember that you're not alone in any of this. You have a lot of people who care about you. Including your family. And you'll find that you can deal with a lot more than you realize." He pauses. "*If* you decide that it's worth it."

There's no doubt in my mind that Brett is worth it.

But will I always be worth it *to him*?

"Did you ever wonder why you? I mean . . . I'm not saying there's anything wrong with *you* or anything, but . . ." I stumble over my words.

His knowing smile calms me. "I was dumbstruck the first time Meryl asked me out for coffee. I was sure the guys at work had coaxed her into playing a practical joke on me."

"But you went anyway?"

"Heck, yeah. She was Meryl Price! I wasn't going to pass up that chance, even if it ended in me tied naked to a pole in the middle of downtown Toronto." He chuckles softly. "I still catch myself wondering if she's going to finally wake up and reconsider, even twenty-eight years later."

I watch quietly as Richard pours batter onto the waffle iron, admiring that easy, relaxed way about him. "Meryl's not like a lot of the people we know in her industry, though. She loves her job and she plays the game well, but she'll never choose fame and wealth over family. I think our kids have a good handle on that, too. Brett, especially. Of course, he's put all of his focus on his career up until now. But that's changing, quickly."

"Do you think he'll play again?"

Richard's mouth curves in a thoughtful frown. "Yes, I do. As well as before? That remains to be seen. But he's a fighter and he doesn't give up easily." With a casual toss of the dirty ladle into the sink, he adds, "And I'm not just talking about hockey."

"Is breafkast ready, yet?" Brenna skips into the kitchen, a spit-polished beater dangling from her fingertips, interrupting our conversation.

"*Breakfast*," I correct her.

"That's what I said. I'm *starving*."

"Well, you *have* been waiting awhile. And so patiently." Richard pulls a waffle from the oven and sets it on a plate.

"Can I have extra whip cream?"

Richard's eyes flash to me and I give a nod.

"Well . . . maybe just this once." He winks at her.

Brett hobbles down the hall toward us, freshly showered and dressed in the T-shirt and track pants I set out for him.

I wish I'd showered, too, or at least had a change of outfit. I did my best to freshen up, wiping smears of eye shadow and liner with my thumb and finger-combing my hair.

He stops beside me, his hand settling on the small of my back as he leans in. "Thanks for the clothes," he murmurs, laying a soft kiss on my mouth.

"You're welcome." Yes, this moment *right here* would be worth all the chaos out there.

When he pulls away, I find Brenna staring up at us, a wide, curious look in her eyes.

She's *never* seen a guy kiss me on the lips before.

I'm saved from any awkward questions when Richard holds a plate out for her that I doubt even Brett could finish.

■ ■ ■

"So? How was it?"

"Not as good as Leroy's but good." Brenna skips off to the couch.

I give Richard an apologetic smile, but he's smiling as he reaches for her plate.

"Here, let me clean up." I move to climb out of my chair but he ushers me back.

"Finish eating! I don't mind. I don't get to cook for anyone anymore, now that my kids are out of the house and Meryl hired a chef."

"She did?" Brett frowns. "Since when?"

"Since she complained that I use too much butter and I refuse to use less."

Brett chuckles. "You know, she may have a valid argument."

Richard wraps the half-finished block of butter and tucks it into the fridge as he peers over his shoulder at us, that same mischievous twinkle in his eye as his son has. "I don't know what you're talking about."

I smile around a mouthful, watching the two of them together. They remind me of Jack and my dad.

Brett sighs with exasperation, his gaze on his phone screen.

"What's wrong?"

"Simone's annoyed."

"When isn't she?" Richard asks. "Who at, this time?"

"Courtney. Apparently she was all over a guy at a club last night."

"Are there pictures?"

"*Of course* there are pictures. Simone wants to issue a statement."

I shake my head. "Why does she have to say anything?" This whole business of having a publicist and making statements about stupid details . . . I don't know that I'll ever get my head around it.

"Because it's better that Simone controls the message than Courtney's people. Simone knows I don't want any of this blowing back to you."

"Would it?" I can't help the wariness in my voice.

Brett's face is lined with concern. "Probably not, but . . ."

But he's so worried about it getting to be too much for me again, and me deciding it's not worth it.

That *he's* not worth it.

I reach out to rest a soothing hand on his knee. "If it does, then we'll deal with it. We can't avoid it forever, right?"

A slow smile curls his lips. "Right."

"So . . . what is Simone going to say in her statement?" I ask, savoring the last chunk of waffle.

"That I'm too busy trying to keep my hands off you to care who Courtney screws," Brett murmurs, punching in a response.

I nearly choke on my mouthful, my face burning at the cavalier way he said that, especially in front of his dad.

"That reminds me, your mom is supposed to call and I left my phone in my room." Richard presses his lips together but it doesn't quite hide the smile as he strolls past us, cuffing Brett on the back of the head on his way by.

"Hey, I'm crippled!"

"And yet still obnoxious," Richard says, as he disappears down the hall.

Chapter 25

...

The familiar mix of vinegar and lemons fills my nostrils when I step inside my parents' house, a fifty-year-old, three-bedroom backsplit that was updated when they bought it thirty years ago and hasn't seen much besides a fresh coat of paint since. They skipped a formal wedding in order to put all of their savings toward the mortgage, choosing a small and practical civil ceremony in Philadelphia instead. Neither had much family anyway, each being only children whose parents had died before I was born.

The house is old, but it's well maintained, the lawn always manicured, the floors barely scratched.

Brenna's heading for the kitchen in a flash. "Grandma!" I hear her exclaim. "Guess what! We slept over at Brett's house in Philadelphia!"

I roll my eyes. *Great.*

A few moments later, my mom appears in the kitchen doorway, a dish towel in her hands.

"Thanks for taking her. It's just for three hours, tops." Two servers called in sick for the dinner shift, and Lou tried everyone else before calling me. I very reluctantly left Brett's at two.

"It's not a problem. I was just about to start dinner and your father is outside in the garden." She pauses. "So you stayed in Philadelphia last night?"

Brenna just told her we did. "Yeah. The storm was too bad to drive home in."

"Hmm." I can see it in her face. She doesn't approve. I sense the words on the tip of her tongue, the caution she's desperate to share. She's deciding how to deliver it, how to get her point across in the most succinct way. She opens her mouth—

"I'm well aware of all the risks, Mom."

Her lips twist. "I can't just sit back and not say something. I know you're old enough now to make your own mistakes. But there's Brenna to think about, too."

"I'm always thinking about Brenna."

"She gets so attached to the men in her life. Have you noticed that?"

"Of course I've noticed. She's my daughter." Jack, Keith . . . They all fill a gap that she doesn't even seem to be aware exists yet.

But there's no use having this conversation with my mom. It'll only end in an ugly fight. "I'll be back by eight to pick her up."

I'm out the door before she has the chance to respond.

■ ■ ■

"Banquet burger, no pickles!" Leroy hollers.

I grab the plate from the warmer and slide it across the counter to Mark, delivering it with a smile. I know it's the trucker's order even without looking. He has the same thing every week when he stops in here.

"How are you doin' these days, Cath?" He nods toward my wrist. "Looks like you healed up all right?"

"As good as new." I roll my right hand around to prove it.

Mark chuckles, showing off the wide gap in between his two front teeth as he whacks at the bottom of the ketchup bottle. A dollop slips out to land on his fries. "Things are finally back to normal around here."

"Finally," I agree.

Mark pauses. "You seem . . . different."

"Do I?" I shrug, feigning indifference.

"You still hear from Madden?" he asks, stuffing a fry into his mouth.

"Here and there," I avert my eyes to wipe up some crumbs. "He's tied up with charity stuff and other appearances, and getting ready for physical therapy . . ." Richard has been busy keeping Brett's mind occupied again this week, signing photos and hockey sticks and jerseys, charity stuff. He even lined up a few appearances at schools and kids' sports team events. Richard may not have an official job, but I'm starting to see that he works harder than any employed man I know.

But even with all that going on, I still get messages from Brett from the moment he wakes up until late into the night.

When I dare look up, Mark is chewing his burger slowly, watching me try to control my expression, the look in his eyes saying he sees right through my bullshit.

I duck my head before the stupid love-struck grin can escape.

"Cath, how many tables do you have?" Lou calls out, her arms loaded with a tray of clean glasses from the kitchen.

"Just three. Two are ready to cash out." The lunch rush passed by swiftly, leaving me with an aching back and a growling stomach.

She drops the glasses on the counter with a loud clatter. "Why don't you go and grab some food, then. I'll close 'em out for you."

"The order for Table Eighteen will be up any minute."

Eighteen.

Brett's number.

I stifle the urge to roll my eyes at myself. What am I, a teenager?

"I'll bring it out to them. And do me a favor . . . check out the paper while you're at it."

"Why?" My eyes are immediately scanning the counter, searching for a copy of the *Tribune*. They're all with customers, though.

"Because there's somethin' in there I think you need to see." She gives me a knowing look. "I left a copy for you on my— What on earth?" Lou's gaze lands somewhere behind me, and she's scowling. "Is that who I think it is?"

I turn.

And watch DJ Harvey stroll into Diamonds, the chain that dangles from his belt loop swinging with each leisurely step. He's gained weight and tattoos, and the golden blond hair he used to wear long and somewhat scraggly has been buzzed off, but there's no mistaking those narrow eyes, that thin-lipped smile, or that swagger.

Unease slithers down my spine as Misty skips across the quiet restaurant toward him like Brenna might when excited. She throws her arms around his neck.

"Good grief. Don't tell me that girl is stupid enough to go back for seconds."

"I wish I could tell you that." From the way she's hanging off him, batting her eyelashes and giggling, it looks like she is exactly that stupid. When did this happen? The last I heard, he had messaged her on Facebook. But she hasn't mentioned him since. Granted, she's been doing a stretch of night shifts lately, and I've been so preoccupied with trying to avoid all talk of Brett—I *still* haven't told her, and I'm likely a horrible friend for that—so maybe there've been signs that I missed. It would definitely explain why she hasn't been hounding me.

Misty catches my eye. "Cath! Look who came to say hi!" Grabbing his hand, she leads him over with a wide grin, oblivious. As if I'd be happy about DJ popping in.

"I'll be in the kitchen before I say somethin' I'll no doubt regret," Lou mutters, vanishing before they reach us and she's forced to be civil.

"Hey." I plaster on a tight, fake smile, trying my best to be polite.

His gaze skitters over me. "How's it goin'?" On first glance, he hasn't changed all that much. He still has that cool, indifferent way about him. Like if he has to talk to you, he will, but he couldn't really be bothered.

Despite his good looks, I never could see what Misty found appealing in him.

"I'm good." I know this is the part where I'm supposed to ask how he's doing, but all I want to do is get away from him.

Uncomfortable silence hangs.

He finally offers, "Saw you on TV. That's one crazy story."

"Right?" Misty's eyes widen. "I still can't believe Cath saved Brett Madden's life. I was really hoping something more would come out of it." She gives me a pointed stare.

Yup. So glad I haven't told her.

Thankfully the kitchen bell dings then. "Hey, Misty, can I get your help with these plates?"

"Sure thing." She grins at DJ. "Why don't you grab an empty table. I'll be there in a sec."

I wait until he's gone and we're by the food warmer. "What are you doing?"

"What do you mean?" She frowns.

"He's a *convict*, Misty. He's not a good guy! And have you forgotten that he cheated on you? *Many* times? Why would you waste your time with him?"

I can already see the shutters closing over her eyes, the ones she is so adept at using to avoid what she doesn't want to face. "He asked if he could come by and visit me one day and I said yeah. It's no big deal. We're just friends."

"Come on, Misty. He doesn't want to be just friends. Don't be stupid."

She flinches, like I slapped her. A long moment passes, and I can't read what's going on inside her head. "So what if I *do* decide I want it to be more? So what? I've *always* stood by you, Cath, no matter what you've done." She drops her voice to a whispered hiss. "I think you're absolutely *insane* for blowing off Brett, but I've kept my mouth shut, haven't I?" I avert my gaze. "And all those months you sat around pining over Scott, even while he was parading around town with his girlfriend, did I ever tell you that you were stupid? No. Even though *everyone* right down to Whiskers could see the truth of it."

Whiskers. Misty's blind cat . . . "You *should* have said something, because I *was* being stupid." I glance over to see DJ seated by a window, his attention on his phone. "I'm saying this to you because you're my friend and I care about you."

Her eyes dart around us. "About me? Or about you know who not finding out he's a father."

"That's not fair."

"No, what's not fair is you standing here and assuming I can't figure things out for myself. You're no different than your mother right now."

My mouth drops open with that well-placed insult. I am *nothing* like my mother! "I can't just sit back and watch him hurt you again without saying something. What kind of friend would I be?"

I stifle my own gasp.

The words feel like an echo of what my mother said last Sunday. Am I turning into Hildy Wright?

If Misty notices my shock, she doesn't let on, a broad smile stretching across her face. "We're not going to fight about this. DJ just wants to be friends, and if he doesn't, well . . . I'll decide what's best for me."

Lou plows through the kitchen door then. "Less gabbing, more moving. Those fries'll get cold."

"I'm gonna take my break now," Misty says, reaching for two of the club sandwiches.

"No, you're not. Cath needs to eat before she leaves to get Brenna. You can go after her and I'll cover your tables."

"But DJ—"

"Can sit there and play with his little chain all day long, for all I care." Lou grabs the other plates in my order. "Cath, get on back there. Leroy set some lunch out. Paper's on my desk."

I shrug at Misty and mouth, "Ten minutes," because Lou is clearly not happy about DJ being here and I'm not about to pick a fight with her when she's in a foul mood. Plus, I'm growing more curious about whatever it is Lou insists I need to read.

A bowl of soup and a Greek salad wait for me on a prep table. I grab them and offer a thanks to Leroy. He merely smiles before turning his attention back to the grill, humming to himself.

I head for the office and, using my hip to bump the door shut, settle in behind the desk. Leroy's tomato-basil soup is one of my favorites and I happily shovel a spoonful of it into my mouth.

And nearly spit it all over Lou's desk when I see Scott Philips's smiling face staring up at me.

Balsam County Realty—his mother's real estate firm—took a full-page color ad spread in the local paper to welcome their latest agent to the firm.

Scott is going to be working for his mother

Which must mean he's moving back to Balsam.

But why? What happened to his job in Memphis?

I drop my spoon into the bowl, sending splashes of soup in every direction. Balsam is too small to have him living here again. But maybe I'll be lucky. Maybe he'll decide to live in Belmont, or Sterling.

The door creaks open. I recognize Lou's heavy sigh without turning around. "I figured you should see it now, in case you run into him in town."

Run into him, or just see his face splashed all over the place. Balsam Realty dominates this county. Very few properties get sold that don't have the Philipses' family fingerprints on the paperwork.

God, I'm going to be seeing Scott's face *everywhere*.

"What happened?"

"Well, from what I heard, he made some sort of deal with the school and the parents of the girl to keep things quiet, and resigned. Who knows what happened there."

Of course he got off.

What a difference, though, between that girl's family and my parents. I can't help but wonder what my life would have been like had my mom wanted to "keep things quiet," too.

I study the picture again. Taken recently, I'm guessing. It's one of those stiff professional head shots—angled pose, business suit, boring blue background. He looks different from the last time I saw him, his wavy hair cropped short and hinting gray at the sides, his face much fuller, his forehead etched with small lines. Older, of course. It's been more than seven years since that day he asked me to show him my latest sketch after school and I felt his fingers slide over mine for the first time. He just turned thirty-eight in April.

His eyes haven't changed much, though. They still have that playful gleam, the one that used to make me blush and stumble over my words.

That he would have used them on a girl half his age makes my skin crawl.

"So he's going to sell houses." He once told me he'd rather spend his days shoveling cow manure at his uncle's farm than work for his mother. "He must be having a hard time getting another teaching job."

Lou drags over a spare chair and sits down beside me. "You do bad things and eventually it'll catch up to you. It *always* catches up with you, one way or another."

I attempt a smile. "You sure seem to have your ear to the ground about him."

"Just lookin' out for you." A long pause hangs in the air. "Is there anything you need to talk about?"

"Like?"

"Oh," she says, feigning mild interest, "just anything at all." Her fingers rap against the desk, a steady drumbeat.

"Brett and I are . . . *talking* a lot."

"Well, yes, who else would you be texting nonstop through your shifts." Her lips twist, but I can tell by her eyes that she's not really upset by it. There's a long pause. "If there's anything else, you know I'll always lend an ear."

"Yeah, I know. Thanks, Lou." I hesitate. "Do you think I'm making a mistake, with Brett? Am I going to end up with a broken heart?"

Lou's never one to hold back her thoughts, but unlike my mother, she never seems compelled to offer her judgment. She has simply always been there with that unwavering support, a sturdy pillar for me to lean on no matter what direction I choose to take.

She frowns in thought. "I think you're a *long* way from seeing the last of him." Climbing out of her chair just as quickly as she settled into it, she adds, "And hopefully that friend of yours is a short way to seeing the last of that dumb-ass sitting at my table out there."

"Ugh." I groan with the reminder.

"I don't want him stirring up any trouble. I have half a mind to kick him out." As much as Lou might want to, she'd never offend Misty like that. She may, however, throw enough eye daggers at him to make him uncomfortable enough to want to leave.

I lean forward to rest my forehead on my palms, my elbows propped on the desk.

Acutely aware of those eyes that stare up at me.

Chapter 26

■ ■ ■

"I heard he's havin' a hard time gettin' clients," John Sanders says from his stool by the counter. He's one of our many regulars, a seventy-two-year-old farmer who puts in six hours of work every day before driving to Diamonds for a late-morning plate of eggs and bacon.

He's not one to gossip idly, either. If he's saying something, it's more than likely accurate.

I duck my head and focus on refilling paper napkins in their dispenser, pretending that I'm not listening to people talk about Scott Philips being back in Balsam. But I've heard every word, and it sounds like he's not getting the warm reception his mother may have expected.

He came back on his own, apparently, staying at his parents' palatial house, no sign of his wife or children. Some speculate it's because the school year hasn't wrapped up yet, but others have pointed out that the school year ends earlier down south. That leads some people to believe that Linda Stovers decided she'd had enough. And of course others to insist that she was stupid enough to marry him in the first place, so she must not be bothered.

It's a swirling pot of gossip.

But, for once, I'm not a key ingredient.

Misty's phone chirps nearby—a deranged clown laugh that she downloaded for her incoming texts—and she rushes to check it. Her face lights up and I know that it's DJ. I don't ask, though. Despite what she said about not wanting to fight, things have been strained between us. And I'm just so horrified that I may be showing signs of Hildy Wright's influence, I don't want to risk saying anything to solidify that fear.

"I don't pay you to be on your phone. Lunch rush is starting soon." Lou's face is less than impressed as she strolls past, glaring at Misty.

"Why do I feel like she's giving me more grief than usual?" Misty moans, more to herself.

Because she is. I open my mouth to lie and tell Misty it's no big deal, that Lou's just having a bad day.

"So, have you thought more about that job offer, Cathy?" Gord's voice booms, startling me. The napkins in my hand scatter over the counter.

Gord showed up about an hour ago, asking to sit in my section. I caught the look Leroy fired through the kitchen window, along with the warning glare Lou threw back. One that said Leroy was not allowed to burn Gord's eggs.

But by the third time Gord waved me over, not to give me his order but to try and strike up conversations about my Escape, about Brenna, about quitting Diamonds and becoming his personal assistant, I was ready to pay Leroy out of my own pocket to char Gord's entire meal.

And since Lou won't bill family, and he's already mentioned with a chuckle that my tip was worked into the deal on my SUV, I stopped making eye contact after collecting his dirty plate.

"Thanks, but I'm not interested in being an assistant."

His face splits into a wide grin, but it's his condescending one. "Now come on, Cathy." He's still smiling as he drops his voice and whispers, "I think it's time you step back and face reality."

I offer him a tight-lipped smile, trying not to crumple the napkins in my hand too much. "Did you need a coffee *for the road*?"

Misty's high-pitched squeal drowns whatever answer Gord gives, startling me. I drop the stack of napkins. Again.

As soon as I see that her wide eyes are locked on the door, I know why, without even needing to look.

Brett just walked into Diamonds.

My heart begins hammering in my chest.

He simply nods at the truckers sitting on their stools up at the counter, their heads tilted to watch him as he leaves Donovan with the hostess and moves toward me.

Gord is saying something, but I ignore him and close the distance toward Brett, my urge to reach out and touch him stifled by all the eyes on us. "What are you doing here?" I whisper, stealing a glance at his good leg, bared in shorts and ridged with muscle. Trying *not* to focus on his injured leg, which is visibly slender by comparison.

"Sid's lending me his place for the weekend and I thought I'd grab a quick bite on my way. I heard the food is good here. And the staff is hot." He does a quick but overt head-to-toe scan of my uniform, making me flush.

His face breaks out in a wide grin.

"People are going to be talking." At least we're near a server station, away from prying ears as long as we keep our voices down.

"About what? Me, saying hello to you and then eating?" He mocks me, his face transforming with an innocent mask. I can only shake my head at him. And try not to let everyone see how enamored I am.

"What time does your shift end?"

"Two-ish. I have to get home in time to pick up Brenna from school. And then I'm back for a dinner shift."

He frowns. "Any chance you can get out of it?"

"Of working? No, I can't do that to Lou." Even though all I want is to toss aside my apron and steal away with him right this moment.

"Do what to me?" Lou appears out of nowhere.

"Nothing. Lou, this is Brett Madden. Brett, this is my boss, Lou."

She gives him a simple nod, as if he's just another customer passing through, but I don't miss the appraising look in her eyes. She has a tendency to dissect people on first impression and make a decision about them then and there. She's rarely wrong.

"Hello, Lou. I was just asking if Cath had to work tonight." Brett smiles.

"Well, funny thing. You wouldn't believe it, but I messed up with the schedule and overstaffed tonight. Tomorrow morning, too."

"*What?*"

"So you can take off for the day when your shift is done."

"But, I *need* to make—"

Her glare makes my complaint drop off. With a nod Brett's way, she marches off.

Leaving me with a grinning Brett. "Well, that worked out well. Now you and Brenna can come up to Sid's place for the night. You'll love it there."

My stomach flutters with the thought of another night with Brett, even as my heart swells with the fact that he automatically included my daughter in our plans. I shake my head. "You sure about wanting her there?"

Those dimples appear. "I've fully accepted the reality of a lot of cold showers in my future, if that's what you mean, yes." His gaze flickers over the diner before coming back to me, dropping to my lips for just a second. "I'm starving. What do you think about letting me grab a table?"

I think that maybe it's time I take advantage of my parents' offer to take Brenna for a night.

"Of course." I lead him to Wendy, the newest hostess—because Lou had to fire yet another one for missing too many shifts.

"Hey, Donovan. Wendy, can you put them at Table Ten."

She frowns a little. "But I thought you were covering—"

"Table Ten." I give her a knowing look.

She shrugs. "Okay!" Her starry eyes flash to Brett before smoothly diverting. "Follow me."

I smile sweetly to him. "Enjoy your lunch." I smile sweetly to him and then head for the swinging door into the kitchen.

"The rush comin' in yet?" Leroy stands at the counter, peeling potatoes—menial work that his staff should be doing, but he finds it therapeutic.

"Not yet."

He watches me pass him and peek out over the food service counter. "What're you up to?"

"A peace offering." I grin, watching Wendy lead Brett and Donovan to their table. "And cheap entertainment."

Misty sees them sit down in her section—because her eyes haven't left Brett since he walked through the door—and her face lights up. Scanning the restaurant, she finally catches my eye.

"Thank you!" she mouths.

Brett is still getting settled when Misty rushes over to greet them and her hands start flapping in that excited way that makes me think of a baby bird trying to fly. I can't hear what she's saying, but her voice is at least five octaves higher than normal borderline squealing.

Donovan, who hides his emotions better than anyone I've ever met, is struggling to maintain his composure.

I can't keep my snort down.

"You are a cruel person, subjecting him to that," Lou mutters, standing next to me to take in the show, her arms folded over her ample chest.

"He loves the attention."

"About as much as a cattle prod up his behind, from the looks of it."

Leroy takes my other side to find out what we're gawking at. His deep chuckle warms my heart. "I don't know many women who would willingly throw Misty at their man. The girl'll be talking about him for the next week."

"He's not my man," I correct him. And oddly, it never even fazed me for a second, the idea of a woman all over him. Perhaps it's because it's Misty, who I don't feel threatened by. Or maybe it's because somewhere along the line, I've decided that I can trust Brett not to hurt me like that.

"Uh-huh." Leroy lets out a loud bark of laughter as Misty bends over to force Brett into a picture. Donovan is busy scanning their surroundings, pretending his client isn't being half mauled by a big-breasted blonde waitress.

"Go on and save him before I have to fire Misty for harassing my customers," Lou scolds, struggling to smother her own smile.

"Well, that would free up your *overbooked* schedule." I don't hide the sarcasm from my tone as I move away from the view of the kitchen window.

Her eyes flash to me once before shifting away.

"I've been here for six and a half years and you've *never* messed up a schedule."

"What can I say? I guess I'm getting old and forgetful. Right, Leroy?"

"Yes, ma'am. She can't remember my name half the time. Keeps callin' me 'fool.'"

"Fool *is* your name half the time, dear."

Clanks sound as the dishwasher, Carl, sets a rack of freshly washed glasses on the table for me to take out front, throwing a wink before ambling back to his station.

"Tell me the truth, did Brett call here and make you give me tonight off?" Because it all seemed to work too smoothly, otherwise.

"When has *anyone* ever made me do anything?" she scoffs.

"Fine. Don't tell me." I head for the front with my arms loaded.

"Looks like I messed up tomorrow afternoon's schedule, too, so you may as well take the whole weekend off."

I sigh, knowing there's no point arguing with her.

And the heady rush of anticipation begins to flow through my veins.

Chapter 27

■ ■ ■

I'm pleasantly surprised to find that Sid Durrand's chalet in the Poconos is a rustic cabin trimmed in maroon detail, rather than the opulent mansion I had prepared myself for on the half-hour drive up. It's also massive—two stories and sprawling—and surrounded by lush trees on a private property that must be several acres in size.

I pull up next to Donovan's SUV, noting that it's the only other vehicle parked here. Brett didn't specify who else was coming tonight, but given he was okay with Brenna tagging along, I'm guessing there aren't plans for a raging hockey team reunion.

The front door creaks open and Brett is filling the doorway, looking oddly comfortable for a guy on crutches. "No problems finding it?"

"None." The dead-end road made it easy not to miss. "This place is . . ." My eyes spy the sparkle of sun catching ripples in water and I let them drift beyond the cabin, to the lake that lies behind. "Thank you for inviting me." I hoist my small duffel bag over my shoulder.

Brett frowns, his gaze searching. "Where's Brenna?"

"Oh." I pick my way up the stone path, admiring the chartreuse-colored creepers weaving through the cracks, until I'm standing before him. "I dropped her off with my parents for the night."

Brett's face flashes with surprise and understanding. "Okay. Well . . ." Minty breath skates across my face with his steady sigh, his gaze drifting over my mouth. But he doesn't lean forward to kiss me. "Come in. Let me show you around."

Inside, thick cedar beams run along the high ceiling, and logs form the walls, making the space feel dark in comparison to the late-afternoon outside. Directly ahead of us is a double-story living room, with a staircase made of cedar climbing to a second story. Everywhere I look is wood, right down to the plank floors.

"Sid wanted to keep this place low-key and relaxed," Brett explains, following my eyes as I take in the worn burgundy leather couches, the old tube TV in the corner, the circa 1980s curtains that drape the windows.

"I think it's great."

"I haven't been up here in over a year. I obviously didn't make it when he had the team last month." Sadness fills his face.

The night of the accident.

"Don took me down the road today, to where it happened. That was my first time being back." There's a long pause. "The flowers are still there. And someone put up a nice cross on the tree." He clears his throat. "Though I don't know how long that tree is going to last."

"Yeah, I heard some townies talking about maybe having to cut it down." I've avoided that stretch of Old Cannery for the most part, taking a busier road that adds five minutes to my commute to work. The one time I did take it—more out of habit than intention—I was left uneasy the entire rest of the day.

Silence hangs for a long moment as Brett gets lost in his thoughts, until finally I reach out and squeeze his hand. "Show me the rest of the place."

He leads me through a similarly rustic dining room and den, and into the kitchen. "This is the only room he actually had renovated."

My eyes take in the cream-colored cupboards and matching cream subway tile, an industrial-size stove like the one Leroy cooks over, and finally land on Donovan, sitting at the island, coffee in hand.

"Why don't you drop your bag." Brett points to a hallway on the other side. "I'll be there in a sec."

I make my way into the all-wood bedroom, smiling with delight at the drab chocolate-brown curtains that line the three windows, a complete contrast to the dusty rose floral bedspread covering a king-size bed.

A small desk sits against one of the windows. I set my duffel bag down next to it as I admire the view of the lake, slightly below us. A long, narrow dock stretches out, where a boat and two kayaks are moored.

A thump sounds. Brett's crutch hitting the doorway on his way into the room.

And my heart skips a beat when I turn around to take him in, as if I hadn't just left him in the kitchen minutes ago, as if I'm only just seeing him now.

Will I ever get used to this?

I hope not.

I hope I feel this same awe every time he walks into a room.

"What's that look for?" A sly smile touches his mouth as he hobbles over to my side of the room to sit down.

"No reason. I love this room. It's cozy and . . ." My words drift as he grasps the hem of my lemon-yellow sundress—a summer staple in my wardrobe—and gently tugs to guide me over to him. The open back of this dress doesn't allow for a bra, and his aqua-blue eyes seem to have picked up on that, lingering on my chest before rising to meet my gaze.

"Where's Donovan?" I whisper, acutely aware of the open door.

Brett's hands settle on the backs of my thighs. "Gone. He won't be back until tomorrow."

"Is anyone else coming, tonight?"

"Nope." His hands tighten their grip but remain where they are, still at a semi-appropriate spot. "What do you wanna do? We can go down to the lake, or sit on the screened-in porch out . . . back." His voice cracks over the last word when I crawl onto the bed. I carefully ease myself onto his lap, curling an arm around his shoulder. Leaning in, I press my lips against his.

One strong arm coils around my body to hold me firm, his skin warming my bare back, his hand settling on the nape of my neck. "Good, I hate nature anyway."

A throaty laugh escapes me, but he silences it a moment later, kissing me deeply, a low, guttural moan rumbling in his chest. "Or we could just do this all night," he suggests, his free hand sliding to the backs of my knees to pull my legs closer, until I'm practically cradled within his arms and he's hardening against my hip.

I've sensed a clock ticking since I pulled into the driveway, counting down these fleeting hours of uninterrupted privacy with Brett. It's oddly liberating not having to worry about a child, not having to consider my responsibilities, and I suddenly feel the overwhelming urge to let go completely.

To find that wild, careless spark that must still be there somewhere.

"I guess we could do *just* this all night." I tease the seam of his lips with my tongue.

His eyes are piercing as they search mine for my meaning. Or, perhaps, to make sure he understood.

I tug at his shirt and he lifts his arms in answer, letting me peel it off him, my fingers sliding over his corded muscles with admiration. He chuckles at my heavy sigh as I stare unabashedly at his chest, my palm memorizing the curves. "I can't help it," I purr, feeling my cheeks heat. "You're just unreal."

"You think so?" His tongue slides over the crook of my neck and I gasp lightly. "I've lost about ten pounds of muscle in the last month. Wait until I'm back to full circuit training."

It's nice to hear him talking positively about his future, but I don't mention it now, happy to soak in the feel of his mouth as it travels along my collarbone, leaving a trail of moisture.

With a deep sigh, he pushes the straps of my dress down over my shoulders to fall and expose my chest for his mouth, leaning my body back enough that he can suck in a peaked nipple.

A low, steady throb grows in the pit of my belly as I let my head hang back. His hand roams my bare legs, sliding in between my thighs, his thumb rubbing against my cotton panties. A soft curse slides against my breast like a caress, sending shivers down to my core, and then his fist is bunching, gathering my dress and sliding it down my legs, off my body. My panties quickly follow, stripping me bare.

Suddenly he stops, and with a sigh, he pulls the bed free of the bedspread, uncovering crisp white sheets beneath. "Can you help me?" he whispers, reaching down to unbuckle his belt.

My breath catches with my nod. *This is really happening.*

Lifting me off his lap with seemingly little effort, he hoists himself up to balance on his good leg. His hands fumble with his zipper, unfastening his shorts. They tumble to the ground.

With a stretch and tug of his briefs, they follow closely. My breath catches in my throat as I take in the sight of Brett naked for the first time.

The mattress springs as he settles back onto the bed, his clothes dangling from his casted foot. "I won't always be so helpless," he promises as I crouch down to carefully remove them, and I sense a hint of bitterness in his voice. I remember how frustrated I was with my wrist, and that was only a sprain.

"I don't mind, at all," I purr. The feel of his eyes raking over my body as I stand in front of him is almost too much. But he seizes my hips and holds me still, pressing his lips against the faint silver lines on my pelvic bone. Stretchmarks that Brenna graced my body with. It's the first time any man has ever seen me naked since having her.

When he finally releases me, I watch his body flex beautifully as he hoists himself back to settle fully into bed, his legs splayed slightly.

Waiting for me to join him.

I simply take him in for a long moment, adoring his perfect form and the human being within.

He almost died.

I almost lost him, without ever getting to know him. Without having these moments with him.

I don't think either of us intended for things to move so quickly after—me, climbing onto the bed to admire his body, first with my hands, and then with my mouth; him, begging me to fish out a condom from the travel bag sitting on the nightstand; me, carefully straddling his hips.

Him, guiding himself into me with a low, guttural moan that I feel right where we are joined.

Me, losing myself in my body as my thighs tense and my hips roll, wanting nothing more than to hear him call my name, to feel his release, to know that he adores me.

Realizing that I've already fallen in love with him.

■ ■ ■

"Come on . . ." Brett's abdominal muscles tense as he pulls himself up, his eyes glued to the TV screen previously tucked away behind armoire doors. It's game seven of the Stanley Cup finals and I have to accept that lying naked in bed next to him while he yells at the players is simply part of the deal.

I'll gladly take it.

So I quietly admire the curves of his back and pick at a slice of the pizza we threw in the oven earlier, while taking a break after three hours of familiarizing ourselves with each other's bodies. I now know that Brett's insanely ticklish around his belly button, barely able to stand being touched there. I know that the seven-inch scar across his forearm is from a skate blade during a collision. I've kissed every one of the six bones he has broken, aside from the ones still protected by his cast. That's actually how I learned one of my most favorite facts about Brett—that no matter how recently he came, kissing him along his collarbone will instantly make him rock-hard.

I've already confirmed that twice tonight, just to be sure. I'm going to be feeling the effects of it for days to come.

Brett groans and falls backward into bed as LA scores a goal against Toronto, making it two to one. "Don't worry. Still one period left."

"Where's their defense tonight?"

When I don't answer, he turns to watch me. "You don't know what I'm talking about, do you?"

I savor a decidedly spicy green olive. "Not really, nope."

His eyes drop to linger over my breasts and my stomach for a moment before returning. "You don't mind me watching the game, do you?"

"Nope." I smile, picking off another olive. This one slips from my fingers before I get it to my mouth, landing just below my belly button.

I giggle as Brett twists his body, free of covers and sprawled out, and scoops up the ring with his tongue to eat it. "Those are good olives." He licks the spot of grease off my skin. His hot breath is a tease, my body silently begging him to shift his attention farther down as I watch his length begin to swell. Briefly considering how he'd react if I took him in my mouth now, while such a pivotal game is on. Would that annoy him?

I'm saved from wondering when the sheets are sliding down and Brett's mouth is on me.

■ ■ ■

I lie in bed and listen to the utter silence of the night, timing my breaths with Brett's as I watch his broad chest rise and fall slowly.

Marveling at the life that courses through those long, strong limbs that I was tangled with, that fuels the kind heart and charming mind that I am enamored with.

Wondering how it's possible to feel *this* close to another human being.

Maybe he's not the one caught up in it all. Maybe it's me who's under a spell. Because I never dreamed that I could feel this way about anyone.

Chapter 28

■ ■ ■

"Why are you *always* at our house now?" Brenna chirps, earning my glare of disapproval. She gives Brett a sheepish smile and then shifts her focus to the chips and cookies that he tossed into the cart when I wasn't looking.

"That'll be a hundred and forty-two even," the teenage cashier says, blatantly staring at Brett as he swiftly moves in with a wad of twenty-dollar bills before I manage to get my wallet out.

"Don't even." He chuckles, nudging me forward toward the cart, treating the cashier to a dimpled smile as he collects his change.

With a heavy sigh, I push the loaded cart out of Weiss, trying to pretend that no one's watching us. The truth is, it's ten on a Sunday morning and *everyone* is watching us. It doesn't seem to faze Brett, though, who casually greets people as he passes.

Since last weekend at Sid Durrand's cabin, Brett has come over four out of five weekdays. Twice during the day while Brenna was at school and I didn't have to work. And then last night, he put his feet up, turned on the baseball game—the hockey season is over, with Toronto taking home the Cup—and simply stayed. We never actually discussed the idea of him staying. It just kind of happened. And it felt right.

Thankfully, it was easy enough to explain why Brett was sleeping in my bed with me—there was nowhere else for him to sleep—and I could rationalize with Brenna about why *she* couldn't sleep with us—she can't risk bumping Brett's leg. That didn't stop her from wandering in at six this morning to wake us both up.

So far, nothing's been reported to the media. No one's lurking behind Rawley's with a camera. It's an oddly . . . normal situation. That's probably because we haven't done anything as public as go grocery shopping together until now. I've definitely heard the whispers, felt the curious smiles.

"Why so tense?" Brett asks as we cross the parking lot.

"I'm not. Brenna, stay close."

His straight white teeth gleam in the morning sun as he grins. "Liar."

"Maybe I *am* a bit tense," I admit softly. "I guess I'm just waiting for someone to jump out of the bushes and shove a camera in my face. You know, ask me when we're getting married."

His grin falls off suddenly. "Whoa . . . Let's not get ahead of ourselves here, Cath."

My cheeks flare with heat. "Oh, I didn't mean *for real*, like that's what I *want*."

He pauses, a frown pulling his brow tight. "You don't want that?"

"Of course I do. I mean, I will. I mean . . ." My mind is spinning as I stumble over my words, searching for the ones to defuse this sudden tension.

Until he begins to chuckle, and I realize he's teasing me.

"You're such a jerk!" I elbow his forearm but I'm smiling.

"Mommy!"

"It's okay. I deserved that," Brett tells her as I root through my purse in search of my keys. "Maybe I should get into acting if this hockey thing doesn't work out."

I roll my eyes at him as I pop the hatch. Brett begins handing me grocery bags, his grin downright devilish, his fingers grazing mine with each pass.

"Have you ever had a dog?" Brenna asks out of nowhere, even while her bright eyes are on the tub of chocolate ice cream that she somehow didn't notice earlier.

"I did. A beagle named Bower. He ran away, though. Never came back."

"Oh." Brenna's face scrunches. "That's a sad story."

"You're right. It is."

"Are you gonna get another one?"

Brett empties the cart of the last two bags. "Funny you should ask. I *have* started thinking about getting a dog lately."

Her eyes widen. *"Really?"*

"Yeah. I just don't know if I can handle walking it right now."

"I can help!"

"Brett lives in Philadelphia, honey," I remind her.

Her face falls. "Oh, yeah . . . I forgot." But the wheels are already churning inside that small head of hers. "I only have one more week of school so I could do it for the summer. I could stay at your house!"

I turn to give Brett a "see what you've done" stare.

He doesn't seem the least bit ruffled. "I'll have to think about it, Brenna. A dog is a huge responsibility."

She's already thinking about it plenty. "I know. But there's three of us. Mommy and I could live with you at your house—"

"No, Brenna."

"Why not? Brett has a big house."

"Just because."

"Because *why?*"

There's no point explaining the more obvious reasons for us not moving in with Brett.

"Because that's a long drive for me to work."

"Why do you *have* to work, anyway?"

I stifle my exasperation. "We've already had this conversation." At least twenty times, the concept still escaping her. "I have to work to make money, so we have somewhere to live, and food on the table, and clothes on our bodies, and—"

"But Owen Mooter said that Brett is super rich so can't he—"

"No!" *That damn Owen Mooter kid again.* I cast an apologetic look Brett's way, but he's merely smiling, as if amused by the entire conversation.

"Brenna, I promise we'll get you a dog when the time is right. Now come on. Help me put the cart away."

She grabs the other side of the handle, chattering on about what kind of dog Brett should get—a boy dog, surely, because Brett is a boy—and what he should name it as we cross the parking lot to the cart station. I let her give it a shove in, and then we're turning to head back to the car.

Scott Philips is just ahead of me.

Chapter 29

■ ■ ■

He wasn't paying attention, his eyes on his phone screen, so by the time Scott notices me, he's a mere four feet away. He stops short. "Catherine?"

He looks like the photo in the newspaper, though less put together, his coffee-colored hair mussed from the light breeze, his jeans and Muse T-shirt casual. That youthful air about him still exists, though dulled considerably.

I'm vaguely aware of the small clammy hand tugging against mine. "Mommy, who is that?"

"No one." I pull Brenna against my thigh, willing my legs to move. In all the times I've played this scenario in my head, I had been able to stroll past him, show him that he's no longer a thought. And yet now my legs are frozen.

Scott lowers his gaze to her, the fine lines across his forehead that were airbrushed out of his picture now clearly visible. "I was your mom's art teacher in high school."

"Really? Did you teach her how to draw houses?"

My stomach twists, watching his hazel eyes twinkle with his familiar smile. "I actually didn't teach your mother all that much. She was a natural artist."

You taught me a lot of other stuff, though.

"Are you still a teacher?"

"I'm taking a break." There's no missing the twinge of bitterness in his voice. I wonder if he's blaming me for this latest turn of events, too. Considering he'd likely still be teaching, his neighborhood blissfully ignorant of the snake living among them, had I not saved Brett.

My anger unexpectedly flares.

"Cath, you okay?"

So distracted by my shock, I haven't noticed Brett making his way over until he's right there. If he's seen pictures of Scott in the news, he doesn't seem to recognize him now, though his face says he knows *something* is wrong. "Yeah. I'm fine. We were just going."

"This was Mommy's teacher," Brenna says, oblivious of the tension. "He taught her how to draw."

Brett's face hardens immediately as he turns to face Scott. He has at least five inches and forty pounds on him, and even supported by crutches, he somehow looms threateningly. I've never seen Brett as anything but kind and charming and gentle, and yet right now, his jaw is clenched so tight, his body so rigid, I'm beginning to wonder if he isn't going to try and beat Scott to a pulp, cast or not.

The wariness on Scott's face makes me think he's wondering the same.

"Brett, let's go." I settle a hand on his chest, pushing him back a touch, adding in a whisper, "People are staring." He doesn't budge. I add even lower, "Brenna."

That snaps Brett out of it almost immediately, his hand settling gently on the top of her head. He peers down at her.

And then back again to Scott, lingering for a long moment, before I'm finally able to usher him toward my Escape. I don't miss Brett's low growl of "Stay away from her" as he passes.

"That teacher was kind of weird," Brenna says as she climbs into her booster seat. Normally I'd ask her why she'd say that, but now I quietly watch her fumble with her seat belt from the rearview mirror.

A warm hand settles on my knee. "You okay?"

I nod. "I knew that would happen sooner or later. Lou warned me that he was back."

"Well, now it's happened and we move on. It's all in the past, right?"

I force a smile. "Right."

"Okay, I'm ready!" Brenna announces, kicking her legs.

Brett turns to regard her for a long moment, a pensive look on his face. I don't pry, though. I'm too busy wondering if we need to move out of Balsam.

Chapter 30

■ ■ ■

"Hold on a sec!" I holler, hugging the towel to my body as I dart from the bathroom to my bedroom, to throw on my pink sundress, my skin still damp from my shower. I glance at the clock: eleven a.m.

Keith's sleeping, so I know it's not him. Besides, he usually lets himself in with his key.

I head for the window, because neither Brenna nor I ever open the door without checking anymore. Actually, Brenna's been banned from opening the door until further notice.

A black Suburban is parked outside.

I hold my breath as I throw open the door.

"What are you doing here?" I sound like I've been running laps, my voice breathless.

Brett grins. "I can't surprise you?"

"Of course you can. But I thought—" My mouth drops open as I finally notice the absence of crutches and the new walking cast that protects his leg. "Oh, my God! They took it off!" I knew he had his eight-week doctor's appointment this morning, but neither of us had expected this.

"Doc said I was ready."

I can't help the squeal as I throw myself at him, my arms coiling around his neck.

That charming laugh of his sails from his lips, warming my chest. "Take it easy. I'm still getting used to this thing."

"I'm sorry. I'm just so happy for you." My face feels like it's about to split from smiling, even as I ask, "So, what did your leg look like when they took it off?"

"Horrible. Withered and scarred. I'll show you later. Come *here*," he whispers, dipping his head to lay a sweet kiss on my lips, his arms circling me, pulling me in tight against him.

He was here only yesterday. I can still feel where he was, deep inside me, and I ache for more. "It's Brenna's last day of school today."

"Yeah, I think I remember her mentioning that." She's been marching around the house for the past week, counting down the days at the top of her lungs.

"That means she's going to be with me pretty much *all* the time."

His breath skates across my lips. "I figured."

"So . . . you're coming in, right?"

He smiles, not missing my meaning. "To celebrate getting my new cast?"

"Sure, whatever you wanna call it."

My whole body shakes with his deep chuckle. "Actually, I thought we could get out for a bit first, before I let you use me for my body."

"Oh, shut up."

"Come on, let's go. Unless . . ." His eyes drift past me, to the baskets of dirty laundry I was about to lug down to the Laundromat, already three days overdue. "Did I catch you at a bad time?"

"Yes. I mean, no, it's not a bad time and yes, we can go."

He reaches out to toy with a strand of my wet hair. "Okay, well . . . the sooner we go, the sooner we can come back." Excitement flickers in his eyes. And perhaps a touch of nervousness.

I grab my keys and purse and trail him out.

The busboy at Rawley's, Gibby, quietly tosses bags of trash into the Dumpster. He's never said much to me, but I offer him a polite wave as usual and then climb into the SUV.

■ ■ ■

"I could have driven us." I admire the lush lilac bush on the corner, the branches sagging under the weight of the conical flowers, still dripping from an early-morning rainfall. Balsam is now in full bloom.

"I wanted to give Don one more day before I get back behind the wheel." A little louder, "You're gonna miss driving my ass around, won't you, Don?"

"It's given my life meaning," the gruff bodyguard replies in a deadpan tone, though I catch his eyes crinkling in the rearview mirror as we coast down the quiet street.

"You're allowed to drive with that?" I nod toward the new cast.

"There's no law against it. I'll still get Don to drive me into Philly for my appointments, but if I'm around here, I can drive myself."

I can't hide my smile. He's talking like he plans on being in Balsam. A lot.

"You know, this is a really nice little town."

"It is," I have to agree. Even overcast, the sun struggling to push through for what the weather claimed would be a "sunny and hot afternoon," it's a pleasant drive. A glimpse of blue water catches my eye. "That's Jasper Lake, up ahead. Donovan, can you take the next left?"

"Yes, ma'am."

"Remember that street I was telling you about? It's the nicest part of Balsam."

"Right." Brett nods, taking in the line of stately Victorian houses on either side.

"I'll bring you here at the holidays so you can see the lights. It's like something out of a Christmas card. It's my favorite time." But truthfully, there isn't a season that doesn't look spectacular here. Oak trees form a canopy over the vast manicured front lawns of old stately homes. It doesn't matter if it's a long, hot, lazy summer day or the frigid dead of winter, Jasper Lane is charming for anyone, visitor or otherwise.

I smile. "And that's the Gingerbread House, up here on the right."

"*This* house?"

"Yeah."

"Hey, pull over, Don."

Donovan stops, allowing us a glimpse where the tall hedge parts for the long paved driveway. I sigh as I take in the three stories of Victorian grandeur. "They must have painted this spring." The buttery yellow siding and white trim details pop against the ebony shingles, also new from the looks of it.

"It's a nice house." Brett's thoughtful gaze rolls over it. "It looks exactly like that picture you drew."

"You remember?"

"I remember *everything* about that night." His chuckle dies off around the same time that my cheeks begin to flush, hoping Donovan doesn't pick up on his meaning.

"You should see the inside. That time they had the open house? I didn't want to leave."

Brett frowns, as if an idea is forming. "Well, let's go and see it, then."

"What?"

"Let's go and see inside."

I'm shaking my head, laughing. "Someone lives there now."

"Who?"

"I don't know. Some rich people."

He grins. "Perfect. Rich people love me. Let's go and introduce ourselves. Don?"

Donovan backs the SUV up and pulls into the driveway.

"*Oh, my God.* You're actually serious?"

"Of course I am. I almost burned to death in a car. After that, I'm not afraid of knocking on a door. I'm surprised you are, actually."

"Yeah, but . . ."

He reaches over to squeeze my knee. "If *you* want to see inside that house, I'm going to make it happen for you."

"They're not going to just let us walk into their house! Besides, no one's home." I'm guessing. There's a detached triple garage off to the side, which could be housing their cars.

He nods toward the puddled divots in the pavement. "Those are tire marks, there."

"Still!"

"Don't worry, I do this all the time."

"You show up at strange people's houses *all the time*?"

He chuckles. "Trust me. You wouldn't believe what people agree to. Plus, you're a local celebrity. What's the worst they can say?"

"But . . . we can't do this!"

Brett pauses, his hand on the door handle. "Why not?"

"I don't know." I don't have a good reason besides that it's crazy and presumptuous.

He pushes his door open and climbs out, that mischievous twinkle in his eye. "Come on."

I shake my head. This is a side of Brett I've never seen before. "Does he do this a lot?"

Donovan smiles but says nothing.

Brett throws open my door and stands there, waiting, his hand out.

"I can't believe you're making me do this," I say, sliding out.

"Don't you want to show it to me?"

"Well, yeah, but—"

"Come on, then." He tugs on my hand, his fingers through mine sending a thrill through my body. "We'll do it together."

I fall into a slow-paced walk with him as we take the path toward the stately wraparound porch, his steps with the new cast tentative. "You're doing all the talking. I'm not saying a single word," I warn him.

That doesn't seem to bother Brett, as he grabs the knocker and bangs against the solid oak door, and I clench my thighs together, a sudden rush of nerves making me feel like I have to pee.

"Hmm . . ." He frowns, cupping his hands around his eyes and leaning against one of the stained-glass panels that bank either side of the door.

I glance around at the neighboring houses, to see if anyone's watching. This feels like the kind of neighborhood where people keep an eye out for each other. Luckily—for us—the houses are spread too far apart and a line of bushes and evergreens separates us from the closest one, blocking the view of the porch. "We should leave. This is trespassing. Can we go?" As anxious as I am, I feel a teensy bit disappointed. Part of me must have hoped this crazy idea of Brett's would work.

"Yeah. I guess." He sighs. "Another time."

I move to lead the way down the steps. The door creaking open stalls me.

I turn around just as Brett steps through the front door, a key sitting in the lock.

Chapter 31

■ ■ ■

"It's way nicer than that sell sheet you showed me," Brett muses, standing in the foyer, the grand spiral staircase that reaches all the way to the third floor in front of him. "You said there was another staircase somewhere?"

They *do* have another staircase—a narrow and steep one to reach the room in the attic. But I can't explain that to him right now, because I'm speechless. My footfalls echo through the wide, vacant place as I wander, my gaze taking in the rooms bare of furniture, the walls empty of art but with rectangular dust marks where the pictures hung. As if someone recently removed them.

"What did you do?" I ask in an eerily calm voice, though I think I already know what Brett did.

Brett bought the Gingerbread House.

"Turns out Mr. and Mrs. Chase were thinking of selling this place. They'd bought it as a summer home for their family, but they could already see that they weren't going to get enough use out of it. Plus, it was too much work for them." Brett strolls over to pick a picture hanger out off the wall.

They were *thinking* of selling it. As in . . . "So you asked them if you could buy it?" How is it possible that Brett Madden bought a house in Balsam and the entire town hasn't heard about it already?

"Yeah. Well, not me. A representative. My lawyer, actually. Signing on my behalf. Kept my name out of the paperwork. That's pretty common. My parents do it all the time."

Okay. I'm trying to wrap my head around this. Brett bought the Gingerbread House.

And Brett knows that this is my and Brenna's dream house.

I'm no idiot. I just can't believe this is happening.

"What?" he asks casually, barely managing to keep a straight face.

"Why did you buy this house?"

He doesn't answer me, instead wandering farther down the hall. "The kitchen could use an update, but it's a good size. What do you think?" I find him standing in the middle of the spacious and bare farmhouse-style kitchen. "Could knock out this wall . . ."

"Brett."

He slides his hand along the surface of the industrial-size stainless steel fridge. "This is new, but the stove needs replacing . . ."

"*Brett.*"

Finally, he stops to look at me. "I was thinking about what you said, about this being a big tourist town and there not being enough of these kinds of places. I figured a little business venture might be a good idea. For *me.*"

"So you're saying that you bought this place . . . for *you*?" I wasn't expecting that answer.

"Yeah." He says it so innocently, I almost believe him.

"*You* want to own an inn."

"Why not?"

"*You*, Brett Madden," my gaze drifts over his muscular six-foot-two frame, "giant NHL hockey legend, son of a Hollywood movie star, want to open an inn in Balsam, Pennsylvania."

He shrugs, still maintaining a neutral expression. "What's wrong with that?"

"Nothing. This is all just a little too *familiar* to me for some reason."

He's on the move again, through the kitchen and into the small den. "This faces east, so I thought it'd be a cool place for guests to have their breakfast."

"Did you, now . . ."

I trail him through a set of French doors and into a room with a fireplace. "And I figure this room could be closed off and converted into a dining room, for small events. I can hire a chef. There are some good local chefs, right?"

I bite my tongue.

"What do you think? Good idea?"

I think that I have this room marked as the dining room in my sketchbook, and, despite being drunk and flipping through it only once, he somehow remembers it. That's what I think.

When I don't answer, he leads me out and around the corner,

down a hallway. "This here was one of the big selling features. For *me*, of course." He pushes the door open. "There's a separate two-bedroom apartment, so I could live here comfortably, away from any guests."

Is he being serious? Or is this all part of whatever game he's playing at? "You're going to live in Balsam?"

He frowns. "Well, yeah. Of course. How else am I going to manage things around here?"

He's so good at screwing with me, I nearly let myself get excited at the prospect of it being true.

"It'll take months to renovate the rest of the place. I've gotta decide on a good contractor. Local, ideally. I've heard that Boyd & Sons are the best around here."

"From Belmont, yeah. They come into Diamonds sometimes," I agree, still in shock, following him into the living room.

He pauses to glance at me. "I've got a few great ideas, too, to make it homey." He reaches up to run a hand through his hair, throwing it into sexy disarray. "I was thinking about a nice forest-green duck wallpaper for this room. Maybe a few stuffed birds mounted on the wall, over there and there. And I'm going to take up hunting in the fall. Hopefully, I'll bag a buck. Or a couple. One head over each table. What do you think?"

When he glances back again to see the horror clearly splayed across my face, his face cracks into a broad grin. "Finally, a reaction! *Jeez!*"

I close my eyes as a giant sigh of relief sails from my lips. "You're joking."

"Fuck! Of course I'm joking. Have you seen my condo? Half the time I'm not sure I should dress myself."

My eyes drift over his gray shorts and black golf shirt. Even in ratty sweatpants, Brett would always looks good.

He slips his hand through mine. "Come on, I want to show you something else. It's another idea I have."

"Oh, *really*." I should be furious with him, but my excitement is overshadowing everything.

He unfastens the lock on the French doors. I inhale the smell of wet grass as we step out onto the covered porch. A large wrought-iron table sits in the center and around it are lounge chairs with plush rust-colored cushions. They're well kept but not brand-new and I know he didn't have these at his condo, so I'm guessing the old owners left them behind.

"When did they move their things out?"

"Tuesday. It closed yesterday."

"That's . . ." I'm still trying to wrap my head around this. He only learned about this house—what it meant to Brenna and me—a few weeks ago. That means he's been negotiating this behind my back all this time, and quickly.

That phone call.

The night we stayed at his condo in Philly, I overheard him talking to someone, telling them to offer whatever they wanted, that he didn't want it getting back to me.

This is what he was talking about.

"That was fast" is all I can manage.

He frowns, scratching at a tiny crack in one of the glass panels of the French door, saying almost absently, "People will do anything for enough money."

I think I'm going to be sick.

Brett must notice my face paling, just imagining what he must have thrown at them to get them to up and move just like that. "It's a smart investment, Cath. *For me.*"

"And sorry, tell me, what were you going to name this inn?"

He twists his lips. "I haven't figured that out yet. I'm sure it'll come to me, though."

"Right . . ."

He gestures at the open space next to the porch, where a flagstone patio currently resides. "I want to build one of those glass rooms over there." His face scrunches up with confusion. "What are they called?"

"A conservatory?"

"Yeah. Exactly. I've always wanted one, and when I looked at that open space, I just knew that's what had to go there."

I can't help the deep belly laugh that slips from my lips as I listen to him regurgitate almost word for word my plans for the Gingerbread House.

"What?" He turns and heads back into the house, but not before I catch the struggle not to smile in his jaw.

"Nothing. It's just . . ." I'm speechless. He's planned this all out perfectly, but I'm not fooled. Not for one second. I'm sure that in an hour or two the shock will wear off, but until then, there's a sizable prickly knot in my throat. "I'm having a very hard time . . ." *Accepting* this, I want to say, but Brett hasn't officially offered anything for me to accept. I settle on ". . . picturing this."

He leads me into the kitchen. "I'm not. Not at all. It's pretty damn obvious to me," he says softly, his eyes full of hope as he closes in on me.

Are we still talking about the Gingerbread House?

I thought the house was quiet before, but now I'd hear a ghost shuffle by in the silence between us.

I clear my throat. "What are you going to do with it when you're on the ice again?"

He reaches up to cradle the back of my head between both hands, so gently. "I can probably find someone to run it. *If* I'm ever back on the ice." That lingering shadow hangs in his gaze. It pushes aside my current anger with him for spending this kind of money on something undoubtedly for me.

I settle my hands on his arms, rubbing his biceps soothingly. "What did they tell you today?"

Brett sighs. "My doctor seems a lot happier with the healing this time around, but that doesn't mean I'll be able to skate like I could before. We just have to wait and see." His thumbs drag along the nape off my neck and I shiver. "So I'm gonna keep myself busy with things. Things that make me happy." Humor touches his lips. "Some smart little kid told me to do that."

"And buying this house made you happy?"

If that crooked smile isn't enough for me right now, the dimple that pops in his cheek sure is. "Buying this house made me the happiest I've been in a long time." He leans in to steal a kiss before pulling away. "Come on, let's go see the rest of it."

Slowly, Brett leads me through the five sizable bedrooms on the second floor, amusing me with "his ideas" for where to build the bathrooms and how to refinish the fireplaces, and then to the third floor, to my favorite room—the attic.

"Did you know you can see the lake from the window" he asks, taking my hand and pulling me to the dormer.

"No. I had *no* idea." I take in the expanse of manicured grass stretching toward the dark blue water, some hundred yards back. A few sailboats drift in the distance. The sell sheet showed a long, narrow dock and a rocky shoreline, but I have yet to see them in person. "Whatever will you do with all this land?" I ask mockingly, picturing the gardens and gazebo I had planned for it. A perfect venue for small weddings.

"Not sure yet. I have so much to focus on in here first." He takes in the vast empty room, his steps echoing. "I've hired Niya Kalpar to help with designing it. She's done some of the inns in Napa Valley. She's going to work off the concept sketches I sent her."

My brows spike. "Sketches?"

"My own, of course. I've been working on them awhile." He's barely able to keep his amusement in check, his nostrils flaring. "Niya says I'm extremely talented."

"Ugh!" I grit my teeth with frustration, even as I'm trying not to laugh at the insanity of all this. I'll yell at him for stealing my sketchbook later. "How long are you going to keep this charade going?"

"As long as necessary." He closes the distance again, dipping down to press his forehead against mine. "Please don't fight me on this."

I shake my head. "I'm furious with you."

"I can tell." He nips at my bottom lip with his teeth, tugging it a bit before he lays a soothing kiss against it. It turns into another, and then another, until I feel myself being sandwiched between the wall and Brett's hard body.

"You're not going to distract me with—"

He cuts off my words with a deep kiss that buckles my knees. I rope my hands around his neck for support. "You sure about that?"

"You can't just go and buy a—" My head thumps softly against the wall as he steals another deep kiss. His calloused hands begin to wander, his fingers tracing my rib cage and then drifting down to squeeze my hips the way he does when I'm riding him. A soft moan escapes me with the thought, earning his groan. He slips his hands under my dress.

And suddenly pulls back, his eyes widing with surprise. "That's efficient."

"You caught me coming out of the shower so I just threw this on," I admit sheepishly, reveling in the caress of his fingertips over my bare curves.

A soft curse slips from his lips. Reaching up, he pushes my spaghetti straps off my shoulders. The light cotton falls to the floor, leaving me completely naked.

"I think I want to catch you coming out of the shower more often." He steps back to admire my body.

My heart is racing. With his words, with the way his eyes touch me.

But the bastard went and bought the Gingerbread House for me! And stole my sketches!

I steel my jaw. "I'm still furious with you."

The corners of his mouth twitch. He reaches over his head to grab the back of his T-shirt and peel it off. "Better?"

"No," I deny, trying to maintain my stern face as I shamelessly stare at his broad, firm chest.

"Fine." His hands make quick work of his belt buckle and zipper, unfastening them to hang open, revealing the prominent bulge beneath. He fishes a condom from his pocket.

"What are you doing?"

His brow quirks playfully. "I'll give you . . . three guesses."

A deep throb begins to ache between my legs as I watch him tear the foil between his teeth and, untucking his hard length from his briefs, sheath himself. "But we *can't*. Not here."

Gripping my backside, he lifts me up to pin me against the wall and guides my legs around his hips. His lips settle on my collarbone. "Why not?"

"How will you . . ." My words fall off with my sharp inhale as he pushes into me. "What about your leg?"

"All my weight's on my good one."

"It's strong enough?"

His deep chuckle vibrates inside my chest. "You really have no idea what kind of endurance I have, do you?"

I *have* noticed he doesn't tire easily . . .

He sinks deeper into me. "Still mad at me?"

"Furious," I whisper, unable to keep the soft moan from slipping out.

His muscles cord beneath my fingertips as he thrusts into me.

And all thoughts besides how intensely I care for this man are swiftly pushed aside.

Chapter 32

...

"If the door is closed, you *have* to knock," I say slowly, hoping that hearing it for a third time will make it finally sink in.

"But I didn't know he'd be changing!" Her bottom lip wobbles.

There's no point reminding Brenna that only three minutes before she strolled in on Brett naked in my bedroom, she had watched him walk out of the shower in nothing but a towel and I specifically told her *not* to go into my room. "It's okay." I push a lock of frizzy hair off her forehead. Unlike my fine strands, which stay poker straight no matter what season, the summer humidity wreaks havoc on Brenna's curls. "But now you know, right?" And now *I* know that we need to install a lock.

She bobs her head up and down. Then frowns. "But what if you're in there, too?"

Then you definitely don't barge in. "If the door is closed, you knock. And *wait*."

She pauses. "Is Brett going to be staying here all summer?"

"He'll probably be here a lot, yeah." I haven't told her about the Gingerbread House yet. I'm not sure how to begin to explain that.

"Why?"

"Because I like spending time with him. And I think he likes spending time with us." I pinch her nose. "And *you* like it when he's here, too, remember? You're the one who kept asking about him."

Her mouth pouts. "But I don't like that I can't cuddle with you at night when he's here."

"Aren't you getting a bit old for that? Don't forget that you're turning six in five days!" I say, even as I tell myself that I'll willingly curl up in bed with her no matter how old she is.

"Are we going to Diamonds for my birthday again?"

I smile. Breakfast at the diner for Brenna's birthday has become a tradition. Some of the regulars even show up with small gifts for her. "Leroy's already talking about the special waffles he's going to make you."

"Yay! What else are we going to do for my birthday?"

"I'm not sure yet. It'll be a surprise. And I know things are changing a little bit. But it's all in the best way." I shut off the light. "Good night."

Brett's lying in my bed when I get to my room. And he doesn't look particularly happy.

"What's wrong?"

With a sigh, he holds his phone out. "Simone just sent me this."

I crawl in next to him.

A picture of Brett and me kissing on my front porch fills the screen, with the caption, "Brett Madden Falls in Love with Good Samaritan."

I try to ignore the way my heart stutters at the love part. "This is from three days ago." I'm in my pink sundress. "How the hell did they . . ." My stomach sinks with realization. "That little asshole, Gibby!" He was back there cleaning up when Brett came. He must have taken the picture. "How did he even know who to sell it to?"

"Somebody probably left their number at Rawley's, told him to call if he got a money shot."

I sink into my pillow with a resigned sigh. "Please tell me I'm not back to security guards and photographers hovering around my driveway at all hours of the day and night."

"No. I don't think it'll turn into that again." Brett sets his phone onto my nightstand. "But you and Brenna should come and stay with me."

"It's too far, Brett. My family's here, my job—"

"Not in Philly. Here, at the house. I told you I was gonna live there."

"I thought you were kidding."

"I have no reason to be in Philly right now. I can drive in for doctor and physical therapy appointments." He rolls onto his side to study me. "So? What do you think?"

"But what will Brenna say? I mean, all of a sudden we're living at the Gingerbread House, with you—"

"And a dog."

"Stop it! I'm being serious."

"So am I."

I shake my head. "*And* a dog. Even better."

"I don't see the problem. She'll love it."

"Exactly." I stare at my ceiling. "She'll fall in love with the house and the dog. She's already completely enamored with you."

"Can't blame her."

He's making jokes and I'm smiling, but it's not really funny. "You can't give something like that to a kid and then take it away."

Brett frowns. "Who's gonna take it away?"

"I don't know. Life. Reality."

The whirl of my noisy secondhand fan fills the long moment of silence in my room. And then calloused fingers seize my chin, steering me back to face his aqua-blue eyes. "Are you planning on going somewhere?"

"No." *Never.*

"Well, then, I don't know what you're worried about."

He doesn't get it. "I'm a mother. I always have to worry about the consequences. I can't do things on a whim."

"This isn't on a whim. Trust me, I like to weigh things out, too. And no one's taking anything away from anyone. Got it?" He leans in to press his lips against my mouth. "I want you and Brenna to stay with me at the house. Tell her it's just for a week or two, if that makes you feel better."

I sigh. "What about her birthday? We always have breakfast at Diamonds, but I don't want to bring her there if there are photographers again."

"We can do something for her at the house, with everyone."

"It's in five days, Brett. There's no furniture at the house."

"There will be by then. Simone ordered a bunch of stuff for me. It's being delivered tomorrow."

"She must have loved doing that."

He chuckles. "She called me an asshole at least a dozen times." Brett's phone vibrates noisily against the nightstand. He groans. "That's her now. They're hounding her for a confirmation." He retrieves his phone and studies the picture again. "Do you think she can pass this off as a friendly greeting?"

I study the way our bodies are pressed flush against each other. "Only if you start groping everyone."

"So . . . what do you want her to say?" He looks to me expectantly. "She can decline to comment, but that usually makes them more annoying."

"Because they'll be looking for the story we're trying to hide."

"Exactly."

"I guess there's really no point hiding this anymore, now that Gibby sold that picture. It's only a matter of time." And I don't feel the same need I did before, to hide my feelings for Brett. A part of me wants to scream about us from the rooftops. Brett is *mine*. Brett wants *me*. "So she should just confirm it," I say, before I can chicken out.

"Works for me." I watch his fingers fly over the keys.

"Oh, my God!" I lunge for his phone, but his reach is too wide and I end up draped over his chest, the screen visible but out of reach. "She knows not to say *that*, right?"

"She's a terrible publicist if she doesn't," he says, chuckling.

I watch as the three dots dance on the screen.

Send me an appropriate response by 9 am tomorrow.

P.S. Really? I wouldn't have guessed that about her.

■ ■ ■

"Where is the birthday girl!" Keith's voice booms dramatically from somewhere unseen, carrying through the giant vacant house, out onto the covered porch.

Brenna squeals as he appears in the doorway, squinting against the setting sun.

"Perfect timing." She's already torn through the presents from my parents, and Lou and Leroy. All that's left is the bike that Jack, Emma, and I went in on, currently hiding in the garage.

"You do that yourself, Singer?" Jack mocks him, nodding at the rectangular box, wrapped in fuchsia paper and adorned with bows.

"My mom did, actually," Keith admits as he sets the box in front of a wired Brenna, earning Jack's burst of laughter.

"Why so late?" I ask.

"I got held up with work." He exchanges a round of greetings, ending with a frown. "Where's Misty?"

"Late as usual," Lou mutters, still picking at her burger. Leroy couldn't get a line cook in to cover off breakfast this morning so we shifted Brenna's little party to dinner and Leroy brought his renowned patties with him.

"Actually, I'm not sure if she's gonna make it."

"She's never missed Brenna's birthday," Keith reminds us.

"Yeah, she had plans in Philly." To visit DJ. And when she suggested bringing him *here*, and I said no, she didn't take it too well. "She may show up later. I gave her the code to the gate."

Brett had an iron gate installed two days ago, along with a small camera, cleverly concealed at the bottom of a coach lantern light, angling down at the end of the driveway. And cameras around the property. And a full security system for the house. I tried to argue that it was overkill, but he politely pointed out that his mother couldn't safely stay here without it. I shut up after that.

"You gave Misty the code?" Keith's brows spike as he turns to Brett. "You might want to think about changing that tonight."

Brett chuckles softly. "Noted."

"Oh, man!" Jack's bark of laughter carries across the long stretch of grass behind us. "You're gonna find her going through your hamper tonight."

"Jack!" my mother scolds.

"Or soaping your back up for you in the shower."

Even my dad and Leroy can't help but laugh.

"All right . . . Leave our slightly crazed friend alone. Hey, Jack?" I nod toward the garage.

"Let me go with you. There's a code to get in." Brett shifts from his spot leaning against the wall, his hand grazing my shoulder gently on the way past.

"I'm coming. I wanna see your Benz." Keith trails the two of them out.

"He's certainly put a lot of money into security for this house," my mother says, obsessively collecting the latest wrapping and paper plates. Leroy had barely put his plate down before it was in the ready trash bag. Lou even made an idle comment about how she wished her staff was half as on top of clearing tables as my mom. While she didn't mean it as a slight, I guess Hildy Wright didn't like being compared to Lou's truck stop diner staff and, well . . . at least it stopped at a tense moment and a dirty look.

I hear the countless unspoken questions and thoughts behind my mother's simple remark.

Mr. and Mrs. Chase may have had no clue who they were selling their old Victorian mansion on Jasper Lane to, but most of the town has figured it out by now, after seeing the gates being installed and me driving in and out of here a few times. The media certainly has, but aside from the occasional car pulling up and a long-lens camera pointed at the house, they haven't been too bad.

I hadn't quite figured out exactly what I was going to tell my family about all this tonight, but then Brenna walked out to the patio with my sketchbook and announced that Brett bought her the Gingerbread House and it was going to be an inn.

"It's his money, and his house," I say, very simply.

The returning look from my mother, as well as Lou and Emma, tells me they're not buying that for a second. Dad and Leroy have the good sense to keep their heads down.

Brenna's pursing her lips as she quietly counts her presents, and I know she's mentally noting that there's nothing from me or her uncle and aunt yet. Wondering if we somehow forgot.

"What's taking them so long?" I wonder.

A nearby neighbor's dog starts barking wildly, followed by a second. And a third, along with some shouts. I'm on my feet, ready to go around front and check.

And then suddenly a ball of white-and-gray fluff comes tearing around to the back, followed quickly by a sprinting Jack and Keith.

The fluff is wearing a pink ribbon.

"Oh, my—"

"Stella!" Brenna takes off running across the lawn, her earlier presents forgotten. The husky puppy veers and darts toward her, its tongue lolling. They tumble in a heap of giggles and fur.

"Sorry, Cath. Keith wanted her out of his truck so he was gonna wait out front with her on a leash." Jack heaves his breaths, like he was just in a race. "But that little shit is fast. We couldn't catch her." He starts to laugh. "I'll bet that photographer got a priceless shot of us trying, though."

"You got Brenna a dog?" I hiss at Keith.

Keith's hands shoot up in a sign of surrender, his own chest heaving. "I'm just the Madden flower and dog delivery boy, remember? *He* got

Brenna the dog." He nods toward Brett, who's only now coming around the corner, a sheepish smile on his face. Keith and Jack promptly move away as I close the distance.

"What have you done?" He's mentioned a dog in passing, but I didn't expect this.

Why didn't I expect this?

"Singer said it's best to just act first and beg for your forgiveness later."

"Yeah, that *is* Keith's MO. I've wanted to murder him a dozen times for it."

"Come on." Brett spins me around by the shoulders and rests his chin on my head. "Look at how happy Brenna is."

"Of course she is. This is *literally* her dream come true." Everything here is. The dog, the house, family and friends surrounding her on her birthday.

"And she deserves to have her dream come true. She's a good kid."

"Mommy, look! It's Stella!" Her smile is wider than I've ever seen it before.

"We're not allowed to have dogs at my house."

"*This* is your house."

"No, this is *your* house," I grumble stubbornly.

"How long are you going to keep up *that* charade?" His voice is thick with amusement as he mimics my words from last week.

We can't get into that discussion right now. I heave a sigh and simply allow myself to listen to Brenna's infectious giggles carry into the night as my throat grows thick with emotion.

"How mad are you at me right now?"

"Furious," I whisper softly, tears threatening. "But thank you. For being in our lives. I've never been this happy."

His arms tighten around my body. "Neither have I." There's a long pause. "By the way, we owe Keith a detailing. She peed in his truck."

I can't help it, I burst out laughing. "We're never going to hear the end of that."

"Misty! Look what I got!" Brenna shrieks.

I turn to see Misty standing in the doorway. And, thankfully, alone. I guess she's not mad enough at me to skip Brenna's birthday. "I should go over there."

"'Kay. Just maybe don't give her the passcode to our house."

"Don't you start, too."

Brett leans over to press a kiss against my cheek. "And I promise you can make me grovel for forgiveness about the dog later."

I grin up at him, even as my blood begins to race. "Don't worry, I will."

I feel Brett's gaze on me as I make my way back to the porch. "Hey! I'm glad you made it." I nod toward the pink gift bag dangling from her fingertips. "We'll have to give that to her later. She's a bit distracted right now."

"I see that." Misty's wide eyes dance from me to everyone now surrounding Brenna and Stella. "You have to show me the porch," she blurts out, already moving back inside.

I trail after her. "We had furniture delivered a few days ago but it's all in here." I lead Misty through to the separate apartment in the back, where the delivery guys dropped a soft charcoal-gray couch and giant flat-screen TV, and two complete bedroom sets—one for Brenna and one for Brett and me. I don't know where Simone ordered it all from, but she has impeccable taste, I'll give her that.

"It's a little eerie, actually. It's so big and empty right now. I don't know how long it'll take for me to get used to—"

"Matt's not Brenna's father, is he?"

My mouth drops open.

"You lied to me." Misty's bottom lip begins to tremble, in that way she gets when she's really upset. And I can see that she is, acute pain shining in her eyes.

"I didn't—"

"DJ said that Matt told him you guys never hooked up. You were talking and laughing, and then he tried kissing you and you shut him down."

I close my eyes as I'm brought back to that night. I remember thinking that if I drank enough, smoked enough, I'd forget all about Scott. "I didn't lie." My voice cracks over that word. "I just didn't correct you when—"

"You've been *lying* to me all these years!" Disbelief fills her eyes. "After *everything* we've been through. I mean . . . I held your hand while Brenna was born!"

My voice is a thick rasp. "Can we please not do this right now? I'll explain it later." If I can just contain this . . .

There's no containing Misty, though, not when she's this upset. "And you let me and Lou—and everyone—believe that Brenna's father was some drug dealing loser? Why?"

"Because it was easier that way."

Tears roll down Misty's face. She's always been emotional, crying over things I might barely notice. Only this time, I can see that I've hurt her gravely.

"It's Scott Philips, isn't it? You slept with him again and you didn't want anyone to know."

"Can we *please* just do this later? When my family isn't outside?" I leave before Misty can push for an answer.

And find a wall of stunned faces—Lou, Emma, Keith, my father, and my mother—at the end of the hall.

"I had a feeling DJ would bring nothing but trouble." Lou's voice is all the more hollow echoing through the cavernous space.

The empty space where voices carry far. And the windows are open. "Brenna!" I whisper frantically. "Where is she?"

"She's with Jack and Leroy. She didn't hear anything." Brett stands in the open doorway that leads out to the covered porch.

But he surely did. It's not shock I see in his face. I can't read exactly what that is. Realization that I'm not so honest after all, perhaps. That I lied to him, along with everyone else.

Whatever it is, I'm certain it means this fairy tale is over.

Chapter 33

• • •

September 2010

The empty soda can topples, clattering noisily against the rocks.

"Shit!" I stumble behind a bush, my eyes on the windows, watching for any signs of movement.

There's nothing besides the dim flicker of a TV.

I release a sigh of relief and hunker back down on my boulder with the giant water bottle I filled with vodka and 7UP. Misty said her dad doesn't care if we drink his booze, as long as we replace it before he's back in three weeks.

The burn of it as it begins to course through my limbs helps against the chill in the night air, but it does little against the eeriness of the darkness that surrounds me. I huddle in my sweatshirt and remind myself that there's nothing besides raccoons and squirrels here in the woods.

And an art teacher.

I didn't actually know if he'd be here when I hopped on my bike, but I remembered him once saying that he comes almost every weekend in autumn to paint the colorful fall foliage. And I didn't know if he'd be alone, or with her. But I'm ecstatic to see only his motorcycle parked next to the dilapidated shed.

The reasonable part of me knows that coming out here is wrong, that I shouldn't be lurking outside the cabin Scott inherited from his grandparents. And yet, here I am.

Guzzling vodka and pretending I have the guts to walk up to that door and knock on it, to remind Scott that I'm eighteen now and no longer a student at Balsam High, effective last Thursday, so no one can stop us anymore.

Fuck it. I'm just going to do it.

I begin moving toward the forest-green door, my heart pounding in my chest, my fist clutching the bottle so tight that the plastic crinkles.

What the hell am I doing? Have I finally lost it?

I need to leave.

I'm fifteen feet away from the cabin door when it swings open without warning. Scott steps out onto the rickety wooden stoop, a joint pinched between his lips.

He finally notices me as he's working to light it, startling slightly. "Catherine?" He reaches inside and suddenly the driveway is bathed in light, highlighting his deep frown. "What are you doing here?"

I don't answer.

He glances around. "How did you get here?"

"I rode my bike. I left it in the bushes, at the end of the driveway." I've brought the rumors to life. I am now officially a crazy stalker girl. "I should go."

"You've been drinking."

I wave the bottle. "A bit."

He pauses. "Who knows you're here?"

"No one." I hesitate, searching for my bravery. "And it doesn't matter if they do anyway."

A sly smile stretches across his lips. "Because you turned eighteen two days ago."

He remembered. "And I don't go to Balsam anymore."

The gravel crunches under his boots as he approaches me unhurriedly, his worn Metallica T-shirt speckled with yellow paint. "So I heard." His gaze roams over my face as he finally lights his joint, takes a haul off it. He hands it to me, our fingertips brushing. My breath catches. "So, why'd you come here, Cath?"

I savor the joint, stalling answering his question. When I finally look up, I meet a knowing look. It's so easy to get caught in those flirty eyes of his, and I do, reveling in them as we pass the joint back and forth wordlessly. It's just a small one, finished in a minute. Scott prefers a light buzz over being outright stoned.

"Where's Linda?"

"Probably baking cookies or praying in church," he mutters. "Don't know, don't really care right now. Truth is, we're close to being done."

Relief swells inside me.

He pushes a curly lock of coffee-colored hair off his forehead. "I don't like the idea of you going home in this state. You should come inside and sober up a bit."

I fight my overwhelming excitement as I trail Scott into the small cabin. The kitchen is to the left, the main room ahead.

He leads me to the right.
To the bedroom.

■ ■ ■

I know it's Brett who's climbing the stairs to the third floor without having to look, his steps slow and careful.

"They must have placed this skylight here intentionally," I murmur into the darkness. I'm sprawled out on the hardwood floor, staring up at the glowing full moon above me. Imagining how amazing it would be to sleep right here. "Is Brenna in bed?"

Brett eases himself onto the floor next to me with some difficulty. "She's arguing with Jack and Keith about crating Stella. She wants to sleep with her."

"She can't. The dog will pee all over the house."

"That's what they're trying to explain to her." Brett's soft chuckle echoes in the room. "But that kid has an answer for everything."

I should really be down there, dealing with it. But I've been hiding out up here for the past hour instead. Trying to hold on to everything for just a little while longer.

"I'm sorry."

He sighs. "I know you are, Cath."

"The day I found out I was pregnant, I was in the restroom at Diamonds, in the middle of my interview. It all happened so fast, and when Misty assumed it was Matt's baby, I just went along with it. I didn't want to admit that it was Scott's. That I'd gone and slept with him after he let me take the brunt of that scandal. How I'd been *stupid* enough to think he'd leave Linda for me."

"Did he tell you he would?"

"Not in those words." I think back to that night, to what he did say and to the look in his lust-filled eyes. "He definitely played me, though, to get what he wanted out of me. Lied right to my face. But I was so sure that I was going to get what *I* wanted." The last laugh, when my mother and all the assholes who swore Scott Philips would never be interested in me saw us strolling hand in hand down the sidewalk, talking about where we should live in Philly. Of course, I kept quiet about it after that night. Waiting for Scott to call, to show up at Misty's doorstep for me.

And then, I heard a week later that Linda and Scott were engaged and they had both accepted teaching jobs in Tennessee, effective immediately. Linda hadn't been baking cookies and praying that weekend. She'd been down in Memphis, arranging an apartment for them.

"It's still embarrassing, thinking how pathetic I was."

"You were barely eighteen."

"It doesn't feel like a good enough excuse." I shake my head. "Honestly, I didn't think the lie would last, but I was happy when it did. I'd had enough of people talking about me and Scott Philips. I figured, who cared if people thought it was Matt? He wasn't going to come around. There was no connection, other than DJ."

"But Scott Philips has money. His family has money. You wouldn't have had to struggle like you did. Plus, if you came out with this, he wouldn't be able to deny something going on between the two of you."

"And then I'd be tied to them forever. And so would Brenna." I've never met Melissa Philips, but Lou had a run-in with her over a property and confirmed she's a controlling, uppity bitch. And I trust Lou's judge of character. But I do know Mr. Philips—Brenna's grandfather. Just picturing him, glowering at me from across the desk in his office, makes me tense. "If his father was willing to corner and coerce a seventeen-year-old girl using his authority, what else would he and his wife be willing to do for their son?" That those two are Brenna's grandparents makes me shudder.

I still haven't found the guts to look over at Brett, but I hear his teeth clench beside me.

"I know that he manipulated me, and he has manipulated others. I don't want a man like Scott in Brenna's life."

"I don't blame you."

I feel the bitter smile touch my lips. "And yet I wouldn't have her if it wasn't for him. It's hard to hate him, when she's what I get because of it. It almost doesn't seem right, that I'd be rewarded with a kid like her."

Silence hangs between us.

"But I can't even blame him, completely. I'm the one who rode my bike over there that night. And I'd like to say that I wouldn't have slept with him if he hadn't lied to me about Linda and him. But if I'm being honest, I don't think it would have mattered. I was in love with him. I would have convinced myself that it was okay no matter what." I've never admitted that out loud to anyone, including myself. "What kind of person does that make me?"

Brett sighs. "A person who has made some big mistakes." His tone is impossible to read. Is he angry? Sad? Frustrated?

Or is that simply the sound of resignation?

A painful lump forms in my throat, as my regret overwhelms me. "I wish I had told you everything."

"And you didn't feel like you could? After everything we've been through?"

"I guess not."

What must be going on inside Brett's head right now? That he's gotten himself into a mess, likely. This isn't going to be as simple as it was when he broke up with Courtney for lying to him. Now there's this massive house to deal with, along with a dog and a kid who won't understand. On top of that, Simone just released a statement that basically said the fairy tale has come true.

A puppy's howl carries through the house. My heart aches, thinking of Brenna, of what this will do to her. "I'll see if my parents can take Stella, just until I can find a place that will let us have a dog." If my mother's even talking to me. I couldn't bring myself to look at anyone as I bolted from the ground floor, near hyperventilating.

"You can stay here. This is your house."

"I don't want to stay here. It wouldn't be the same without you." Brett is now firmly tied to every thought I have of the Gingerbread House. Even this attic . . . My gaze wanders to the wall he had me pressed up against.

"Why? Where am *I* going?"

I turn to find Brett frowning.

"I just thought . . ." I've been lying to him, to my entire family—to everyone. Lying is what ended things for him and Courtney, he said so himself.

The light from the full moon casts a glow over his face, highlighting those stunning blue eyes as they rove over my face. "I knew."

"What?"

"Well . . . I guessed, anyway." He shifts onto his back. "That day at the grocery store, when we ran into him."

"You think she looks like him?" Panic stirs inside me. I'd always banked on the fact that, despite the olive skin tone, her curls, and the ring of hazel around her pupils, she really does take after me.

"No. But I saw something familiar in his eyes. A look, I think. I can't pinpoint it, exactly, but it was uncanny. That's when I started to wonder if you were telling the truth about that other guy. It would make sense, why you would avoid talking about Brenna's father, even with me."

"Why didn't you ask me?"

"Because I figured you had a good reason for lying."

"You said there was never a good reason for lying." *Not to someone you love.*

"And yet here you were, lying to everyone. So I figured that you really believed you had no choice."

What is Brett saying? "So you bought this house and got the dog and asked us to stay with you . . . even though you knew?"

A soft smile touches his lips. "Yeah."

"So . . . you're not ending this?" I hold my breath.

He slides his arm beneath my neck and pulls my body against him. "No. I don't think I could, even if I wanted to. I'm in too deep, with you and your little hellion. But I don't want to."

The crushing weight suddenly lifts from my chest, as tears of relief begin streaming. I feel his arms tighten around me as I sob softly against him.

"You've been carrying that for a long time," he says soothingly, stroking my hair.

I never realized how much guilt had settled on my shoulders until now. Will everyone forgive me as quickly and easily as Brett seemingly has, though? "How angry are they?"

"I don't think anyone's angry. Not at you, anyway. And Lou already knew."

I shouldn't be shocked, but I am. "How?"

"She said she always wondered, and then when she saw that real estate ad in the newspaper, she was sure."

Of course. "Did anyone else figure it out?"

"No. Your mom tried coming up here to talk to you about it, but Keith and your dad blocked the stairs."

"Has she mentioned a lawsuit yet?"

"I believe I might have heard that word, yeah." My body shakes with his chuckle. "Your dad said not to worry, though. She's just angry, but she won't risk losing you again. No one's saying a word to anyone about this. They've all agreed to keep it quiet."

"But if Misty said something to DJ—"

"She didn't."

"Are you sure? Because he's the kind of slimeball who would sell this story to a tabloid." And right now, the tabloids would be all over this juicy bit of gossip.

"You'd have to ask her that." He pauses. "But if I figured it out and Lou figured it out, and now that jackass is here . . . You have to be ready for it if it comes out. And because we're together, that will make it a bigger deal."

"I know. I'm just not sure what I'll do if it happens."

He brushes my tears away. "Don't worry about that. I can promise you that we have better lawyers and more money than those assholes. If he or his parents even try to come after Brenna, I'll make them regret it." He smiles. "I'm sure his mother already hates me, anyway."

"Why?" I ask curiously.

"The Chases tried to use her for the sale and we told them that the deal was off if the Philips name was anywhere on the paperwork. She would have figured out by now why."

"Was that what you were talking about, that night you said you didn't want someone to get a dime?"

He pauses. "Were you eavesdropping on my private phone conversation?"

"No." I avert my gaze. It all makes sense now.

A commotion sounds beneath us—of footsteps running through the rooms on the second floor, Keith and Jack taking turns calling hyper Stella's name as they chase her.

"Did Keith *really* not know?" The night he grilled me outside my house, he asked me why I couldn't just move on, if I was still hung up on Scott. I was so sure that he would take that next step and figure out exactly what's always been hanging over my head.

The fact that we share a daughter.

"He was as shocked as the rest of them. Jack told him he was a shitty cop for missing that."

Tears still stream from eyes, even as I giggle. "And you?" I skate the tip of my nose across the hard line of his jaw, relishing the feel of his body pressed against mine. I don't ever want to let go of him again. "You're really not angry with me?"

"Me?" A slow grin stretches across Brett's face. "I'm furious."

■ ■ ■

October 2017

"For the road."

My hands drop with the weight of the Styrofoam container. "Seriously, Leroy!" I flip open the lid to find it stuffed with blueberry pancakes and strips of bacon. "He can't eat like this all the time!"

Leroy's face splits into a wide grin. "The boy needs his calories."

"If his trainer complains, I'm sending him to you."

"You do that. I'll put some meat on his trainer's bones, too." Leroy tosses two plates up on the counter and slams a hand down on the bell.

"Can you send some cute hockey players this way, too?" Misty chirps, collecting the plates. "I could really use one right about now." She broke up with DJ the day after Brenna's birthday, afraid that having him in her life could cause turmoil in Brenna's and mine. She finally understood why I was so apprehensive about having DJ around, aside from just not liking him as a person. And, if Misty is good at one thing, it's not holding a grudge against me.

I smile. "I'll keep on the lookout."

"Cath? Can you come in here for a sec?" Lou calls from her office.

I cringe, checking the clock. Brett will be here any second and I haven't changed out of my uniform yet. But what am I going to say? "Sure. What's up?"

She nods toward the door.

I push it shut. "Thanks for letting me take off early."

"No problem." She frowns at her computer screen before leaning back, sliding her reading glasses off her nose. "Is Brenna at your parents' place?"

"No. Our place, with them. And Stella."

She chuckles. "Hildy get over the fiasco in the backyard yet?"

"Not exactly . . ." Call it a severe lapse in good judgment, but my dad decided to leave four-month-old Stella uncrated and in their backyard while he made a quick run to the store with Brenna a few weekends ago.

They came home to uprooted gardens and a mud-covered puppy. Brenna said she's never seen Grandma's face so scary before.

"Oh, well. Some chaos will do that woman good. How are the renovation plans coming along?"

"They're starting soon." I can't hide the excitement from my voice. "Niya came over yesterday to go over all the final designs with us." With me, really. The thirty-two-year-old designer from New York and I have been trading emails and ideas back and forth, to bring my sketchbook to life. And then she goes to Brett to discuss the costs, because they both know I'll say no to everything if I see the price tag. But I'm done arguing with him about spending money because I know he's going to spend it either way. "The permits should be approved next week."

"How long do you think it'll take?"

"They said four months so I'm guessing eight? Double whatever they say, right?" We're lucky that we can close ourselves off completely in our apartment, but we won't be able to avoid the dust and noise completely.

"And that other little side project that she asked you to do?"

"I should be done with it next week." Niya's been hired to remodel a house in the Hamptons. She said she's swamped and asked if I'd like to throw together a preliminary design idea for the master bedroom. She's paying me, but I can't help but feel like it's also a test.

"That's something you think you could do? You know, aside from the whole *inn* thing."

"Yeah. I think so. I mean, I don't know what kind of schooling I'd need but . . . yeah, I could make it work." Funny, I never thought that a loose-leaf real estate flyer on my doorstep would eventually lead me here.

"You should look into that, then."

My phone chirps with a text from Brett.

Lou's eyes dart to my pocket. "You have to go?"

"He's probably outside, waiting. And I still have to change." I'm not about to show up at the ice rink in my diner's dress. I watch her expectantly, wondering why she called me in, besides just catching up.

"I heard there's a warrant out for Scott Philips's arrest in Memphis."

"Oh?" That catches me off guard. I've managed not to run into him again, though we've seen his face on real estate signs plenty. And every time we do, Brenna points out "my art teacher."

"Seems a sixteen-year-old student has come forward with a damning statement."

"It wouldn't be the first time."

"Well, this time they have several witnesses, too. And it doesn't sound like the girl or her family wants to back down. This one might stick."

I shake my head at his brazenness. "Let's hope so." Aside from a single conversation the week after Brenna's birthday, the topic of Scott Philips being Brenna's father has not come up, oddly enough. Even my mother has stayed quiet. Possibly for fear of this exact situation. She doesn't want her granddaughter associated with a man who chases teenage girls.

"Okay, I should get—"

"Wait." Lou purses her lips.

She's been beating around the bush, I realize. That's really not like Lou. Unease stirs inside me.

"So, here's the thing. You've got all this stuff goin' on in your life now—renos and this designer stuff, maybe school on the horizon; you've got Brenna to care for and that wild dog of hers. And don't forget that man, who's going to have to be in Philadelphia a lot more going forward, especially if today works out for him . . ."

My stomach tightens at the idea that my days of curling up next to Brett every night are over. It's been almost five months since the accident. His walking cast is finally off, he's been working with a physical therapist to strengthen his leg, which, though healed, is not the same.

But the doctors have given him the green light to put on skates again. Sid Durrand, Coach Roth, and everyone else on the Flyers team are frothing at the mouth to see what will come of it.

"So, I'm gonna give you two options, Cath: Either you quit or I fire you."

I simply stare at her, looking for her stern face to crack into a smile. It doesn't.

She eases out of her chair to round the desk, smoothing out the front of her uniform. "Listen here, I love you like I love my own child. *More*, actually, than my own child, though that's not too hard." Her eyes flare with meaning. "And I know that this is not the life I want for you, sluggin' plates of food and pourin' coffees for strangers. You have all these wonderful things happenin' for you now and you don't need this place anymore."

"But I need a job for—"

"Don't you dare bring up money to me, Catherine. You will be just fine. Let him take care of you while you focus on *you*."

As if Brett has given me any choice, as much as I fight it. He won't let me pay a single bill, including the rent on my little clapboard cottage, though I've finally agreed to give my notice to vacate. And last month, I found a bank and credit card tied to his accounts in my wallet. I haven't used them, much to his frustration.

"I'll give you three days to decide how you want it to go, but either way"—Lou blinks away the sudden glossiness from her eyes—"Leroy and me don't wanna see you in here with this uniform on after that, and that's final."

My phone chirps again.

"Get goin'. He's waiting for you." Lou practically pushes me out of her office. I'm in a daze as I change out of my uniform, spending a few minutes freshening my makeup. By the time my phone chirps a third time, I'm rushing to the front.

Brett's standing by the counter in track pants and one of those clingy long-sleeve shirts that show off an upper body he's been training heavily over the last month. He's chuckling with a couple of the regulars who are talking his ear off, wishing him luck with his first skate today. Even though people have started getting used to having him in here by now, I can still see the excitement in their eyes.

Much like the excitement in mine, I guess, because Brett still steals my breath at first sight.

"I'm sorry. I got caught up." I'll have to tell him about that bombshell later. If he doesn't already know, that is.

He leans down to kiss me and I automatically inhale the scent of him—a mixture of soap and cologne.

"This is for you." I thrust the container of pancakes and bacon into his hands.

He checks the window for Leroy and, seeing his grinning face, throws a wave and a "Thanks." "Okay, we've gotta go."

I trail after him, enjoying the sight of his strong back and his long strides. He still seems to favor his left leg a touch, but the doctor thinks that'll work itself out. "Nervous?"

"Nope."

I smile. "Liar."

"What, you don't think I'm strong enough?"

"Of course I think you're strong enough." I've noticed how much muscle he's put back on, just over the past month. "I just—Ah!" Suddenly I find myself scooped into one of Brett's arms and being carried across the parking lot toward the black Suburban he bought—off, of all people, Gord Mayberry. "Put me down!" I shriek, though I can't help but laugh.

But he merely adjusts so he's cradling me in both arms. "Don't knock the container out of my hand," he warns sternly. "I love Leroy's pancakes."

A phone is aimed at us from a booth in the diner. "Oh, my God. People are taking pictures now."

"Better smile and pretend you love me, then."

"I *do* lo—" I cut myself off right before I say it, feeling my cheeks burn. We have yet to say those words to each other, though they're on the tip of my tongue every day from morning until night. Brett seems to have made a game of it, wanting me to say it before he does.

We reach the hood of the SUV, and instead of putting me down, he leans in to kiss me deeply right on the lips, taking his time and giving them a good angle.

"Why are you so insane today?"

He releases me to the ground. "Maybe I'm a bit nervous."

"A bit?"

"Okay. More nervous than I was playing my first NHL game." His jaw tenses. "Thank you for coming with me."

"Of course I'm going to be there for you." I smooth my hand over his jaw. I love the feel of his skin when it's so freshly shaven. "You've got this."

He leans forward to press his forehead against mine. "But what if I don't?"

"Then . . ." I sigh. "You've got *me*. I know it's not the same, but you've got me either way."

"No, you're right. It's not the same." He folds me into his arms, and I revel in the feel of his body—warm and powerful, and *alive*. And all mine. "It's better."

EPILOGUE

■ ■ ■

"Hey! We're on the TV!"

I look over at the flat-screen in time to see Brenna waving her arms wildly back and forth at the cameras, my parents, Emma, and Jack sitting on either side of her in the front row of the luxury suite seats.

"She's certainly not shy, is she?" Meryl says with a soft chuckle.

"No, she's not." Unlike Emma, who's pretending to search for something in her purse, trying to avoid the attention.

"We might have another actress in the family," Michelle adds, winking at her mother. Brett's sister is a younger replica of Meryl, right down to the same shade of silky blonde hair and exact height. And she's just as nice. I got to know her pretty well over the Christmas holidays, when we flew out to Malibu.

"God help us all, if that's the case," Richard says around a sip of his beer, though he's grinning. "How's the house coming?"

"It's . . . coming." I chuckle. "It's chaotic right now. We're in Philly most weekends." To spend time with Brett as much as avoid the dust. He can't come back to Balsam every night, the drive too much given his hectic training schedule and the snow. And now that he'll be traveling with the team again . . .

"They're about to go on!" Jack hollers.

I take a deep breath and try to calm my nerves as I make my way down. Wishing I could talk to Brett right now. But he's somewhere below, in the bowels of this giant arena with his team, getting ready to play his first game, eight months after the car accident that nearly killed him. He's done well, his ankle standing up to the test of daily practices and intensive strength training. He's ready.

But he was also pacing around the condo for hours last night. The crowd comes to life as lights in the arena begin flashing and changing colors, and the announcer's deep voice blasts through the speakers.

"I'm embarrassed to admit that I haven't been to one of his games in almost two years," Meryl says, throwing a smile and wave at the camera that's once again trained on our suite. Brett prepared me to expect that a lot tonight.

"It's not exactly easy for you, is it?" I glance over my shoulder at the security detail—there's one giant man by the door and another one standing just outside the suite entrance. Meryl will leave through a restricted exit at the end of the night.

"Still . . . I think the accident was a good reminder to take advantage of what's in front of us today, because it might not be there tomorrow, right?" She takes a deep breath. "But now that we're back on the East Coast again, I'm going to be here more. Assuming things go well tonight."

"They will."

She ropes her arm around my shoulders and squeezes me tight against her once, before letting me go.

"Here he comes!" Michelle squeals.

The announcer is talking, but whether it's the noise from the crowd or the way his voice reverberates, I'm struggling to understand him.

Until he calls out, "Number Eighteen, Brett Madden!"

My heart soars as I watch Brett skate out, as the arena vibrates with the welcoming roar of the crowd. The energy doesn't die down either, only growing as two lines of players form, one of the Flyers and the other the Bruins.

We stand for the national anthem.

And then the players square off at center ice.

"I think I'm going to be sick," I mumble to no one in particular.

My dad chuckles. "We'll make a hockey fan out of you yet."

"Whoa, we don't want her using those season tickets, remember," Jack mock-whispers.

"Oh, you're right." Dad's face grows stern. "Good call, son."

I ignore them, turning my focus to Brett at center. And I pray, to whoever was listening the night I pulled Brett out of that car, that they're watching over him tonight, too.

The puck drops and I take a deep breath.

Thirty-two seconds later, Brett scores his first goal.

ACKNOWLEDGMENTS

■ ■ ■

I needed to write this story. It's very different from the ones I've written recently. It's light (for me), it could be called trope-y (by others), it's full of love and family and laughter, and it has left me with a broad smile and a sigh of content. I hope you have enjoyed experiencing Catherine Wright's adventure.

To my readers, thank you for giving me a chance. Many of you continue along with me on this journey, whether it be with a lighthearted romance or a nail-biting suspense story, trusting me enough to allow me a few precious hours of your life.

A special thanks to Jennifer Wiers Severino, for allowing me to pick your brain over legal stuff so I could sort out my plot and simplify things. I *always* complicate things for myself. Having you as a sounding board for this was an enormous help.

To Amélie, Sarah, and Tami, the very best readers and Facebook group admins a person could ask for. Thank you for *always* being excited to read my latest books.

To Stacey Donaghy of Donaghy Literary Group, for our shared love of coffee, crispy bacon, and laughter. We joke about how I give you the first half of my books and then let you hang for several weeks, waiting for the rest. You're right, it is a special form of torture. I'm glad it's you and not me experiencing it.

To KP Simmon of Inkslinger PR, for always being so willing to brainstorm ideas and chase after opportunities, no matter what time of day or night.

To Sarah Cantin, you are a cornerstone of my writing career. What I have learned from you is invaluable. Thank you for your willingness to edit a swoony story and your patience when I decided that something just wasn't right (at the eleventh hour).

To Judith Curr and the team at Atria Books: Suzanne Donahue, Ariele Fredman, Tory Lowy, Kimberly Goldstein, Alysha Bullock,

Cynthia Merman, and Albert Tang. Eleven beautifully packaged books, yo! (I keep losing count.)

To my girls, who make creating adorable, lovable, sweet, smart, funny kids a breeze, just by being themselves. You two continue to give me so much inspiration.

To my husband, for taking care of our adorable, lovable, sweet, smart, funny kids, even when they're not so adorable, lovable, or sweet, so I can toil away in my cave.

And, finally, to my fellow Toronto Maple Leaf fans, as if I wasn't going to let them take home the Cup.